BOOKS BY KRISTIE COOK

— SOUL SAVERS SERIES —
www.SOULSAVERSSERIES.com

Promise
Purpose
Devotion
Power
Genesis: A Soul Savers Novella
Wrath

— THE BOOK OF PHOENIX SERIES —
www.THEBOOKOFPHOENIX.com

The Space Between
The Space Beyond
The Space Within

FIND THE AUTHOR AT
www.KRISTIECOOK.com

WHEN DARKNESS
THREATENS, WHAT
MATTERS MOST LIES IN
THE SPACE WITHIN

THE
SPACE
WITHIN

BESTSELLING AUTHOR
OF THE *SOUL SAVERS* SERIES

KRISTIE COOK

PART THREE IN THE BOOK OF PHOENIX

Published by
Ang'dora Productions, LLC
15275 Collier Blvd
#201-300
Naples, FL 34119

Ang'dora Productions and associated logos are trademarks and/or registered
trademarks of Ang'dora Productions, LLC

Cover design by Regina Wamba at MaeIDesign and Photography, L.L.C.
Formatting by Nadège Richards at Inkstain Interior Book Designing.

This book is a work of fiction. Names, characters, and events are either products
of the author's imagination or are used fictitiously and any resemblance to actual
persons, living or dead, is entirely coincidental.

First Edition July 2014

Print ISBN 978-1-939859-11-2
EPUB ISBN 978-1-939859-10-5

Printed in the United States of America

ACKNOWLEDGEMENTS

Thank you first to the Maker and His Son, who have blessed me in so many ways. With Him, the possibilities truly are endless.

Thank you to my boys–Shawn, Zakary, Austin, and Nathan–for your support, your love, and your inspiration. Without you, I wouldn't know things like "turtling up." Seriously, you are true gifts in my life, and I thank God every morning and night for you. Thank you to my parents for life.

Thank you to Chrissi Jackson for all that you have done. To Tammi Swartz for keeping me on track and real.

So much appreciation goes to Regina Wamba at Mae I Design for the photo shoot and gorgeous cover designs; to Nadège Richards for the beautiful print interiors; and to Jen Trammell and Kristen Yard for finding my bloopers and polishing my words to a shine.

More thanks to my beta readers—Stacey Nixon, Julie Bromley, Debbie Poole, Jessie de Schepper, Inga Kupp-Silberg, and Heather Wakefield—for making me think. An extra thanks to Debbie for helping with the Liverpool scene. For all of their support and cheerleading, I thank my fabulous street team, Kristie's Warriors: Stacey Nixon, Julie Bromley, Inga Kupp-Silberg, Jessie de Schepper, Claire Downes, Debbie Poole, Marissa Feidelbaum, Christina Silcox, Heather Wakefield, Jeana Todd, Lisa Reeves, Chloe Billingham, Josephine Militello, Christina Madison, Kate Wilson, Char Wilcoxson, Jill Cruz, Zee Hayat, Kelly Victorine, Lisa Ammari, Megan Elworthy, Michele Luker, Mindy Janicke, Katherine Murphy, Jenny Finnigan, Annmarie Spiby, Wendy John Jahnke, Heather Brandt, Felicia Filion, Sue Van, Meshell Blackborow, Jennifer Murray, Dawn

Sutphin, and Georgee Olivia Leigh Frost. And thank you to all of the book bloggers who do so much for authors *and* readers.

There are no words to express my appreciation to you, dear reader. Thank you for spending your very precious time and hard-earned money on this world I have created. Thank you for supporting not only me, but all authors. *You* are our life force.

Until we meet again...

TO MY READERS—
WHO BRING ME LOVE, LIGHT
& HOPE EVERY DAY

CHAPTER 1

Leni HUNCHED OVER TO push against the wind that tore across the desert terrain, I contemplated what would kill me first—the Darkness tainting my soul because half of it was worlds away, or the ugliness of this place called Erde. I'd yet to see anything but gray sand on the ground and swirling in the gusts that whipped my curls against my cheeks, the occasional gray tree permanently bent in the relentless wind, and the rare gray pond that was barely more than a puddle. No color here, only shades of gray. Even the sky, without a cloud in it, was the color of concrete. As Hayden and I hauled our measly findings—what he called food and a raggedy blanket—from our supply run, the sun seared down on us, hot and scorching, yet its warmth never penetrated beyond the sweater I wore. The rays blistered any uncovered skin, but couldn't heat the coldness within.

At night, the grays disappeared ... only to be replaced by varying shades of black. No moon lit the sky, and although more stars could be seen here than on Earth, their lights were dim, far away. No matter how hot the day felt, the temperatures plummeted to a freezing cold like none I'd ever experienced in the several places I'd lived on Earth. The bone-chilling cold of eternal Darkness.

Along with the cold and blackness, night brought the screaming.

The wind screamed through the cracks in the rocky cave that gave us shelter. Creatures I'd yet to see but Hayden had warned us about screamed as they hunted, becoming prey to even more wretched beings that bellowed with their victories. Bex, overcome by nightmares, screamed in the night, too, and Brock and I often joined her.

At least Bex had her Twin Flame to comfort her when she woke.

Brock and I may never see ours again.

The chill in my bones didn't compare with the ice seeping into my soul. The Darkness of this world and of being Separated from Jeric grew heavier and colder with each passing day—at least five of them so far, although we couldn't always leave the protection of our cave, so there could have been more. I didn't know how many Earth days that equaled, but even one felt painfully long as we waited for Jeric and Asia to find us. Since they hadn't rescued us yet, I began to worry they never would. They didn't know how to use the Book of Phoenix, which had brought us here through a Gate portal but hadn't returned us home. I'd lost the Book when we came through and could only hope Jeric and Asia had found it and would figure out how to use its powers. Soon.

"How did you survive so long with this pain in your soul?" I asked Hayden. His muscular form, clothed in a threadbare brown sweater and holey jeans, led me as we headed back to our cave. It was the same one he'd brought us to the night we landed in the pond that had shrunk into a mud puddle now. Because of Bex's condition, we hadn't been able to move yet, which made Hayden tense—he wasn't used to staying in one place for so long, he'd said. But her health and well-being were more important to him than anything.

Either Brock or I had accompanied him on a couple of supply runs while the other hung back to watch over Bex, who spent most of her time sleeping. Hayden had loaned Brock a hoodie, and the first trip they'd made out, they brought back clothes for Bex and me. My shorts and flip-flops wouldn't have cut it here, and Bex's clothes were a bloody, shredded mess because an asshole coward who supposedly loved her had nearly killed her. Hayden and Brock had been able to find each of us a pair of pants, boots, and a sweater, but no coats. I wore everything, including my own clothes under the oversized, black pants, with one of Hayden's knives hanging from my belt. He never let us go out unarmed, although we hadn't come across any other living thing yet. Hayden said that was both good and bad—creatures meant food, but could also mean death. I didn't doubt it by the screaming we heard every night.

"The pain and suffering ... they were different for me," Hayden answered with an accent that reminded me of Australian, but wasn't quite the same. He reached down from the charcoal colored boulder he'd just climbed to take the burlap sack of treasure I carried. I followed him up and took the sack back. "I didn't know my Twin Flame in this lifetime. I hadn't even known she existed until Enyxa reminded me. The evil bitch gave me memories of our past lives ... along with the despair of our Separation."

"How nice of her," I muttered.

"Not exactly," Hayden said, and I didn't know if my sarcasm was lost on him or if he was returning it. "Eventually, the memories would begin to fade and the pain would dull to an annoying ache that I would accept as a part of me. As soon as I learned to live with it, though, Enyxa returned to refresh my memory and renew the pain."

"What'd you do to piss her off so bad?"

Hayden looked at me with his brows pinched together. The contrast of his light eyes against his tanned skin was sometimes unnerving, especially with the sharp angles of his high cheekbones and jaw. Even if he weren't as tall as he was, way over six feet, he'd be intimidating. He kept his light brown hair military short, and if we were home on Earth, I'd expect to see dog tags hanging around his neck. He had that look to him.

"Piss her off?" he asked. "As in urinate on her? I can't deny I'd considered the idea, but have never actually done so."

I snorted at his comment and the miscommunication. This world was supposedly a near duplicate, although Darker, version of Earth, if what Enyxa, leader of the Dark worlds, told Hayden was true. The air was breathable and the water hadn't poisoned us yet. Hayden looked like us, dressed similarly, and even spoke English, although with that unusual accent. He said most of the "intelligent" (I imagined air quotes the way he'd said it) beings here were the same. But there were differences, and this was one of them.

Hayden spoke English, but our languages weren't exactly the same. If our worlds were nearly identical, I figured our continents and countries were similar, too, but what Hayden called the place we were at now was no name I'd heard on Earth. The terrain and climate somewhat resembled the southwest United States, but could have just as easily been the Sahara Desert, somewhere in the Middle East, or the Australian outback. He'd said climate change and the humans—that was what they called themselves, too—had altered the geography of the world centuries ago, so I'd probably never know for sure anyway.

Although he seemed to use sarcasm at appropriate times, he didn't always get ours. And slang terms were often lost on him. Like just now. He knew piss had to do with pee, but apparently they didn't use "piss off" with an alternate meaning here.

"In our world, *pissing off* means making someone mad," I explained.

"Ah. Yeah." He chuckled, a sound that fell flat in this flat world. "I used to wonder myself what I'd done to her. Sometimes it does feel like she singles me out more than anyone else, like she deliberately hunts me down for a specific kind of torture, but I think it's really just who she is. She probably chooses favorites as souls cycle through to keep the boredom away, and maybe I happen to be that right now." He shrugged. "Or maybe not. She did me a favor. Knowing Rebethannah existed and that we have a love that transcends time and even worlds kept my hope alive. Hope that I'd somehow be with her again before it was too late. And look what happened."

He had more firsthand experience with Enyxa than I did, but my memories of her ripping our souls apart didn't lead me to believe she'd intentionally reward him with something like hope. In fact, it seemed like that was the last thing she'd want if she desired his soul to go Dark. Did this mean Hayden was stronger than Enyxa had anticipated and his hope was an unexpected consequence? Or did she have other plans, maybe using the hope to make him fall further and harder? The latter was probably the case, but I liked to believe in the former. I needed that kind of hope and strength myself.

"Hayden, do you think it was that hope that allowed you to communicate with us?" I asked.

I'd been hounding him with questions every chance I had since we'd arrived, trying to find clues that would lead our way home. He'd been able to leave us messages in the Book of Phoenix when we'd been on Earth, allowing us to know Bex was his other half and to bring her to him. He'd shared some of the memories Enyxa had given him, such as being part of the Original Seven, but he knew nothing more elaborate to share. I'd asked him about the Original Seven, wondering if it was the same as the Sacred Seven the Phoenix knew on Earth. Well, we didn't know much—just that we were all somehow a part of the Seven, Jeric and me, Asia and Brock, and Bex and Hayden. So it was probably the same Seven, but the memories Enyxa had given Hayden were incomplete. He couldn't remember what might have made us original or sacred, anything about the Book or what clues and powers we'd given it, or other potentially helpful details. Enyxa had apparently blocked any of his memories she knew would aid us in escape. Talk about selective memory.

"I'm sure hope didn't hurt anything," he said as we began the ascent up the hill to the opening of our cave. "Like I keep telling you and Brock, I don't know exactly how I was able to project my soul, as you put it. It wasn't like I do with Bex now—not all the way out of my body like that—but enough to feel disconnected from the physical world. And when I did that, yeah, I felt like maybe there was a chance of finding her. Belief ... hope ... whatever you want to call it, I'm sure it helped."

"I just wish we could figure out how to do it," I muttered.

"I can't say it enough—if I could help more, I would. All I can say is it took time to feel that loosening, but once I did, it got easier to push out ... beyond my body. And that's when I felt there was something more than the here and now. Enyxa had been showing me for years that my soul has existed in other bodies and on other worlds, but I didn't know what that had to do with my life now. Not until I felt that separation from my physical self and this world. I'm assuming that's how I made the connection with you and Bex, but I can't be certain."

Brock and I had both felt the loosening of our souls from our bodies when we'd tried, but probably because we were used to the feeling of completely projecting. Neither of us had been able to push our souls out, though. Projecting was supposed to be impossible without your other half, but if we could push just enough to disconnect from the physical world, as Hayden had explained, maybe we could communicate with Jeric and Asia through the Book. Maybe we could at least feel them and know if they were on their way to rescue us. And if they weren't because they didn't know how, I could explain how to use the Book to do so. Of course, that was assuming they'd found the Book after we left.

"When I felt you," Hayden said, "especially her, that's when I felt the most hope ... but also became my most desperate."

"And the more desperate you were, the clearer your messages came."

He shrugged. "I guess so."

"You were pretty desperate when you knew something was wrong with her."

He answered with a rumble of choice words.

If desperation was the key to unlocking the messaging powers of the Book, we should have already been communicating with Jeric and Asia. With the despair of being Separated a crushing force on our souls, I couldn't imagine being more desperate than we already were.

Especially when we entered the cave and Bex's joy for Hayden's return filled the small space with an almost tangible thickness. I was happy they'd found each other and shared so much love, but it made my heart ache for Jeric all the more.

"Did you talk to her?" Bex asked Hayden, her voice barely more than a whisper, as he knelt beside her, evaluating her wounds. The swelling in her face had gone down quite a bit, but there was still a lot of bruising. We'd bandaged her arm as best as we could to set it. Hayden seemed to know quite a bit about emergency first aid and wound treatment, learned during his harsh life here where the only halfway decent medical care, he said, was in the cities. The cities that were overrun by Darkness, which meant anything humane like medical care was difficult to obtain and came with a hefty price.

A look of discomfort passed over Hayden's face. "No. Not yet," he answered in hushed tones. "Where's Brock?"

"He went outside to take a leak. And why not? We both feel it. She—"

"Because it doesn't matter right now. You're in no condition to travel."

"Um." I cleared my throat. "I'm right here. What's going on?"

They exchanged a look, and after a moment Hayden seemed to acquiesce because he looked away first. Bex moved to prop herself up on her good elbow so she could see me better in the dim firelight. I moved closer to her pallet of blankets. They'd been Bonding their souls every night, which seemed to help her healing along—or at least keep infection at bay—but they really needed to Forge to do her the most good. And to Forge, they needed a Gate, and we had no clue where to find the nearest Gate.

"We've been feeling this strange, uh ..." Bex's big blue eyes slid to Hayden, but when he failed to provide the word she sought, they came back to me. "I guess a tug? Kind of like we've been hooked on a fishin' pole and someone's reelin' us in like a big ol' catfish."

My breath caught, and I sprang across the five paces separating us to fall to my knees next to Bex. "Seriously? Like an urgent need to go somewhere that comes all the way from your soul?"

"Yes!" Bex nearly squealed, the loudest sound I'd heard from her since we'd been here. She looked up at Hayden. "I told you she'd know."

I clapped my hand over my mouth. "It's a Gate! You're being pulled to a Gate so you can be Forged. And you *have* to go or you'll both die. How far away do you think it is?"

"It's to the east," Hayden answered with reluctance. He blew out a sigh. "If it's where I feel like it is, about a three-days' walk. If we're lucky and don't have any problems, which is unlikely."

I wanted to squeal like Bex. A Gate! They knew where to go to find a Gate, which meant they'd not only be stronger by being Forged, but Brock and I could get back home. I didn't squeal, though. Only nodded.

"We need to leave as soon as we can," I said. I thought about the screaming creatures we heard at night. "It's better to travel in daylight, right?"

"We're not going anywhere until Bex is fully healed and ready to travel."

"She'll heal faster once you're Forged at the Gate. We'll have to help her."

"I can—" Bex started.

"I said *no*." Hayden stood and put his hands on his hips as he towered over us. "We're not going anywhere. Not yet."

I rose to my feet to face him. Unfortunately, I was vertically challenged and he definitely was not, so I had to tilt my head back to look him in the eye. "Didn't you hear me? You *have* to. If you don't—"

"I don't like sitting here any more than you do, but we're not moving until Bex is ready. She's not ready yet."

"You're going to run out of time! If we don't get you two to the Gate in time, your souls will start to reject your bodies. And if your physical bodies die before we can get your souls to the Gate and to the Space Between, the Darkness here will overtake you. All of this will be for nothing!"

I didn't know how much of that was actually true here on this Dark world—if things worked the same way they did on Earth. I didn't know if a Gate here *could* Forge them with all of the Darkness surrounding it. Unless Brock and I somehow figured out how to project, I didn't know how we could get their souls to the Gate if it came to that. Would we be able to stay in our physical bodies, like we did when we passed through the Book's portal? Would Lakari try to stop them or us? So far, the Dark souls didn't seem to care much about Brock and me or that Nathayden and Rebethannah had already started the Bonding process—they hadn't attacked us yet. I didn't know anything, really, except that a Gate held a lot more promise than anything else in this world. The news that they'd been feeling that pull was the best news we'd had since arriving.

Hayden's eyes narrowed, and he pointed a finger at me. "You have no idea what it's like out there."

"We just came from out there," I said through clenched teeth, glowering at his finger. Yeah, the climate sucked. So did the scenery. I did have an idea what it was like outside.

"That was a quick supply run," he snapped. "We got lucky by seeing nothing. Or by nothing seeing us! Shelters like this are rare, and if we get trapped by a gozzard or a Weiran or even a human, Bex can't fight and she can't run. We're dead anyway!"

He glared at me, and I glared back. I'd heard the sounds at night that came from creatures Hayden called gozzards and alien races with names like Weiran. But we'd yet to see or hear them during the day. Before we could continue our argument, monster-like screams came from outside.

"Ah, shit, what the hell is *that?*" Brock yelled as his footsteps tromped through the outer cave, quickly coming closer to us. "*Hayden!*"

His terrified yell for help was drowned out by a deafening roar.

"Oh, fuck," Hayden said as he leapt to immediate action. Four-letter words were apparently universal.

He snatched up one of his bags and pulled a dagger out of it, although he already had one in hand.

"Arm yourselves!" he ordered as he took his place in front of Bex.

He'd given her a blade to keep under her bedding, just in case. She pulled it out, but she could barely stand steady on her feet. Hayden and I both positioned ourselves to guard her. I already had my knife out of its sheath, the blade's mere six inches seeming like nothing more than a pocket knife compared to what I expected we'd be facing based on that roar. We were prepared in the two seconds it took Brock to come flying through the narrow passageway that connected the outer room with the inner cavern. He had a katana-like sword in hand that he'd found on their supply run the other day.

"Looks like a dragon fucked an elephant," Brock said, his voice shaking and his chest heaving with pants as he shoved a hand into his dark hair. Seeing someone built like Brock—as tall and muscular as Jeric and whose fighting skills ranked at the top of the Guardians—showing so much fear was enough to scare the shit out of you.

"A dragon and a *what?*" Hayden asked.

"An elephant. I mean, it's huge as an elephant and with a long trunk for a nose." He held his arm in front of his face to imitate an elephant's trunk. "But it's scaly and has a bunch of horns. And it breathes. Fucking. *Fire!*" His eyes were wild as they remained trained on the opening. "It can't fit through that passage, though ... right?"

"A gozzard," Hayden said, understanding now, "and yes—"

He didn't have to finish his sentence to answer Brock's question. A long, black, scaly, tube-like thing, kind of like an elephant's trunk, slithered into the cavern from the passageway. It lifted into the air, its end wiggling, as though smelling for us. It swung for Brock.

"Whatever you do, don't cut—" Hayden began to warn, but he fell silent when Brock's katana blade sliced through the tentacle or trunk or whatever it was.

The piece fell to the cave floor and burst into little wormy bits that hopped in the air like Mexican jumping beans. As though they could smell us, they swarmed toward Bex and me. One hit my leg and latched on with piercing little needles that sank into my skin. The main body of the beast remained on the other end of the passage, and flames and smoke shot through the opening into our room. The part of the trunk that was still attached to the body split into four parts, peeling back an opening. Several tentacle-like things—these thin, white, and slimy—flared out of the hole, and their ends opened up to little mouths full of spindly teeth. The little black pieces on the ground jumped for us as the white tentacles swayed and swung, the mouths snapping for our faces.

My heart kicked into overdrive and my body into action. I swung my blade in the air while I grabbed the slug-like things on my legs and threw them on the ground, then stomped on them until they fell still. Hayden and Brock jumped and hopped from foot to foot to avoid the little leeches while slicing at the tentacles trying to bite us. Bex screamed behind me, and I spun to find the black things attacking her, and with only one working hand, she was barely able to fight them off, let alone smash them until dead. I left the tentacles to the guys while I helped Bex, yanking the gross little bastards off of her skin and stomping them to death. When she was clean of them all, she looked behind me, her eyes huge. She screamed and tried to jump backward, but she fell on her butt. A louder scream of pain ripped from her mouth—the injuries between her legs hadn't fully healed yet. I spun to find a mouth snapping at me. I swung my knife at it, severing the mouth from the rest of the tentacle. The creature's bellows filled the cavern, but it looked like we'd amputated all of its pieces and the thing was retreating.

Hayden ran for the passage. "Follow me! Aim for its eye, nice and deep!"

He ran into the darkness, and I followed. Brock cursed behind me, but his footsteps were right on my heels. We flew into the smaller entryway of the cave. Almost all light was blocked out by an enormous, black, scaly beast with half of its face missing where a nose or snout should have been. Five horns protruded from its head over eyes the size of my fists that glared at us angrily. Its bottom jaw, jutting with tusks longer than my arm, stretched open and flames flew out. I ducked and rolled. When I came back to my knees, I couldn't see Brock or Hayden on this side of the beast. But I could see its eye. I sprang to my feet, and as it opened its mouth to spit more fire, I jumped into the air, kicked off the cave wall and came down with both hands gripping the hilt of my knife. With the full force of my body weight, I plunged it as deep as it would go into the creature's eye. Black, inky shit spewed out at me. More black fountained on the other side of its head, and the creature screamed one more time before it collapsed to the ground.

Hayden stared at me from the other side of its head.

"Nice work," he said, his voice filled with awe.

"Comes with being a Phoenix," I said. "If you and Bex get Forged, you'll be amazed at what the both of you can do."

His eyes narrowed for a second, but instead of responding, his gaze dropped to the beast between us. "Dinner."

Brock and I exchanged a look. We were going to *eat* this? But then Brock shrugged. "Looks like we'll have plenty to eat for the next few days."

I left the guys to cut up the meat and found Bex collapsed on her bedding. Her whole body trembled. Tears filled her eyes, and she blinked them back. The way she gnawed on her bottom lip, though, I knew she was in a lot of pain—physical and emotional. She'd already been through so much. I dropped down to her to clean any new wounds as well as my own.

"I'm okay," she said, though her voice shook.

"No, you're not," I said.

"I *am*. As far as Hayden knows, I'm just peachy." She ducked her head to catch my attention and looked me in the eyes. "I don't have much to go back home to, you told me that, but I woke up on another damn *world*. This is all just blowin' my mind. I got my Hayden now, and I really ... I really just want to go home."

"I know, sweetie. I'm right there with you, trust me."

"We have to get to that Gate, Leni. I can *feel* it. And I know you and Brock need it, too, right? Because it will get you back to Jeric and Asia?"

I nodded, then went back to dabbing at the little pinpricks of blood on her legs. "Yeah, but Hayden's right. You need to heal. You need to be able to at least defend yourself."

She lay back on the bedding with a sigh and stared at the dim ceiling. Her eyelids fluttered rapidly, but a tear slipped down her temple anyway. "We might not make it that long, though. We might not ever make it home."

"We *have* to," I said simply. I patted her on the knee. "Right now, don't you worry about anything, but getting better. We'll figure the rest out."

If she could hear the doubt in my voice, she didn't say anything, although I was probably making empty promises. Hayden was right: Bex was definitely in no shape to travel. But if we didn't make it to the Gate in time, we'd all be in trouble. And the clock had already started counting down—probably the moment we arrived.

CHAPTER 2

Jeric "WHAT ARE WE going to do, Jeric?" Asia asked me from my side, her voice edged with the same agony I felt. Her hair had become black as night, matching her black clothes and our black moods. Her thin arms were wrapped around her tiny waist as though hugging herself, but she did it because she felt that if she let go, she'd fall apart. I knew this because I had the same feeling that I was missing pieces of myself. That I was incomplete.

We both held what had become our usual spots on the water's edge, watching and waiting. The Phoenix manor loomed behind us, an old plantation-style mansion with an eight-story, abandoned hotel built around it. The sun hung low in the western sky to our right, causing the small waves of Tampa Bay to shine gold and pink. We needed the gold light to come from below, though, from the Gate that would bring our Twin Flames home to us.

"Whatever Leni did for the Book to take them through the Gate, she apparently can't do it again to bring them back," she said when I provided no answer.

I crossed my arms over my chest, not wanting to believe it, but after three days of waiting, the truth of Asia's statement had become clear. Something was wrong, with either Leni or Brock or the Book. Otherwise, they'd be back by now. My jaw clenched and popped. Asia, not normally the touchy-feely type, placed a tiny hand on my tight bicep and squeezed. I looked down at her, and she returned my stare with round, dark eyes that seemed too big for her elf-like face and shining with the desperate sorrow we shared.

"We have to do *something*," she said. Nearly begged. We both knew what that something was, but she looked to me to make the decision. We were part of the Sacred Seven, and I was supposed to be the leader of not only the Phoenix, but of the Seven, too. I didn't know how I could do that when I was missing half my soul. I pressed my lips together and blew a lungful of air out of my nose before giving her a short nod.

"We don't have much choice," I finally said. "We just have to convince everyone else."

With one last look to the water where Leni and Brock had disappeared, I dropped my arm over Asia's shoulders and turned her toward the manor, where a small army of Guardians waited. Someone must have been watching us from inside the manor and warned everyone we were coming, because when Asia and I entered, all was silent. I hated the way the other Guardians looked at us—it was like going back to school all over again after the accident that had taken my family and my hearing. Expressions of sympathy mixed with blame and fear: fear that Asia and I would lose our shit and also fear of losing their own halves as we had. The other expression I didn't know quite so intimately was one I figured cancer patients were familiar with.

"They look at us like we're dying," Asia whispered, noticing it, too.

"Aren't we?" I said.

Her head snapped up to look at me. "No, Jeric," she said sharply. "We don't have time for that attitude. We're going to get them back. Whatever it takes."

Whatever it took ... Unless the Lakari had backed off the Gates, doing whatever it took to bring our other halves back could mean jeopardizing all of Earth's souls, and not even I was that selfish. I knew Asia wasn't, either, but sometimes pushing the pain away to see clearly became impossible. We just had to hope something had changed.

Most of the Guardians were gathered in the old hotel's ballroom, waiting for us. They silently created an opening for Asia and me to walk through, like Moses parting the Red Sea, until we reached the front of the room.

The Phoenix consisted of the Guardians of Earth's seven Gates to the Space Between—the place where souls go when their physical bodies die so they can begin their next journey—and to other worlds. Each Gate had a loose hierarchy of Guardians based on seniority, which was a relative term. No Guardians were over the age of thirty-five, and the older ones had only lived that long because they were healers and rarely went on missions, although they still often had to fight. Guardians didn't have the luxury of normal lives with families and living to old age with our other halves. Our lives were dangerous and our life spans short. Nobody had survived more than six missions in one lifetime in thousands of years. Or so the rumor went.

No one really remembered or understood why, but Jeremicah, Jacquelena, Broderick, and Anastasia held special status over all of them. Rebethannah and Nathayden supposedly did, too, although neither of them had made it to an Earth Gate in several lifetimes. We'd all been part of the Sacred Seven, which meant little to us right now. The true meaning of what this entailed or how it had happened had been lost over generations. All that remained was a vague notion that we were elite among the Phoenix and intended to lead them. Other Guardians said their souls felt our superior status, but we hadn't felt this instinctively at all.

Still, they insisted that we take our positions as leaders. Even those with seniority at Gates other than ours looked to us now that we were here and the Phoenix were in crisis. In other words, nobody else wanted to make the hard choices. Nobody else desired to make the decision to open the Gates and risk all of Earth's souls, or to keep them closed and lose us—their supposed leaders—to the Darkness and Enyxa's control.

Some of those with authority stood at the head of the room and watched us with curiosity, including Melinda and Uri, healers who had the most seniority at our Gate. My eyes scanned over all of their expectant faces as I made my way to the front, but I didn't stop to discuss my decision with any of them. Instead, I climbed the three steps to the dais in one stride, and Asia followed. We stepped to the front of the low stage and stared out at the sea of faces. I stood with my feet shoulder-width apart, my back straight, and my hands clasped behind my ass. From the corner of my eye, I could see Asia taking the same confident stance. Once everyone settled from our passing through, the room's silence became complete, as solid as when I was deaf. Hundreds of eyes stared at us, waiting.

"We're opening our Gate," I announced without beating around the bush. The deadly silent room exploded into chaos.

"The Lakari will swarm through!" someone yelled, and that was everyone's concern.

I held up my hand, and the room fell quiet again. Huh. No wonder some people became addicted to power. It came in handy sometimes.

"I have a plan," I said. "If the Lakari are still waiting to swarm in—which we won't know until we actually open a Gate—we *will* have to fight. But my plan will keep the fighting to a minimum, and hopefully, the only souls truly at risk are mine and Asia's. And we're pretty much lost causes anyway, aren't we?"

Nobody argued with that statement. Instead, they all looked away—at their feet, at the walls, at each other, anywhere but at Asia and me.

"What's your plan?" Yoshi asked. He was a senior Guardian from the Gate near Tokyo who'd arrived just today to meet us and help us figure out what to do. He'd planted the idea in my head of bringing in other Guardians from around the world.

"I'm taking your advice," I said. "We need to bring in as many Guardians as we can get here in the next day. Then we open only this Gate to see what, if anything, is waiting to get in. If the Lakari are still gathering and any push through, they should be easily handled with the number of fighters we'll have here."

"And then what?" Uri asked.

"If I know Brock and Leni, they're waiting for us on the other side of the Gate," Asia answered. "The Book probably couldn't bring them back because the Gate's been closed. We have to try this."

"And if they're not?" Melinda countered.

"Then Asia and I go through the Gate and hope the Space Between has mercy on us and sends us to our Twin Flames," I said.

Yoshi squinted his narrow eyes and stroked and pulled at the dark goatee that hung to his chest. "That's quite the risk."

"One we're willing to take." I waited for somebody to challenge me, but nobody did. They all had to understand where Asia and I were coming from. Surely they'd all be willing to take the same risk if they were in our position. When I knew for sure I wouldn't have to argue this further, my muscles relaxed. "We need to do this anyway. We need to know if the Lakari are still swarming, or if we can open the Gates. We can't help the Lost and the Broken here when the Gates are sealed like they are. With any luck, the Lakari have moved on or gone back to whatever hell they're from."

Everyone eventually came around to accepting our plan and began calling for reinforcements. Without having much of a choice, I'd taken my first real step as a leader, and so far, so good. Leni would have been proud.

The direct reminder of her and her absence sent a new stab through my heart that made my lungs seize. This had to work. She and Brock had to be waiting for us, or we'd have to find our way to them, because I didn't know how much longer I could live like this. The unknown was worse than anything. When I tried to imagine where she was and what she was doing, I came up blank. I couldn't even be positive she was with Brock, or if Bex had even survived, let alone if she was with them. Had they found Nathayden? Were they all together? I hoped they'd accomplished their mission, and this wasn't all in vain. I prayed they at least had each other, although if they were on Nathayden's world, it was a Dark one. I knew nothing for certain. I could feel Leni's pain, but nothing else. And I hated feeling her pain. I hated knowing she was *in* pain. All because of me.

If I hadn't been arguing with her and had followed her like she'd said, we'd at least have been together, if not on this world. Asia and I would have been close enough to them to have gone wherever they had. I'd been trying to learn to follow her instinct as I was supposed to, but when it really counted, I'd failed. And now look where we were: fighting for our very souls.

The pride of my leadership decision deflated. I had to get out of here, where all the dyads were gathered in their perfect, loving pairs.

"We do it tomorrow at noon," I told Melinda and Uri before pushing my way back through the crowd. Asia followed me.

"I'll do whatever needs to be done," she said once we were alone, outside again, watching the water. Just in case. It was better than sitting inside, in our rooms, where we shouldn't be alone. "But if we need to go through the Gate, how do you plan on doing that since we can't project our souls?"

"They left with their bodies. So why can't we?"

"The Gate's under the water, though. We could drown before we even get there, and if not, we will while we wait for it to open."

I looked down at her. "Ever scuba-dived before?"

A bit of light came to her eyes. "Yeah, actually, I have. Do you think it will work?"

I shrugged. "I can only hope. So … you think you can teach me, because I never have."

We spent the next several hours renting equipment and Asia teaching me how to scuba dive, a good and necessary distraction. Knowing we had a plan and were already acting on it gave us hope, too, which we needed more than anything.

"What if this doesn't work?" Asia asked as we climbed the stairs to our rooms on the top floor, finally overcome with sheer exhaustion that should make sleeping possible.

"Then we come up with another plan," I said. "Whatever it takes, right?"

We entered the hallway of our floor and stopped. She nodded. "Whatever it takes."

I looked down the hall toward my room, but hesitated. I turned back toward the girl with the slight frame but the strength and resolve to do something most grown men could never do. "And when we're back with them, you need to tell Brock."

"Tell him what?" she asked innocently, though I was sure she knew.

"What happened."

She narrowed her eyes. Yep, she knew. "Or what? You'll tell on me?"

I cocked my head and put a hand on her shoulder. "I'm not talking about what happened at Mason's condo. I'm talking about what happened to you. Brock deserves to know. Your relationship deserves it."

She shrugged my hand off her shoulder and strode down the hallway.

"You don't know what you're talking about, Jeric," she said over her shoulder before opening her door and disappearing inside.

I did know, though. Leni and I didn't keep secrets from each other, and I knew Asia had confided that she and Brock didn't have the same relationship we did. There was a wedge between them that shouldn't exist between Twin Flames. Something big and bad had happened to Asia that had driven her to stab that broken bottleneck into Mason's balls. Something significant enough that it had probably changed her. Brock deserved to know what made her the woman she was with him.

With the unhesitating vehemence she acted with, I had a pretty good idea what it had been. Another fucking coward bully who'd probably claimed to love her.

Men like those made me wonder why I should even care about Earth's souls. They were all doomed anyway.

THE NEXT DAY found hundreds of Guardians gathered to give my plan a try. The number who came had surprised me at first, but Melinda and Uri made a good point when I said something at breakfast—with the Gates sealed, the Guardians really had no purpose. They had nothing to guard, and they had no way to help the Lost and Broken souls. Their former lives had been wiped out, so they couldn't go back to those. And the thought of being able to live normally and maybe even long sounded nice, except that's not who we were. Not as long as the Lakari were still here, threatening Earth's souls. It had taken me a while to accept it myself, but I knew deep down what I was.

What we all were. We were warriors, and we had a purpose, and without purpose, there's not much to life at all.

We needed the large numbers, because we needed some pairs to project to fight the Dark souls, others to guard those bodies, and more to fight any physical Shadowmen that dropped into human form. Asia and I were the only ones who had to swim out to the Gate. For such a tiny thing, weighed down with the equipment, she had no problem making the swim halfway across the bay. More proof we could never lead ordinary lives again: our bodies were altered. We were meant to fight and to protect, whether it was against assholes like Mason Hayes or Dark souls that belonged in the realms of Hell.

Once we reached the island where the weeping willow stood, Asia and I dove down to the bottom of the bay. Several dozen ghost-like figures stood at attention—Guardians' projected souls waiting for us. As soon as Asia and I were in place, I gave the signal. Two of the Guardians opened the Gate.

Bright light flared up around Asia and me. We both tensed for the fight. Lakari would come through in spirit form, so it would be difficult to fight them like this, but we had to be prepared for anything. When the Gate took us through, we didn't know what we could end up facing. Hopefully, we'd be facing Leni and Brock, or, at least, the Space Between that would lead us to Leni and Brock.

All we needed was for the walls to close completely around us and the Gate to sweep us away without any interference. As the light reached higher toward the water's surface, it began to thicken. Asia looked at me with hope in her dark eyes. I gave her a tight smile. Our surroundings faded away as the wall of light solidified. My smile began to grow real when the water drained away, down through the sand below our feet. We both removed our air regulators.

"No Lakari," Asia said. "They're gone!"

A hole stretched open behind her, and I nodded at it. "There it is. Get ready."

We both prepared to be sucked into the hole. I could barely see through the small opening, but light shone through it, not darkness. Lakari weren't waiting to swarm through. The Gate was working for us, helping us to reunite with our Twin Flames. I had no idea what to expect once we passed through, but relief already flooded over me. Not long from now, I'd be holding Leni again.

The hole widened. It grew taller than Asia and wider than both of us standing side-by-side, and I began to wonder if it would suck us in after all, or if we needed to jump through it. I couldn't tell if we stared at a gray sky or a gray wall or gray water. It didn't matter.

"We better go through," I said. "Before it's too late."

Asia gave a sharp nod, and we both tensed to jump. But something large and dark flew at us through the hole. A rush of Lakari souls, but that wasn't all. A giant human-ish body with a torso the size of a truck, bulging limbs as thick as redwoods, and a reptilian-like head with multiple horns, everything covered in a green, leathery skin. It charged through the hole in the Gate.

The light walls cracked and disintegrated, and water rushed over us. I tried to find my regulator, while also reaching for Asia's to help her. The hole from another world somehow remained open, though, with Darkness filling it and trying to push through. Guardians fought back, keeping as many as possible from entering our world. Especially that beast.

Once the regulator was back in my mouth and I could breathe again, I pushed off the bay floor and shoved at the thing's head with my whole body. It pushed back with a force stronger than anything I'd faced before. I palmed the knife strapped to my leg and yanked it out. As Asia and the Guardians' souls held the creature half in and half out of the hole, I stabbed it in the eye and plunged the blade deep into its brain— assuming it had one. It fell still, its head hanging through the gap in the Gate's wall as a thick, black substance swirled into the water around us. We shoved the creature back through, and the hole closed up. Several Guardians shut down the lights of the Gate and sealed it up again. Others took off after the Lakari souls that had made it through and had already soared for the Earth's surface. Asia and I swam back for shore slower than we'd come, impeded not so much from the physicality of the fight, but from the defeat weighing heavy in our souls.

How could that thing be so solid and pass through? We'd thought only spirit forms could enter the Gate, and Asia and I had been banking on a slim bit of hope that it would take us since it had taken Leni, Brock, and Bex in their bodies. We hadn't considered physical bodies coming *in*, however. This changed everything. If huge beasts like this could get through to Earth, what would we truly be up against?

By the time we waded out of the water, the fight with the Lakari was over and most of the projected souls had returned to their bodies. Dozens of Guardians stood by the water's edge, waiting for us.

"What the hell was that thing?" I demanded as soon as I could talk. I yanked the equipment off and threw it on the ground.

"Nobody knows," Kel, a Guardian from our Gate, said.

"Never seen anything like it," Yoshi added. "Nobody has."

I scanned over the dozens of faces in front of me. "*Nobody* remembers anything like that? Not from any world you've ever been on? Any life?"

Silence met my question.

"So where did it come from?" Mat, Kel's boyfriend, asked. "Because that's not something easily forgotten. I know *I'd* remember it, and I don't care how long ago the past life was. That thing was fucked up and something that would stick." He jabbed at his temple as he said it.

Several people murmured in agreement. I was right there with him. We only had glimpses of past lives and worlds, but that thing would be one of the first memories I'd be able to recall. No doubt about it.

"It's obvious," Asia said, her voice heavy. "It came with the Lakari, none of us remember seeing one before, and its Darkness was ... *solid*. It had to have come from one of the lowest worlds. One of the Darkest."

"If any of those get all the way through, Earth will go Dark fast," Kel said. "We can't allow them in."

"Damn straight," Mat agreed, crossing his arms over his chest. "It was *solid*. In. Its. Body. We can't let that shit into this world."

Everyone nodded in consent, and some shouted it out.

"Sorry, Jeric, but there's only one thing we can do," Melinda said. "We have to keep the Gates sealed. We have no choice."

Asia and I looked at each other. Her eyes filled with the same mix of emotions roiling through me. I pushed my hands through my hair, blew out an angry breath and stalked off. My chest felt like cement had filled my lungs. My heart was tight and small. I'd never felt such an overwhelming sense of loss, not even when my parents and sister had died.

With long, forceful strides, I walked until I was far enough away to be out of sight. When I stopped, one hand dropped to my hip and the other squeezed the bridge of my nose. I had to compel myself to breathe, the air tearing through my lungs as they tried to inflate against the thousand-pound pressure on my chest. My eyes squeezed shut against the burn in them, only to see Leni's face and those beautiful sea-green eyes on the backs of my lids. A sob pushed at my throat.

I may never see her again. We may never be together—not just in this lifetime, but ever. Our souls would be lost to the Darkness. Because if the Gate had been trying to connect Asia and me to where Brock and Leni were, then they were stuck in the same world where that evil beast had come from. They were in the lowest realms of Hell, and we had no way of getting them back.

CHAPTER 3

Leni

TWO MORE DAYS had passed that felt like two lifetimes. When I wasn't taking Bex outside to pee, I remained curled in a ball by the fire with my one measly blanket wrapped tightly around me, as if it could hold the pieces of me together. My chest ached. My stomach remained in a tight knot. My muscles felt weak and quaky when I used them, and my skin constantly crawled like something lived underneath it. I couldn't believe I'd become addicted to a damn man—a man!—but here I was, having serious physical withdrawals. Sometimes this Twin Flames crap was really screwed up.

I couldn't say if Brock was handling it better or worse than I was. He was taking it like a man—with anger. He constantly paced around the cavern, threw punches at the air or even the wall, and muttered or yelled obscenities. He should have been bald by now from all of the pulling he did at his dark hair while he groaned from the pain living inside him.

The agony of being apart from our other halves had become a living and breathing beast within us. It clawed at our hearts and ate on our souls, never satiating itself but definitely growing. Before long, it would consume us whole. Sometimes, letting it devour me felt so easy. I'd wanted to succumb so many times. But that was the Darkness of the world niggling its way in. I couldn't allow that. If I gave into the Dark, Jeric would be forced to, as well. I couldn't do that to him.

Bex and Hayden weren't much better off than Brock and me. Although her injuries were healing miraculously fast, their souls were not. The effects of their Bonding every day kept them from worsening, but the melding no longer provided improvement against the Darkness. I could feel it settling in on them almost as quickly as it had on Brock and me. Before long, their bodies would start failing.

"Hayden, we have to go soon," I said, my voice raspy from another night of whimpering and sobbing. Or a day of it. I'd lost track of time, but it seemed like it had been a while since the screaming that came at night. "We can't stay here much longer."

"We have enough meat to last a few more days yet," he said from his spot next to Bex on the other side of the fire, where he drew lines in the dirt floor with the tip of his dagger. The gozzard may have been huge, but only certain parts of it were edible, and the four of us had been starving before it followed Brock into our lair. The meat didn't last long. "That gives Bex a few more days to heal. She's still too weak."

"But we're all going down," I said. I glanced over at Brock, who, for once, wasn't pacing, but sat with his knees drawn tightly to his chest, his eyes glazed over as he stared at the flames. "In a few days, we'll *all* be too weak to travel."

"She's right," Bex said, straightening to sit up on her own rather than leaning on Hayden, as though to prove herself. "I'm doing a lot better. I can walk, and I think I can even run. And this tug in our guts has gotten crazy strong. I don't think we can fight it much longer."

"You can't defend yourself with a broken arm," Hayden said.

"We'll have to do it for her," I said. "Isn't it better to have one of us a little weak than all of us? Right now, we can look out for her. But the way we're going, I can't say we'll be able to do that in a few days. Not even you, Hayden. Once the soul-sickness sets in, you'll go down fast. Both of you. Do you really want to risk Bex's soul after all of this?"

Hayden didn't answer me. He continued dragging the point of his dagger through the dirt.

"What if your mates finally come looking for you and you're gone?" he asked. "Waiting here for them to get us off this world is a lot safer than searching for a Gate, especially since we're not exactly sure where it is."

"Instinct will guide you," I said. "And if Jeric and Asia figure it out, they'll be able to come to us wherever we are. We were able to find you."

"Have you even tried to contact them?" he demanded. His tone raised my hackles.

"Every minute of the day! I'm *constantly* reaching out for Jeric. And I'm getting no response. I can't feel anything from him except the pain in his soul. However you were able to send us messages, it's not working for me. Which means there's a good chance the Book's not working for them at all, and they'll never get here. We have to go, Hayden. Sooner, not later."

"Jacquelena's our leader," Brock said, his words surprising me. His eyes had focused beyond the fire, straight onto Hayden. "And you know she's right. We need to go before we're all taken by the Darkness. Including your Rebethannah."

We all watched Hayden expectantly. He stopped drawing in the dirt, but gave no response. Instead, he rose to his feet and took over Brock's usual pacing, his hands on his hips.

"We can leave in the morning," Bex said when Hayden still didn't concede. "That gives us another night of rest and food, and you and I can do that thing with our souls to make us stronger, Hayden. And then we need to make like a tree and leave." He turned his head to look over his shoulder at her and opened his mouth, presumably to protest again, but she held up a hand and cocked a brow. "No arguin' with me now. Just shut that trap of yours and listen. We don't have a choice. I feel it, and I know you do, too. We've been through too much to get here only to lose each other all over again. Besides, Leni and Brock risked themselves—and Asia and Jeric, too—for *us*. We owe them, Hayden. We're not gonna let them down. We all need this, and you know it."

When a Southern woman was as serious as she was, a smart man didn't argue with her. Hayden may not know Southern, but he was obviously a smart man. Finally, we'd be on our way.

We packed up and headed out at first light the next morning. We followed the pull of their souls in the direction of the Gate, moving slowly at first as Bex pushed through the ache of her healing wounds. After a while, she must have grown accustomed to the pain because she began to move faster. She was the only one not carrying a bag of supplies—Hayden carried hers for her. Mine was strapped to my back, over my raggedy sweater that was too tight across my boobs, and my knife hung from the belt that scrunched up the waist of the black pants that were too big for me. At least my boots fit fairly well, and their fit was more important than anything. We had a long walk ahead of us.

I mentally snorted at myself. Barely more than a year ago, I'd been auditioning to be a ballerina in New York City. Only a few months ago, I was dancing on stage in Italy. And here I was now, trekking through some post-apocalyptic world, prepared to fight alien creatures so I could get home to a man whose soul I shared. Since meeting Jeric, life had become so weird, but I couldn't imagine living without him. Well, I could since I was doing it now. But this wasn't living. This was struggling to survive until we could be together again.

We'd been traveling for what felt like a few hours over the gray, desert-like terrain when a forest appeared in the distance ahead of us.

"We don't want to go in there," Hayden said. "We need to go around."

"How big is it?" I asked. "Won't going around take longer?"

"Yeah, but trust me, we don't want to be in that for—ahhhh."

All three of my traveling companions screamed and clutched their heads as they fell to the ground around me. I spun in a circle, my stomach clenching with panic. Their faces twisted and their bodies thrashed as though they were in a great deal of pain, but I had no idea what caused it. I had no idea what to do.

A woman's laugh carried across the land. My head whipped in the direction it came from. Four figures emerged from the forest, quickly headed straight for us. My extra sharp eyesight gained from the Forging must have been fading—I could barely make them out from here. Three appeared to be huge monsters, and the other quite smaller, possibly human, but I couldn't be sure. All of them seemed to be gliding rather than running.

"Come on," I said, tugging at Hayden. He yanked his arm out of my grip and rolled away, moaning. "Someone's coming, Hayden! Please get up!"

"Noooo," Bex cried, her eyes squeezed shut as she, too, rolled on the ground. "Sisssssssy …"

"Asia, please," Brock begged.

"What's wrong with you guys?" I demanded, my neck prickling with fear. My heart raced at the thought of having to fight alone. I'd never be able to do it. "Get up!"

More laughter from the woman. Then I was suddenly not in the gray desert, but sitting in a motel room, on my cell phone, listening to my daddy tell me he didn't have a daughter. Hearing him threaten to call the police if I bothered him or my mother again. And then I was on a street corner in Juneau, Alaska, facing my mama who had no recognition of my face at all. My heart broke as it had the other times I'd gone through the complete rejection by my own parents.

"Lovely memories, yes?" a woman said from nearby, her voice as icy as the nights on Erde.

I jerked out of the visions and refocused on my surroundings. Brock, Bex, and Hayden still lay on the gray, sandy ground, whimpering. The four figures stood a few yards away from us. The three big ones looked like gigantic dogs, but with three heads each the size of a small car. Drool hung from fangs longer than my arm, and eyes rolled wildly in their sockets. They all sat on their haunches, growling and snapping at the air. In front of them stood an average-sized woman with big, snow-white hair that reached her butt, streaked with thick chunks of jet black, perfectly clear skin as white as her hair, and eyes blacker than night. She wore a shiny, black, one-piece suit that appeared to be painted over her voluptuous body, and black, stiletto boots that reached her thighs. She looked like a villainess straight out of a comic book. She was an evil nemesis all right, but very real.

Although I couldn't remember ever seeing her in physical form, my soul recognized her black one instantaneously.

"Enyxa," I breathed.

Her red, full lips quirked up into a smirk. "Jacquelena. It's been a long time."

"Not long enough," I said, pushing down my fear and putting on my mask of courage.

The creatures snarled.

"Watch it," Enyxa warned as she reached up and raked her long fingernails down the mangy neck of one of the monsters. "My hellhounds don't take well to a challenge. I wouldn't try to run, either, although they'd *love* the chase."

I swallowed hard against the lump in my throat and tensed my thigh muscles to keep my knees from knocking together. Trust me, I wasn't running. Especially as my friends still lay on the ground, helpless. "What did you do to them?"

She glanced down at them, and her grin widened. "Ah, just showing them the way."

I cocked my head. "To where?"

"To Darkness, my dear." She gave a hand signal to her hounds, then began walking a circle around us, while the monsters remained seated. "That's why you're here, and what I do—escort souls to the Dark. By forcing them to relive all of the pain they suffered *and* the hurt they caused others, physical and emotional." She stopped across the circle from me, and her dark gaze swept over the three people on the ground between us. "With as much pain and suffering you've all been through, your souls will go quickly. Hayden's been a difficult one, but with Bex here in my world, they'll both go fast."

They all cried out. She must have given them another bad memory.

"Except for me," I said, trying to pull her attention away from them. "My life hasn't been so bad, and I have no loved ones to really care about. You have little to use against me, don't you?"

She looked up at me and tilted her head as she studied my face. The smile returned as she continued her walk, coming closer.

"Oh, Jacquelena, you poor dear. You had no real love in your life this time around, did you? Did you ever think there's a reason for that? Maybe because last time you caused the fire that killed your parents, pushed away the one man who did love you, your so-called Pops, and led your best friend to be murdered? Even in this life, you've rejected Theodethan, the person besides Jeremicah who cares about you most, just as your parents denied you."

My stomach fell, and tears stung my eyes. I'd never thought about things in that way, but I could see the truth in them. *Feel the truth.* And it hurt so much. The realization of how horrible I'd been as Jacey and Leni sent my emotions crashing over me in a tidal wave. She didn't have to make me relive it all to Darken my soul. I could already feel it tainting.

Enyxa stopped in front of me and raised her hand near my head. I flinched as she drew a fingernail down my cheek.

"Don't worry, darling, you have *lifetimes* of pain and hurt to relive," she drawled. "But there's more from this one than you realize."

White-hot pain suddenly seared through my head, blinding me. When the brightness faded, several memories ran through my mind—pushed through it by Enyxa. Memories of me shoving my fist in my mouth to stick my finger down my throat, making myself purge all the calories I'd eaten behind my mother's back. Memories of her forcing me to dance on a stress fracture in my foot. Memories of learning I didn't get into a company or earn a part in a production, and other memories of girls' faces full of hurt when they saw I was awarded a part over them. Memories of sitting in the corner of a dark closet where my mother had locked me up when I was little, my punishment for not mastering the pirouette yet.

"Besides, I have my own special plans for you, Jacquelena," Enyxa said, wiping out the visions. She gripped my chin in her hand now as she looked down her nose at me, her eyes such a deep black, I didn't know if it ever ended. "Plans that have been in the works for eons. After all, you're the cause of *all* of everyone's pain. Too bad you couldn't figure out all the ways to use that Book of yours, which is pretty stupid of you, considering *you* created it." She let me go and strode over to her hellhounds. "Have fun trying to escape the Dark worlds. As I said, my babies love a good hunt, and they *always* find their prey. So ... I leave you with this until next time."

She snapped her fingers, and she and her monsters disappeared into thin air, and my surroundings vanished once again. I was in Mason's apartment, lying on my back, looking up at him as he hovered over me, a shard of glass carving into my breast. Except it wasn't mine, of course. I was reliving Bex's memory. Reliving her physical pain and her emotional hopelessness. Then I was transported again, now sitting in the driver's seat of a car at twilight, witnessing an accident—a truck T-boning a small sedan in front of me. My heart buckled along with the bodies of the vehicles, folding in on itself just like the metal of the cars, becoming something much smaller and crushed until it was no longer recognizable. No way could anyone have survived that crash or the fire that exploded. A female wailed "Nooo! Oh, God, no!" next to me. She sounded like Asia, but the memory vanished before I could know for sure, leaving only agony in my heart.

Somehow, I was still standing when I returned to the present. Not for long, though. I fell to my knees and bawled. Ugly, snotty, gut-wrenching sobs tore through me until I no longer knew why I cried. With one arm held tightly against my stomach, I scrubbed at the wetness on my face. I couldn't remember the last time I'd sobbed so hard. Probably never—my mother wouldn't have allowed it. My eyes burned, and my skin felt gritty from the sand that had stuck to the tears. I tried breathing deep breaths, but the air hitched all the way in and all the way out. My heart and soul weighed so heavily with the spots of Darkness Enyxa had left, I didn't know if I could even stand and support their weight.

"Fucking bitch," Hayden groaned from my right. He rolled onto his knees and braced the weight of his upper body with his hands on his thighs. His head hung between his arms.

Bex and Brock came around, too, also rolling to their knees.

"What the hell was that?" Brock asked.

"The worst thing ever," Bex said through heavy breaths.

"Enyxa paid us a visit," I explained. "She told me we'd be reliving every pain we'd ever experienced and we'd ever caused. From all of our lifetimes."

"That's what she does," Hayden said. "Leads us into the Darkness."

"At this rate, we'll be Dark in no time," Brock said as his hand pressed against his chest.

I assumed the accident had been his memory, but I didn't know what exactly happened that hurt him so much. He hadn't actually been *in* the accident. Had he and Asia known the people in one of the vehicles? Or had they somehow caused the wreck? They'd never spoken much about how they'd met. I didn't know their story. I had a feeling Enyxa was going to make sure I relived it myself. She said I'd caused all their pain. Had *I* been the reason for the accident? I didn't know how that was possible, but my stomach tightened anyway at the thought.

Bex hiccupped with another ragged breath. "As if living through it once hadn't been bad enough."

My stomach heaved with the reminder of what Bex had just gone through. Again.

"Brock's right," I said. "I can't remember everything about all of my lives, but I know they haven't been paradise. We'll never survive the Darkness if we don't get out of here."

Nobody argued any more. We all pushed to our feet and stumbled a few steps before taking off in the direction of the Gate—but staying far away from the forest.

CHAPTER 4

Jeric I LEANED MY elbows on the wooden conference table in the small meeting room, dropped my head between my arms, and rubbed my hands over the back of it. The news kept getting worse and worse.

"You don't have to make a decision today, Jeric," Asia said from across the table.

"So far, the Guardians have been able to protect all the Gates," Yoshi agreed from my right, "but if the souls from the Dark worlds grow any more persistent in opening them, I don't know how long we'll be able to keep the Gates sealed."

"And if sealing them doesn't keep the Lakari out, our only option is collapsing all of the Gates?" I clarified. "We're sure there's no other way?"

"Not that anyone knows of," Melinda said quietly. She and Uri sat on the other side of the table by Asia.

I banged my fists on the table, making everyone jump. "There *has* to be, damn it! There must be a way for us to pass through or we wouldn't be able to help the Broken and the Lost."

"He's right," Asia said. "Why would the angels, or whoever they are, give us this job without alternative passages for times like this? If God and the universe work in mysterious ways to help us with other problems, why not with this?"

Nobody could provide an answer.

"I can't believe there are no records," I said. "*Nothing?* Nowhere?"

"If there are, nobody remembers," Uri said. "The information got lost between generations somewhere along the way."

"Well, then, we need to fucking remember," I growled. "Aren't there hypnotists who do age regression? Maybe they can help. Or, here's an idea—maybe Leni wasn't the only one smart enough to create something to leave clues. Maybe there are more journals ... somewhere."

"There are items, but Leni's not the only one who's forgotten what they do or how to use them," Tasha, Yoshi's other half, said, her English strong, though edged with a Japanese accent. "It's the curse of the Guardians. No matter how hard we try to keep the information flowing generation to generation, it gets lost or jumbled up. It's part of our test in each life to figure everything out."

I shook my head. "I don't buy that. If guarding the Gate and helping the Darkening, Lost, and Broken souls are so important, why wouldn't we be armed with as much knowledge as possible? Why make our jobs more difficult than they already are?"

Again, silence answered my question.

"It seems to happen after we go to another world," Yoshi finally said.

"What does?" I demanded.

"The forgetting."

I cocked my head toward him. I'd never heard a plausible theory that explained why the Guardians couldn't seem to keep their shit together when it came to remembering past lives.

"I'm all ears," I said.

Yoshi lifted his hands. "There's not much more to say. We've all noticed that every time we come back after a life on Earth, it's easier and faster to remember things, especially our need to go to the Gate. True?"

I nodded—it had been easier and faster for Leni and I to remember than it had been for Jacey and Micah. Everyone but Asia nodded also, or agreed aloud. She only shrugged. Why was that?

"But after several lifetimes on Earth, we move up to higher worlds," Yoshi continued. "And it's always once we come back to Earth that we seem to have forgotten everything and have to start over."

"Why can't the Guardians who've been on Earth for a few cycles be able to tell them everything?" Asia asked. "That's what doesn't make sense. There's always Guardians here to pass on information. But not even the Guides remember."

Yoshi shrugged. "Good question. Except when Tasha and I came back to Earth two lifetimes ago, all of the Guardians in this world were either newer—soul mates still making their way to the higher worlds, and therefore never knew our full history—or Twin Flames, Separated and back to start over. All of them on their first or second cycle since being Separated. None of them able to remember anything useful from previous times on Earth."

"In fact, all they could remember clearly was back to their Separation," Tasha said.

I scrubbed my hand over the stubble on my jaw. Leni and I had only been able to remember back to our Separation, as well. We remembered being on that world and some of its specifics, but we clearly recalled Enyxa's Lakari sweeping in and the bitch herself following, ripping our soul apart. Memories of any lives before that, whether on Earth or on other worlds, only came in bits and pieces. Brock and Asia had said the same, confirming Yoshi and Tasha's observation.

"So coming back here from other worlds causes us to lose our memories of this one?" Asia clarified.

"Or Enyxa does something when she Separates us," I suggested.

Everyone in the room reacted to this theory, but Asia and I exchanged a look. Either of these explanations meant that even if we could get Brock and Leni back to Earth, they may not remember anything, including us.

"Whether it's the Gate, or other worlds, or Enyxa who does this to us, though, we can't be the first ones to figure this out," I said. "There must be something somewhere that can give us more answers."

"Well, that Book of yours is a good start," Melinda said. "As part of the Sacred Seven, surely you all would have kept the best records."

"The Book went with Leni," I muttered. "She had it with her when shit hit the fan."

"And since we don't know what the Sacred Seven even means, who says we're the keeper of records?" Asia asked. "Maybe we're too *sacred* to be recorded."

I snorted, catching her sarcasm. We weren't elite or special or anything. In fact, being apart from our other halves, we were pretty damn useless as Guardians. Only good for making the decisions nobody else wanted to make.

"You know how Asia and I feel about collapsing the Gates," I said. "It'll probably end up killing us and our other halves, so we're not too fond of the idea. But it means more than that. It affects everyone—all of the Guardians who will no longer be able to do their jobs and the souls of Earth. So I'm not taking this decision lightly, and I'm not making it on my own." I stood up and leaned my hands on the table. "We're taking a vote."

All of the others in the room looked at each other and back at me.

"Who's voting?" Tasha asked.

"If there were a way to get the whole world to, all of Earth's souls since they're all affected," I said. "But since that's impossible and illogical, all of the Guardians."

Nobody argued. They only stared at me for another long moment. Then they dove into conversation about how to make a vote happen, which meant calling all Guardians in from their missions. They seemed to be on board with this idea.

Some might call me a coward for failing to make the decision myself, but that was their problem. Maybe I wasn't the leader they expected me to be, but I wasn't stupid and power-hungry. They all had a right to weigh in because collapsing the Gates permanently could mean an end to the Phoenix Guardians.

"What do we do if they vote to collapse them?" Asia asked me later that day as we ate dinner. Or, more accurately, pushed the food around our plates, unable to actually eat it.

"I don't know yet, but I'm thinking we go through before they do it."

"We won't be able to come back," Asia said.

"True. But neither will Brock and Leni. So hopefully we can find them through the Gate."

"But what if they do? What if they use the Book to come back? Then we're the ones trapped in the Beyond, and they're here."

THE NEXT DAY, while the Guardian leaders worked on setting up a vote, Asia and I stood outside at our usual places by the water's edge. A brown, rectangular object tumbling at the crest of a wave caught our attention. When it washed ashore, Asia ran for it and brought it back to me. Her eyes had grown wide and watery, and her chin trembled. I opened my mouth to ask what it was, but when my gaze dropped to her hands, my jaw snapped shut.

She held the Book of Phoenix.

My heart skipped a beat as the thought that Leni and Brock must have made it back jumped into my mind. But then it sank to my feet with the realization that we would have felt their return. The brown leather and paper were waterlogged, dripping all over Asia's feet. The Book hadn't recently arrived, bringing our other halves with it. It had obviously been in the bay for a while. Which meant Leni had never taken it with them. And that meant she couldn't use it to bring them back.

I sank into a squatting position, and then fell backwards on my ass. I dropped my head into my hands with defeat.

"Fuck," I muttered under my breath. The Book had been my last hope. If the Guardians voted to collapse the Gates, I'd been banking on Leni using the Book to bring her and Brock back. Now that hope was crushed, along with my soul.

"Stop it, Jeric," Asia said sharply. I looked up at her questioningly. "You're not going to feel sorry for yourself. We'll figure this out."

"Figure out what? It's not up to us anymore. The Guardians are going to vote, and Leni and Brock can't use the Book to return. There's not a whole hell of a lot we can do."

"Sure there is," she said as she jerked the old journal in the air, shaking the water out of it. "We need to figure out how to use the Book like Leni did. Surely she can't be the only one who can make it do whatever she made it do."

I arched a brow. "She used it to get from place to place on Earth. That's not going to help us."

She returned my skeptical expression. "Who says? Maybe the Gate didn't move like we thought it had that night, but Leni used the Book to open up a different portal. One to another world."

I stared at Asia for a long moment, then out over the water while rubbing my brow ring. "She did have it with her," I murmured. "I guess she could have triggered something ..."

"Exactly," Asia said, plopping down next to me. "We just have to figure out what."

She handed the journal to me. The old, brown leather cover looked darker than usual from its dampness, except in parts of the image embossed on it—a weeping willow with a phoenix carved into the trunk that stood on a small island surrounded by water. That area that was supposed to be the water gave off a kind of glow, almost like that part of the leather had a different, smoother texture than the rest, although that wasn't the case.

"Do you know what Leni did?" Asia asked when I'd failed to try anything.

"All I know is she put her finger on the phoenix, like this." I pressed my finger against the bird in the trunk. Nothing happened. No smoke-like, colorful phoenix rose from the cover and surrounded us like it had when Leni had done the same thing. No sparks or ash or bright light. No transporting of Asia and me to a different place, let alone a different world.

"Hmph," Asia said. "That obviously wasn't *all* she did."

"Then you figure it out," I snapped, and I tossed the journal into her lap. "For all we know, it only works for Leni."

"I don't think so. She said she remembered making it for us—the Sacred Seven—right? Or, at least, those of us who've been around lately—you guys, us, and Rebethannah and Nathayden. We may not know what the Sacred Seven means, but why would she say that if only she could use it?"

I shook my head and lifted my shoulders in a half-assed shrug because I had no answer for her. The Book had always been a mystery to me. Leni was always the one figuring things out. But I supposed that didn't mean she was the only one who *could* figure things out.

"Nathayden used it, right?" Asia continued, as though arguing with herself since I hadn't given her anything. "He communicated with it. So that must mean the rest of us can use it."

She lifted the Book up to her face and studied it closely. Her fingers trailed over the parts of the image. She pressed a tip to the phoenix, but still, nothing happened. She wiped her thumb over other parts of the cover. Then she scooped some sand on top of it.

"What are you doing?" I asked.

"I had a thought …" She rubbed the sand around the cover. Again, nothing happened. So she proceeded to push the entire book into the sand, face down.

"What the hell, Asia?"

"Remember how we told you we'd found the Book when Brock and I first met, too?"

"Yeah, but it didn't have your previous story in it. You read ours from our last life—Jacey and Micah."

"Right. And later, something happened with it. The Book did something, but I don't know how. I was trying to recreate that." She sighed when she pulled it out. "It's not working, though."

My stomach shriveled tighter than ever. "Do you think it's ruined from soaking in the bay all this time?"

She gnawed on her bottom lip. "Let's hope not. Maybe it needs to dry out first."

"Yo, bitches," Mat called from behind us.

Asia brushed the Book off before we both stood and turned to face the manor. He and Kel were headed out to us.

"The Guardians have decided," Kel said as they still walked our way. While he was thick with muscle and kept his hair buzzed, his boyfriend was his complete opposite. Mat's muscles were long and sinewy, keeping his body thinner though strong, and his dark hair flopped over his eyes and hung to his shoulders. He reminded me of the look of my band mates and me long ago, while Kel was closer to the post-accident, sick-of-bullies me.

"What do you mean?" I asked as they approached. "They've voted already?"

"How?" Asia asked.

Mat and Kel both shook their heads.

"There's not going to be a vote," Mat said, tossing the hair out of his eyes.

I stared at them for a long moment, realized they were serious, and pushed past them to stalk toward the manor. Yoshi, Tasha,

Melinda, Uri, and some other "senior" Guardians met me at the big, wooden doors, with Asia, Mat, and Kel right behind me.

"What do you mean there's not going to be a vote?" I demanded of them.

"The Guardians don't need to vote," Melinda said. "Word's already passed around to all the Gates and everyone's feelings are the same."

Asia pushed past Mat and Kel to stand next to me.

"They can't choose anyone's soul over others," Uri said. "They won't choose Earth's souls over yours or vice versa."

I groaned. My hands flew to the back of my head, where they clasped as I paced a few times. I could feel everyone's eyes on me.

"Nice. How the hell did I get here?" I muttered. Barely more than a year ago I was modeling in France. Not exactly my cup of tea, but I'd trade anything to go back to that instead of where I was now: leader of some Sacred Seven bullshit that led this faction of people who were responsible for Earth's souls. And now I had to make a choice that could destroy our world either way I decided. My agents and business managers had always talked about win-win situations. Well, I was in a lose-lose one, and had no fucking idea what to do.

"They're not going to make you choose, either," Melinda said.

I turned on her. "Someone's got to!"

She shook her head. "Nope. The Guardians have unanimously agreed to fight."

Asia inhaled sharply. "Seriously?"

Tasha gave her a smile—the type that was meant to be kind, not full of happiness. "Seriously."

Yoshi shrugged and offered a smirk rather than a smile. "Sure. We'll just put on double or triple the forces at each Gate, twenty-four seven. We can handle this."

Mat let out a whoop.

"The Lakari got nothing on us," Kel said.

Other Guardians had gathered around us, and they all began whooping and hollering. Letting out their battle cries. I blew out a breath. A small part of me thought this was a stupid idea. We didn't know what we'd be facing—what could try to push through the Gate. But another part of me knew this was the best option, at least for now. Maybe the Lakari would back off the Gates when they realized we weren't giving up, and we'd never know that if we collapsed the Gates. Maybe we could figure out another solution in the meantime. Maybe we could find more information from our past selves to help us out. We needed more time to figure out all these maybes, and the Guardians had given it to us.

A third part of me, a very big part, was the fighter in me. I wanted to pump my fist in the air and prepare for battle myself. Without Leni, however, I wouldn't be able to guard the Gate. I could fight Lakari on land, but that was about it. Neither Asia nor I would be part of the battles that might come.

"We have our own priority," Asia said, as if she could read my mind. She turned toward me with the Book of Phoenix in her hands, held up between us. "I'm going to go dry this out. You and I need to figure out all the clues this Book contains, including how to use it to bring our Twin Flames home. Preferably before the Guardians change their minds."

I nodded, and she took off. My expectations remained low, though. While I was proud and thankful the Guardians were willing to fight for us and knew I'd figure out a way to help, I'd also made the decision no one else could: If the pressure of the Lakari became too much and we were losing too many souls, I'd make the final call to collapse the Gates. I could only hope it wouldn't come to that, or if it did, the Book would be able to help us anyway.

Otherwise, my Leni was gone from me forever.

CHAPTER 5

Leni

"SO WHAT'S WRONG with Ty?" Bex asked as we climbed our way up a gray sand hill.

Hayden hiked ahead of us, leading the way and scouting for trouble. Brock remained right behind us, covering our backs.

I cringed at her question and shifted my bag to my other shoulder in an attempt to hide it. She was probably trying to distract herself from her physical pain, but I didn't think now was the time to have her worrying about Ty.

"What do you mean?" I asked, striving to sound oblivious. "Nothing, as far as I know."

Which was true. I obviously had no idea what was happening on Earth. Ty could have been fine and dandy for all I knew right now.

"Don't piss on my leg and tell me it's rainin'. Every time I mention him, you and Brock get a look on your faces. Especially Brock. And you ignore my questions."

I glanced over my shoulder at Brock. He scowled at me, but gave no opinion on whether to tell her the little bit I did know.

"He's been missing," I finally blurted.

"*Missing?*" Bex practically screeched. Hayden paused and looked back at us, his face full of alarm. Bex muttered something under her breath, then called to him, "I'm okay, sweetie. Just something from back home." She twisted her head to level me with her blue eyes and said in a harsh whisper, "What do you mean *missing*?"

"I don't know if that's the right word," I said quickly. "He's a grown man, and it's not the first time he's gone off on his own for a while, right?"

"He has been known to do that," Bex admitted. "As soon as he could drive, he'd go off to get away from his daddy."

"Okay, so, he'd been gone a while, and we didn't know where," I said. "That doesn't mean *nobody* knows where he is, especially now. I'm sure he's fine."

"Did you ask around?"

"We don't exactly know all of Ty's friends," I said. "We know he has that friend in Gainesville, so maybe he's there."

That wouldn't have explained why Ty hadn't returned any of Jeric's phone calls, but I wasn't about to tell her that. The poor girl didn't need that kind of worry. She'd been through enough right before coming here, and we were all helpless when it came to anything happening on Earth anyway.

"Who knows, maybe he's home by now," I added.

"Why don't you tell her the truth?" Brock snarled from behind me.

I peered back at him with an eyebrow raised.

"She should know," he said. "May as well yank the Band-Aid off now."

"What are you talking about?" I asked.

"I should know what?" Bex demanded.

Brock's eyes narrowed at me. "Jeric didn't tell you what I'd texted him right before we went to save Bex?"

His tone indicated he was trying to remind me of something, but I had no idea what.

"We didn't exactly have time to talk about anything but Bex and Hayden."

Brock scowled again and then shifted his dark gaze onto Bex. "Someone said they found his truck in the swamps near the springs of Lake Haven."

Bex gasped, and her good hand went to her throat. "Oh, no," she choked. "That's no good. People die in those springs! Did they ... did they find his body like the others?"

Brock's brows pushed together. "I don't know. Asia and I found out right before Jeric called about you. And then we ended up in this god-forsaken place."

Bex's face had gone completely white, causing her greenish-yellow bruises to stand out in stark relief. I returned Brock's constant scowl at him before trying to settle Bex down. I'd always sensed a layer of deep pain in Brock, but he usually kept it hidden under the surface, masking it with jokes and a laid-back attitude. That comfort blanket had been removed, though, uncovering a side of him I didn't particularly like. It wasn't like him to be so direct and hurtful. The Darkness of this world had already begun to claim his soul.

"He's probably dead," Bex cried. "Just like Sissy and Mama ... everyone I love ... my family ... dead."

"You don't know that, Bex," I tried to soothe. "And you still have Hayden. And us."

She swiped at her tears and nodded, but she didn't force her usual smile. Her chest heaved as she tried to fight the emotions, but heartache showed through her eyes. The Darkness was getting to her, too.

Hayden had stopped right below the top edge of the dune we'd been climbing to wait for us. As we came closer, Bex gasped, and her hand flew to her chest.

"Ohmagosh, we're here," she said, picking up speed to reach Hayden. "I *feel* it."

I felt something tugging in my own chest, and it could only be the pull of the Gate. Finally. We'd been traveling for three days, stopping for only a few hours at a time to rest at the tops of trees and under the ledge of a cliff—the only kind of shelter we'd found. My legs ached, my chest burned from trying to breathe normally, and my head throbbed from the weight of the Darkness. I could only imagine how Bex felt, although she hadn't complained once. Probably because she knew Hayden would make us stop, and we couldn't afford to do that. Brock's pace picked up into a near jog, and I pushed myself to move faster, too, and we all caught up to Hayden right below the crest. As soon as we reached the top of the hill, Hayden swore.

"Get down!" he barked in a whisper, dropping to his knees behind the top of the hill.

We all dropped, too, and crawled up on our bellies to look over the dune. My breath caught at the sight.

Off to our right, maybe five or so miles away, stood a city of black, gothic buildings with a multitude of towers and sharp-pointed spires reaching for the sky. Like the cathedrals of old Europe, but if those were places of worship, I didn't want to know *who* the congregation praised. A wall of black stone enclosed the entire city, and from our vantage point, I saw no break in the barrier, no gate to pass inside. Not that I really wanted to get inside. The city sat at the edge of a huge body of black water—perhaps a large lake or bay or maybe even a sea because I couldn't see the other side—that stretched down toward us. Besides that, nothing but gray desert lay between us and the city.

Below the dune, though, about a quarter-mile away and on the edge of the water, was an encampment of ... monsters. Gozzards, giant troll-like men that stood at least twenty feet tall with muscular limbs thicker than a Redwood trunk and skin the color of peas, and smaller beasts that looked like lizards but were the size of lions. People intermingled among them, all dressed in long, black Victorian-style coats, knee-high lace-up boots, and scarves, hats, and goggles on their heads, as though they'd walked off the set of a steampunk Sherlock Holmes movie. And all apparently female. Tents made of a black material were set up around the area, and several fires burned in barrels.

A black haze hovered in the air, stretching from here to the city. It churned and bubbled and moved not like a cloud on a current, but as though individual particles moved on their own. It was a swarm of Dark souls in spirit form, swooshing to and from the city, some coming down and wrapping the monsters and women in a black mist before gusting upwards to the mass above.

"If the pull in my gut is right," Hayden said, "the Gate's on the other side of them, in the water."

"Makes sense," I whispered.

"Who—or what—are those things, and what are they doing?" Bex asked.

"Good question," Hayden said. "I've never seen so many in one place except in battles. With each other."

"Battles?" Bex echoed.

"They're at war?" Brock asked.

"We're always at war," Hayden murmured. "Those who've gone Dark are always fighting for power and greed, throwing each other off the thrones every few months or so, it seems. They're really just feeding Enyxa's insatiable lust for chaos and mayhem. The rest of us, who haven't gone completely Dark, live away on our own in the wilds, staying out of their wars as much as we can."

"Where are the men?" I asked.

"Who knows? Enyxa takes them away."

"*What?*" Brock demanded.

"The only male humans are those of us who haven't gone completely Dark yet," Hayden explained. "Enyxa uses these female Dark ones to help us along. More temptation, in more ways than one. If you get up close, they'll mesmerize you with their beauty. It's only on the surface, though. Their promises are alluring, but only good until you fall into complete Darkness. Then they cast you aside like trash for Enyxa to clean up."

"Sounds like most of the women I dated," Brock muttered.

Hayden ignored him, the sarcasm once again lost on him. "Enyxa enslaves them as her army, but they don't think they're slaves because they have rank over the other creatures, which is why they're always fighting. Once we men go Dark, she takes us away, presumably to use for some other purpose."

I knew the other purpose. Brock did, too. Enyxa used them to make souls on other worlds go Dark. When the Lakari dropped into human form on Earth, they were always men, so apparently Enyxa kept the female souls in the Dark worlds with her and sent the males to the other worlds. I couldn't help but wonder why.

"This group doesn't look quite friendly, but definitely not at war with each other," Brock said.

"Obviously," Hayden agreed.

"So what are they doing here?" Bex asked again.

We watched the gathering silently for a few moments longer as the sky began to darken with nightfall, and the air grew noticeably cooler. Several of the monsters stood in a line along the shore, their backs to us as they faced the water. The mist of Dark souls spread across the sea, swirling and churning restlessly.

My stomach sank with the answer. "They're guarding the Gate."

Brock's head twisted sharply to glare at me, and then he looked back at the encampment. He scooted up a little farther, as though that would give him any better of a view.

"Why, though?" he asked. "Wouldn't they want souls to come through so they could be Darkened?"

"They're not here to keep souls from coming *in*," I said, my voice heavy.

"Damn." Brock had caught on. "They're waiting for their opportunity. For the Gate to open somewhere else so they can go through."

My throat thickened, making my next words even harder to force out. "They're waiting on us to open it for them. They know we're here."

We all scooted down the dune a few feet to keep ourselves out of sight—as if that helped when Dark souls flew overhead.

"What are we going to do?" Bex asked as she flipped onto her back. She held her good arm against her chest in the same way Brock and I did, as though what we felt within was a physical sensation. "The pull to go there is even stronger."

"I say we get the hell out of here," Hayden said. "We can take on one or two of them, but not that many."

I rolled onto my back and stared at the sky that had become a slate gray in the last few minutes. Before long, the sun would disappear, and I'd learned these recent nights of being out in the wild that no one on Earth knew the black of night like it was here. The freezing cold would settle into our bones. We definitely couldn't stay on the side of this hill. We wouldn't last for more than a few hours—less if they saw us.

"Will they hunt at night?" I asked him.

"Yes," Hayden said, "and here we are in plain sight for them."

"So that can be when we make our move," I said. "We can sneak past them."

"And then what?" Hayden asked. "That water is black for a reason. It's not clean, fresh water. All kinds of things have been dumped into it."

"We don't have a choice," Bex said. She shuddered, though, and I didn't know if that was from the thought of swimming in black, mucky water, or from the air already cooling down. "You know we don't, Hayden. You feel it, too."

"We have to sneak past them, swim through gross-ass water, and then somehow figure out how to open the Gate,"

Brock said, his voice a near growl. "All without those ... *things* ... getting through it, too. Impossible."

"We have to figure it out," I said. "If we could project, it might be easier, but then we'd be leaving our bodies behind."

Brock rubbed his scruffy chin. His tone lightened some as he said, "Hayden and Bex can project. They could sneak out there and open the Gate, and we could carry their bodies to them."

I considered this for a moment, then shook my head. "They're not Forged. We don't know if they can even open the Gate, or if they can fight off that massive mist of Dark souls. They're not strong enough."

Brock huffed and rolled onto his back. "Then I'm out of ideas. Maybe Hayden's right. We should just get the hell out of here."

I sat up and stared at him. "You are *not* giving up, Brock. We will figure this out, and we will get through that Gate, and you *will* get back to Asia. We promised each other." When he didn't answer—didn't even look at me—I turned to Hayden. "Is there any way to camouflage ourselves? Maybe we could steal some clothes and try to pass through the camp?"

Hayden snorted. "You and Bex, maybe, but Brock and I will never pass."

"It doesn't have to be perfect. We can stay on the outskirts of the camp, and it's only until we reach the water."

"We could do it!" Bex said excitedly. "And once we hit the water, it's pretty much balls to the walls to get out to the Gate anyway, right? Not like we're taking a moonlit dip in that shit."

Hayden groaned, expressing his dislike for our plan, but he knew it *was* a plan. The only one we had. So we huddled together as night fell completely, shivering against the cold. At least half of the beastly creatures left camp to hunt, and by the grace of God, they hadn't sniffed us out already, but had headed away from us. Before their noses did lead them in our direction, we slid down the other side of the dune and crept to the first dark tent on the edge of camp. Bex and I snuck in while Hayden and Brock kept watch behind a burning barrel. At least it gave them a bit of warmth, too.

"There's no way these are going to fit the guys," Bex whispered as she held up a jacket inside the tent that would barely fit me, let alone Brock or Hayden.

"We'll have to do the best we can," I said.

The tent contained two beds, two trunks, a table with a dim lantern on it, and a chair. I could only hope the woman who slept on my side of the tent was larger boned. Her size was definitely bigger, but the guys were going to look ridiculous. No way would we be able to fool anyone.

"Hey, look at these," Bex said. "They'll work, right?"

Now she held up what looked like a cape. No, a poncho. She pointed to another one draped over the chair.

"Perfect," I said. "Let's get out of here."

We threw on the coats we'd found, buttoned them up, and pulled the hoods over our heads. They both reached to our knees, with a tighter bodice and waist and then flaring over the hips. I'd found some goggles, too, to hide us a little more and also help us to blend in. The goggles would have been nice when we were traveling through the desert, but maybe they could help in the water, too.

After a quick peek through the door to check for others, we walked out like we belonged and headed straight for the barrel where the guys hid. They grumbled quietly about the clothing we gave them.

"Beggars can't be choosers," I snapped. "Hurry up."

Both of them were tall and broad-shouldered, and neither could pass for women, so we stayed on the very edge of the camp and hurried toward the shore. We were almost there when two giggling women emerged from a tent right in front of us, both of them completely naked, their skin glowing in the darkness. Both of them just as beautiful as Hayden had said they would be. Except their eyes. Although one had blond hair and paler skin while the other was a brunette with a darker undertone to her flesh, both had the same eye color: ink black. They stood in front of us, smiles on their faces, arms around each other while their free hands roamed over the other's body. Right in front of us.

"Why do you have all those clothes on?" the brunette asked with an accent like Hayden's, while staring at me. I kept my head averted, as we all did, so they wouldn't see the unusual colors of our eyes—unusual for these humans anyway, who were completely Dark. I rolled my eyes up to peek at them through my lashes.

"Yeah, aren't you hot?" the blond asked. She reached out for Bex's jacket, her arm skating over Bex's boob, the same one Mason had mauled, making her flinch. The woman cocked her head for a moment, then laughed. "You even have gloves on! I don't know how you can wear all that. The cold feels so good." She lifted her arms above her head, raising her full breasts, and spun in a small circle before wrapping herself around her partner again, one hand landing on the other's breast and the other hand sliding over her stomach, downward. "I can never wait until that fucking sun drops so I can take it all off and feel the air on my skin and see all the sexiness of my girls."

The other woman giggled as her friend pinched and pulled at her nipple. "Me, too. You should come join us in our tent. The more the merrier, right?"

They batted their eyelashes at us as they smiled seductively, then turned to each other and proceeded to make out right there in front of us, their hands groping and stroking the other's body in the most intimate places while they moaned into each other's mouths. Without breaking their kiss, one of them reached out, about to grab my arm.

I carefully tucked it close against my body, out of reach. "We're going to shed these clothes first. We'll be back."

I gave my head a small jerk as a sign to the others, and they began moving. I must have said something wrong, though. Or maybe it was my poor attempt at mimicking their accent.

"Wait," the blonde said, extricating herself from the other's embrace. She studied us more carefully, first Bex and me, and then her gaze fell hard on Brock and Hayden. In a flash, her hand flew out and knocked the hood of Hayden's poncho down. "You're a man! And your eyes ..."

Her mouth fell wide open, but not to express her shock. A shrieking, siren-like sound exploded from her.

"Run!" Hayden barked, and the four of us took off toward the shore.

Hearts pounding and legs pumping, we sprinted through the camp and broke through its edge, onto the beach. A half-dozen monsters barreled toward us. Without slowing down, we all pulled our weapons out. A Weiran, the green-skinned giants that reminded me of the Incredible Hulk, shook the ground as he ran toward us, swinging a mace. Hayden stepped in front of Bex and exchanged a look with me before we both craned our necks to look up at the beast. We lunged at the same time, Hayden's two swords slicing into the Weiran's tree-trunk of a leg and my knife cutting a gash into the arch of its other foot. The thing howled and immediately fell on its butt, making the ground quake beneath our feet.

"Run!" Hayden ordered again.

Before the Weiran could react or the other creatures could reach us, we raced again across the beach. Several round objects that I thought were rocks were scattered on the sand. Hayden picked one up and threw it at Bex.

"Put this on," he commanded. He grabbed another and pulled it down over his head. Brock and I each picked one up and did the same as we continued running, splashing into the water.

As soon as the water touched it, the jacket I'd stolen tightened up around me, becoming a second skin, as thick and reptilian-like as the gozzards' hide. Good thing, too, because even it began sizzling and disintegrating in the water. It wasn't mucky and oily as I'd expected, but apparently acidic. I could barely breathe in the helmet at first, but then it sealed up, too, and oxygen came from somewhere. The protection would only last so long, though—everything was peeling away in thin layers—so I swam as hard as I could. Hayden and Brock took turns helping Bex, but eventually she must have realized they were moving too slow, because she began to use her broken arm to swim.

We swam for what felt like hours but had probably been only minutes. Then finally an island with a tree, permanently bent over from the wind like all of the trees on Erde, came into view. Brock turned back to me and gave me a thumbs-up. My pounding heart slowed minutely. But just because we'd found the Gate didn't mean we could open it. Big splashes and waves behind us meant the monsters had followed us in. Part of the black sky above fell toward us—Dark souls. I pointed my knife downward. We needed to dive.

As soon as we were all under the water, a light emerged from the depths. The Gate! It recognized us as Guardians! I could have squealed with joy. But Darkness pressed down from above. The Dark souls were funneling into the water, and their physical counterparts were right behind us.

"Hurry!" I yelled at the others, although I didn't know if they could hear me through the helmets.

Right before the light reached us, everything around me changed. We fell into more painful memories, reliving them as if we were there, in the past again. Except not mine. Bex's, Hayden's, and Brock's memories enveloped me. Their heartbreak engulfed me. I didn't know how much real time passed, but Brock and I relived several weeks, from the moment he met Asia and through the rocky beginnings of their relationship. Although we both knew that wasn't the end of their story, the emotional agony Brock felt and poured into me meant that wasn't the worst of it.

As the bright light of the Gate returned, and we entered into it, I was able to pull one full, lucid thought through the pain:

Enyxa was near. She was going to follow us through the Gate, along with all of her minions.

We could *not* bring them to Earth.

CHAPTER 6

Aria   I AWOKE WITH a gasp, my fists gripping the sheet and my head still in the dream I'd been having. Except whatever I'd been dreaming about had ended with a memory—a very clear, very real one. One I preferred not to relive again, but there it was. Still playing in my mind even as I came fully awake.

I lay on my stomach, my face buried in the pillow. I pressed my hands into the mattress and pushed myself up to roll over. Only when I blinked and my lashes stuck together did I realize I'd been crying.

The dream—the memory—had been too real.

And like that day, when Brock had said I couldn't be in his life, I was again completely alone. My heart and soul ached, I couldn't help but wonder if it ached for him or ... for something else.

With a shake of my head—I didn't need to be thinking those thoughts—I swiped my hands over my face, and then reached over and tugged the chain for the bedside lamp. There was no point in trying to sleep after that. My mind wouldn't clear those images so easily, and even if I could fall back to sleep, I was afraid I'd be right back in that memory again. A glance at the clock on the nightstand told me I shouldn't be in bed anyway. The blackout curtains hid the daylight, but it was surely another beautiful fall day in Tampa, Florida. Another day I didn't want to face. Not alone.

Only the thought of the Book of Phoenix was able to drag me out of bed. After a quick stop in the bathroom, I padded over to the in-wall air conditioning unit under the window and picked up the Book. I'd set it on end over the vents before going to bed, hoping the air would blow up through the pages and dry them out. Jeric had left it with me to try to discover any clues, but it had been too wet last night, and I was afraid I'd ruin the pages by trying to peel them apart from each other. My fingers gripped the leather cover, which was now dry. I picked up the Book and carried it over to the bed, snuggled under the covers again, and opened the lock. As I flipped through the pages, my heart sank.

Everything had been washed away.

Jacey's story, Jeric's drawings, Nathayden's messages ... all were gone.

At least, until I held the Book directly under the lamp. I could barely see the handwriting, only a shade darker than the paper itself. And the harder I squinted at it, the more I realized that not only did Jacey's neat cursive fill the page, but there appeared to be other words, too. Ghosts of other stories?

As I stared, my face only inches from the paper to see better, new words began scrolling across the page in black ink. With a gasp, I jerked back. A lump formed in my throat. I recognized that handwriting.

"Brock?" I squeaked. "Is that you?"

My heart stopped as I waited for an answer. More words continued filling the page, and then the next one.

"*When the doorbell rang, Mom called out to me to answer it while she was undoubtedly still organizing what she needed for the interview. She'd talked about canceling it because of my sudden appearance on my parents' doorstep a few days before, but that was the last thing she needed to do, so I convinced her* to keep it. I loved her, but the woman's life was out of control, which was exactly why she needed to have this meeting. My own hands were full, of course, and I wasn't even dressed completely, but I went and answered the door anyway. When I did, my heart did this weird seesaw thing at the sight in front of me ..."

My hand had gone to my throat as a smile crept across my face from the memory, but a beep from my phone nearly had me jumping out of my skin. A text message from Jeric: "Coming to your room."

Good news maybe? I sprang out of bed again and threw on a pair of pajama pants, just in time, too. My fingers fumbled with the drawstring when there was a knock at the door. I yanked the door open and lasered my focus onto Jeric's face. Crap. No, not good news. Not if his piercing blue eyes or the downward pull of his mouth were any indication. His hand was fisted at his temple, and he rubbed his thumb over the ring in his eyebrow as he stared back at me.

"What's up?" I asked, not knowing whether I should invite him into my room or if this would be quick. It would feel weird to have another guy in here when Brock wasn't.

He leaned against the doorjamb and crossed his thick, tatted up arms over his chest. "There was more activity in the Gate early this morning."

My eyebrows leapt, and my heart stuttered with the tiniest bit of hope. "And ...?"

Of course, if Brock and Leni had returned, I would have known. I surely would have felt it in my soul the instant Brock was back. And judging by the look on Jeric's face, he wasn't about to tell me anything I really wanted to hear. My hands came together in front of me, twisting and turning. What if they *had* come back ... but were dead?

"Nobody came through," he said quickly. He must have seen the fear on my face and knew I'd been thinking of the monstrous beast that had come through the Gate the other day.

"But the Lakari on this side had grown pretty excited, I guess. I wasn't there, but that's what Mat and Kel told me. They said the Gate lit up and a hole began to open as if someone was trying to come to our world. There was a lot of movement and noise from the other side, and I guess it didn't sound good, but the hole tightened up before any Dark souls came through."

"Okay." I nodded. "Well, that's good. Right?"

Jeric sighed and pushed himself to stand up straight. "Yeah, for now. I guess. But Asia?"

He paused, and I felt his gaze piercing into me. I looked up into his face.

His eyes traveled over mine as he pressed his lips together. "I feel like I need to tell you this, just so we're clear."

My throat tightened. I wrung my hands tighter in front of me. His tone scared the shit out of me. "What?"

He broke his gaze from my face and looked down the hall for a long moment before returning his eyes to me. "If things get really bad, I won't have a choice but to order the Gates to be collapsed. As much as they're willing to fight, I can't allow Guardians to die for us."

I forced my throat to swallow and then nodded. "I know, Jeric."

I'd tried to sound strong, but my voice betrayed me, cracking on the words.

He blew out a breath and nodded. "I just wanted to be sure …"

He trailed off, realizing I didn't expect him to explain. I didn't need him to. We both knew what he'd have to do if it came down to it, and I couldn't argue with him. We had a responsibility much bigger than ourselves, as much as it sucked.

Apparently with nothing more to say, he shoved his hands into his pockets, turned and walked away, down the corridor toward his room. I shut the door and leaned against it. My whole body trembled. I slid down the door until my butt hit the floor and then pulled my knees into my chest and curled myself over them. I couldn't breathe. The air was too thick. Too Dark.

A deep sadness settled over me, and I began to wonder what it would feel like when the Darkness took over completely. Would it be painful? I couldn't imagine any worse emotional pain than I was already in—a pain so deep and thorough, it felt physical. Worse than the utter misery of major depression.

I remembered too easily my bout of depression and the feeling it brought that nothing in the world could ever be right again. All I could see then were days and months and years ahead of me of living at the bottom of a black pit that I could never climb my way out of. Where every day consisted of the exact same desolation because nothing would ever change. I didn't deserve anything different anyway, I'd thought then. I was too weak and ignorant and ugly and skinny and selfish and vain and irresponsible and bitchy ... and just plain stupid to deserve happiness. I *belonged* at the bottom of that pit, far away from the intelligent, beautiful, happy people of the world who shouldn't be subjected to the damage my presence would do to them. I didn't deserve their love or any kind of joy of my own.

I walked the rim of that pit every day, always fearful of falling back in, and I felt now that same weight of negativity and despair tugging me downward again, heavier than ever. The Darkness had already begun to seep in, coloring my soul. How much longer before I succumbed to it? Maybe it would be easier for both Brock and me if I just gave in now. Maybe if I freed him from this Bond ...

"No," I said aloud. "I can't think like that."

I'd let my mind go down that path for the second time since waking up only fifteen minutes ago. I knew it was the Darkness taking me there. And I knew I had to fight it.

I forced myself to my feet, shuffled back to bed, and returned to my position under the covers with the Book of Phoenix. More of Brock's handwriting filled another page with his memories of when we'd first met, but no more than that. Had he cut off the memory? Or had the magic of the Book failed again? I went back to the first page and read the beginning of our story as my Twin Flame told it. The Darkness lifted some. I could breathe again, and my chest didn't feel like a two-ton weight sat on it. Or that there was a giant hole in me that a car could pass through. My heart and soul felt lighter, in more ways than one, as my own mind recalled the memories Brock shared, wanting to pick up where he left off. Of course, my perspective was different from his, but reading about it from his point of view was nice. It made me feel closer to him than I'd felt since the night they disappeared.

I wondered if that meant they *were* closer to us. Maybe they'd been the ones in the Gate, trying to get through this morning. Maybe the Gate had been sealed too tightly for them to find this world. Which meant they could be stuck in the Space Between, or worse, somewhere else, like where that monstrous beast had come from.

Panic rose. Breathing came harder again. The weight returned. Thinking of these increasingly horrible possibilities brought the Darkness back.

"Focus on the Light," I murmured to myself, but my soul was already sinking again. Tears made my vision blurry. *Memories.* Remembering when we'd first met had been good. Much better than wallowing in my sorrow. And obviously better than letting the Darkness take hold, even when I knew the memories themselves would quickly turn bad. I sucked in a jagged breath and nodded to myself. "The past is better than the present, at least."

I wasn't really so sure about that, but I was trying hard to convince myself because I needed a good place to go to. And being with Brock, if only in my head, was much better than being here alone. So damn alone.

I lifted the Book, but was unable to see his words through the tears, so I pressed it against my chest as I sunk down into the pillows. And I allowed myself to be carried off by my own version of our story.

For me, our story started before it did for Brock, back several months in fact. I couldn't believe it had been over a year ago. More than fifteen months since what had been the worst day of my life at the time. Maybe still was. No, that wasn't a good memory, and thinking about what could have been if that day had never happened didn't help my psyche, either. I fast-forwarded a few months, to a year ago almost to the day, to the first time I met Brock.

CHAPTER 7

1 YEAR AGO

Asia I LEANED OVER and looked out the passenger side window at the large, cream-colored, two-story home, then back at my phone to double-check the address. Another glance at the house number confirmed this was the place. I turned right into the driveway, shaded by two enormous palm trees, stopped in front of the iron gate that blocked the rest of the driveway and presumably the backyard from visitors, and slid the gearshift into park. Then I smoothed my hands over my blond hair that finally reached my shoulders again, took a few cleansing breaths, and forced myself out of the car and into the heat of fall in Florida.

I seriously needed this job. The drive from Boston to here and living in hotels proved to be expensive, and my savings was draining away quickly. I wouldn't be able to survive much longer, and I wasn't about to call home for money. Not only did this position pay a weekly salary, but it also provided private living quarters. Nice ones, by the looks of the place.

With lush, green grass, plenty of tropical bushes and flowers, and a variety of palm trees, the grounds were certainly beautiful, and so was the Spanish-style house with its elegant arches and orange, ceramic-tiled roof. Although huge, the size paled in comparison to my parents' home, but considering it was near the water on Florida's famous Gold Coast, it may have been worth nearly as much. I'd left home and school to escape this nauseating lifestyle, but a job was a job and beggars can't be choosers. If I didn't find work fast, I would certainly be a bona fide beggar on the streets.

My legs wobbled on my high heels as I walked up to the front door. I'd already become used to my Doc Martens, and I now felt vulnerable and naked without them. Not too long ago, I'd been a typical rich girl fashionista who could walk five malls in a day and still go clubbing in shoes like these. But life happened, my priorities shifted, and then my whole world was basically flushed down the toilet in a massive mess that had left me hollow inside. My ass-kicker boots were one of many ways I'd found to protect myself from ever going through such hell again. Now wearing one of only two outfits I'd kept from that previous life, I felt completely out of sorts and wanted to jump back in my car, drive back to the motel, and hide under the covers.

Instead, I jabbed the doorbell with my finger. And wiped my sweaty hands on my skirt as I waited. And forced myself to breathe normally.

When the door opened, I completely forgot how to do that last part.

I expected the woman I'd spoken to on the phone to answer the door. Instead, a hunk of a guy about my own age stood there in jeans and nothing else. No shirt, no shoes, no socks. Bare chested and bare footed. Holy mother-effin cow, what a view he provided. Broad shoulders, bulky and well-defined arm and chest muscles, washboard abs, and a narrow waist with that V shape that made smart women stupid. Like I was being right now as my thoughts ran away with what it would be like to lick all those muscles. Heat flushing my cheeks, I forced my eyes up to his face. He looked down at me with a raised brow—a dark brow over dark but playful eyes that matched his disheveled dark hair.

And in one perfectly sculpted arm, he held a baby.

As my brain caught up to the view, my eyes immediately went to the tiny human, cradled between the thick forearm and bare chest. The world froze, and my gaze became stuck on its little head with a shock of dark hair and an angelic, sleeping face. My heart wobbled. My stomach clenched. A newborn, I thought. Barely a month old, I guessed. Wearing a onesie, with soft, pink arms and legs curled into itself as it slept comfortably. For a moment, breathing became even harder than it had already been.

"You're here to see my mom?" the guy asked, and my nerves jolted as if they'd been given an electric shock.

I tore my eyes from the infant's peaceful little face and cleared my throat as I looked back up. "Um, yes. I'm Asia?"

Why did it sound like a question? He smiled. Shit. I had to remind myself where I was and who he was. Not that I knew him, but I didn't have to. He was rich and hot and that's exactly what I needed to stay away from. But damn, what a smile.

"Are you sure about that?" he asked. The baby squirmed and opened its mouth in a big yawn. I didn't know which unnerved me more—the teasing tone in his voice or the little one in the crook of his arm.

"Brock?" a female voice called from somewhere in the house behind him. I recognized it as the one I'd heard on the phone. "Is it my twelve o'clock?"

He glanced over his shoulder. "She thinks she's Asia. Does that sound right to you?"

A woman appeared behind him, looking around his arm. She may have been middle-aged, but she'd arrived there gracefully. Her dark hair, streaked with gray, was pulled back in an up-do, and she wore only enough makeup to accentuate her gorgeous dark eyes, which her son obviously inherited from her.

"Oh, stop giving her a hard time," she said before smiling at me. "Ignore him, dear. He always likes to tease the pretty ones."

I pressed my lips together. Brock rolled his eyes.

"Are you going to let her in, son, or stand there and gawk?" she asked as she turned and already began walking away.

The smile I'd been fighting slid away when my gaze returned to his face. She didn't mean gawking at me. He was staring past me, at the driveway.

"Your car?" he asked before turning and stepping to the side to finally let me in.

I looked over my shoulder at my yellow Camaro, the only thing my mom and stepfather had given me that I'd kept. "That's my baby."

As soon as the words were out, I wanted to suck them back in. Or change them. Or do anything because they suddenly sounded all wrong and awkward, and probably only to me, but still ...

"Nice," he said appreciatively as he held his arm out in a welcoming gesture. Or shooing me in, I wasn't sure.

Once the door closed and blocked out the bright sunlight, my eyes adjusted to the sunny grand foyer with its tile floors, sweeping staircases to each side, and multiple archways to other rooms. Brock's mother—my potential future boss—stood in the middle with her arm extended to me. She wore a loose top and miniskirt on a body that defied her age more than her face did.

"Hope Verdor," she said when I took her hand for a quick shake. As if I didn't know, and not just because she'd told me on the phone. "Romance author—" she waved a hand in Brock's direction "—mother to Brock and—"

The baby took that moment to introduce itself with a loud cry. She hurried over and tried to scoop it out of Brock's arms.

"Let me have my little sweet 'ums," she said.

"Mom, you have a meeting. I'm pretty sure I can take care of him for more than a few minutes," Brock said, turning away from his mother. I couldn't help but notice his nicely shaped butt and how his back muscles pulled as he walked off.

Mrs. Verdor put her hands on her hips and pouted as she watched them disappear into an adjacent room, and then she let out a sigh.

"That was baby Connor. Truly unexpected, both of them, but my pride and joy nonetheless." She turned toward me, and I had to clench my jaw to keep it from hanging open. I couldn't believe she'd just said that about her own children. I'm sure it was weird to have kids so far apart in age, although I didn't know if she had any more in between, but to just blurt that out to a stranger floored me. She went on as if such comments were normal. I instantly felt a little bad for her children. "So tell me about yourself, Asia."

She began walking down a corridor, and I followed as I gave her a brief overview of myself, trying not to be distracted by the row of windows on our left that looked out onto a courtyard with colorful plants and a fountain in the center. Was I really in Hope Verdor's home? I wasn't the squealing type anymore, but I'd almost reverted to it. Romance wasn't exactly my favorite genre, but since scheduling the interview three days ago, I'd been devouring as many of her books as possible, and her characters had converted me—at least to paranormal romance.

"I just moved to the area from up north," I started, and then it all poured out in one long gush. "I hope to enroll in classes again for the spring semester, but first, I really need a job and a place to live. I love reading and writing, and I'm good with computers and social media, and very organized to the point of being a little OCD, so when I saw your ad for a personal assistant, I had to call."

We stopped in front of a door, and she waved at me to go inside. We entered what was obviously her office, with an entire wall of bookshelves crammed full, a desk piled with teetering stacks of notebooks and more books, a sitting area with two salmon colored, velvet-upholstered armchairs and a table in between them, and pictures all over the walls of her with other people, some of them famous authors and celebrities I recognized.

"This is where the magic happens?" I asked, trying and failing to keep the awe out of my voice.

She snickered. "Not exactly. This is where I do the business stuff. I can't stand to write in here. It kills my creativity. Have a seat."

I sat on the edge of one of the chairs and she sank into the other, tucking her legs under her.

"So tell me about yourself."

I stared at her while clasping my hands together tightly in my lap. I thought I did that already?

One side of her mouth pulled up in a half-smile. "You didn't tell me anything really. I think I know five things about you and nothing personal."

"There's not much else to tell." Not anything she needed to know anyway.

"Oh, please. We're all characters with backstories, motivations, and goals. I don't need your biography, but at least tell me about your goals and why they're important to you. If you want, you can share your hobbies. A personal assistant is *personal*. We have to like each other at least somewhat."

I sucked my lips in, not sure if I was offended by her directness or appreciated it. I thought a little of both.

"Mrs. Verdor, I'm being totally honest," I said. "My current goals are to get a job and a place to live, because I can't do anything else until I accomplish those. I'd love to tell you that I still want to complete my degree, land my perfect job, and have my dream life, but I've learned that the world doesn't work that way. Life happens and priorities change. I can only focus on what's right before me and what I can control, and right now, that's being able to support myself. I'm sure you've had a lot of applicants, but I can promise you no one will work as hard as I will."

"Please call me Hope," she said as her only reply for several long moments. She leaned her elbow on the chair's arm, rested her chin onto her fist, and stared at me, her eyes tightening with each beat of my heart. Then a smile spread across her face. "I like that! You have a good head on your shoulders, I can tell. I looked over the résumé you emailed me—by the way, you're the only person who sent one—and it's kind of sparse, but that's okay. I'd rather teach you my ways than have to unteach you someone else's first."

She listed out the main job duties, and for each one, I told her about my experience doing it, or how I might approach it, emphasizing that I'd always do it her preferred way, whatever "it" was. She appreciated my answers, and I seemed to be acing this interview. I tried to suppress my hopes, but if nobody else had applied, I surely had this job.

"The OCD thing is exactly what I need, because I'm pretty much a mess," she said as she waved a hand toward her chaotic desk that had me twitching inside every time I looked at it. "I need someone who can keep up my calendar and make sure I'm where I need to be with everything I need to have for whatever I'm doing. There will be travel—I do a lot of events and signings—and that may include Connor, too, although I haven't figured that out yet."

She paused and let out a long sigh.

"But that's the problem right there," she said, and again I couldn't believe she'd said that about her own child. "Oh, no, not Connor. He's not a problem. Not really. Anyway, the problem is, as you said, life happened and priorities have changed. I've had to clear my calendar from travel and deadlines until I can work some things out. With Brock showing up like he did when he's supposed to be up north at college, and the baby, and everything that's going on ... everything's changed. I don't even have the private living quarters available now. I need a PA more than ever, but I'm afraid throwing another person into the disarray is also the last thing I need. I just can't see how I can make it all work at this time."

Shit. My hopes had already risen, but my interview and the promise of a job and home were on a sinking ship before I'd even arrived, and it was going down fast.

"I promise I'm a fast learner," I said, spewing out words, trying to save any possibility of changing her mind. "I can help you get control over whatever you have going on and take a lot off of your plate. I'm excellent at juggling and multi-tasking, and will do anything you need me to do. I can even—" I paused, not believing I was about to say this, but I *really* needed this job "—I can even help with Connor, if that's what you need. Please, Mrs. Verdor, I like you, and you seem to like me. We can help each other out here."

She gave me a smile, but it didn't reach her eyes, and then she stood up and walked for the door. I bit my bottom lip to keep from frowning as I stood, too, and followed her back through the house to the foyer.

"I'll have to give it a lot of consideration, Asia," she said when we reached the front door. "I wish I could make it work, and if I can, I'll call you. Family's first, though, and I have to remember that."

I nodded and held my hand out to shake hers. "I understand. You have my number."

My thoughts and emotions were all over the place as I slid into my car and drove back to the motel I called home. She wasn't going to hire me, I knew already, and I couldn't decide if I was disappointed or relieved. In a way, the job would have been perfect for me, and I couldn't imagine not loving it. I liked Hope, even if she was unexpectedly direct, but I could get used to that. I wasn't so sure about Brock. Although nice eye candy, I felt uncomfortable around him, and it wasn't his looks or build that intimidated me. It was all that he represented. And then there was baby Connor.

My chest tightened at the thought of the sweet little face scrunching up and letting out a howl, his tiny fists waving in the air and bare little feet kicking. Part of me had wanted to sweep him into my arms as much as Hope had, press him against my shoulder, and soothe him back to sleep. But a much bigger part of me had panicked inside and wanted to bolt.

Which was what convinced me, as I slid my key card in and out of the slot and opened the door to my room, that the job wasn't meant to be mine.

After I dropped my purse on the table and pulled off my heels with a sigh, I changed into shorts and my favorite Batman t-shirt, grabbed my laptop, and sat on the bed. Back to square one and more job hunting. If my luck didn't change soon, though, I'd have to take drastic measures.

AS CHRISTMAS APPROACHED two months later, the time for drastic measures had come. Well, actually, the time came a couple of weeks ago when I'd started sleeping in my car. It wasn't so bad really—I'd park at the beach, roll the windows halfway down for the breeze coming off the ocean, and let the sound of the waves lull me to sleep. There were public bathrooms with showers nearby, too. I even had company in the form of a white cat that hopped into my car every night and curled up in the back window until morning, when it would disappear as if knowing I couldn't feed it. Safety was an issue, but I picked the beaches near the upscale neighborhoods, kept my weapons handy, and never took off my steel-toed ass-kickers. The real problem was during the day. My pale skin didn't equip me for life as a beach bum, although it wasn't as pale as it had been when I moved down here.

I'd been able to catch an odd job here and there, enough to make food money. Just not enough to keep a roof over my head.

I did land a job as an "appointment setter," which, turned out, meant I was cold-calling people and trying to convince them to schedule an appointment to have their air conditioning system inspected and maintained. That lasted a week. This girl could only take so many times of being hung up on or cussed out, especially since my income was based on how many people made—and kept—an appointment. That definitely wasn't the job for me. Then I'd started training to be one of those girls who went around to restaurants and bars, selling roses to men to give to their ladies. Except after a couple of weeks of that, the boss-woman said my youth and my body would be perfect for the night clubs, and when she showed me the skimpy costume I'd have to wear, I was out of there. I'd never be that desperate.

Completely out of money, I'd had to move out of the weekly motel room then and into my car. I'd been putting off the decision forever because I didn't want to admit that my life had come to this, but it was time to decide whether to give in and go home to the obnoxiously sized estate up north where I had an entire wing to myself ... or to sell my car. The decision wasn't really that hard to make. Following through on it was a different story.

But when my phone rang and I recognized the number, I couldn't prolong the decision any longer.

"This is the girl I talked to yesterday?" the guy on the other end asked. I wondered if he looked as sexy as he sounded, but quickly shut off that thought. "About the car?"

"Yeah, it's me," I said, hearing the dejection in my own voice.

"My friend's definitely interested if you still have it. Can we meet somewhere so we can take a look?"

I swallowed against the lump in my throat.

I loved my canary yellow Camaro. I'd wanted one since I was twelve, but my parents had given me a boring BMW for my Sweet Sixteen instead. Mom thought it would be safer for me. Exactly why it was boring. I mean, I was grateful to have anything with wheels, of course, but my heart had longed for the sports car. They bought the Camaro for me not too long ago. A make-up gift of sorts. The only one I'd actually accepted. And then I left them in it, not planning to see them ever again. The car still held a lot of value, which meant I could buy myself an old beater and have enough money remaining to survive another several months. Surely by then I'd have found a real job.

"Yeah, sure," I finally said, and with a sinking heart, I told him where to meet me.

As much as I hated giving her up, this plan was definitely better than going home.

A few hours later, I sat in my car in a busy public parking lot, wondering if it was the last time I'd be doing so. I stroked her black dashboard and leather seats as if she were a puppy I was about to give away and not an inanimate object whose main purpose was to get me from Point A to Point B. She'd been more than that for me, though—the only thing I could depend on for months. An Audi, not unlike the BMW I'd had before but black and a little sportier looking, pulled up next to me. If that was any indication, then the caller likely had the finances to buy my girl. My heart sank further—I'd kind of been hoping he was only window-shopping—but then it did a strange little skip when the two guys climbed out.

The dark-haired, more muscular one who'd emerged from the driver's side looked at me and smiled with the same familiarity I felt.

"Asia, right?" he asked. Shit. He remembered my name? That was impressive. Especially since I couldn't remember his. He must have realized this. "Brock Verdor. Hope Verdor's son?"

Oh, geez, how did I forget that?

"That's right," I said, grinning and nodding like an idiot.

"This is Brandon," Brock said, nodding at his friend with the shaggy, strawberry-blond hair who was already circling my car.

"Hey," he muttered distractedly. "This car is sick."

Brock walked around the back of his Audi to stand next to me and shoved his hands into his khaki shorts pockets. "I can't believe you're selling it."

"Yeah, well, I don't have a choice," I said, but I suddenly couldn't bring myself to say I needed the money. My brain spun for a reason that wasn't as embarrassing. Well, not so much embarrassing as an admission of defeat. I guess I didn't want him thinking that his mom and the job she'd never offered had anything to do with my situation. "I need something that gets better gas mileage."

"Can I get in?" Brandon asked as he stood at the driver's side, his hand already on the handle.

"Of course," I said with a nod. "Go ahead and move the seat back, if you can. I kind of have a lot of stuff back there."

Brandon chuckled when he inspected the back seat. "Yeah, you do. There aren't any holes in the leather back there, are there?"

I scowled. "No! She's practically brand new, and I take excellent care of her! If you want to take everything out to see for yourself, feel free."

Brock had walked closer to the car, leaned his arms on the roof, and hung his head over the window while his friend made himself comfortable in my seat. I mean, in the driver's seat.

"Damn," Brock said, "you lucky son of a bitch. You know this is what I wanted."

Brandon grinned as he gripped the steering wheel, and he looked over his right shoulder. "There's plenty of room back there. You could have done it. But you snooze, you lose. This one's mine."

"The keys are in the ignition. Feel free to turn her over," I said, my voice thick through my tight throat. He was already claiming my girl.

Brock's head ducked down as he seemed to inspect the interior closer. A V formed between his eyebrows as his gaze traveled to the back seat where pretty much everything I owned was piled. The rest was in the trunk, which I popped open when Brandon got out and circled the car again.

"It's pretty roomy," I said, motioning my hand toward the trunk.

Brandon nodded appreciatively, but Brock's dark brows pushed together again. He turned his head toward me, and his chocolate eyes narrowed. Something about his gaze caused a shiver up my spine.

"Um ... do you want to take her for a test drive?" I asked as I looked back at Brandon. The thought made me nervous, getting into the car with a strange guy, but I didn't have much choice unless I let him take it on his own, along with my life's possessions.

"Definitely," he said eagerly. I almost rolled my eyes. The dude obviously wasn't used to negotiating—I could already tell I'd get my asking price from him. That probably came from growing up as a spoiled brat. I was surprised he was even looking at a used car in the first place, even if she was souped up with top-of-the-line bells and whistles and had fewer than ten thousand miles on her.

"Hold on a second," Brock said, lifting his hand toward Brandon while his narrowed gaze remained focused on me.

The same hand moved toward me, and I flinched. When his fingers wrapped around my upper arm in a gentle but firm hold, my own hand fisted, ready to punch him in the stomach if necessary. Except I'd lost all control over my body at his touch. An odd sensation tumbled through me, and my bones felt as though they were melting into liquid within my flesh. My mind blocked out everything except the feeling of his skin against mine. As he pulled me a few feet away from Brandon and the car, something tugged at my subconscious, as if trying to pull it through the surface of a memory. But the sensation fled as soon as he let go of me. It had all been so quick, I was sure I'd imagined everything.

"Are you living out of your car?" Brock demanded. I blinked, and any remnant of the odd feeling disappeared. Sheesh. I'd thought his mother was direct!

I crossed my arms over my chest and lifted my chin. "No."

His brows shot up, wrinkling his forehead. "So you're telling me you always keep all that stuff in there?"

"I'm in the process of moving," I said defiantly.

His hands went to his hips, and he leaned toward me.

"Where?" he challenged.

"None of your business," I snapped. "Do you really think I'm going to tell two strange guys where I live?"

His dark eyes studied me for a long moment, and then he pulled back. "Touché. So what kind of job did you find?"

He was taking another angle. How had he figured all of this out? I'd met him for two minutes, talked to his mom for maybe twenty, and he acted like he knew everything about me.

Now my eyes narrowed. "Again—none of your business."

He stared at me for another ridiculously long moment until I had to look away because of the awkwardness. And maybe because of the look in his eyes that had me shivering and melting at the same time.

"You're not getting the car, Brandon," he said while his gaze stayed trained on me. I could feel the burn of it, as though he bore holes into the side of my head.

"Bullshit," Brandon said, leaning against the Camaro as though he already owned it. "You may have seen the sign first, but you gotta be responsible, remember?"

"I'm not buying it either," Brock said.

My head snapped toward him. "What the hell? Who do you think you are? Brandon, if you'd like to take her for a drive, let's go."

I strode for the passenger's side.

"Brandon, if you get in that car, I'm never helping your ass again," Brock said.

Brandon stalked over to his friend who towered over his shorter and thinner frame. Still, he bowed up. "Dude, what the hell is wrong with you?"

Brock dropped his voice to the point where I couldn't hear him, and they argued for a few moments in hushed tones. Brandon peered over his shoulder at me and turned back to Brock with a scowl, but then he nodded. Brock headed over to his Audi.

"Let's go for that test drive," Brandon said to me as he walked back over to my car. I supposed he won that argument.

Facing the reality of getting into the car with him in control caused a nervous band of butterflies to flutter in my stomach. Not the good kind either. I was about to change my mind about the whole transaction, but was able to force myself into the passenger seat. I needed the money. And surely Brock wouldn't be associated with a psychopath, right? Wouldn't that be really bad for his mother's celebrity status? Of course, I knew firsthand what guys with their kind of money could get away with and keep silenced from the public. Which was why I kept a handgun in the glove compartment and my hands on my knees for the entire ride, only inches from the latch.

"So?" I asked after we'd been driving for about ten minutes. "She drives nice, right?"

"Yeah," Brandon muttered. "She's great."

His voice was off. Something had changed his mind. When we turned into a familiar neighborhood, my hand slid closer to the glove compartment. Maybe this really had been a ruse. When he pulled into Brock's driveway and climbed out without a word, the butterflies became eagles, making my stomach clench. Brock pulled up next to us, and Brandon gave him a nod then sauntered down the street. Anger replaced the fear. I jumped out of the car.

"What the hell did you do?" I demanded of Brock, who'd made his way around his car by now. "I needed to make this sale! Who do you think you are, anyway, you arrogant son of a—"

"Asia?" called a female voice from behind me. I spun around to find Hope outside with her baby, who'd grown so much already, on her hip. "I heard you still need a job."

CHAPTER 8

THE SEMI-FAMOUS AUTHOR stood on the front walk in jeans and a red t-shirt, her hair again swept up and clipped to the back of her head, and her face void of makeup. And yet, she was still stunning. She held one arm under the baby's butt and her other hand against his back and head as he leaned against her shoulder. I supposed enough time had finally passed that I didn't have quite the same reaction to him as I did last time, but I still had an overwhelming desire to hold him ... and to run away, too.

Hope stared at me expectantly. I stared back for a long moment as everything computed, and then I turned toward Brock. He wore a proud grin.

"You both have a problem, and you're each other's solution," he said.

I turned back toward Hope. "I'm sorry, Mrs. Verdor. This was not at all ... I didn't plan ... I had no idea ..."

I stopped, unable to form coherent sentences as a bazillion thoughts ran through my mind.

Hope tilted her head, then moved her gaze to her son. "Brock, what did you do? You said—"

"Mom," Brock interrupted, and he paused briefly as he rubbed the back of his neck. "You seriously need help. You're trying to do it all, and making yourself insane, along with the rest of us. If family is really your first priority, do us all a favor and hire the assistant you know you need."

His mother stared at him with her mouth partly open. Before she could say anything Brock turned to me.

"Asia, you obviously need a job. You're selling the car, which you called your *baby*, for the money, aren't you?"

Heat rose to my cheeks. Hope's open-mouthed stare turned on me now. I flushed even harder.

"Do you remember what I said about this being none of your damn business?" I hissed through clenched teeth.

"Just listen for a moment," he pleaded. "Mom loved you. Told me everything about the interview, and she really wanted to hire you, but shit was weird here for a while. It's settled down now, and she needs you so damn bad that if she doesn't hire you herself, I'll do it for her."

"Brock, if she doesn't want to work for me," Hope began.

I couldn't help the little noise that escaped my throat.

"Do you?" Hope asked me.

I swallowed. "I ... I would love to. But please don't feel obligated."

Hope sighed and shifted the baby to her other arm. "I *do* need help. And Brock's right. I thought you were perfect for the job. If you still want it—"

"Oh, yes," I gushed.

She smiled. "When can you start?"

"Immediately."

"Tomorrow then. I'm afraid I can't offer you the living quarters anymore, though."

"Why not?" Brock asked.

Hope arched a brow. "Because you're living there."

He rolled his eyes. "Hardly. My stuff is in there, but I'm always over here anyway. Let Asia have the apartment over the garage."

"You really want to move back in with your parents?" Hope asked skeptically.

"I pretty much already have anyway," Brock said. "And it's only for a little while, Mom. You and Dad will get your space soon enough. Not like you don't have enough as it is ..."

"You *will* finish college, and you *will* go to med school—"

I cleared my throat, interrupting. "Please, I don't want to cause problems. I'm very grateful for the job, and I'll be here tomorrow. I can find a place to live."

Brock cocked his head at me and smirked. "I thought you said—"

"I'm in the process of moving," I finished sharply, not wanting to give him the satisfaction of being right about living in my car. "I am. I didn't like the place I was staying at, so I left. I ... uh ... just haven't found another place yet."

"So you like to go to the beach in the middle of the night?"

My mouth popped open.

"Yeah, I've seen your car there on my way home, except I wasn't positive it was yours, and, well ... ." He made a fake-cough sound and hurried on. "Anyway, how do you think I knew it was for sale? When I passed again the next morning, it was still parked in the same space, and I saw the sign in the window. And everything you own is in that car, isn't it?"

Hope gasped. "Asia, have you been living in your car?"

As if my skin couldn't grow any hotter in the sun. I'd never been so embarrassed in my life, and it choked me up, flustering me so no words could come out. My eyes stung, causing me to blink rapidly and look away.

"Oh, no, dear," she said softly. "That's not acceptable. Decision's made. I said before that the job includes private living quarters, and that's what you'll get, utilities included, plus a salary of two thousand a month. Will you please accept my offer?"

I blinked for the hundredth time and looked back at her. My eyes filled again, but now with tears of gratitude, and a heavy weight suddenly lifted from my shoulders.

Two hours later, Brock had moved all of his belongings—not many—and a few baby items out of the apartment over the detached garage and into the main house.

"I think baby things make their own babies," he muttered with the last haul. "For such a little dude, he fills every space."

After Hope's housekeeper had come in and cleaned the apartment, Brock emptied my car into the one-bedroom space. My few belongings barely covered the dark green sofa in the small living room that was adjacent to the open kitchen. He told me the code to the gate, where to find the nearest grocery store, and the names of the best places to have pizza or Chinese delivered.

"So I guess I'll let you get settled in," he said as he stood in the doorway, hesitating as though he didn't want to leave. I wondered if he was regretting his decision to give up the apartment for me.

"Are you sure about this?" I asked.

His lips pulled into a slow smile, and I fleetingly wondered what they tasted like. "I've never been surer about anything in my life."

My throat went dry. "But why?"

His grin widened. "I didn't want to see you give up your baby."

I logically knew what he meant, but my breath caught and my stomach tilted at his words anyway. The room suddenly felt way too small for the two of us as I tried to breathe the heavy air.

"I mean your car?" Brock said, the tone of his voice indicating that he'd sensed my distress.

"Um ... yeah," I choked out. I forced an inhale, my body shaking with it. As I exhaled, I imagined expelling the gray cloud that had just threatened to shut me down, along with the air.

"I hated to see you have to sell it, especially to Brandon who would have totaled it in a month or less," he clarified further. "His dad refused to buy him anything new anymore because he's such a dumbass."

"Well ... thank you," I said, my senses returning and my head clearing. "For everything. It really was sweet of you."

He lifted one shoulder in a shrug. "Like I said, you both needed help. I couldn't *not* do it and live with myself. Or with my mother."

I smiled. "It was still sweet of you. I don't know how I can ever pay you back."

He gave me that warm, teasing smile that made me suddenly stupid.

"Oh, I'll find a way." He backed out of my apartment as he kept his gaze on me, sending chills down my spine, before finally turning for the steps. But then he appeared back in the doorway. "Asia?"

"Yeah?"

"My mom was right that I only tease the pretty ones."

I blinked. Huh? He disappeared down the steps, leaving me gaping. What the hell did that mean? Why had he even said it? He hadn't teased me at all today, had he? Or was that what he meant? Since he hadn't teased me, he must have been saying he didn't find me pretty. *Well, eff you, Brock Verdor. I don't really care what you think.*

I tried to convince myself of that, but it wasn't entirely true. Although he was exactly the type I'd vowed to stay away from— wealthy, hot, and a little too sure of himself—I couldn't help but feel attracted to him ... and wish he was attracted to me. So it was probably a good thing he wasn't.

With an internal groan at myself, I switched gears and inspected my new place. The door, which had a window next to it, opened directly into the living room that consisted of an end table under the window, a coffee table, a chair, and a couch facing a flat-screen TV hanging on the opposite wall. On the far end of the room was the kitchen with an L-shaped granite-top counter, blond wood cabinets, a small refrigerator, an oven range with two burners, and a dishwasher I'd probably never use. Beyond the kitchen was the door to the bedroom that consisted of a queen-sized bed, a nightstand, and a dresser, and the bathroom with a standard sink, toilet, and shower-tub combo. The entire apartment had a Mediterranean-style décor, making me wonder if Brock had stripped down posters of half-naked girls and beer signs. As it was now, it wasn't exactly a typical bachelor-pad for a college guy, although I thought I could smell a hint of something that might have been his cologne lingering over the fumes of cleaning products. I sniffed harder, enjoying it, and then chastised myself for being so girly.

Within an hour I'd found a place for everything I owned in the bedroom and bathroom. I didn't possess anything to put away in the kitchen, but I discovered the cabinets to be stocked with all of the pots and pans, dishes, and silverware I'd ever need living by myself. For now, I only really needed a knife and a glass.

Since I'd run out of peanut butter the day before and was almost out of bread, I tied my Doc Martens on to head to the store. As I threw open the door, I collided with a sexy, muscled, *shirtless* body, but his raised fist had me flinching and jumping backwards.

"Oh, shit, sorry!" Brock said when I gasped audibly. His hand gently wrapped around my upper arm, just above the elbow, to catch me before I tripped over my own feet. "I was just about to knock."

I pressed my hand to my chest as though I could still my pounding heart. The shock of running into him and the ridiculous fear of his fist had been enough, but the touch of his palm on my skin was pushing me over the edge. A pulsing heat through my arm sent a wave of goose bumps over my flesh. I'd never reacted to a guy's touch like this, and although it was pleasurable, it was also unnerving. I tried to jerk my arm from his grip, but he tightened it. I would have gone into immediate defense mode, but my body betrayed my brain. I narrowed my eyes and slid them up his bare torso to glare at his face, but I found his own gaze meandering over my body. At the same time, the gentle squeeze he'd given my elbow turned into a light brush down my arm as he released me, and the goose bumps spread further ... until the heated look in his eyes turned cold and his lips pressed into a scowl as his eyes came back to mine.

"I was heading out for a run and saw this on the ground. It must have fallen from a box I carried up. Sorry." He shoved something into my hands, turned on his heel, and pounded down the stairs and across the driveway before I could even take a breath.

Not that I could breathe if I wanted to. The boy was *built*. Of course, I'd seen him shirtless the first time I met him and knew he was big, but seeing him now as he jogged down the driveway in basketball shorts, running shoes, and nothing else gave me a whole new appreciation.

Pull it together, idiot, I silently snapped as I shook myself out of it. As if I didn't already know that someone like Brock was the last thing I needed right now, Brock's sporadic behavior gave proof that I didn't need *him* specifically in my life. One moment he was nice, the next teasing, and the one after that downright rude. He'd saved me from having to sell my car, helped me get a job, and moved me in, and then treated me like I had the plague. Not that I was surprised. Guys like him were all douchebags.

I deserved better.

As I walked back inside to put away whatever he'd dropped, I finally looked down at the object he'd shoved into my hands. A brown leather-bound book, quite old looking, that I'd never seen before in my life. Brock had been mistaken—this had not come from any of my boxes. He'd already ran out of sight, though, so I placed the book on the end table close to the door and headed out.

Once I found the grocery store, I used my last few dollars to buy bread, peanut butter, and milk that would last the rest of the week, when I hoped I'd receive my first paycheck. Merry Christmas to me. By sunset, I was sitting on the couch of my own little apartment and able to connect my laptop to the Internet without worrying about a barista shooing me away because I wasn't a paying customer. Tomorrow I started a real job that I just knew I would love, even if it meant I might have had to deal with my boss's sons—both of them. Surely it'd be worth it.

Life was good.

When I opened a private message on Facebook, my good mood faltered for a moment. The message came from someone named Kami and read:

"Asia, I didn't have your phone number or email, and I had to scroll a bit through the search results here to find you. I'm so glad I did! I've been thinking very hard on what you said that day we ran into each other a month or so ago, and I think I'm going to follow your advice. I have some things I have to get straightened out first, but hopefully, everything will work out. So I really wanted to say thank you. Ever since making this decision, I've felt in my heart it's the right thing to do. I hope one day you'll find what you're looking for, too."

I read the cryptic message twice, and neither time did it make sense to me. The avatar for this Kami girl was a cat, so that didn't help. I clicked through to her profile. We weren't friends, and the girl smartly kept most of her profile private, so I couldn't see much on her page. The only clue was that she attended the same university I had in Boston, until I'd dropped out at the beginning of the semester—over two months ago. So there was no way I could have run into her "a month or so ago."

I tapped out a quick reply to say I was sorry but she must have had the wrong Asia. Not that there were a lot of Asia's running around, but she had to have meant someone else. I kind of wished she'd meant me. Her message had been so full of gratitude, and the other Asia had done something right by her. If anything, that would have at least explained the good karma I was receiving now.

For the first time in months, I took a shower in a decidedly clean bathroom and settled into a real bed that I didn't feel compelled to check for bedbugs every hour. I opened Hope's book that I'd put aside after our interview and read until my eyes couldn't stay open any longer. I might have fallen asleep with a smile on my face.

MY APARTMENT CONSISTED of the second floor of a detached four-car garage, which sat in the corner of the fenced-in backyard. My commute to work entailed crossing the lusciously landscaped backyard, skirting the custom pool, and entering the main house through the rear wing, then turning left and circling the courtyard until I was halfway to the front wing. Those were the directions I'd been given to find Hope's office, which I presumed to be the same one where she'd interviewed me. I got a little distracted on my way, though, as I passed the pool and glanced through the tall windows of the room nearest the back door—a home gym, complete with a treadmill, elliptical, stationary bike, weight machines, and the standard hot guy that should come with all home gyms.

He wasn't on any of the machines or the weight bench, though. He was in an empty part of the room, going through what looked like karate moves to my ignorant eye, punching and kicking the air. When his dark eyes glanced up and caught me halted in mid-stride and staring, I instantly looked away and hurried for the door. I entered and made my left turn, and then became distracted all over again. The door to the gym was open, providing another view of the beauty within. I simply couldn't help but gawk.

When he moved to a punching bag, a thought occurred to me.

I cleared my throat, and Brock stopped his workout and turned toward me. A slow smile crossed his face, making my stomach drop an inch or two. The sweat glistening on his tanned skin and dripping down the crevice between his abs made my mouth dry.

"Good morning," he said, as kind as could be, as if he'd forgotten his rude departure last night.

"Good morning," I said, trying to return the warmth, mostly because I had a favor to ask. I hesitated, though, after remembering just how bipolar he'd been with me.

"Did you forget how to find Mom's office?" His tone remained kind, but I couldn't help but wonder if he was teasing me. Arrogant jerk.

"Um ... actually, I saw you doing the martial arts thing and was wondering where you learned it." That sounded stupid and not at all what I was thinking. "I mean, I was wondering where *I* might be able to learn."

He walked toward me a few steps and crinkled his forehead. "You want to learn martial arts?"

I pulled the book I'd brought back closer to my chest, hugging it. "More like self-defense?"

His gaze skipped over my tiny frame, and he nodded. "Probably not a bad idea." His eyes returned to my face as the corner of his lip lifted. I didn't know if he was about to smile or smirk. With him, it could easily be either. "I could teach you a few moves. I don't have a lot of time to give lengthy lessons, but there are really only a few things you need to know to protect yourself."

I stared at him for a long moment, not knowing at first if he was truly offering this or was about to do another one-eighty on me.

"Tomorrow evening," he said when I didn't respond. "Mom's always dying for time with Connor by five-thirty, so how about then?"

"It's not exactly what I meant," I said, still skeptical. "I meant lessons ... at a gym ... after I get paid, of course."

Brock rolled his eyes. "Save your money. I can teach you everything you need to know, in this gym. No charge. Consider it a Christmas present."

"A Christmas present? We just met. And I already owe you for getting me this job and my apartment. What ever could I give you in return?"

The corners of his mouth jumped upward, and his eyes sparked. "I'm not worried. I'm sure you'll come up with something."

I pressed my lips together, but after another long moment of consideration, I nodded. "Okay. Tomorrow after work." I glanced down at the book in my arms. "Oh, and this isn't mine. Maybe it's your mom's or dad's."

I placed the book on the top of a small shelf unit by the door that held some towels. Before his warm and helpful attitude became icy again, I hurried off, not wanting to be late. Decked in greens and all kinds of beautiful Christmas decorations, the house barely looked the same as when I'd first been here, but I found Hope's office, where she greeted me with loads of excitement and a mile-long to-do list.

My first day went as well as first days could go. At one time not so long ago, rubbing elbows with a celebrity would have had me gushing, but I wasn't like that any longer. Still, I kept catching myself in awe that I was spending my day with Hope Verdor. It wasn't so much her fame that awed me as much as the actual job itself. In truth, Hope Verdor wasn't a household name. She was a *New York Times* bestseller and many romance fans would know her and all of her books in an instant. Even some readers of other genres might. However, she was no Stephen King or J.K. Rowling. But working behind the scenes with a bona fide author thrilled me way more than her celebrity status.

It didn't take long to realize just how much she needed me—the business side of an author was completely overwhelming, and she'd been drowning. I'd have fires to put out for weeks before we could ever start to bring everything under control. If I could pull it off, that meant job security, but by the end of my second day and my "appointment" with Brock, I was ready to work off some stress.

After I changed into shorts and my black Batman t-shirt, I met Brock in the home gym.

"Nice shirt," he said with a smile as soon as I walked in. Once again, I didn't know if he teased or meant it. After years of hiding the nerdy side of me, though, I proudly owned it now.

"Thanks," I said with my own smile, smoothing my hand over my stomach.

"I took you for a Wonder Woman type, though."

"I have one of those, too. And Superman."

"Well, Batman's better anyway. He has that badass edgy side to him that he uses for good."

I shrugged. "That's the only reason I like him. Otherwise, he'd be just another rich asshole breaking all the rules and getting away with it."

He gave me a funny look, and then motioned toward the mats on the floor. We began by stretching.

"Besides the moves I'm going to teach you, the best thing you can do to protect yourself is make your body stronger," he said as I sat on a mat and reached for my toes. "Do some strength training. You're free to use this room whenever you'd like."

I lifted my head enough to look around at the machines. I'd always been blessed with a thin body—or cursed, depending on how you looked at it—so I'd never had much use for such things. I'd gone to the gym at college maybe three times because a friend told me the stair-climber would make my butt rounder. She also told me I "glowed" when I sweat, which was a downright lie; I looked like a pig. So I never returned. That was before ... when I cared about such things. Now the idea of being small but strong piqued my interest.

"I used to be skinny like you," Brock said, his gaze raking over my body.

I snickered as I returned his examination with my own. "Really?"

"When I was twelve," he said, and I rolled my eyes. Another jab at me. Although I wasn't exactly stacked, he'd change his mind about my body looking like a prepubescent boy's if he saw me dressed the way I used to, flaunting all I had. Like that would ever happen. "Seriously. I was a scrawny little thing. I grew up as a book nerd. Total geek. But I was always getting picked on, so Mom put me in karate classes to start with. Besides reading, it became my second favorite thing to do. I've trained in all kinds of martial arts since then."

I pulled myself up to sitting and then to my feet. "And that kept the bullies away?"

"Once I kicked a few of their asses, yeah. But it wasn't until I bulked up that they really stayed away. They don't even start when you're bigger than them."

I jutted a leg out and put my hands on my hips. "I'll never be bigger than most men. I just need to know how to protect myself."

"No, but I'm not talking about size and intimidation when it comes to you. I'm talking about giving yourself the best chance in any situation. The stronger you are, the more efficient and effective your kicks and punches will be. The faster you are, the more likely you'll get away."

He proved his point over and over as he showed me some basic self-defense techniques. Once I understood each move, we'd practice it with Brock using his size and strength more and more to his advantage each time. He was right: I could know how to do everything in perfect form, but someone bigger and stronger would always be able to overpower me. My best bet would be to run away, but I wasn't exactly a fast runner. And I didn't like the idea of running away. I wanted to be able to fight back. To kick a bully's ass.

Of course, if I were ever in a situation again that required me to protect myself, I hoped adrenaline would give me a boost of unnatural strength. Working with Brock created quite the opposite effect. My muscles wanted to go soft, my bones wanted to melt, and my whole body wanted to surrender to his demands, especially if it meant we'd end up with him on top of me. It took every bit of concentration I had to remain focused on fighting back, because every time he touched my skin, a distracting warmth pulsed through my body.

And that's how I ended up on my back with Brock on top of me, his mouth only an inch away from mine.

I hadn't been paying attention, and he'd twisted me around, hooked his leg around mine, and toppled us both to the floor. He caught himself on his forearms before his full weight fell on me, his breath hot on my lips as his dark eyes caught mine for only a moment. The next thing I knew, his body pressed fully on mine, and our lips locked.

An unrecognizable feeling swept through me—the feeling of true pleasure. A tingling sensation that rippled from our joined lips, across my jaw, down my neck, over my breasts, and into the pit of my stomach. All thoughts left my mind, leaving it numb. All I knew was that I wanted more. More of this feeling. More of this man. More of the taste that his heady scent promised. My lips parted, Brock's tongue gently prodded, and mine met it, tasted it, tangled with it. I reached my hands into his hair. My boobs ached with a new heaviness, and my nipples hardened against my sports bra, little marbles against his chest as I pulled him closer. The tingling grew as our mouths melded, becoming a ball of heat in my stomach that surged through my body and out to his. I suddenly felt like I might explode from my own body. I needed air. I slipped my hands between our chests and pushed on Brock's. He sprang backward at the same time, already feet away that felt like miles.

Our eyes held each other's as we stared for a long moment.

"I'm sorry," we both said.

"That wasn't supposed to happen," he said.

"This can't happen," I said at the same time.

Yet the energy between us remained charged. An electrical connection I'd never felt before that kept me from taking anything more than the shallowest of breaths. Brock's broad, cut chest lifted as he also seemed to have trouble breathing. Not until he pushed his hands through his thick, dark hair and looked away, breaking the lock of our gazes, could either of us catch a breath. My heart finally slowed. Brock stood and held his hand out to me, but I had a feeling touching him again wouldn't be a good idea. I rolled to my knees and stood on shaking legs. I pressed my hand to my quivering belly and strode for the door.

"Asia," Brock said, stopping me in the doorway, although I didn't turn around. "I like you. A lot. I just can't do this right now."

I closed my eyes, and then snorted. "It's not you, it's me—did you really just say that?"

"It's true, though. My life—it's too complicated right now."

I shook my head and chuckled. "Don't worry. I can't do this either. Not with you, especially. Let's just agree it was an accident. It won't happen again."

"Agreed," Brock said from behind me, and I didn't know if I imagined the hurt in his voice, or if it was real.

It didn't matter. I had to get out of here. Without a look back, I rushed out of the room and the main house, across the back yard, and up the steps to my apartment. My hand shook as I fumbled to get the door open. Not until I was inside the dark apartment, my back pressed against the door, could I finally breathe again. Once my heart settled, I immediately headed to the bathroom, stripping as I walked, and stepped into the coldest shower I could stand.

I tried to remove all thoughts of Brock, his hard body, and the heated charge between us from my mind, but I couldn't erase the memory of how it all felt. I thought what I'd had in the past, especially with Drew, had been nothing more than lust, but that paled in comparison to the desire I felt for Brock. A deep-seated need that penetrated through every cell of my body, perhaps even into my soul. A lust like no other. And that's all it could be.

Needing a distraction, I sat on the couch in my short pajama shorts and a tank top, crossed my legs, and opened my laptop. Facebook was still open in my browser, so I took a peek to see if anything was new. Another message from that Kami girl waited:

"I know we met only a couple of times, but I'm pretty sure you're the Asia I know. We met first at the support group on campus. I think it was your first time then, and I didn't go back after that. But then before you left, we ran into each other at the coffee shop. You said you were taking a break from classes and headed out of town. You had everything packed up in your Camaro. If this is you, I hope you'll accept my friend request. I think we can both use a good friend, right?"

The memory of the girl with the long, brown hair and sad blue eyes filled my mind. The day I left Boston and headed south to Florida, we'd literally run into each other, both of us spilling coffee down our arms. By then, we both appeared normal from the outside—your typical college girls—but we were destroyed on the inside. I knew I was, of course, and I could feel it in her. See it in her eyes. Something unspoken had passed between us the first time we'd met, but neither of us had done anything about it. We hadn't seen each other again until that moment and something told me to take a minute to sit down and chat with her before rushing off to the new life I needed to start.

I confirmed her friend request and was able to see her pictures. Definitely the same girl, although the most recent photo showed a spark of life in her eyes I'd never seen before. Was that what she'd been thanking me for? I wished I could remember what I might have said that seemed to have changed her life. I'd just finished typing a reply out to her and closing my laptop when a knock sounded on my door.

My heart stopped as I took in the sight on the other side. Brock had apparently showered, too, his dark brown hair still damp and standing up in towel-dried spikes. He wore nothing but jeans—his chest and even his feet bare, just like the day I'd met him. My mouth immediately felt like the desert. When his eyes skipped down my body, I had to swallow and cross my arms over my chest. My nipples pressed into my arms through the thin material of my tank top, and by the way his eyes tightened and his tongue slid over his lips, he'd obviously noticed now that I wasn't exactly built like a twelve-year-old boy.

"I, uh ..." He cleared his throat and locked his eyes on my face with a focus that felt forced to keep his gaze from wandering again. "I know you said this isn't yours, but it's not mine, although when I tried to get rid of it, it appeared on my dresser in my room, and I just have to be sure it's not yours because the damn thing is driving me crazy, especially because I can't open it to find out where the hell it came from ..."

He trailed off as I stared at him and blinked. He must have realized he'd been babbling. He thrust the leather-bound book at me, and I had no choice but to take it. Needing to break my gaze from his, I looked at the book in my hands, studying the clasp. There was no hole for a key, not that we had a key, but no way to jimmy it open with a paperclip or anything.

"Did you, um, try cutting it?" I asked, turning my back to him and walking the four steps to the kitchen, feeling the heat of his eyes on me the whole time. I opened a drawer and pulled out a knife.

"With scissors and a knife. Nothing will cut through that leather."

I spun around, surprised to find him inside my apartment and the door closed. My heart rate ratcheted up several notches. He seemed to fill the entire living room. His eyes darted to the knife I held, pointed toward him. With a difficult breath, I placed the book on the counter and tried to saw through the leather. He was right. I couldn't even nick it.

I turned back toward him and tried to give a nonchalant shrug. "I don't know. Are you sure it's not your mom's or dad's or anyone else's?"

He took a step closer to me. I swallowed hard and stepped back, pressing my lower back into the counter. Our eyes locked.

"I don't think …" He paused. Licked his lips. And as he did, his gaze dropped to my mouth. "Damn it, Asia. I brought the book over as an excuse. I can't … I can't stop thinking about you … and your lips … and that accidental kiss that wasn't really an accident."

He slowly lifted his eyes back to mine, where they held for a long moment. Then he crossed the space between us, slid his muscular arms around me, and pulled me against his hard body as his mouth crashed down on mine. And I was powerless to stop him. My resolve vanished as soon as he admitted what I'd already felt—the kiss before hadn't been an accident. I'd wanted it. I'd wanted to feel it again. And here he was, kissing me again like I'd never been kissed before. As though he felt the same deep need I did, from our very cores. As though we could only be satisfied if we devoured the other.

His lips moved perfectly with mine, as if they were made for each other. Our mouths parted at the same time and our tongues intertwined, completely in sync. His hands skated up and down my back, sending wave after wave of chills over my skin. One pushed underneath my hair and cradled the back of my neck. His fingers curled into my locks and tugged my head backwards, tipping my mouth at a better angle for the kiss that was making my knees weak.

My own hands slid up his bare chest, over his broad shoulders, and up along his neck until I could rub the stubble dusting his chin and jaw. I clasped his face in both hands and pulled him even closer. I swore everywhere our skin touched singed with the heat of a million suns. But it was a warmth I wanted, ached for, needed like my lungs needed air. His lips, his tongue, his skin against mine filled a well within me that I'd never realized had been empty until now. I felt more alive than I had in months, and the way he was giving and taking, feeding me while feeding himself, I had a feeling I did the same for him.

As the kiss deepened, it also became more urgent. A driving lust for more. My legs began to tremble, both from the intensity and from standing on my toes. Brock's hands clamped on my waist, and he effortlessly lifted me to sit on the counter so he wouldn't have to bend down and I wouldn't have to reach so high. My butt landed on something—the book—and I pushed it away before bringing both arms around Brock's neck. His hands gripped my knees, scorching the bare skin, and he spread my legs so he could step between them. I fought the urge to wrap them around his waist and let them hang instead.

Sensing my need to keep things above the belt, his hands moved to my shoulders, clutching them for a moment as though he was afraid if he let go, I might disappear. Then they slid to my back, one up into my hair while the other trailed lightly up and down my spine, sending a shiver through my heated body. Our mouths remained locked as we devoured each other as though our souls had been starving for this connection. I moaned into Brock's mouth, and he growled in return, before nipping my bottom lip and breaking the kiss. He pressed his forehead against mine, and his hand slid from the back of my head to cradle my face.

"Your mouth is like a life force," he whispered as his thumb swept over my lips.

CHAPTER 9

NOW

Asia MY FINGERS ON one hand skimmed over my lips, remembering the feeling of Brock's doing the same, as the pads on my other hand skated over the words on the journal's page. Words I hadn't written. I could only figure Brock had somehow added them to the story I'd begun writing in the Book, because they obviously came from his memory:

"Her mouth tasted like cherries and mint, but the longer we kissed, the more she tasted like heaven. Like the single answer to everything I ever needed. Not that she was the solution to every problem. But somehow, kissing Asia and holding her in my arms, feeling her small body pressed against mine, made me believe I could take on any problem in the world, hers and mine, and come out triumphant. Made me feel that together we could take on anything.

"But maybe that was false hope from the heat of the moment."

Something tickled the tip of my nose and not until I swiped at it did I realize it was a tear. More were streaming down my cheeks. My chest felt tight as it tried to contain the sob that was already building toward my throat, pushing upward, making my breasts heave and forcing a choking sound from my mouth.

At last, I could no longer hold back. I cried for Brock and me, for us now and for us then. I cried for his words and his doubts. I didn't know if the uncertainty came from what he felt then or what he felt now as he reflected on our story, knowing what came next ... and after that ... and until now, as we remained Separated across worlds.

What had come next was Hope knocking on my door, baby Connor on her hip. She and her husband had a dinner that night, which, of course, I'd known about, and she needed to hand off Connor to Brock. He sweetly cuddled the tiny baby in his strong arms that only moments ago had been embracing me, and with little more than an apology to me, ran off for the house, leaving me confused and uncertain of where we stood. And knowing we shouldn't have stood anywhere. Regardless of him being the very type I'd vowed to stay away from, he had also been my boss's son. A disaster waiting to happen, I'd thought, and I'd lose my job and home in the process. I didn't know then how much worse it would be.

But I was getting ahead of myself. Of our story. I needed to relish in the good parts, not let the bad ones bring the Darkness faster. It would come soon enough.

We had some happy times. They felt insignificant now, but they'd existed. Like reading Jacey's journal together.

See, a while after Brock had left that night and I'd been locking the front door, I noticed the brown leather book still sitting on the counter, where I'd pushed it to the edge. Somehow, the clasp had fallen open. Of course, I knew now that I must have touched the metal lock while Brock and I had been melded together at the mouths, but at the time, the book became even more of an enigma.

I scrubbed at my wet cheeks and sank into the memory of texting him immediately and how he'd been just as excited as I'd been to find out what was inside and to whom it belonged. He made me promise, though, to wait for him before opening the mysterious book. I hadn't known until this moment, feeling it from him now, that he'd felt bad for having to push me to the side. Knowing what I did now, though, I couldn't blame him one bit. In fact, I would have been disappointed if he'd done anything else.

Before losing myself again in writing our story, I stroked my fingertips over the script on the page—Brock's script, where he'd somehow added that part about our kiss. When I did, I could almost, *almost* feel his presence. Not anything physical like his hand touching mine or anything, but in my soul. I closed my eyes and concentrated on the feeling. *Brock*, I silently called out. The slightest sensation rippled through me, like the lightest breeze, there and gone again before I could even be sure I felt it.

A knock at the door jarred me back to reality.

Jeric stood on the other side, one hand clasping the back of his neck and the other shoved into his jeans pocket. His blue eyes pierced into mine for a moment, then he looked away, at a point over my shoulder.

"Are you okay?" he asked. "I haven't seen you all day."

I glanced down the hall at the window at the end, which was black. I'd had the curtains pulled closed over my window, blocking out the sun, and hadn't realized night had fallen.

"Yeah, I'm fine," I said as I wrapped my arms around my midsection. "As fine as can be expected."

He nodded, but his gaze still stayed away from my face. He almost seemed to be looking for something.

"Have you found anything in the Book?" he asked, and I realized that was probably what he searched for. He hadn't even tried to mask the hope in his voice.

I swallowed, not wanting to tell him. "What had been in there before ... Jacey's story, your drawings, everything ... it had all apparently washed out."

Jeric's sharp eyes finally came back to me, and his brows pushed together as his mouth pressed into a scowl. Although I relished being able to read Brock's words, my heart hurt and my eyes stung for Jeric and Leni and what they'd lost. The pages may have held the memories of what had been written on them before, but without any idea of how to bring them back, the words and pictures may as well have been gone forever.

"That fucking sucks. I, uh, I thought …" He paused, looked away again, then back at me, and lifted a shoulder in a sort of shrug. "I've been wandering the entire manor all day, feeling lost. I keep finding myself back at your door without even realizing I'd taken the steps to get here. It's like a pull. I'd hoped … I thought maybe it was the Book. Or something you found in it. I was trying to give you time and space to go through it, but here I am … again."

The pain etched into his eyes—the same agony filling my soul—had me stepping to the side and inviting him in. "There's something I want to show you."

Jeric hesitated for a long moment. I was sure he felt as strange as I did being here, in my room, without Brock or Leni serving as a buffer. Jeric was hot, but he wasn't my type. In fact, the only type I had any more was Brock. Even though I struggled to understand exactly what we had together, I knew I'd never want anyone else. I also knew Jeric completely loved Leni. They were the definition of soul mates, the embodiment of Twin Flames. Always had been. I certainly didn't have to worry about him trying anything.

I strode past Jeric and over to the bed. I picked up the Book of Phoenix, held open to the page I'd been reading, and handed it to him. He glanced down, then back up at me.

"I thought you said everything had been washed away," he said.

"Right. I started writing in it, though. About how Brock and I met, since it'd never been recorded, as far as I know."

Jeric's eyes tightened slightly.

"What?" I asked.

"Nothing. I just … uh … I've been getting what I can only call visions. Of how you and Brock met."

My breath caught. "That's wonderful!"

His brows rose.

"It confirms what I've been thinking. Look here." I pointed to the page. "That's Brock's handwriting. Like he's adding to my story. Like he can feel it, too!"

Jeric studied the page closer. "This just started appearing?"

I gave him a small smile. "Yeah. And that's not all. I swear, I kind of … I sometimes think I can feel *him*, Jeric." I pressed my fisted hand against my chest, over my heart. "I feel him almost like a ghost in my soul. But more than that … more than a memory. It's almost like the Book's trying to connect us through more than just words."

"Like a bridge across worlds?" he asked, his voice full of hope.

"Maybe. I mean, Nathayden was able to feel Bex, right? Or see her or something. I don't remember exactly what he said and his messages are gone now, but he knew she had red hair and blue eyes. He knew she'd been reading it. And he was able to communicate with us. So maybe …" I paused and sighed, then muttered, "Or maybe it's just wishful thinking."

Jeric sat on the bed, his gaze focused on the Book as he ran his fingers over the outside cover. "It makes sense, though. If I'm getting your story without reading it … Brock's able to add to it … Nathayden had felt something from us and sent us messages in return … Leni thinks we gave the Book powers in a past life. We just have to try to remember them."

He turned back to the page where I'd left off, his finger holding the spot the whole time. He closed his eyes, like I had before, and skimmed his fingertips slowly over the paper. Several beats of my heart passed before a slow smile began to spread over his face, revealing his dimples that made him look more boyish and less intimidating. With his eyes still closed, he pressed his palm against the page and lifted his other hand to his chest.

"I feel her," he said, his voice more of a croak than anything. "Barely, but I do. She's alive, at least."

CHAPTER 10

Leni JERIC'S VOICE CALLING out my name swirled through me, and for a moment, I thought I could actually feel him again, his soul a part of mine. *Leni!*

Jeric! I called back to him, reaching for him with everything inside me. *I'm coming, babe! I'm coming home.*

I didn't know if he heard or felt me, or if I really heard or felt him. The sensation could have been no more than the Gate pulling me in and spitting me back out. The sound of his voice wishful thinking, like the mirage of an oasis in the middle of a desert. Regardless, I lost it all as soon as I landed in another body of water.

Unable to breathe, I jerked the helmet off of me, not thinking or caring that the air of this new place could possibly kill me. It didn't. The water wasn't acidic like it had been on Erde, either. It was a small, murky lake, and I'd landed waist-deep not too far from shore. The sun beat down from high in the sky, where bodies fell from and splashed into the water around me. Bex, then Hayden, then Brock.

Why had we fallen from the sky again, like we had when we arrived at Erde? Why hadn't we emerged from an underwater

Gate? I'd thought last time had been because we'd used the Book of Phoenix to transport us directly to where Nathayden was—that the Book had used or even created a portal. But this time we'd gone through an actual Gate on Erde. Shouldn't it have spit us out through the other side? No lights of a Gate shone under the water, though. Did each Gate work differently? I'd never thought to ask, and no one had ever mentioned this, but it seemed pretty plausible now.

A massive form blotted out the light of the sun before I had a chance to say anything, and we all looked up. We weren't the only ones to have passed through the Gate.

"Run!" Hayden yelled as soon as he tugged his own helmet off.

We sprinted for the shore, nearly there when an enormous wave of water almost knocked us down and the beast bellowed behind us. I looked over my shoulder at the gozzard that had followed us, its elephant-like trunk raised, sniffing the unfamiliar air. Nothing else seemed to have come through with it, thank God for small miracles. But bringing the monster from Erde to this new world, whatever it was, was bad enough. A look around as we continued running across the marsh made me think we'd made it back to Earth ... and brought a freakin' gozzard with us. But wouldn't I feel Jeric if we were on Earth? Maybe we just weren't close enough to each other.

We ran into the green jungle surrounding the lake, where near darkness immediately engulfed us, the pounding of the gozzard's footsteps behind us as it chased after. Chirps, buzzes, and hums filled the air, as well as the sound of dripping water on leaves. Our feet squelched in the muddy jungle floor as we trudged across it, and the putrid smell of rotting potatoes forced me to take quick, shallow breaths so I wouldn't gag. We clipped through the light-dappled jungle as quickly as possible, each of us taking turns in stumbling over a root or rock and pushing hanging vines out of our way. I tried hard not to think about the gigantic spider webs we passed ... or the creatures that made them ... but I couldn't help my hand from continuously swiping at the back of my neck, feeling creepy-crawlies all over me when there were none. Except for mosquitoes the size of birds that I swatted on my arms.

The air was thick and heavy with humid heat, and I'd started to shed the acid-eaten jacket I wore that was now nothing more than a membrane clinging to my body, but Brock stopped me.

"That thin material could be all that's keeping those mosquitoes from sucking every ounce of your blood," he said as he waved his hand in the air and smacked one away.

"Good point," I muttered, and I left the jacket on although sweat poured from my scalp and down my back.

My legs felt like tree trunks, as heavy as a gozzard's, when we finally broke through the edge of the jungle and halted in our tracks. Night had fallen, and the low, almost full moon reflected off the water in front of us. A sea. Waves beat at the shore that stretched to our right and left as far as we could see.

We each bent over, bracing ourselves with our hands on our knees, and tried to catch our breaths. We'd lost the gozzard a long time ago, but kept moving to put as much distance between it and us as possible. Now we were trapped between the raging sea and the jungle with the monster and who knew what other creatures. We hadn't seen any but certainly had heard them.

"Is this ... Earth?" Hayden panted.

"Possibly," Bex said. "Like the Amazon or something?"

"It's hard to say," I said. "I thought I'd feel Jeric as soon as we came through, but if I really did, which I'm not so sure, it was only for a moment."

"I felt Asia," Brock said, and my heart leapt as I spun to look at him. "I swear I feel her every now and then, but ..." He paused and frowned. "I could easily be lying to myself."

I shook my head, not letting him lose hope. "Maybe we're just not close enough to feel them."

"Do you have any idea where we are then?" Hayden asked. "Or do we need to find shelter for the night?"

I wracked my brain to remember all of the Gates' locations on Earth. I knew there were two in the U.S. and one in every other continent except Antarctica, but I didn't know if that even mattered.

"We could be in South America or Africa," I suggested, based on the jungle. "I don't know if we actually exited through a real Gate, so we could be anywhere in the tropics."

"Maybe even Australia?" Bex suggested.

Brock shook his head. "I don't think there are any jungles like that in Australia. Nowhere I've been, anyway."

"But this does look like a place on Earth?" Hayden tried to confirm. "Are we near civilization?"

"I could only say based on pictures I've seen, not actual experience," I admitted. "I've seen nothing here to say for sure that we're on Earth. And if we are, there's still no telling about civilization."

"There could be people around, but that doesn't mean they're civilized," Brock added.

"Then I say we find shelter for the night and hope we can learn more in the light of day." A shadow passed over Hayden's face, and my heart jumped. The last time darkness blotted out the light, a gozzard had dropped from the sky. This time it was only a cloud that had moved across the moon. More clouds were building in the distance and lightning flashed. "Looks like we better hurry, too."

We followed Hayden's lead, who might not know Earth, but had much more experience than the rest of us in living off the land. Because the rest of us had none. Using branches, palm fronds, and other foliage he could find, he and Brock built a shelter barely big enough for the four of us to cram into. Just in time, too, as the storm crashed overhead. We huddled together like four human balls, water dripping through the leaves here and there and sliding down our heads and backs. My body ached and jolts of pain shot through my hips and knees from old dance injuries feeling the strain of today's run and the humidity. My eyelids felt like five-pound weights hung from them, pulling them down over my gritty eyeballs. But nightfall and the storm had brought a chill to the air, and I couldn't sleep with the wet cold making me shiver. Without breaking the forms of our scrunched up bodies, Bex and I squirmed closer together, and the guys tried to warm us from the sides but with cold and clammy skin, they weren't exactly space heaters themselves.

After what felt like several dreadful hours of lightning, thunder, and downpours, the rain let off and the clouds began to thin, the moon's light shining through.

"Does your moon usually stay in the same place so long?" Hayden wondered as we still sat on the sand under the shelter, our legs stretched out in front of us now that it wasn't raining.

I rubbed my forehead as his meaning set in. The moon still hovered over the horizon, reflecting off the water in the same place it had been when we'd first emerged from the jungle. Granted, a cold, wet storm could make minutes feel like hours, but I'd seen for myself that the moon had risen in the sky while Hayden and Brock had built the shelter and Bex and I had collected firewood (that was now soaked).

Brock growled. "It's not the same moon."

He jerked his head toward our right, where another round, white light hung much higher in the sky. A third shone from a place over the tops of the jungle trees behind us. My heart sank, and tears pricked. We weren't on Earth. For all I knew, I was no closer to Jeric than I'd been on Erde.

"Should have known it wasn't her," Brock muttered under his breath before he pushed himself to his feet and strode down the beach.

"Asia?" Bex asked from beside me.

"I can only assume so," I said. "He thought he'd felt her a couple of times. I thought I'd felt Jeric, too, so I know what he means. In our souls."

"Not if we're nowhere near them," Brock said as he paced back toward us.

"Was it while we were in the Gate?" Bex asked. "Maybe a connection through there?"

Brock growled and shook his head. "It's been more than once."

I watched him pace a few times, then rose to my feet and did some yoga poses we used to do to stretch after rehearsals. While doing a standing forward bend to loosen my hips and back, a thought occurred to me.

"Maybe we're feeling them through the Book," I said to my shins. I lifted my head and looked up to see if anyone heard me. Brock had stopped his pacing, his head cocked. I slowly pulled myself upright to find all of them staring at me, the moons' light reflecting off their faces. "We already know we can communicate through the Book, right? I mean, Hayden, you sensed us when we were writing and drawing in the Book. You even knew what Bex looked like. So maybe Jeric and Asia finally figured it out, and they're trying to do the same. Maybe *they're* feeling *us* at the same time we're feeling them."

"I could feel you, yes, especially my Twin Flame," Hayden said. "But I'm not sure what you mean by this book. You've mentioned it before."

"Is this the same book you'd dropped in my car?" Bex asked. "The one with the drawing of Hayden? All of the Nathaydens?" She gasped. "It is, isn't it? And Jacey's story ... I remember now! That Bex *was* me! Leni, we'd been best friends and roomies before."

I gave her a small smile as she began to recall.

"We've been sisters before, too, haven't we?" she said. "No wonder I felt close to you."

"I'm still confused," Hayden pointed out. "I vaguely recall what a book is. There are printed words in them, yes?"

We confirmed Hayden's memory of a book, and he explained they didn't exist on Erde. They'd been banned generations ago. I told him, as well as Bex, more specifically about the Book of Phoenix and what I thought it could do. Hayden rubbed his chin and stared out at the water while I spoke, and I thought he hadn't been listening.

"The Book seems important to Enyxa," he said after I finished by telling them how the Book had brought us to Erde, but it had remained on Earth. "I can't remember why, though ..."

We fell silent as we all seemed to consider this seemingly unhelpful piece of information. What could Enyxa want with the Book of Phoenix?

"I think we were all involved in creating the Book, so maybe if we all keep our thinking caps on, we'll remember more about it," I suggested. "But we definitely need to keep trying to reach out to Jeric and Asia. They may be our only chance of going home."

With the weather calm and the tide low, we finally settled down for sleep after deciding on shifts. Brock took the first one. I fell asleep faster than I thought possible, only to be awoken a while later by a heart-wrenching scream.

"NOOOOO!"

I bolted upright, my heart in a gallop. Bex was already sitting up, too, but her arms and legs thrashed about.

"NO!" she screamed again, terror filling her voice.

"Bex, love," Hayden whispered, now also awake and sitting on her other side. He tried to put an arm around her to calm her down.

Her eyes, vacant and distant, widened and filled with fear. She shoved him away. "No! Don't you touch me!"

"It's me, love," he said, his voice soft and soothing. "You're okay."

"LEAVE ME ALONE!" she screamed. She jumped to her feet and spun to face us, her knees bent slightly, her hands out in front of her, her fingers curled in like claws. And her blue eyes wild with fear.

Hayden looked over at me, at a loss.

"She's going to attract animals," Brock hissed from where he sat a few feet away from the shelter, his katana laying next to him. He was on his knees, as though he'd begun to get up to help her, but had decided against it. Probably a wise decision.

Being the least likely to be mistaken for Mason, I sprang to my feet and wrapped my arm around her shoulder. "Bex, honey, it's me, Leni."

She tried to fight me at first, but I grabbed her chin and turned her head toward me.

"Look at me. See? It's just me. You're okay."

The wild look in her eyes began to fade.

"That's right," I soothed, rubbing my hand up and down her back. "You're safe. You're with me, and Brock, and Hayden. That's all. Nobody else. Nobody here wants to hurt you."

She looked around and nodded, but only when her eyes came back to me did they show any trust. Along with a deep sadness. Her hands reached out and clutched my shoulders. She threw her full weight on me, her knees buckling, and dragged us both to the ground. I wrapped my arms around her and held her as she cried.

"It's okay, you're okay," I repeated over and over, tears filling my own eyes. I honestly didn't know if she'd ever be truly okay.

"I'm not," she choked out at one point. "I'll never be okay again."

"Yes, you will," I whispered in her ear. She shook her head against my shoulder. "You *will*, and you know why? Because you're strong. You're stronger than that bastard. You won't let him ruin your life. You won't let what he did to you define you. Right?"

She sniffled and eventually nodded.

"And your love with Hayden is strong, too, right? Stronger than anything you face."

She sniffed again and pulled away from me, looking over my shoulder at where her Twin Flame sat.

"Oh, Hayden," she cried, "I'm so sorry."

I shifted to the side so she could crawl to him.

"Nothing to be sorry about, love," he said as he took her into his arms.

"There's everything to sorry about!" Bex's voice took on a new tone, one of total despair. "I'll never be right for you. He took that. He took *everything*."

"No, love—"

She pushed away from him, but not out of fear now. Something else filled her eyes.

"Yes! He destroyed everything! He destroyed me! I can't be with you, Hayden. I can't be with anyone. There's nothing left in me worth fighting for."

"Bex," I said, "that's the Darkness talking. You and Hayden haven't been Forged yet, so it's getting to you, too."

She shook her head vehemently. "It's the truth."

"It's the Darkness," I said more firmly. "Don't let it win."

"Funny thing about Darkness—it has a way of bringing the truth out," said a taunting female voice.

We all jumped to our feet as Enyxa emerged from the jungle, the moonlight bouncing off her white and black hair and sleek, form-fitting outfit. She grinned at the looks on our faces.

"You didn't think I'd let you stay in one of my worlds without another warm welcome, did you?" she asked. My heart sank at this knowledge, and she beamed even bigger. "Oh, yes, this world is mine, too. Not quite as dismal as Erde, but the souls are all mine." She turned bodily toward Bex and reached a hand out toward her face. "Are you ready to be mine, too, dear?"

Hayden jumped between them, a knife in each hand, one of them slicing toward Enyxa's outstretched arm. She jerked her hand back and hissed. Hayden fell to his knees. He pressed his fists to his temples and let out a feral, snarling sound. His face twisted as though he were in physical agony.

"No, please, stop!" he moaned.

"Oh, aren't you cute," Bex seethed at Enyxa, and then she went down, too, the fear and pain returned to her face. She curled over her thighs, moaning and sobbing.

Brock had moved to the evil bitch's back, his katana in hand. He silently swung it upward into position. Before he could move another inch, though, the long blade slid from his fists. He grasped his head and fell to his knees screaming, just like the other two.

Enyxa finally turned toward me. My heart pounded in my chest, but I tried to show nothing but calm. She had a weakness. We only needed to figure it out.

"What do you want from us?" I demanded as I stood with my feet shoulder-width apart and my hands clasped behind my back. They trembled, but at least she couldn't see them.

Her black eyes narrowed. "Your souls, of course."

I tilted my head. "I think there's more."

Her lips slowly tilted up into a smile. "You should know, Jacquelena. Maybe if you tried hard enough, you'd remember. If not—" She shrugged. "I'll give you the memory one of these times. For now, I just want to watch you all suffer as I did so many eons ago. Watch the Darkness take over you little by little, in the most painful way possible."

She disappeared then, along with the whole other world we were on. I was back in the ballet studio, with its scruffy hardwood floors, floor-to-ceiling mirrors, and the bar that stretched across the middle of two walls. The studio was empty and mostly dark except for the light that shone directly over me as I stood in front of the mirror in fifth position en pointe, wearing a light pink leotard, tights, and toe shoes. My round butt protruded significantly, hard and defined under the leotard. My breasts were full, too, so I was probably about seventeen. Something thin and sharp whipped out and cracked against my thighs. Through gritted teeth, I maintained position and held in the scream, but a whimper still escaped.

"You need to *lengthen*," Mama said as she ran the edge of the yardstick down my back and over my butt. She brought it to my front and pressed it against my breasts as though trying to slice them off. Their newness already made them tight and tender, but the pressure of the ruler made me bite my tongue against the pain. "Your lines are unacceptable. *You* are unacceptable like this."

The words hurt more than the sting of the yardstick as she once again whipped it against the backs of my thighs. Only after she walked away into the darkness, leaving me alone, did I crumple to the floor and cry. The insults of my own mother would echo in my mind for the next several years as I tried in vain to please her, while binging and purging behind her back.

Before she left, Enyxa made me feel one last hurt, and it wasn't mine. It was the pain my mother felt every time she looked at me and knew I'd never be the ballerina she'd devoted so much time and energy into raising.

And that hurt my heart more than any of the memories.

When my lucidity returned, I found myself curled in a ball on my side, staring at the water with a heaviness in my heart and soul I'd never felt before. I felt tainted. Stained. Darkened. I'd never meant to hurt my mama, or even disappoint her, but intentions meant nothing to her. My very existence had been the biggest agony of her life, and now Enyxa made sure I felt it.

The moans and cries of my friends around me subsided as the sun rose over the water and the sky lightened. None of us moved, though, too weighed down by the Darkness.

"We need something good to think about," I said, my voice thick and raspy. "Something light and with love to push this Darkness away."

"Not much of that for me to share," Hayden said.

"I've got nothin'," Bex agreed. She rolled to her back and turned her head toward Brock. "What about you, Brock? What's your and Asia's story?"

He snorted from his position on his back as he stared at the gray sky overhead. "It's not light and lovely."

"We know it has a good ending," I hedged.

"Does it?" he muttered.

I sighed. "Point taken."

"That's all you need to know."

"Come on, Brock," Bex pushed. "Tell us the whole story."

"Leave him alone," Hayden said. "Decent guys don't kiss and tell."

"We already know the beginning," Bex countered. "I know ya'll have been gettin' it from Asia like I have, right?"

She looked at Brock, then Hayden and me. I nodded. Besides the parts Enyxa gave me, I'd been *feeling* their story from Asia. Almost as if she were right here telling it to us. I could only hope that meant she was using the Book, and we were receiving her communication.

"Then get the rest from her," Brock grumbled, confirming that what we'd been feeling had been pretty accurate. At least from Asia's point of view. "Because I'm not telling you shit."

We all lay in silence for a few minutes, and it was almost as if Asia could hear us, because her story continued, giving us what we needed—an escape from our miserable present.

CHAPTER 11

10 MONTHS AGO

Aria MY CURIOSITY ABOUT the secrets the book held had grown to ridiculous levels since finding the lock open last night after Brock had left. I'd promised him in a text message that I'd wait to open it until he could come back over tonight, but I was admittedly weak and had peeked inside the front cover before I'd even gone to bed. I knew it was a journal, and although part of me thought we shouldn't pry into some stranger's privacy, another part of me pointed out how ancient the book looked and that the Jacey and Micah mentioned on the first page could be old or even dead, for all we knew. Whoever had dropped the book in the driveway certainly didn't seem to miss it since nobody had come by to claim it.

Hope had left me to work alone all day so she could write, which was good. I didn't know what Brock might have told her last night after they'd left ... after her knock on the door had interrupted our kiss. I hoped he'd told her nothing, that he'd given her some excuse for being at my place. I needed this job and kissing the boss's son probably wasn't a good idea. I was grateful I didn't have to face a humiliating warning to stay away from him today. I'd already given one to myself and dreaded the awkward but necessary we-can-only-be-friends talk.

So as I waited for Brock, curiosity and anxiety warred within me. He'd said he'd be over no later than 5:30, and when my phone showed 5:40, my foot was already bouncing. By 6:00, I began to think he had second thoughts about coming over, which was probably good, and by 6:15, my stomach was growling. I'd just finished making myself a peanut butter sandwich when there was finally a knock at the door.

"I'm really sorry," Brock said as soon as I opened it, standing there with purple smudges under his eyes and his dark hair disheveled as though he'd had a tough day. Thankfully, he wore a shirt this time, although the lavender polo did little to disguise the perfection I already knew hid beneath. "Mom was on a roll with her writing, and I learned as a kid to never interrupt her unless there's a fire or profuse amounts of blood. And I didn't want to bother you with Connor."

"He wouldn't have been a bother," I said automatically around a bite of sandwich.

"Oh, trust me. Today he would have been. Mom thinks he's teething or colicky. He was a cranky little bastard all day."

His tone was filled with love, so I knew he meant it as an endearment. Guys were weird like that. I gave him the expected smile as I stepped to the side to let him in.

My words had been more of a nicety than the truth anyway. I hadn't had to spend time with the baby yet to know how I'd react to him. Had I overcome the panic by now from the first time I'd seen him? Had enough time passed to heal my wounds? Or would I freak out again and want to run away, possibly with him in my arms? Either way, I didn't think having a baby in my small apartment with no way for an escape was a good test of how I'd respond.

I held up my sandwich with a bite taken out of it. "I was just eating dinner. You want a sandwich?"

Brock lifted a brow over his chocolate-brown eyes as he sat down on the couch. "A peanut butter sandwich is your dinner?"

"And a glass of milk," I said as I walked over to the counter and grabbed my cup. I took a long swig to wash down the sticky bite. "Protein, grains, and dairy. Cheap, easy, and at least a little healthy."

He shook his head. "I should take you out to dinner."

Uh-oh. Here we go. I drew in a deep breath.

"We can't do that," I blurted. "The whole dating thing. Kissing ... I can't—"

He held a hand up, stopping me before I could go on. "I know, I know. I can't either. I can't do that to you or me or everyone else involved. But we can be friends, right?"

I sucked my lips between my teeth, hesitating. That's what I'd wanted, too, a friend, but seeing him here in all his rugged beauty, I didn't know how that was going to work out. Especially with the way he was looking at me now.

He closed his eyes. "Okay, I admit, I was just thinking friends with benefits, but you don't deserve that. Just friends. I promise."

He opened his eyes and stared at me until I finally nodded.

"Friends," I confirmed as I grabbed my sandwich, glass, and the book and sat down beside him on the couch.

I placed my cup and the book on the coffee table, took a bite of my sandwich, and chewed and swallowed it before reaching to open the cover. As I did, my thigh pressed against Brock's and my arm brushed over his knee. We both tensed, and I wondered if he felt the same charge I did.

He cleared his throat. "If we're going to be friends, we can't sit like this."

Yes, he did. I sprang to my feet, nodding, and hopped over to the armchair. He slid the book closer to me and turned it at an angle so we could both look at it as he flipped the cover open.

"Jacey and Micah," he said as he studied the words I'd already peeked at, and then he turned the page. A date was handwritten at the top, along with a lengthy journal entry. I'd been right about it being old, but not as old as I'd expected.

"A diary from 1989?" Brock looked up at me. "Should we read it?"

"Definitely!"

He smiled with a twinkle in his eye like a boy about to cause mischief. "It's kind of wrong, isn't it?"

"It's old. They're old by now, maybe even dead. Let's at least see if there's anything interesting in it." My gaze dropped to the page, and after silently skimming the first couple of sentences, I pointed to them. "It even says, 'I hope that writing this down here will help us. And if not us, then someone else who might be reading it.' See? They *want* us to read it."

Brock chuckled and leaned back on the couch. "You're kind of naughty. But go ahead. Read it to me."

I eyed him, part of my mind stuck on how naughty I wanted to be with him. *Friends. We're only friends.* I couldn't let myself be so easily distracted. "You want me to read it to you out loud?"

He shrugged, a small smile playing on his full lips. "I've always enjoyed a good story."

I picked up the book and settled into the chair while he stretched out his legs and propped his feet on the coffee table. I felt his eyes on me as I read, and once when I glanced up, his gaze was focused intently on my mouth. I stumbled over whatever words I'd been reading, and his eyes popped up to mine. He gave me a guilty smile and motioned his hand to continue. The next time I looked up, only about ten pages in, his eyes were closed. I paused, watching his chest lift slowly, and he didn't seem to notice that I'd stopped.

"Aliens came and promised us all big boobs and endless kegs of beer."

Brock didn't reply, and if that phrase didn't catch his attention, it only meant one thing. He'd fallen asleep on me!

He'd looked exhausted before, and I hated waking him up, so I watched him sleep for a while instead, his dark lashes pressed against his cheekbones, and his mouth soft, the corners lifted slightly. After about fifteen minutes passed and he still didn't stir, I marked my spot in the journal and placed it on the table.

"Um ... Brock?" I said softly.

He startled awake, making me jump, too.

"Sorry!" I said guiltily. "I just figured your bed is probably more comfortable than my couch."

He straightened up and rubbed a hand over his face and then the back of his head. "No, no. *I'm* sorry. I can't believe I fell asleep on you."

"Well, more like on Jacey. Is she that boring?"

"Nah. It was kind of interesting, although pretty sad, too. I just ... I had a rough night. Lots of rough nights. It's hard, you know, trying to do it all."

I sat back in my chair and tucked my legs under me. "Do what all?"

He shrugged. "You know. Everything. Life."

I tilted my head. "We're friends, remember? If you want to talk, I can be a good listener."

He seemed to consider this for a moment. "Meh. I don't really want to talk about it. I'd been looking forward to this all day. It was kind of like an escape from reality and talking about my problems doesn't make for much of an escape, does it?"

"Do you want me to keep reading?"

He glanced at the stove and frowned. "My time's up. Need to get back to real life. Studies and responsibilities and all that."

"You should probably go to bed, don't you think?"

"That cat nap should do me for a while. That and a cup of coffee." He smiled warmly, the heat going straight through my body. "Thanks for your concern, though."

He stood, and I stood, and we both stood there awkwardly for a moment.

"Sorry again for the late start," he said as he moved for the door. "Hopefully it won't be so late tomorrow. We'll do it again, right? I want to find out what happens with Jacey."

I nodded, probably too enthusiastically, looking like one of those bobble heads. "Yeah, sure."

"Same bat time? Same bat channel?"

I laughed and pushed him out the door. "Earlier time, remember? Now go, you dork. Go get smarter."

He looked over his shoulder at me, and his gaze fell to my mouth. He let out a heavy sigh and turned back for the stairs again, rushing off before we did anything stupid.

The next evening, he showed up earlier and brought with him a large bowl of pasta with sausage and homemade sauce, a Caesar salad, and half a loaf of garlic bread.

"Friends bring food to each other, right?" he asked as he unloaded his bag onto my small kitchen counter.

The food smelled divine, making my mouth water and my stomach growl at an embarrassingly high decibel. No way in hell could I deny the bounty in front of me. Not after weeks of little more than peanut butter sandwiches and the occasional plate of cheese, crackers, and fruit Hope shared with me. That hadn't happened for the past two days, though, because she'd locked herself in her writing room. The apartment didn't have a dining table, so Brock sat on the couch and I took a seat on the floor on the opposite side of the coffee table. I tried to take my time eating and not looking like a disgusting pig with no manners shoveling in the forkfuls, but damn, it was too good.

"I guess you like it?" Brock asked as he eyed my half-empty plate.

"Like it?" I echoed after swallowing a bite. "I want to roll around naked in it."

He grinned, a gleam in his dark eyes. "I wouldn't mind watching that."

Heat rose to my cheeks. I wouldn't have minded him watching ... or joining. And then we could lick the deliciousness off of each other. *Damn it, Asia, stop it!*

I stabbed at a tube of ziti. "Your mom's an excellent cook."

He burst out laughing. "Hardly. I don't even remember the last time I've seen her cook."

"Oh, well, then, your chef is excellent."

He chuckled again. "I made this."

I practically choked on the bite I'd stuffed into my mouth. "You cook?"

"Another love, after reading and martial arts. I had to learn. Mom sucks at it, but she was always holed up in what she calls her writing cave anyway. Dad's a great cook, but he works a lot and travels all the time. He taught me the basics, and I took it from there."

I stared at him wide-eyed. He loved to read and cooked like a pro, both of which were sexy as hell, even if he didn't have a face and body to die for. Could he get any better? *Rich. Spoiled. Used to getting everything he wants. Could probably get away with murder.* I had to break open a few old wounds to remind myself that I couldn't want Brock. That guys like him were nothing but trouble wrapped up in a shiny package. Or worse. Except ... he wasn't like all the boys I'd grown up with. He was kind. Generous. Seemingly genuine. I mean, he had that moodiness going on for a while, but I thought that probably had something to do with his attraction to me that he obviously felt. Now that we'd kind of broken the ice there, he knew we were both fighting it, which I supposed made it easier to deal with.

"What?" he asked as I continued to stare at him.

I smiled and shook my head. "There just might be the makings of a good husband in you."

His face clouded over, and his eyes darkened. "Not likely."

I about dropped my fork. "Not with me! I didn't mean that!" Oh, god, this was embarrassing. "I just meant … with someone. In the future."

The dark cloud left his face, and he gave me a small smile. "I know. Don't worry. But it's still not likely. It'll take someone special to put up with me and everything I bring to the table."

His tone was heavy, lingering with the same darkness that had filled his eyes a moment ago. I wanted to ask what he meant, but I also liked what he'd said last night about our time together being an escape for him. Maybe some day he'd tell me an escape from what, but for now, I'd give him what he needed. So I tried to lighten the mood.

"Bringing food like this to the table is a pretty damn good thing. Especially when it tastes like heaven."

"I think anything not made of peanut butter and bread would taste like heaven to you."

I shrugged. "True. But seriously. This is impressive, Brock. Unless … is this all you can make? Your one signature dish?"

He chuckled. "It's just my go-to meal. I don't have to think about making it, which means I can do other things at the same time. I've been making it a lot the past few months."

I leaned back and rubbed my hand over my stuffed belly. "I think I could eat it a lot. All the time. I wouldn't even mind getting fat from it because it'd be worth it."

"You know, I don't think I've ever heard a girl say those words."

"Well, unfortunately, it's not all that likely. Unlike most girls, I have trouble putting weight on. I can eat like a horse—like this—all the time and never gain. I'm like my mom in that way. She's tinier than me."

"You must not have had any girl friends."

I snorted. "Yeah. I thought my best friend got over it when she realized it was just as hard for me to maintain a normal weight as it was for her. At least she got curves. I barely got any." Except for a few months last summer, but I wasn't going there.

Nothing Brock ever needed to know about. "But when her curves tried to become rolls and she had to work her ass off at the gym, she became more jealous than ever. It was stupid. And then shit kind of happened, and I got over all the superficial drama. I haven't talked to her in ages. Don't really care to, either."

"Do you keep in touch with any friends back home? Where is that anyway?"

"D.C. suburbs. And no. No real friends there."

I shoved the last bite of garlic bread into my mouth, but it suddenly became hard to swallow. My throat had thickened, and I had to force it down. I pushed my plate away.

"No wonder you want to be friends with me so much," Brock teased. "You don't have any."

Now it was his turn to lighten the mood. Bless him for noticing.

I smiled. "Yeah. Suppose I could use one. But you already knew that when you and your friend showed up to buy my car."

"Brandon. I guess you could say he's my friend, except he's not much more than a neighbor these days. I'd had a lot of friends at one time, but we all drifted apart since high school. Gone off to different colleges. I went the farthest away, but now that I'm back, they don't get me at all any more." He shrugged. "Different lives now. They're still into the drinking and fraternity things. I've had to grow up faster, which makes them stay far away."

His tone had darkened again, and once more I had to fight the urge to pry. To offer an ear that he seemed to need. Maybe if he were a girl, I would have asked, but guys were different. They didn't like to talk about feelings and shit. And that's one thing I liked about them these days.

"So I'm not the only one who's friendless, eh?" I teased.

He laughed and rose to his feet, then began collecting our dishes. "Yeah. We're quite the pair, aren't we?"

We cleaned up together, and he stuck the leftovers in my refrigerator. I was surprised there were any. I felt like I'd eaten enough for four.

Taking our same spots as last night, I read aloud again, and this time Brock didn't fall asleep. We had to stop for the night when his phone beeped with a text.

"Back to reality?" I asked after he glanced at the screen and frowned. "Again tomorrow?"

"No friends. No life. Remember?"

"So I'll see you tomorrow." This time it wasn't a question.

The next evening was the same. Brock brought over a scrumptious chicken and rice dish, and after we finished eating, he listened to me read the journal for about an hour or so, and then his phone beeped, signaling his time of escape was over. I was surprised he came over the next night. Yeah, he admitted to not having much of a life either, but he grew up around here. Surely someone like him could find something to do on a Friday night. But here he was, sitting with me for the fourth night in a row, an almost empty box of pizza sitting on the coffee table between us.

"Sorry," he said when his phone gave the tone.

"Even on a Friday?"

"No rest for the wicked." He gave me a smile to match the phrase, making my heart stutter, and then stood and stretched. "So what do you think's going on with these guys? Pretty weird, right?"

I marked the page and placed the book on the coffee table before standing, too.

"Who knows? Honestly, I'm starting to wonder if we're reading a real diary or somebody's fiction."

He groaned as he headed for the door. "Damn. That figures. We got all excited, and the book probably came from some new writer who'd figured out Mom's address and left it for her, hoping to get some kind of response."

I frowned. "She gets emails like that. I've already seen them from writers thinking she has some kind of special power to give them a publishing contract. But this book came with no contact information. Why would they bother?"

"Good point. But people are fucked up. They probably have some diabolical plan."

I laughed. "Let's hope not. Maybe we'll find out more tomorrow."

He opened the door and turned back to me with an apologetic look. "I can't do tomorrow. Probably not the whole weekend." He paused, and then cocked his head. "Sunday is Christmas Eve and a family dinner, though. You should join us."

My eyes widened, and I stopped in place. I hadn't even realized I'd been moving closer to him. "Um ... I don't think so. I'm your mom's employee. Not family."

"You're my friend, too, remember? I've had friends over before."

"For Christmas?" I said doubtfully, and I shook my head. "Thanks, but I think I'll pass."

"You want to be alone for Christmas?"

I shrugged. "All of my Christmases have been spent at a ski lodge with strangers. It'll be nice to be alone for once."

He looked at me skeptically, but gave in. Thank God. I really didn't want to make such a big deal over the holiday.

"Okay, then. Your loss. I'm cooking," he taunted.

"Very tempting," I admitted. "But no thanks."

He studied my face for a long time, and, as usual, his gaze dropped to my mouth. I couldn't help but lick my lips. His nostrils flared before he turned away, muttering something about being friends sucked as he trotted down the steps.

I wasn't sure if I agreed or not. I liked being friends with Brock. He was fun to hang out with, and there was no emotional pressure of a more intimate relationship, no wondering what the next step was, no freaking out about whether we were moving too fast or too slow. But I also liked kissing him. A lot. A *fucking* lot. The feel of his lips on mine was firmly planted in my memory, and part of me wanted to make it real again.

Shit. I was falling for him.

So badly that I couldn't stop thinking about him Saturday morning. I hadn't left Hope's property since the day I moved in, and I seriously needed some time away from there. And from Brock. I went to the beach for a few hours, and then to the grocery store, armed with my first paycheck. It was about time that I cooked for Brock. Too bad that wouldn't be for another few days.

Crap. There I went again, thinking about him and looking forward to our next rendezvous. I seriously needed a life.

That night, I was good, though, when Brock texted me at eleven, asking if I was awake. Not wanting my boredom and desperation for company to show through, I suppressed the urge to reply. But I had no control over the giddiness in my belly or how long it took me to fall asleep because he was thinking about me.

After spending a whole hour cleaning my entire apartment on Sunday morning, I took Brock's advice and worked out in their home gym. Or tried to anyway. I didn't really know how to use the weight machine, so I did the best I could, while constantly glancing around the room as I searched for cameras. I was sure someone was somewhere laughing at me. Like Brock. Right when I'd given up and was about to head back to my apartment, Hope walked in.

She was dressed in workout pants and a tank top with her hair pulled back in a ponytail. Earphones hung around her neck.

"Oh, Asia," she gasped when she saw me. "I didn't—"

"I'm sorry!" I jumped to my feet and grabbed my towel to wipe the sweat off my neck and chest. "Brock said it was okay to use the gym, but I didn't mean to intrude."

She gave me a warm smile. Even without makeup and at her age, she was beautiful. "No, that's fine. You're welcome any time. I just hadn't expected you is all. It startled me."

I scooted toward the door. "Well, I'm done anyway. It's all yours. I mean, of course it is, but, um … I think I'll leave now."

Why was I acting so stupid? I felt like I'd been caught with my hand in the cookie jar—even worse than when she'd knocked on my door while I was kissing her son.

"Asia, wait," she said, and I paused, drew in a deep breath, and turned around. "I haven't seen you much the last few days, I know. But I wanted to say thank you."

Um… "You're welcome?" It sounded like a question because I wasn't sure what she was thanking me for. It had to be all the organizing I did of her files while she was writing. "I mean, it's my job. It's what you hired me for, right?"

"I meant for Brock."

My breath caught. My face heated. Oh, god, here we go. The conversation I'd been dreading where she'd tell me to lay off her beautiful, perfect son while I tried to sink into the floor and become invisible.

"We're just friends," I blurted.

She smiled. "I know. It's okay, hun. Even if you were more than friends. I think you two would be good with each other."

I imagined my eyes bugging out of my face like a cartoon character's. "What? I mean, really?" I shook my head. "No, I mean, we're friends. Nothing more. That's all."

"I kind of have this sixth sense about people who should be together. Maybe because of all the romance writing, you know? And I think you two kind of need each other." She lifted her shoulder in a shrug. "Whether friends or anything else, I'm glad he has you. He needs someone like you. Not his guy buddies, but a real friend. He has a lot on his plate right now, and you seem to understand that. That's why I haven't minded him ditching Connor and me for dinner all this week."

My face flushed even hotter. "I'm sorry. I didn't mean to cause problems."

"Asia, please stop apologizing. I'm thanking you. I *want* you to be his friend ... or whatever."

I frowned, and my heart clenched. "I'm afraid I haven't been much of a friend, though. I don't even know what you mean by all that he has on his plate right now. I've tried to ask, but he never wants to talk about it, and I didn't want to pry."

"Well, most of it's pretty obvious, isn't it?" She let out a little snort. "But that's my Brock. Always playing down the hard stuff."

"He's kind of great," I admitted.

Her mouth stretched beyond a grin this time to outright beaming. "He really is. I *knew* you thought so, too. I told you—I'm good like that. He'll need a lot of time and patience, though, Asia. Even if you are just friends." She winked. "He has his priorities, though. I don't see him ever purposely messing up, but he's a boy. A male. He'll screw up plenty enough by accident. They just can't help it. I only ask that you be the girl I think you are and keep him on track."

So that was her warning. Not exactly what I'd been expecting—I thought for sure she'd tell me to stay away from him and remember I was here to work and nothing else—but a warning nonetheless not to become his top priority. Not to be a distraction.

"That's what he needs most from you," she continued, and then she chuckled. "That's what all men need most from their women."

"Like I said, we're just friends," I assured one more time before turning back for the door.

"For now," Hope said from behind me. "Oh, Asia, why don't you join us tonight for family dinner? You can finally meet my mister. The one *I* have to keep on track."

"I already told Brock—"

"I don't care what you told Brock. *I'm* asking you to join my family for dinner. It's Christmas Eve, and you shouldn't be alone. Please come."

Well. How could I say no to that? Especially since she was my boss.

"What time?"

"We won't eat until after Connor goes down for bed, so around 7:30."

We actually didn't eat until nearly eight, but I arrived a little before 7:30 and helped Brock and his dad in the kitchen as much as I could while Hope tried to put a cranky Connor to bed. Mr. Verdor traveled constantly for business and was only home on some weekends and apparently holidays, which had been one of the reasons I hadn't wanted to intrude on their dinner—they had such little time together as a family as it was. But I was glad to have met him. Although, I did feel envious of Brock over his very cool parents. They were obviously successful and could have been snotty jerks, but they were complete opposites of my always proper (except behind closed doors) asshole of a stepfather and my wimpy, wilted mother who couldn't make a decision for herself.

Disregarding my protests that it wasn't necessary and reminders that I lived right behind the house, Brock insisted on walking me home, all the way up the stairs and to the door.

"I never thought any girl would ever be able to earn them, but you have my parents' blessings," he said as I opened the door.

I froze with my back to him. "Oh, really?"

I felt him move closer to me. Felt the energy charging between us.

"Oh, definitely. Especially my mom. She said she talked to you earlier today."

I closed my eyes and held my breath. What had she told him? Our entire conversation? Oh, god, I hoped not. Brock moved even closer. I could sense every inch of his body only centimeters from mine.

"Asia," he whispered, my name a sigh on his lips. "I really don't know if this is right ... or best ... or anything. But, I can't help it. I can't be friends with you."

My breath leaked out, and I slowly nodded. "I know. You have priorities."

"I don't think you understand." He was so close now, I felt his breath on my neck as it fluttered my hair. "I can't be *just* friends with you. I want you too badly."

His hand landed on my shoulder and slid down my arm until his fingers tangled between mine. His chest pressed lightly against my shoulders, and his mouth was so close, I could already feel it on my skin although his lips hadn't actually touched me. My heart raced, and my stomach tilted.

"Do you want me?" he breathed against my ear, sending goose bumps over my skin. Powerless to do anything else, I only nodded. "Good."

With one hand still holding mine, his free one came to my waist and held me as his mouth skimmed from my ear down my neck stopping at the hollow at my shoulder. There his lips parted, and his tongue swirled over my skin. My knees turned to jelly, and I leaned back, wanting to melt into him. But he kept his hand steady on my waist as he stepped away from me. I turned around to face him, wondering why he stopped before he even started.

"I'm going to do this right, though," he said. "Slowly and on purpose. No more accidental kisses. Every one will be deliberate. Meant for only you."

I could only stare at him and blink. Eventually I nodded. He returned my affirmation, and then lifted our hands so his thumb could brush over my lips.

"Merry Christmas, Asia," he murmured, and the next thing I knew, he was free from me and halfway down the steps.

The following two weeks he courted me almost in an old-fashioned way, taking things slow and deliberate as he'd promised. We only read Jacey's journal a couple of times, not getting very far, because he kept insisting on taking me out for dinner or at least ice cream and walks on the beach. We were always home by seven-thirty, though, when his phone would beep, letting us know his free time was over. I didn't mind. I remembered what Hope had said about keeping him on track. I knew it was important to both of them that he finish college and then med school, and since we'd only started dating, I wasn't about to become the co-dependent whiner. Then he promised me Friday night to celebrate my twenty-first birthday with a full date and staying out later than dark, and I became ridiculously excited.

When I'd gone to work Friday morning, I'd forgotten the dishes from the dinner he'd made me the night before so I brought them over a little before our date was to begin. I wasn't ready to go out yet, and I was sure Brock wasn't either, but I heard him in the family room, so I popped my head around the corner to say hi.

And everything crashed down on me.

He lay on the brown leather sofa in jeans and nothing else with his knees bent up and closed together. In his lap, leaning against his thighs, was Connor with his little fists waving in the air. And the way Brock was looking at him, smiling at him, showing complete adoration and protection, I suddenly knew what Hope had meant. It hadn't been obvious. Not to me. Not until now.

But seriously. How had I not known?

"Who's Daddy's big boy?" Brock cooed as he picked Connor up and snuggled his nose into the baby's neck.

Into his *son's* neck.

CHAPTER 12

9 MONTHS AGO

Asia

"OH, MY GOD," I gasped aloud as my hand flew to cover my mouth.

"There's our birthday girl," Brock said in his daddy-to-baby voice. My heart stopped even before he turned to look at me, a broad smile on his face. As he took in my shocked expression, his brows pinched together, and the corners of his mouth turned down. "What's wrong, babe?"

I shook my head, still unable to breathe, unable to think, unable to do anything but stare. When he swung his legs around to the floor and stood with Connor sitting on his muscled arm, I bolted to the kitchen toward the back door.

"Asia, wait!" Brock commanded as I cornered the granite-topped island in the gourmet kitchen. I stopped in my tracks and drew in a deep breath as I kept my back to him. "What's the matter? You look like you caught me in bed with another girl or something."

Heh. *That* would have been easy to comprehend. Wouldn't have been the first time, and I'd know what to do. This, though. This had me in complete shock.

I turned around to find Brock only a couple of feet away from me, both his and Connor's dark eyes staring at me.

"He's—" My throat felt thick and dry. I swallowed down the lump in it as I looked at the baby and back at Brock. I'd thought the resemblance had been because they were brothers. Not this. "He's ... yours."

It didn't even come out as a question, because it was painfully obvious now.

"Well, yeah." Brock looked at me with the same confusion I felt. After a moment, his head cocked and his eyes squinted. "Wait. You didn't know?"

I shook my head. Gathered my hair in hands and tugged. All kinds of emotions swirled through me, and I felt a panic attack beginning to rise. My chest constricted, and my lungs fought for air. My stomach twisted and turned, and stars began to dance in front of my eyes as a dizzy spell came on.

"I have to get out of here." I spun and ran through the kitchen, out the back door, and up to my apartment, ignoring Brock's pleas to stop and come back.

Once inside my apartment, I fell to my hands and knees on the floor, gulping in much needed air. When I could finally breathe properly and I felt sure my heart wasn't going to pound its way up my throat and out my mouth, I collapsed and rolled over. I lay on my back, knees in the air, and stared at the ceiling.

How could I have been so fucking *stupid?*

So blind? How had I not even considered that Connor belonged to Brock and not Hope? It couldn't have been because of his age or that he was single, because I, of all people, knew that meant nothing. Or maybe I'd assumed most people weren't as stupid and careless as me? I knew better than that, too, though. So how had I ignored this possibility, especially when Brock "babysat" Connor so much? He wasn't actually babysitting. He was simply taking care of his own son.

A sob began to push in my throat as his love for Connor hit me hard, reminding me of what could have been .... If only ...

Brock's shape filled the window by the door at the same time a knock sounded on it. He must have peaked in and saw me on the floor because he didn't wait for me to respond, but entered on his own. I stared at him as he stood over me, focusing on his bare chest and arms that were so damn exquisite, because I couldn't bring myself to focus on anything else. After a long moment of studying my face, he dropped to his knees next to me and pulled me off the floor and into his lap, hugging me close to him. I didn't even know how to respond. I couldn't hold my ignorance against him. But I couldn't bring myself to return the embrace. My arms hung loosely at my sides.

"I'm sorry you didn't know," he whispered. "I honestly thought you did. Please don't think I was lying to you."

I shook my head. "It was my own damn stupidity. I thought you were brothers. That Hope had a baby late in life. An oops baby. I assumed, and you know how that always works out."

"So you're not mad at me?"

I pulled back to look into his eyes. "How could I be mad at you for having a son, Brock?"

"But you ran away ..."

"I was in shock. I still am. I don't even know how to process this. What to think any more." I pushed off his lap and to my feet. I needed to separate myself from him, so I walked over to the couch and sat in the corner, pulling my knees to my chest.

"I know it's a lot to accept." He scratched at his cheek before his arms fell to his sides. "I honestly thought you already had. Now that I think about it, though, I realize how stupid I'd been to think you'd accept it. Sometimes I find it hard to believe myself."

"How?" I asked.

"How what?"

"How did it happen?"

He lifted a brow. I rolled my eyes.

"I mean, how did you end up here, a single dad?" For some reason, I felt the need to hear his story. Right now. Probably because I knew it would prolong having to focus on my own. On the multitude of emotions storming through me.

Brock came over and sat on the other end of the couch. He pulled one knee up and turned so his back rested against the couch's arm, allowing him to face me. His chest rose as he drew in a deep breath and fell as he blew it out.

"We've been skating around our pasts long enough, huh?" he asked as though avoiding having to tell me. I nodded. "Okay, then. Well … I met his mom at a party at college. When I was up north."

"New York, right?" I asked, sure he'd mentioned that before.

"Yeah, upstate. I'd spent freshman year enjoying life as a 19-year-old college boy should—joined a fraternity, barely passed classes, drank way too much beer, and chased after girls. We hooked up at a party early fall semester my second year, and she gave me her number. I didn't think much of it, but I was bored one night and gave her a call." He shrugged, showing his nonchalance at the time. "We had some fun for a while, hanging out on the weekends when neither of us had anything else to do. By the end of the semester, my grades weren't what they should have been. I realized I needed to take my studies a lot more seriously if I was ever going to get into med school, and I thought dating someone exclusively would help keep me from the parties. So I asked her. It wasn't all that serious, though. I mean, definitely not love or anything. We never talked about the future except our career goals. We never got to that point, and then I didn't hear from her for a few weeks, until around spring break of last year. When she finally called again, it was to tell me she was pregnant."

"And you were sure it was yours? At the time, I mean? He's obviously yours, looking at him now."

"We may not have loved each other, but we did care for each other. She wasn't a slut. In fact, I was only the second guy she'd ever been with." He frowned, his gaze dropping to watch as his thumbnail flicked at the hem of his jeans. "I didn't love her, but I offered to marry her anyway. I was brought up to do the right thing, you know? I thought maybe someday we'd grow to love each other. But she didn't want any of that. She didn't want me giving up on my dreams of being a doctor. She didn't want to give up on her own dreams either."

My heart stuttered as I felt her pain. "She was thinking abortion, wasn't she?"

"She brought it up, but I was against it, and so was she. She talked about adoption, but I didn't approve of that option either. I was going to take responsibility for my child. End of story. And then she dropped off the face of the Earth." He shook his head, his dark hair flopping over his forehead. "I couldn't reach her anywhere. Not at her place, not on her cell phone, not through email. I drove the two hours to her parents' home every weekend throughout the summer, figuring she'd gone there, but could never catch her. I thought I'd never see my child. I was scared that she'd aborted him. Last semester started, and I tried to go on as usual. I was in my own place by then, hoping that I could get her to move in with me. If I could only find her. Her due date came and went, and I still couldn't reach her. I hated not being there for her ... for him. Not being there for his birth."

"Wow. I can't believe she did that to you." My heart squeezed for Brock and what he must have been going through.

"Yeah, it sucked. When I still hadn't heard from her a few weeks after her due date, I figured I wasn't going to. I prayed that she hadn't aborted the baby, but that she'd decided to keep him and maybe one day she'd let me into his life. Or, at least, that she'd put him up for adoption. Even if that meant she hadn't put my name on the birth certificate, and I'd never know my own child, at least I'd know he was alive and well somewhere.

It was that hope that got me through it. And then I refocused on my studies, trying to forget."

"Which is impossible."

"Yeah." He nodded. "I tried to fool myself, but failed. But what could I do? I could only believe in what Mom always told me: things happen the way they're supposed to."

"Which they obviously did ..."

"Right. So, she'd apparently received all of my messages and had tracked me down in my new place, because one day I was sitting at home, working on chem homework when I got a text from her to open my front door. My heart had gone crazy. I crossed the living room in three long strides. I was so excited to see her again, and, hopefully our baby. Or at least to find out what she'd done. I figured if she'd had an abortion against my wishes, she wouldn't dare show her face at my door. So, I threw it open expectantly."

He paused. His last words had come thickly, as though his throat had closed up.

"And?" I coaxed.

"And there he was. The most beautiful but tiniest human I'd ever seen. He was sitting in a car seat with a diaper bag next to him, sound asleep. A car engine gunned in the distance as it took off out of the parking lot, but I paid it no attention at the time. But then another text message came through: 'I can't do it,' it said. 'You wanted him. He's all yours. His name is Connor. I hope that's okay with you.'"

My breath caught audibly.

"Oh, my god! She just *left* him at your door?" What had she been thinking? How could any mother do such a thing?

"She obviously knew I was home."

"But, still ... What did you do?"

He shrugged. "I brought him inside, of course. It took me a while to process as I stared at his sweet little face, but when he woke up crying, reality hit. I was suddenly a daddy. And I had no clue what to do."

"So you came home."

"Yep. Mom and Dad were on their way back from Europe. I couldn't get a hold of them, but I didn't know what else to do, so I dropped my on-campus classes and only kept the online ones, packed the important stuff and moved back here. A buddy helped me make the drive, but he didn't want to stick around for when I broke the news to Mom, so I dropped him off at the airport as soon as we were in town. The whole way here, I dreaded her reaction. But she took one look at us and promised I would never have to do it all alone. As long as I stayed in school, she'd take care of us. So ... here we are. That was less than a week before you showed up to interview for a job."

I thought back to that first day I'd met them. "Damn," I breathed as I flopped against the couch. I hadn't realized how tensed up I'd become from listening to his story. "So many things make much more sense now."

He pressed his lips together and nodded. We held each other's gazes for a long time.

"So ..." he said, and his voice trailed off.

"So ..." I echoed. "You, uh, have a baby."

"Yep. I do. He's my world. That changes things, doesn't it?"

I chuckled. "Uh, yeah, that changes a lot. I don't ... I don't even know what to think right now, Brock."

His story had distracted me, allowing my emotions to calm, but now we'd returned full circle to the subject of us. Trying to think of us—*three* of us—was impossible, because my brain went one way, while my heart kept traveling to different feelings and memories, and my soul wanted to pull Brock into my arms and tell him it'd all be okay. We'd be okay. We'd find our way through this.

He rose to his feet. "So, uh, you should probably take some time to think about this. I'll take a rain check on our date for tonight."

My heart sank, but I nodded. "Yeah, that'd be best. I definitely need time. What we have—had—it's all different now. I ... I just don't know right now."

A muscle in his face twitched, but his eyes turned distant. "I get it, Asia. Trust me, I get it."

He left then, and I listened to his footsteps trudge down the stairs until I could hear him no more, and then I leaned my head back on the couch cushion and blew out a sigh weighed down with life. I stared at the ceiling again, and a single tear leaked from the corner of my eye and trailed down my temple into my hair. I squeezed my eyes shut to prevent any more from falling, but my heart was taking the rest of me down the path I didn't want to go. To my own horrible summer of difficult decisions, hopes, and fear of the unknown. To a time I wished I could return to and do things differently.

But like Brock's, my life was how it was meant to be.

Unlike Brock's, it was completely lonely.

Along with my job, he'd filled the huge void I'd been living with since leaving my old life behind four months ago in October. Actually, since losing what was most precious to me last summer. For the past month or so, I hadn't felt empty like I had before. And it wasn't just his presence that filled the gaps, but the feeling that he appreciated me in his life as much as I did him in mine. He *wanted* to be with me. He'd called me his escape. He looked forward to seeing me every evening as though I were a luxury to enjoy. I understood more fully that I really was. He didn't have time or room in his life for a girlfriend, but he'd made it for me. And he thought I was the exception to most girls our age who wouldn't be so accepting of a pre-made family.

I didn't know if I was, though. I certainly didn't deserve to be revered as a luxury. Regardless, the real question was whether I was truly an exception to all the other girls.

Letting Brock go and returning to my empty life scared me more now than that same life had when I actually lived it. Something deep within me twisted painfully as I considered the idea, balking at the possibility of breaking up with Brock. But if he filled me, made me feel complete, what would bringing Connor into the equation do? Was there room? Could I make more space in my heart for him? He could never push out the piece of my heart held for the baby I could never have, but maybe there was another place he could fill.

I just didn't know. I liked Brock. A lot. As in, I could easily see myself falling in love with him. Maybe I already had and just couldn't admit to it, and that was why this decision came so hard. I'd never felt so lost and confused. Well, actually I had, but this took a close second.

Taking my time to figure things out, I avoided Brock for the following week and beyond. I pretty much knew his schedule, so I made sure I walked over to Hope's office when he'd be upstairs showering and getting ready for his day. I made the quick journey home during what I'd previously called his afternoon babysitting duty, but now knew was his father-son time. When he called, I let it go to voicemail. When he texted, I didn't reply until I knew he was in class or sleeping and couldn't text me back right away. I simply didn't know what to say yet.

I spent my evenings with extra social media work for Hope, which brought me to Facebook and another message from Kami:

"Hi, Asia, Sorry it's taken so long for me to reply. I'm still trying to get my ducks in a row, which is taking a lot longer than I thought it would. I dropped my classes for the semester, and I've been working full time to save up some money for my new life. I want to make sure I can be independent and live on my own, because you never know how things will turn out. I know you understand. After all, it was you who inspired me to do this in the first place. I hope everything is good with you, wherever you are. You never did tell me where you ended up. Anyway, thanks again for telling me to take charge of my life and to make things happen instead of letting them happen. I'm almost there. I mean, I've already taken a lot of steps, but sometimes it's hard. I miss being a kid sometimes, you know? But I also hate the person I'd become before. So, yeah. I'm taking charge. Maybe by the time I can reply again, I'll be on the road. Please keep in touch."

The full conversation we'd had at the coffee shop came back to me now, and I dropped my head into my hands and massaged my temples. I remembered her telling me about how she'd always been able to coast through life, never having to make a big decision on her own, which had led her to end up in the same support group as the one I'd found on campus. Only, after we each left that one meeting we'd both been at, our lives had taken very different paths. She still hadn't been able to decide her next step, and my decision was ripped away from me. Until that day when I'd made several life-changing decisions, including packing everything I owned, quitting classes, and driving to Florida.

She hadn't told me what her ultimate decision had been that day in the coffee shop. We hadn't grown that close in the ten minutes we sat with each other. But she did tell me she regretted it. Her eyes told me more—that it would haunt her until her dying day. And that's when I'd told her that I'd finally made the decision to take my own life into my hands and suggested she consider doing the same.

"Stop letting others make decisions for you that *you* have to live with," I'd said. "It's *your* life. Own it."

I rubbed the pressure points on my forehead for another minute, and then I wrote back to her:

"Hi, Kami ~ No problem on the delayed reply. I have to apologize, too. I only get on here for my boss and usually through her account as she dictates what she wants me to post. I'm glad things are going well for you. I guess they are here, too. I met a guy. A super guy. I thought he was going to be like all the rich, arrogant jerk-offs I'd grown up with, but he's not. Just the opposite. Only, he has baggage. Pretty big baggage. As big as we have. I just found out last week, and I've put us in a holding pattern until I can figure out what to do. I mean, I don't fault or blame him. I just don't know if I can help him carry his load. I think I want to, but after everything I've been through, I don't know if I can yet. You're probably the only person I know who can understand that."

Tears pricked my eyes as I realized the truth in that last statement. As I'd been typing, I'd wondered why I was even telling a near stranger all of this. I avoided giving too many details since everything stays on the Internet forever and a day. Even if it was a private message, I didn't trust the Internet gods to keep it private into eternity. When I typed out that last sentence, though, I knew why I was spilling to Kami. We may have been mere acquaintances, but she really was the only person I knew in the world who would understand exactly where I was coming from with the Brock and Connor situation.

I wiped at my eyes before I reviewed what I'd already written and continued:

"Anyway, you've kind of inspired me now to take my own advice and make a damn decision. If I don't, it'll be made for me, and I probably won't like it. That's how things go, right? Let's make a pact with each other that we'll both stop letting others make all of our decisions. Sound good? Good luck with getting your ducks in a row. You keep in touch, too, and let me know when you start your new life. ~ Asia"

I signed off, closed the laptop, and set it on the coffee table next to Jacey's old journal, which had remained there since the last time Brock and I had read it together. I picked up the book and ran my fingertips over the image embossed into the leather. I gasped as a tingling pulsed through my fingers. The feeling wasn't unpleasant, and I closed my eyes automatically, wanting to relish in the strange sensation.

By the time I opened them, my decision was made, based on something I felt deep in my soul. I felt the truth in it so strongly now, I couldn't believe it had taken me as long as it had to figure it out. A knock on my door made me jump—it was nearly midnight—and when I opened it to find Brock on the other side, I couldn't help but wonder if he'd somehow sensed that I was finally ready to talk. Except I wasn't *quite* ready. Although my decision was made, I hadn't yet figured out the best way to execute it, and now here he was, all rugged and gorgeous as usual, making my mind wander when I really needed it to focus. At least he wore a shirt. I never thought that would be a positive, but at the moment, it was.

His gaze skimmed down my tank top and pajama bottoms and back up, where they caught for a brief moment on my boobs, freed from their confines of a bra at the moment. I crossed my arms over my chest when I realized I was totally nipping out, and not because it was cold.

"You, uh, want to come in?" I asked, and his eyes jumped up to mine.

He shook his head. "No, it's late. I just couldn't wait another moment to talk to you. I'm letting you off the hook."

My brows scrunched together. "What?"

His gaze dropped as he rubbed his thumb over his eyebrow. "I've been thinking hard about everything, as I'm sure you have. I really thought you knew from the beginning, and I'm truly sorry if you felt led on."

"I already told you—it's not your fault. I was too blind to see the clues, and I didn't ask enough questions. Please don't blame yourself for this. It was a misunderstanding."

He snorted. "A pretty serious misunderstanding."

I nodded. "Kind of."

"Yeah, well, there's more that makes it bigger. See, not only did I think you knew, but I thought you actually were okay with it." He chuckled, but I heard no humor in the sound. "That was stupid of me, I know. Why would you want to take on something like a baby? I mean, I know he's mine, but that means he's part of my whole package. And who wants that? You obviously don't. I'd been living in a fantasy world, and I see that now."

"Brock—"

"Please," he interrupted, "just let me get this out because it's been killing me for days." He watched me for confirmation before he went on. "Your reaction, Asia, your need to take this long to think about it, tells me you're not ready for this life. For what I have to offer. And as much as it kills me to say it, I'm letting you go. You can stop freaking out and worrying about it. I'm not going to beg you to stay in something you don't want to be in. I did that enough in the past. I won't do that to you. I care about you too much. I care about my son too much to be with someone who doesn't really want us."

I'd frozen in front of him, my heart folding in on itself with each word he uttered. I could only manage to stare at him. No words came to me. Only feelings, hordes of them, crashing down on me. So after a long moment, he turned and jogged down the steps and into the darkness.

"Fuck!" I said aloud as I closed the door and leaned against it.

I hadn't been fast enough, and the decision had been made for me. Again. And as I'd suspected, it wasn't the choice I would have made. I couldn't say that to Brock now, though. It had obviously pained him to come to this decision. Although he showed no evidence of a broken heart as he delivered his little speech, I could feel it. Actually feel his pain deep in my own soul. I also felt his strong belief that letting me go was the best thing for all three of us, and I could no longer argue with him.

My short stint of happiness was over.

How had I ever lived with such emptiness? Had I felt this hollow before I met him, when living on my own with no friends and family? I didn't think so. I didn't think I'd been so bare and vacant since last summer. How could I feel such a big void after such a short time with one person? I never thought I was this girl. Not even in the *before*. But here I was, letting the days and weeks pass by with little notice or participation from me except for my work. Depression and its endless pit of darkness began to take a stronghold in my life again. Like last time, when I wasn't working, I lost myself in books—in other worlds and lives that were much worse than my own but somehow more enjoyable.

Except for the leather-bound book that still sat on my coffee table, untouched. I couldn't bring myself to open the journal again. Reading Jacey's story had been something I shared with Brock. It had no meaning any more now that he wasn't here to listen, too. I should have tossed the book, but I couldn't bring myself to do that. It became part of the scenery.

Although we were often in the same house for hours on end, we managed to avoid each other for weeks. I could always feel him when he was nearby, however, like my soul was more complete. Still hurting, but at least not empty. When he was gone, though—at classes or taking Connor out—I didn't feel exactly sad, especially as time passed, but somewhat hollow. As if something had perforated my soul and part of it leaked out, returning only when Brock did. As stupid as it all sounded, I couldn't shake the feeling. It wasn't a mental or emotional woe-is-me depression. It was physical, and not something I could help no matter how many times I told myself to get over it.

"This is ridiculous," Hope said one day as we were packing for a book convention.

This would be the first event I'd attend with her, and I was excited about it, but not as much as I should have been. For the first time in my entire life, I felt anxious about traveling so far away from home. We traveled all the time when I was growing up, going to the mountains or the beaches or out of the country—the more exotic the better, my parents thought—nearly every Christmas, Spring Break, and a good chunk of the summer. I'd looked forward to every trip as an adventure. For this trip, I'd be working, but I could finally show my inner nerd and be surrounded by people who shared the love of books and reading. But for some reason, my stomach turned every time I thought about boarding the plane.

"It *is* a lot of stuff," I agreed, sitting on my knees as Hope handed me another costume to somehow fit in the suitcase with her others. She said not all events were like this one, where all of the authors participated in cosplay of their own characters. Hope had decided to play a different character for each of the three days of the convention, requiring all kinds of dresses and accessories.

"Oh, this isn't ridiculous. Well, maybe a little, but it's always fun. I was talking about you and Brock." She looked at me with a single brow raised. "You both mope around this house, only yards away from each other but galaxies apart. The atmosphere's perfect for writing angsty love stories, but not for your real lives."

"I don't know what I'm supposed to do about it," I said as I tucked a sleeve of the dress into the suitcase. "Brock doesn't need a girl in his life right now."

Standing over me in jeans and a simple t-shirt, she put her hands on her hips and nodded. "Any girl? No, he doesn't. He doesn't need to be running around like a man-whore when he has a baby to take care of and medical school to prepare for. But you're not any girl, Asia. And from what I've seen, and what I know in my own heart and soul, you both need each other in your lives."

I dropped my gaze from her and fiddled with a feather on a hat that sat in front of me, still needing to be packed. "You've said that before. I don't understand. Shouldn't you be protecting him? Keeping him from making another stupid mistake?"

"Exactly. That's what I'm doing. *You* are not a mistake, Asia. His ex was, yeah, but we have Connor now, so I can't even regret that. But you are the opposite of a mistake. You and

Brock *belong* together. I believe you always have and just needed—how did you put it that first day?—that's right, life to happen and priorities to shift to bring you two together."

I pondered this for a moment, and then looked up at her, my head cocked to the side. I tried to choose my words carefully because Hope was, after all, my boss first and foremost, and I didn't want to piss her off.

"I can't be what he needs and what you want for him and Connor. I can't fill the shoes of Connor's mom."

"I certainly don't expect that! Yeah, Connor needs a mom. *His* mom. That's what would be best for him, of course. But he also needs his dad—a happy dad who can serve as a good role model. Right now, Brock's not happy." She pressed her lips together, and the corners lifted slightly. "You should have seen him that day he brought Connor home. He didn't even walk in the back door like usual, but rang the doorbell at the front of the house. When I opened the door, I was in shock. There was my son who was supposed to be over a thousand miles north standing on my front step. His hair stuck up all over the place, dark circles were under his eyes, and a baby seat with a tiny bundle in it sat at his feet. He stared at the ground at first, shifting foot to foot as he refused to look at me, but when he finally did, I could see the fear in Brock's eyes—fear of the unknown of being a dad just as much as the fear of my reaction. I did the only thing I could do. I threw my arms around him and welcomed them both home." She wiped a thumb under her eye. "His relief was immediate, but he wasn't really happy until you came along, Asia. And when he was happy, he was a better dad to his son."

I opened my mouth, but she continued.

"That's how parenting works best. Parents always think they need to make sacrifices for the well-being of their kids, and that's absolutely true. But we all forget that sometimes we also need to do what's right for ourselves for the benefit of our children. What happens to children who only witnesses misery as they're growing up? They become miserable adults themselves, not knowing any better. I want Connor to grow up witnessing and knowing love." She took a much needed deep breath and then chuckled. "I'm sorry. Didn't mean to get on my soapbox. I know too many people who've grown up in a dark world, only to lead dark lives themselves. I've done my best to show Brock only love, and I hope he can do the same for his son."

Heat rose to my face.

"Um ... love? I don't think—"

"Never deny the possibility of something good like love. The world's a dark enough place as it is. We need to let the light in every chance we can." She smiled. "And that's all I'm going to say. Conversation over, I promise. Just think about it. Maybe reach out to Brock. I know he regrets letting you go."

Both of my brows shot up. This was news to me. She sucked her lips in and shook her head.

"You didn't hear that from me," she said with a conspiratorial wink. "But, seriously, talk to him. For everyone's benefit."

"I thought this conversation was over."

"Right. It is." She nodded. "Think about it while we're gone, at least. I bet you come home with a better idea of what to do."

I had little better to do than think about it while we were gone because I was sick the whole time we were in Chicago. The plane hadn't crashed, as I'd feared, and the hotel never burnt down, but I sure felt like I'd died and returned as a zombie. I spent the entire convention curled in a ball in bed, except when I was hunched over the toilet. Every cell of my body ached, and my skin was like a radiator. And for some stupid reason, all I could think about was Brock and how I wished he were there to hold me and care for me. Stupid, stupid, stupid. Why was *he*, of all people, the one I thought about when feeling my worst?

"I'm so sorry," I muttered to Hope as we took our first-class seats for the flight home. I curled into my spot and closed my eyes against the brightness of daylight that didn't help my aching head. "I wasn't one bit of help. A hindrance more than anything."

"No worries," she said, patting my knee. "I've always done these things alone before. One more time didn't kill me. I'm just sorry you didn't get to enjoy all the fun. I'm sure you'll feel better as soon as you get home, though."

She was right. I hadn't been home and in my own bed for more than a few hours when my aches dissolved and my twisting stomach finally settled. I was even able to drink some Sprite and eat a few crackers Hope had brought over when we'd arrived home, the first solid food I'd eaten since we'd left. By the next morning, I was back to normal. Thank God for that. I'd never been so sick in my life.

Even my appearance—I hadn't only felt like a zombie but had looked like one, too—had improved overnight, I noticed as I brushed my teeth. I ran a hand through my hair, which had grown even more. When I'd been in my deepest depression, I'd dyed my hair black to match my mood, but then shortly after, regretted it, so I'd chopped it all off. I also regretted that. It's not that I missed my once beautiful, waist-length, golden-colored hair all that much. I'd worn my hair like that for as long as I could remember, and I'd become as sick of it as I had the rest of that life. I just hated that drastic measures had to be taken to make a change, and then it took forever to grow it out to something I could change again. When Hope had needed an idea for her book and asked me if I could have a superpower, being able to change my hair color and style at whim was what I'd blurted out.

"It's stupid, I know," I'd admitted. "It was just the first thing that came to mind when you asked, besides all the obvious ones."

She'd tapped her pen against her lips. "I guess it would be useful for instantaneous disguises."

"Or for empowerment. You know what they say—a new hairstyle can change a girl's life. Or at least her outlook on it," I'd said with a snort, paraphrasing all the fashion magazines I used to devour like I consumed full novels now. "For me, though, I'd do it just because I could and nobody else can. It's different, I guess."

Hope had eyed me, as if something had occurred to her, and then disappeared, back to her writing cave. I'd assumed I'd helped her figure out whatever she'd been stuck on with her book.

Now, I brushed the blond strands back, but it still wasn't long enough for a decent ponytail, so I put it up in a clip. I was beginning to feel human again.

Not sure about a strenuous workout in Hope's gym yet, I took a long walk to the beach that evening, reconsidering one more time the conversation I'd planned to have with Brock instead of actually finding him to start it. I still felt the sting of his first rejection and feared Hope was wrong about him regretting that he'd let me go. Or even if she wasn't wrong, what if he'd changed his mind? She'd told me that nearly a week ago. A lot could have changed in that time. Maybe my absence had allowed him to clear out the cobwebs of our relationship, and he was completely over it now. He'd probably moved on and didn't even think about me any more.

Yeah, I was good at psyching myself out.

In fact, by the time I headed for home, I'd pretty much convinced myself that approaching Brock would be disastrous. He'd send me on my way and break my heart again. If he really wanted to be with me, he'd have to come to me ... even if I was the one who never spoke up to share my feelings in the first place. Hope said he was giving me space, not wanting to force me into something I didn't want, which was pretty much what he'd told me, too. But if he really regretted saying that, maybe I needed to make him fight for me to prove it.

Sheesh. Relationships were stupidly complicated.

I crossed my arms over my chest as I walked the three blocks home from the beach. The day had been much warmer than the near freezing temperatures in Chicago that I hadn't missed at all, but after the sun dropped below the horizon and darkness fell, the cool, winter air sent a chill over my skin. So did the feeling of being followed.

I rubbed my hands over my bare arms and glanced over my shoulder. I thought I saw a shadow shift down the street, but there was no one around to make it and the overhead street lighting was all wrong for the direction it moved. Then a white cat darted across the street, and I had to laugh at myself. *You're imagining things. Freaking yourself out.* Still, I picked up my pace and mentally went over the self-defense moves Brock had taught me, trying my hardest to focus on the steps I was supposed to take for various types of attacks, and not on the memories of his arms wrapped around me ... or that accidental kiss.

As Hope's house came into view, the feeling grew stronger. I peered over my shoulder again. A man was running toward me. I walked faster, but still tried to convince myself it meant nothing. I couldn't have been in a safer neighborhood. People go running all the time. Even at night. I took off into a jog, anyway, as the footsteps came closer, my heart pounding much harder than it should have been. Why wasn't I wearing my steel-toed Doc Martens? I'd become complacent again, instead wearing flip-flops or tennis shoes. I wore the latter now, with their mesh material and rubber toes. Not very protective except maybe against shin splints.

I turned into the Verdors' driveway, anxious for the security of being within their fence. The man's footsteps came much louder and faster, following me into the driveway. My fingers shook as I keyed in the code for the people gate, and as soon as I was inside, I punched the button to close it as fast as possible. But it wasn't fast enough. The man squeezed through.

I could barely see him in the darkness, only his form. What happened to the security lights? The floodlights that usually lit up when there was movement in the backyard? Adrenaline pumped through me, and I burst into a sprint and sucked in a breath to scream. As I circled the pool, running for the main house, a hand landed on my shoulder. An electric jolt charged through me, and the scream erupted. Remembering what Brock told me, I reached back and grabbed his wrist with both hands, threw my shoulder backwards into his chest, bent my knees, and thrust. He flipped around and over, headed for the pool.

"Hey!" he barked, grabbing at me for balance. He managed to grasp my wrist, and I screamed again as I fell in after him.

CHAPTER 13

WATER IMMEDIATELY FILLED my mouth and lungs, choking and drowning me. My arms flailed, and my legs kicked. Darkness surrounded me, and I couldn't find my way up to the surface, to the sweet air above. The man's hand gripped my arm, tugging at me, and I kicked harder hoping to connect with some part of his body—his balls would suffice—while I tried to escape. Bubbles surrounded us, and muffled sounds swooshed in my ears. His arm wrapped around my waist, too strong for me to fight, and he pulled me farther down, pushing my head toward the bottom. I was going to die.

When I expected to hit my head against the unforgiving concrete, cool air suddenly blasted me instead.

I coughed and spurted water as my attacker's head broke the surface. More liquid spewed from my mouth as his arm tightened around me, and he swam me over to the underwater seat in the corner of the deep end. His hands gripped my waist as he sat me on the ledge. I gasped again as I stared into Brock's face with wide eyes, water dripping down my forehead, into my eyes, and over my face.

"Are you okay?" he asked as he bobbed in front of me, his breaths coming out hard and fast.

I coughed some more, clearing the rest of the water from my lungs, eventually nodded, and then threw my arms around him. My body shook from both fear and relief, as well as the chill in the air. His arms were warm around me, his body hot against mine. The heated pool made the water much warmer than the air, so I slid off the seat to submerse myself so only my head remained above the surface, inches from Brock's.

"I'm so sorry," I breathed as he tread water, and I held onto him. "I didn't know it was you."

He chuckled, and I thrilled at the sound I'd missed more than I cared to admit. "Glad to see my lessons stuck. Nice trick, by the way, landing me in the water. If you wanted to be back in my arms, you only needed to tell me, though."

My eyes rounded, and I tried to squirm away from him. "I didn't mean to. I swear. I didn't even know—"

"Asia," he said quietly, reeling me back against him, "*please* tell me you want to be back in my arms. Because this is exactly where I want to be."

I stared at him, my heart pounding in my chest for a new reason now. Chills swept over me, and not from the cool air any more.

"In the pool in your clothes?" I asked. "That's where you want to be?"

"In the pool or anywhere, if that's where you are," he murmured. "Preferably not in my clothes, though."

Our eyes locked for a moment, his inquiring. I had all kinds of questions, too, but also answers. Especially the one he sought.

"I want to be here, too," I admitted in a barely audible whisper, but he must have heard me loud and clear because his mouth crashed into mine.

His lips were soft and warm and wet, urgently moving against mine as though he'd been the one drowning and I was his breath of air. And I returned the kiss just as urgently because he *was* the breath I'd needed for so long. His tongue swept out, licking the water from my lips before pressing against the seam between them. I parted my mouth, letting him in, wanting all of him in and a part of me. As our kiss deepened, and we sank lower into the water, all of the backyard lights suddenly came on, including the pool light.

"Hello?" Hope called out, and we broke the kiss to look at her. "Is someone out—oh! Sorry! Carry on!"

The yard returned to darkness, and a giggle tumbled over the air right before the door closed. Brock and I turned back to each other, and he chuckled before coming in for another kiss. Hot and desperate again, as though that brief moment apart had been a lifetime. He pulled me closer to him, and I wrapped my legs around his waist, pressing my boobs against his hard chest. As our mouths moved together, he swam us over to the side of the pool where he could stand, although I couldn't. He used his body to pin me against the side, our heads below the pool's edge and our shoulders still under water. His hands cupped my face, and his thumbs slid over my cheeks, pushing the wet strands of hair out of the way. Each stroke was like the strike of a match against my skin, enflaming me with heat.

His mouth slid away from my lips and down to my chin, then up along my jawline.

"God, I've missed you so much," he murmured against the curve of my jaw just below my ear, sending shivers through my body.

"I've missed you, too," I said as I arched my neck toward him. The movement caused my hard nipples to push into his chest, and I couldn't help the moan.

"Damn, girl. I want you so badly." He rocked his hips, showing me how much. His erection pushed against the thin material of our shorts, the hardness rubbing me in just the right spot between my open legs. I tightened them around his waist, returning the stroke against him. Now he moaned. "I fucking *need* you so badly, Asia."

His mouth returned to mine, open, his tongue probing. Mine met it, swirled against it, tasting him, and trying to drink him in as he tried to devour me. His fingertips skated over my shoulders and down my sides until his hands gripped my waist, his thumbs sliding between us and pressing into the sensitive area of where my thighs met my pelvis. The tickle caused my hips to jerk toward him, and we both groaned with the pressure against our most sensitive parts.

My hands made their way down his muscular back to the hem of his t-shirt and under. The heat of his skin under my touch electrified me, and I rocked against him again. He returned the stroke, and we continued sliding and thrusting against each other, moaning and whimpering as our mouths remained locked and our hands explored under the other's shirt. His palm cupped my ribs, and his thumb stroked over the thin material of my bra, then pushed its way under. Our thrusts came harder and faster, my back scraping against the side of the pool, but I didn't care. I broke away from the kiss to gasp for air. I was going to come, and he hadn't even touched me there.

"You feel amazing already," he murmured as his lips slid over my cheekbone. "I don't have a condom with me, but I want to—"

I froze. He tensed against me.

"We can't do this," I panted as rationality finally edged its way into the overload of hormones.

"I know," he said, even as he rocked against me, wracking another wave of bliss over me. "We can go up to my room. I have some up there."

I shook my head. "No, Brock. *This.* Any of this. I can't—I won't. I won't be your fuck buddy or booty call."

He pulled slightly back, enough to look at me. Now that we'd been out here long enough, it didn't seem as dark. Light from Hope's kitchen windows provided enough for me to see his face and the tilt of his lips and pull of his brows low over his eyes as he studied me.

"Asia, you will never be a fuck buddy or booty call to me." He leaned in closer and pressed his forehead against mine. "You mean so much more to me than anyone ever has."

"Anyone?" I challenged, my tone clear about Connor ... and possibly his baby's mama.

"You know what I mean." He pressed his lips lightly to mine and didn't move away as he spoke. "I was about to say I want to make love to you, Asia. I've never made love to anyone, but I want to make love to you. I want to know every part of you, outside and in, including your heart. Because you're already embedded in mine. Into my fucking soul."

If I'd been standing on land, I might have collapsed due to my bones liquefying. Instead, I melted against him, kissing him again, but softly this time. I pulled away when it became urgent and heated again.

"I want to make love to you, too, Brock. But not now. Not yet. I want—I *need*—to know that this is what we both really want. That it's not an accident because we're both lonely and horny and out of control."

"I promise you it's not an accident. I told you before that everything I do with you would be on purpose." He sucked my bottom lip. "Although I am fucking horny, thanks to you."

I kissed him one more time, then dropped my legs from his waist and pushed him back. I slid to the side as he floated away. "Seriously. I need to know this is what we both want when you don't have a damn hard-on, and I don't feel like a cat in heat."

He laughed. "You have such a way with words."

"I'm learning from your mom." I swam for the steps, but as soon as I climbed out, I regretted it. Although the temperature was probably in the sixties, the air made the water on my skin feel like ice.

"There are towels in the laundry room," Brock said as he hoisted himself out on the side of the pool.

"There are towels in my apartment, too," I said, shivering. "And that's where I'm going."

"Me, too." He stood right in front of me now, and his arms enveloped my trembling body.

I crossed my arms over my nipped out boobs before they pressed against him. "You're going to your home. You're going to cool off before you try to convince me this is what you really want."

"I'm already fucking cooled off," he said, his teeth chattering.

I ducked out of his embrace. "Go home, Brock. Put some dry clothes on. You know what I want now, but you need to think hard about it." I jogged for the garage and the steps on the side of it, my soggy shoes squelching the whole way, and then called over my shoulder, "I'm really sorry for dumping you in the pool."

Once up the stairs and inside, I ran for the bathroom, turned on the hot water, and had barely pulled out a towel when my phone beeped from the kitchen counter with a text message. Brock had already sent four. The first one was kind of long, for a text anyway:

"I miss you. Terribly. I shouldn't have said what I did and pushed you away. I made the decision for you, and I'm sorry. Please forgive me. If you don't want to be with me, I understand, and I'll leave you alone. But if you do at all, just give me a sign, and I'm there."

The second was much shorter: "In fact, I'll probably be there anyway because I'm a fighter, and I'll fight for you. That's who I am. I'll do whatever it takes."

Sheesh. How had he texted all of this already? He must have had super-thumbs.

The third: "Shit. You're not answering. I hope I didn't scare you off. I'm going for a run so I can hopefully stop thinking about you. I doubt I will, though, so I'm leaving my phone here so I'll at least stop bothering you."

I scrolled back up to the first message and the time showed those three had come in over an hour ago. The last one had come just now:

"I've been thinking about this for a month. I'm done thinking. I already know what I want...the same thing I've wanted since the day I met you. My hard-on's gone. In fact, my dick's turtled up. So when you're done feeling like a cat in heat, lemme know."

Another text dinged: "Shit. I'm hard again. Sorry. Can't help it. Thinking of you."

I laughed as I walked over to the window, feeling a pull toward it. I pushed the sheer curtain to the side and looked down toward the main house's kitchen window, where a large form stood. Brock's, without a doubt. I held my hand to the glass, and he did the same. With my other hand, I replied to his text.

"We need to talk."

I watched as he looked down at his palm for a long moment, and then he turned away from the window. My phone vibrated in my hand.

"On my way."

I shook my head and headed for the bathroom that had filled with steam, unable to help the smile on my face. I used my feet to push off my wet shoes and socks while pulling the shower curtain to the side. I couldn't stand one more minute of shivering to try to remove my wet clothes, so I stepped into the shower still wearing my shirt and shorts. When I went to draw the shower curtain shut, a hand closed over mine, making me jump.

"Oh, my god, you scared me!" I gasped. Brock climbed into the shower with me, also still wearing his running shorts and shirt. "I could have been naked!"

"I was hoping," he said with a smile, his dark eyes full of mischief … and promises. I looked at him with a raised brow. "I knew you weren't. I saw you getting in."

I kept my eyes open and on him as I stepped backwards into the spraying water. The heat felt like heaven, and my body immediately relaxed. Brock moved closer, his skin covered in goose bumps, and I reached up to move the showerhead to include him. Our arms slid around each other, and we stood silently under the water until both of our bodies stopped shivering.

At least … shivering from the cold, because then we began trembling from each other's touches.

Brock's hands moved up to my cheeks, cupping them gently as he tilted my head up toward his. His smoldering gaze alone sent a flame of heat through me. Water flattened his hair and flowed down his face, off his nose and over his full lips, and I wanted to lick it off. I slid my tongue out, catching the falling water. His eyes flared even more before he leaned in with puckered lips and sucked the water off my mouth, drawing my bottom lip in, too. A new chill ran through me at the same time that a ball of warmth blossomed in my belly. I gripped his face in return and licked and sucked the water tumbling over his mouth. Our lips meshed, our tongues lapped, our bodies pressed closer and closer together until no space remained between us.

My heart galloped away at breakneck speed, my lungs striving to keep up as I drew in small shallow breaths between kisses, until finally I had to lean my head back to draw in more air. Brock seized the opportunity, moving one hand to the nape of my neck, cradling me while sliding his mouth over my jaw and using his other hand against my lower back to lift me upward, closer to him. His hot lips on my skin, his tongue swirling against my throat, his mouth sucking at me and the water did nothing to help the whole breathing thing. And his desire growing between us only fueled the ball of fire in my belly whose flames now licked downward.

Brock's arms slid around me, and he lifted me fully off my feet. I wrapped my legs around his waist and whimpered in his strong arms as his lips traveled back up to my ear and his erection pressed into my shorts.

"This is better," he murmured as he straightened, not having to hunch over me to plant his mouth against mine again.

The steam from the shower, rising from our bodies, the heat within as his tongue plunged my mouth intoxicated me. I became lost in the sensuality, in the way his full, soft lips moved with mine, how his fingers slid softly over my skin, how he was gentle and hot and urgent all at the same time. He made me drunk with his kisses, and I think I made him drunk with mine. There was no thinking. No more talking. Only kissing and licking and caressing.

Our hands slid under each other's shirts at the same time, and we peeled them off within seconds. My fingers skittered over the fine contours of his torso, exploring the hills and valleys of his muscles as his mouth and tongue learned the dips and edges of my collarbone and shoulder. When he found one of my most sensitive places, where my neck curved into my shoulder, and his lips sucked as his tongue swirled, I moaned and pressed myself against him, rubbing against his tip. His teeth nipped at me before his lips clamped down, and my pelvis involuntarily rocked against him. His erection became rock hard between us. My breasts felt full and tight, my nipples little marbles straining against my bra.

I unwrapped my legs from his waist and slid down his body to my feet, the friction of my breasts against him fueling the flames. His hands slid up my bare sides and ribs and pushed under the sports bra, lifting it, freeing my breasts from the confines. He brought it over my head, then dropped it with the other wet clothing that was piling up at the other end of the bathtub. Our gazes locked and held as we removed our shorts and then stood there, the shower raining down on our naked bodies, steam rising from our feverish skin.

Brock's hand reached out, and every inch of my skin tightened, aching for his touch. His fingertips brushed my wrist and lightly trailed up my arm, over my collarbone, down my sternum, between my breasts, and over my flat stomach. He stroked a circle around my belly button, and the fire exploded, making my knees knock and my thighs clench. I circled my hands over his wrist and pushed it downward, between my legs. His fingers stroked the edges at first, making me whimper, and finally one delved further inward. My mouth parted with a moan, and my eyelids fell halfway down, but never did his eyes leave mine.

His other hand slid over the small of my back, his fingers over my ass, and he pulled me a step closer, causing my belly to rub against his erection and his fingers to slide inside me. We both moaned now, and what had felt like a sensual dream in the clouds of steam instantly became urgent, frenzied. Our mouths couldn't devour the other fast enough. Our hands moved frantically, wanting to touch every bit of the other person at once. He backed me into the wall, and reached around me to turn off the water as he looked down into my eyes. My skin screamed for his touch, and my insides ached for him to fill me, but my heart and soul were drowning in those beautiful, deep, dark eyes that invited me to gaze through them, into his soul.

"I love you, Asia," he said, his voice thick and husky. "I'm sure of it. I don't need to think about it a second longer, so please don't force me to. Don't turn me away again. Because I most definitely know I want to make love to you."

I stared up at him, into his chocolate eyes that didn't shine with mischief or twinkle with a tease. Only sincerity came through now, firm and genuine. He didn't look expectant, either, as though waiting for me to say it back. But I did anyway.

"I love you, Brock, and want to share it with you. Everything."
I sucked my bottom lip in. "But, uh, we need a condom."

With only a smile for a reply, he yanked the shower curtain open, swept me into his arms and carried me to the bed. He laid me down on it before dipping his hand in the large, decorative vase that stood next to the nightstand, holding tall reeds of dry grass.

"What are you doing?" I asked as I propped myself up on my elbows. "I thought you were getting a condom."

He pulled his hand out with a square, foil package dangling between his fingers and a big grin on his face. "I've always kept a few of these hidden in the apartment since middle school. You know ... just in case."

I threw my head back and laughed, my insides quivering, making me giddy. "Since middle school?"

"I had high hopes."

"Please tell me that's not that old."

"Nah. I threw this one in before I moved out ... and you moved in."

I lifted an eyebrow. He smiled as he stepped up to the bed between my legs, his full nakedness giving me quite the view.

"As I said—high hopes."

I returned his grin as I sat up and took him in my hands. "Well, I have high expectations."

I helped roll the condom on, then scooted back on the bed as he crawled on over me. I spread my legs so he could move between them. His head dipped down, and he licked his way up my belly, around the swell of my breast, and over my hard nipple. Then he sucked the swollen tip into his mouth, and my lids fell closed as my back arched off the bed, my whole body wanting to feel the heat and wet of his mouth and tongue. I whimpered when he pulled away, needing more, but he inched his way higher until he hovered directly over me.

He lowered himself down to my body, flesh against flesh, and his mouth claimed mine as his thick maleness claimed the rest of me. He only prodded at first, as though testing. I opened my legs further in answer, wet and hot, ready for him. With a small push, he slid in, hard as steel, and began to fill me a little at a time, slow at first, until I was convulsing around him. And then he pulled almost all the way out, his head pulsating at my opening, teasing both of us, before pushing in faster and further than before. He repeated this, each time thrusting deeper and sending a wrack of shudders through me. We moaned into each other's mouths as he stroked in and out, and my hips lifted to meet his. Our rhythm became faster, our movements harder, and our cries louder until our mouths had to break apart as we both arched into the other, aching for the release that was coming. A wave of chills swept over my skin. My belly soared and then plummeted. He plunged into me one more time, and my toes curled as I screamed, and I swore my soul flew out of my mouth.

I couldn't believe what I felt—like I'd left my body and hovered over it on a bigger high than I'd ever experienced in my life. And I swore I could feel Brock floating next to me, even when I could see both of us on the bed, our mouths open and our eyes closed as we reached our climaxes together. My soul and his somehow mingling together, like they were one. Then I was suddenly back, feeling through both my body and soul, the most amazing, belly-dropping, bone-shattering orgasm I'd ever had.

"Damn, Asia," Brock panted as his arms gave out and he collapsed on top of me. "I knew we'd be perfect together, but ... *fuck*."

I laughed against the weight of his body. "Yeah ... me, too."

He rolled over onto his back and turned his head to look at me. "Expectations met?"

I smiled. "Hopes fulfilled?"

He returned my grin with a beautiful, satisfied one of his own. "Exceeded."

"My expectations, too."

He inched his arm over, slid his hand under my palm, and intertwined his fingers with mine. "Mom has Connor all night."

I gave his fingers a squeeze. "I love your mom."

"Yeah, she's pretty awesome. But, let's not talk about her when we're naked, okay?"

I laughed and rolled into his body, pressing the full length of mine against his side. He wrapped his arm around my back, and we lay together peacefully for a while. Well, for a few minutes, anyway, before we caressed each other into another round of bliss.

Happiness had returned, and not just for Brock and me. The next day he brought me to the main house for breakfast, and Hope beamed at us. It was still awkward because she obviously knew what we'd done—what *I'd* done with her son—but the woman seemed almost as content as we felt. As if she'd accomplished something. I supposed she had, though. If she hadn't been so supportive, we would have probably never found our way back to each other.

March brought perfect weather to South Florida while people back home and at school suffered through more blizzards, but Brock and I had our own heat no matter where we were. Even though we'd said The Three Words to each other, I often wondered if we really only felt lust. My feelings were so strong for him and his seemed to be the same for me that I could hardly believe they were real. Then I'd find him doing something special and unexpected for me—little things like bringing over a book I'd mentioned I wanted to read or buying a TV series box set of DVDs because I hadn't been able to watch the last season of my favorite shows. And I'd do the same, like picking up a six-pack of his favorite beer and bringing home his preferred study snacks. But they were such little things, I could easily convince myself that we did them simply because we were thinking about each other, more physically than anything.

Maybe I was too broken to know real love.

We returned to reading Jacey's journal and finally finished it. Only to find out both she and Micah died.

"I can't believe that's the end!" I growled as I stared at the page as though more words would magically start filling it.

Brock shook his head. "That's really fucked up. It has to be fiction. I mean, the stuff that happened to them? How they died? No way is that a real diary. It was probably some writer trying to get Mom's attention after all."

I tossed the journal on the table, leaned back, and crossed my arms over my chest. "I doubt she'll like it. She prefers HEAs."

His eyes cut sideways at me since he was sitting next to me on my couch. "That's horny ever after, right?"

I laughed and pushed my shoulder against his. "*Happily* ever after."

"Right. Until they get married, and then he's horny ever after."

I rolled my eyes. "What are we going to do about the journal? I can't bring myself to let your mom read it."

"Me neither. She'll cry for days, and then complain about her writing mojo being ruined for weeks. Maybe we should just toss it."

I considered that for a moment and already knew I wouldn't be able to simply throw the book away. It was a *book*, no matter how weird or sad the story was. A leather-bound book, soft and smooth from age, with a beautiful image embossed on both the front and back. Not exactly something disposable.

"Maybe we should put it on Craigslist or something as a found item," I suggested. "Someone could have dropped it in the driveway and be looking for it. Or, at least, maybe the writer will come back and claim it."

Brock's phone toned for him to return home to put Connor to bed and then tackle his studies. He stuffed his phone in his back pocket and stood. "Do whatever you want with it. I gotta go."

He leaned over to grab my hand and pulled me up next to him so he could kiss me goodbye.

"I could help you put Connor to bed," I suggested.

Brock had been great about not pushing that part of his life on me, saying he wanted to take it slow. He did everything he could to prove that he wasn't just looking for someone to take care of him and Connor. But like he'd said—he and Connor were a package. They came together. And as time had passed, my mixed feelings about babies, especially Connor, had evened out. He'd never be my baby, but that didn't mean we couldn't grow to be important in each other's lives. So I tried to make more effort to show Brock that I accepted both of them.

Bedtime was special, though, as much for Daddy as for baby.

"I appreciate that. I do." He bent down and pressed his lips lightly to mine. "Why don't we take him to the park tomorrow?"

I smiled and agreed before sending him on his way, but not until after he kissed me crazy. Once he left, I picked up the old book and stared at it as I fell back onto the couch. I ran my fingers over the uneven leather of the cover. With such a strange story that sounded impossible, how could I feel like it was real? Not only real, but that in some way, it was even kind of familiar? Not the people or the events—I hadn't even been alive back then—but some of the details of the story. Something wavered in the very far corners of my mind, like a fleeting memory that refused to come to the surface. I couldn't place it, but as I held my palm against the cover, I felt certain there was more to the book than the story inside. I just had no idea what.

After too much time of actually considering this, I laughed at myself.

"You're such a dork," I said aloud. "Letting the bizarre tale get to you."

I took the book into my room and placed it on top of the dresser. I didn't know what to do with it, but neither throwing it away nor trying to find its owner were options. I'd figure it out later.

In April, we celebrated Connor's half-year birthday. He really was a sweet little guy, and at six months, a lot of fun. He could sit up and kind of scoot around and play with toys. His face was constantly full of wonder. Brock brought him into our time together more and more, and I was falling just as much in love with him as I was with his dad. Or maybe more, since I still couldn't be sure what Brock and I had was truly love.

Whatever it was, we were happy together. We had a good time. Whether it was lust or love, I felt whole and didn't think I'd ever need more than this.

"You got him?" Brock asked as I headed for the driveway with Connor on my hip one April afternoon.

"Yeah, we're fine," I said over my shoulder. Brock was dragging a cart full of towels, blankets, toys, and other beach supplies. Taking a baby anywhere was like bringing half the house. When I walked through the gate, though, I was anything but fine. My jaw dropped, and I stopped in my tracks. Brock ran into me, making me take another couple of steps forward. Then he stopped, too, at the sight of the girl in front of us, who stared glassy eyed at Connor. "*Kami?*"

Her eyes flew to my face, and her brows shot to her hairline. "Asia? What—" She looked behind me, and her voice fell several octaves to a near whisper. "Brock."

"What are you doing here?" he demanded from behind me, his voice harsher than I'd ever heard it. He stepped up next to me, looking between Kami and me. "Wait. You two know each other?"

Kami tilted her head, looked at me, and then at Connor. I didn't think it possible, but her eyes grew even wider and her mouth stretched into a large O.

And then the truth hit me.

"Oh. My. God." The words came out thickly as I choked on the realization. I shook my head in denial. "You ... it can't be. Not you."

Tears stung my eyes. Everything was about to change.

"Yeah, we know each other," Kami finally said in answer to Brock's question as she crossed her arms over her chest, her eyes locked on me. "We met in a Single and Pregnant support group back at school."

CHAPTER 14

Jeric THE OTHER GUARDIANS still treated us like we had a contagious disease, so Asia sat in the corner of the dining room by herself, her head in her hand, and her jet-black hair curtaining her face. Her breakfast remained untouched. I stuck my tablet under my arm, grabbed a plate, and put a few random items from the buffet on it—a couple of hardboiled eggs for protein, a slice of multigrain toast, a banana, and an apple. The thought of putting anything in my mouth and actually swallowing it set off my gag reflex, but I needed to try to keep my energy up. The food would do nothing for the emptiness I felt in my gut. I just hoped it wouldn't make the pain that never lessened any worse.

I set my plate and tablet across the table from Asia before going over to the beverage station to pour a cup of coffee and a glass of orange juice. The coffee was much needed. Asia and Brock's story had filled my mind last night, as if I didn't have enough shit already keeping me awake. At least it provided a distraction from my own misery.

Without a word, I sat down and stared at my plate. I sprinkled some salt and pepper on the eggs and lifted one of the slippery spheres to my mouth. My stomach heaved. Fuck. It'd been too long since the last time I'd eaten. Fighting and modeling had taught me good nutrition, and I'd been violating every rule since the night Leni disappeared. I sucked in a deep breath and stuffed the egg into my mouth, forcing myself to take a bite, to chew, to swallow. I shoved the second half in right after, chasing down the rubber bits and dry, pasty shit with a swig of orange juice. Then I sat for a moment, waiting to make sure it didn't come back up. My stomach twisted and turned, but the egg stayed down.

"That looked painful," Asia said.

My eyes shot up to her. I hadn't realized she'd been watching me, because she'd been so engrossed in the Book of Phoenix. She hadn't been writing in it, but studying it intensely.

"Yep. Pretty much." I glanced at the Book and back up to her, lifting my brow.

"I don't want to talk about it," she muttered, understanding my question.

"Good."

She narrowed her eyes at me. I shrugged.

"I'm a guy. Talking's not my thing, especially after not talking for so many years."

She gave me a weak smile that I thought was supposed to be appreciative.

"But, you know, the shit I've been picking up on, which I can only assume came from that journal, is pretty serious, Asia. If you do need to talk, I'll do my best to listen."

She grimaced. "You're getting it *all*?"

"How would I know? Every story has holes, so I can't say for sure, but it seems like it. Yeah, I got the pool and the shower part."

She groaned. "How embarrassing. I was just trying to reach out to Brock. Thought those parts might be enough to get a reaction from him. Something I could feel, you know?"

I chuckled. "If you knew what I used to be like, you'd know there's no reason to be embarrassed. So did you feel him?"

She sighed. "Kind of. I think. I just don't know if it's real or because I want to so bad. He's not adding to it any more, though. If he is, his writing's not showing up in the Book. But I think he's pulling away, Jeric. He doesn't want to remember what comes next, I'm sure. And if he does … I don't know what it'll do to him. I honestly don't know if I can take it, either. It's bad. Dark. And I'm already feeling so Dark."

"Maybe you should stop writing it down then."

"I don't know if I can. It may be painful, but it's therapeutic. And, well, whether I'm imagining it or not, it makes me feel closer to Brock. Even the bad stuff."

I tilted my head forward and looked up at her. "Don't go Dark on me, Asia. I need you. If you go, I don't think I'll be able to hold my shit together."

"I'm doing my best." Her voice cracked on the last word, and the smile she tried to give me was watered down.

I nodded, taking what I could get because that's all we could do any more, and picked up the apple. I reluctantly took a bite. It went down a little easier than the dry and rubbery egg, but my stomach still tightened when I swallowed. I sat for another moment, waiting. When I felt safe, I turned my tablet on. The screen I wanted was already open. I slid it over to Asia.

"Here's some good news to cheer us up. Mason's facing murder charges," I said before she had a chance to read the article or watch the video from the Orlando news station. "For Sissy. Of course, nobody knows about the attempted murder on Bex."

"Yeah, I guess she can't press charges where she is now." Her tone was bitter. She read the article on the screen, and then handed the tablet back to me before wiping at her eyes. "Poor Sissy. She shouldn't have been involved."

I rested my head in my hand and rubbed my temple. My knuckle slid back and forth over my brow ring. "In the wrong place at the wrong time. I could never really figure her out, but she didn't deserve that."

"The asshole murdered her. Almost killed Bex." Asia's tone had grown even sourer than my stomach felt. "He'll probably get off easy with the death penalty when he deserves to rot in jail."

"Probably not. He'll buy his way out."

"Of course he will. Dickhead. I hope he gets butt-fucked enough while he's still in there to cause incontinence for the rest of his life."

My nose wrinkled automatically. The chick was brutal. "Oh, I'm sure he'll have issues, all right, with what you did."

Asia crossed her arms on the table, leaned forward, and narrowed her eyes. She jabbed a finger in my direction. "No, Jeric. Don't go there."

I watched her silently as she glared at me, her eyes becoming watery. She finally looked away, shaking her head.

"No," she repeated.

She still wasn't going to talk about it. Although that night had been less than a week ago, it felt like it'd been months or even years since we'd found Bex bloody, bruised, and unconscious on Mason's bed. He'd been standing over her, jerking off, when I walked in. The beating I gave him on Bex's behalf was nothing compared to what Asia did to him. She wouldn't tell me then what had driven her to stab him in the balls with a broken bottle, and she wasn't going to tell me now. I was pretty sure not even Brock knew.

"Fine. I just can't help but wonder what happened to you to make you hate men so much."

"I don't hate men, Jeric. Not *real* men. I don't like coward assholes, okay?"

"Rich assholes, you mean."

"Them, too."

"Except Brock."

Her eyes widened, and then her face crumpled. Shit. I'd pushed her too far. I had a bad habit of doing that with women.

"Brock is always the exception," she said quietly. She looked away for a long moment, and I let it go. I forced another few bites of apple down the pie hole before she turned back to me. She pointed at the tablet. "Any news on Ty in there?"

I shook my head. "Nothing. I can't even find the report about his truck being out at the Lake Haven springs. Are you sure Brock got it right?"

She lifted a thin shoulder in a shrug. "He overheard the police scanner. Maybe it was someone else's big, black truck. There's enough of them in the South."

"I guess we can hope."

Something flickered in her eyes before she looked away again. Hope was hard to come by these days.

"I think Yoshi's looking for you." Asia tilted her head so her chin pointed to the entrance to the dining room.

I looked over my shoulder in that direction. Yoshi stood in the doorway with his hands on his hips, his black hair sticking up as if he'd stuck his finger in a socket. I waved a hand at him, and he nodded before heading our way. He was thinner and shorter than me, but his white t-shirt and black cargo pants were snug over a cut body. Regardless of his size, he gave off the air of a formidable opponent. At least I wasn't one of those.

"Hey," he said as he stood in front of our table, eyeing our plates. "You two need to take care of yourselves."

Neither of us replied. What could we say? It's nothing we didn't know already. The follow through was the hard part.

"Tasha and I and our people are taking off," he continued as he pulled at his long goatee.

I bit my cheek to keep from scowling. Not that we'd become best friends or anything, but Yoshi was the closest I'd felt to having an equal here besides Asia. He didn't treat us like we were any different the way everyone else did, expecting us to have all the answers. He at least gave some input, even if he left the final decision making to us. To me, more specifically.

"Our Gate needs us," he finished when we still hadn't said anything. He clapped a hand on my shoulder. "But no worries. I'm only a phone call away."

I stood up and returned the hand on the shoulder thing. "Thanks, dude. You've been a big help."

He bowed his head. "Glad to do what we can."

"Keep in touch. If shit gets hairy there in Tokyo, let me know."

"Will do. It's not good, but so far, nothing we can't handle. We might be all right on this, Jeric. You just need to figure out how to get your other halves back as soon as possible."

"No shit," I muttered.

"Until next time, Asia. Tasha says bye, too."

"Sayonara," Asia replied.

Yoshi bowed his head again to her, and then to me. "Dewa mata."

He turned on his heel like a soldier would and strode off. I wondered if we'd ever see him again.

"Not even ten in the morning and our day's been nothing but a bag of shit, huh?" I said as I grabbed my tablet.

"Welcome to our new reality," Asia muttered.

"Things can only get better." My lame-ass attempt at trying to keep a positive attitude. After all, Yoshi and his people were returning to Japan to guard their Gate. To fight if necessary. Which meant they still stood behind us instead of demanding to collapse the Gates. Until Leni and Brock were back, that was the most we could ask for.

CHAPTER 15

Zeni "I CAN'T BELIEVE Asia hadn't told him she'd been pregnant," Bex said quietly as we sat on the shore at the edge of the jungle. Apparently we'd all been feeling, for lack of a better word, Asia telling her and Brock's story. Brock had been silent all day, a hard set to his jaw as he and Hayden waded in the water looking for some kind of marine life we could eat.

"We don't know that she was," I said. "We can't jump to conclusions until we get the rest of the story."

"I almost feel like I'm readin' a good book, ya know? But more than that. Almost like living it in a way ... but not. It's so weird."

"Yeah, it is," I agreed.

I knew she meant how we "received" the story—a feeling that came through our souls—but everything about Brock and Asia's relationship was strange. At least, different from most Guardian Twin Flames, as far as I knew. They'd said before that they'd had a lot of ups-and-downs in their relationship before realizing they were Twin Flames, but I hadn't expected it had been as tumultuous as it actually had. And I knew we hadn't even heard half the story yet. I figured they'd be dying of soul sickness by now, or attacked by the Lakari. How had they Bonded and not attracted the Dark souls' attention? It was almost as if they'd been somehow protected. I was just as curious as Bex to find out what happened next.

"Everything about this life is weird," she added.

I snorted. "Now that's an understatement. You're taking it better than I expected."

"Ha! My nightmares and all."

"*Those* are expected. You went through hell, girl. And you're handling that like a boss. But the weird stuff ... the Twin Flames, projection, reincarnation stuff ... you're kind of taking it all in stride."

"Hayden's helped with that. Connecting with him like we do—with our souls, I guess—helps me remember everything, which makes it difficult to deny." She let out a laugh, a good sound that was rare in all of our misery. "I just remembered that conversation you and I had when we were packing my angels. Damn, I was so naïve then." She shook her head, her red hair swinging over her shoulders. Hard to believe we'd been packing for her move to Mason's apartment only a couple of weeks ago, in Earth time anyway. Her voice came out darker and thicker with her next sentence. "Not just naïve, but stupid in some ways."

"Don't go there, Bex," I warned. "You will *not* blame yourself."

She nodded but didn't say anything more. Her whole aura changed, became dark and heavy once again. And that brought my own misery to the forefront of my mind. Helping Bex and learning Brock and Asia's story had been a good distraction, but the ache always remained close by, ready to take center stage in quiet times like now. I wished Asia would continue writing or doing whatever she'd been doing to distract us again.

Or, even better, that she and Jeric would suddenly appear in front of us, ready to take us home. Away from these foreign worlds that were too much like Earth, but not. Away from the misery and Darkness that settled deeper into our souls with each passing moment. Away from Enyxa and the horrible memories she insisted we relive.

"We need to find the Gate on this world," I said to the others later as we stood on the beach, staring over the water at the horizon, where one of the three moons rose although the sun remained high in the sky behind us.

"We need to find something to eat," Hayden growled.

He and Brock hadn't caught anything in the water, but I thought he and maybe Bex were the only ones who cared. I knew the pain in my stomach from missing my other half would make eating impossible. But I also knew we had to keep our energy levels up if we were to survive.

Bex turned toward him, opened her mouth to say something, but then her blue eyes grew the size of beach balls as she looked behind us.

"Son of a biscuit eatin' bitch," she croaked. "Somethin' found *us* to eat!"

We all swung around. Two bright orange, anaconda-sized snakes had slithered out of the jungle. Part of them remained hidden in the trees' shadows, but all of what we could see lifted several feet in the air above us. They waggled toward us, as though catching our scents. We all backed up, but paused when the snakes came farther onto the beach, our breaths trapped, too scared to move. Scratch that. Not snakes. Those were only the antennae attached to a long, thin body that never stopped rippling out of the jungle. Hundreds of translucent legs propelled it along like a centipede the size of a tractor-trailer truck. The front portion of its body reared up, its snaky antennae wiggled, and dozens of legs as thick as my own undulated in the air, reaching toward us.

Fear seized me in place. My breath froze in my lungs. The gigantic spiders in the movies would have been dinner for this thing. But they weren't here. We were.

"RUN!" Brock yelled, kicking the fight-or-flight response into gear for all of us.

He sprinted down the beach, and the rest of us dashed after him. When the strip of sand narrowed so that the water lapped at the trees' roots, we turned into the jungle, running back the way we'd come yesterday. We were slower and more awkward than we'd been just one day ago, tripping over roots and letting hanging vines hit our heads and shoulders. The trees were too tall to see their tops, and the foliage too thick to allow more than a dim, green-filtered light to reach the ground. The jungle felt more alive than it had last time we'd run through it. Glowing butterflies and other bugs flittered about. Animals that moved too fast for me to see raced along the branches high overhead from tree to tree. Birds chirped and squawked, and what sounded like monkeys chattered loudly. My skin wouldn't stop crawling with the thought of one of those monstrous centipedes falling from a tree and landing on my back. An occasional roar sounded through the air, making my heart race faster than it already was.

As we passed under one tree, vines hanging from branches thirty feet high became like tentacles and swung and cracked the air. They whipped at us, lashing at our flesh hard enough to break the skin. The pain knocked me to my knees. Brock grabbed my elbow to pull me up, but another vine snapped against his back. He arched forward with a yell, and stumbled, dragging me with him. Hayden wrapped an arm around Bex and tried to use his body to protect her, taking all the lashes himself. By the time we found our way out, our acid-eaten clothes now sported new cuts, which were staining with blood from the gashes in our skin.

"We gotta keep going," Hayden panted. "I don't think that thing followed us, but it's not the only creature in this bush."

He swung Bex into his arms and took off again. Brock and I glanced at each other. The look in his eyes reflected what I felt.

There was only so much of a beating our bodies and souls could take. We wanted to give up. Let the trees whip us. Let the jungle kill us. The Darkness was too heavy to bear with everything else. It'd be so much easier to just give in to it. We were fools for thinking we'd ever get back to our Twin Flames, back to the Light. Why fight it any longer?

Laaaaaay-kneeeeeeee. Jeric's beautiful voice floated in my head in a song sang only for me. *Loooooove youuuuuuu.*

I didn't know if it was real or something my survival instincts threw at me, but it was enough to keep me going.

"We'll ... get back to them," I huffed at Brock as I grabbed his thick forearm and pulled him forward. He stumbled a few steps, and then stopped.

He put his hands on his hips and bent over, panting and shaking his head. "I can't ... go on. I don't ... *want* ... to go on."

"What about Asia?"

"Asia deserves better than me!" he barked.

I crossed the two paces between us and slapped him across the face. "Bullshit! Stop that right now, Broderick. You and Anastasia are made for each other, and you *will* be together again. Now stop being a fucking pansy and pull your shit together. We can do this!"

He stared at me with widened eyes and his mouth slightly open. He shook his head again, and I thought about punching him this time, but he straightened up and resumed walking, muttering something under his breath about Jeric wearing off on me. I wished I'd been channeling Jeric just now, but it was probably more the Darkness wearing on my last nerves.

We jogged after Hayden and Bex, but they ran so far ahead, we couldn't see them any more. Great. The last thing we needed right now was to get separated in this god-awful jungle. A scream from Bex kicked us into a sprint, following the direction it came from. A familiar screech followed right after it.

"Shit. The gozzard," I said as we ran. I could see its huge shape fifty yards ahead of us.

"Dinner!" Hayden yelled from above us as we came closer. He and Bex were both in a tree with branches lower than most of the others. She sat on a branch higher than the one he stood on. He was inching his way out, over the gozzard who had swung its head and elephant-like trunk toward Brock and me.

"Don't cut its trunk this time," I reminded Brock as we pulled our weapons and bent our knees into a crouch.

"I'm not eating that thing raw," Bex said.

"Don't worry, love." Hayden stopped as the branch he was on lowered with his weight, almost touching the gozzard's back. "You two be ready."

The gozzard took a step toward Brock and me, causing the ground to shake. Hayden yelled, catching its attention, and at the same time dropped down on its back haunch. With knives out, he sliced along the beast's sides as he ran toward its front horns. The gozzard let out a bone-chilling roar and whipped its head around, trying to get to Hayden.

"Grab the meat," Hayden yelled as slices of flesh fell from the monster. "Throw it in front of its face. We only get one chance!"

Brock and I dashed for the pieces Hayden had sliced off and threw it as instructed. The flesh hadn't even hit the ground when Hayden drove a dagger into the side of the gozzard's throat. Fire flew out of its mouth. The trunk whipped back toward Hayden, one of those thin, white tentacles flying out of it. It wrapped around Hayden's leg and yanked him off the monster's back.

"The eye," Hayden yelled at us as he swung a dagger at the tentacle.

I ran, jumped, and plunged my blade into its eye. The gozzard collapsed, quaking the ground. I collapsed next to it with no more energy to move. Hayden dropped to the ground beside me, his face twisted in agony. The white tentacle, severed from its owner, was still wrapped around his leg like a tight string, digging into his skin. His flesh sizzled and smoked all around it. I tried to lift my arm, but it came up slowly as though it weighed eight-hundred pounds. Brock beat me to it and sliced the tentacle off of Hayden's leg. He moaned and groaned and rolled on the ground.

Bex slid down the tree trunk, holding her bad arm close to her chest. As soon as her feet touched the ground, she ran over to Hayden.

"We have to help him!" She winced through her own pain as she grabbed Hayden's shoulders with both hands and pinned him to the ground. "Tell us what to do."

"Leave me to die," Hayden moaned as he writhed under her weight.

"Not happenin'. Now tell us what to do!"

"The venom will kill me. There's nothing you *can* do."

"Can we suck it out?" I asked.

"It'll kill *you.*"

"We'll spit it out."

"As much as there is, you'll undoubtedly swallow some. Too much and you'll be as bad as me."

"Then we'll take turns," Brock said. "Between the three of us, we can handle it."

"Don't be stupid," Hayden said. "It's too risky." His eyes glassed over as he looked up, behind Bex's head. "Ohhhh, mountains. So beautiful. I've never seen colored mountains like that."

We all looked in the same direction, but only saw more jungle. He was hallucinating. We had no choice but to take turns sucking on Hayden's wounds and spitting out the venom. The sour, putrid taste made me gag, and I couldn't spit it out fast enough. I didn't think it possible to accidentally swallow any.

"Think we got it all?" I asked, my tongue feeling thick in my mouth from all the sucking and spitting.

I looked up at the others, but they were all gone. Instead, the most wonderful sight ever stood in front of me.

"*Jeric?*" I shrieked. I jumped up for him, suddenly filled with all kinds of energy.

He caught me in his arms and wrapped them around me, hugging me to his chest. Tears streamed down my face.

"You made it," I sobbed as I held him tighter. "You found us."

I pulled back to take a good look at him, to make sure he was really here. I laughed at the sight of him. Why the hell was he wearing a girl's hot pink tube top and shorts made out of a United States flag?

"You look ridiculous, but beautiful to me." I sprang back into his arms and dropped kisses all over his face, on his brow ring, on his cheekbones, on his dimples. His skin felt rough under my lips. He probably hadn't shaved in days, since I'd left.

As my hands slid down his chest, though, the roughness was enough to scrape against my palms. I pulled back again. Jeric was gone. I was clinging to a damned tree. I slid to my knees on the ground and sobbed.

"Here." Bex pushed a piece of charred gozzard meat in front of me. "Hayden says it'll help."

I shook my head. "Don't want to eat. Want to die."

"Not if I can help it," she said, and she stuffed the meat into my mouth.

I had no choice but to chew and swallow. I thought my stomach would protest and heave it back out, but it actually seemed to welcome the substance. Almost immediately my head cleared. Bex handed me a larger piece of meat, cooked by its owner before we'd killed it. As I sat up and looked at the others, they all looked away.

"God," I moaned.

Bex laughed. "Don't worry. You weren't as hilarious as Brock starting to strip while dry humping that tree root over there."

Brock growled as he pulled his shirt back over his head, and I really tried hard not to laugh, honest I did. But I couldn't contain it. The sound bubbled up on its own accord and burst from my mouth. In seconds, we were all rolling on the ground, even Brock. I'd never done drugs, but if the high was anything like this, I thought I might take up smoking pot.

"It's the after effects," Hayden said once we settled down. "From the venom. The hallucinations come first, and if you're lucky enough to survive them and get some meat into you, the high comes next."

"We have to get home," Bex said. "I thought ya'll were gonna die on me, and no way am I gonna survive here by myself. Especially without you, Hayden."

She'd never spoken such truer words.

Once we ate all of the cooked gozzard meat, which wasn't much but enough to give us some energy, we made our way through the rest of the jungle. We came out where we'd entered yesterday, and I felt the Gate in the water. Maybe we shouldn't have run off so fast, after all. Then again, we'd thought maybe we were on Earth, and there was that gozzard that had been dropping from the sky, too.

"I feel it," Bex confirmed.

"This is where we landed," Hayden said. "The same Gate, right? Won't it just take us back to Erde?"

I gnawed on my bottom lip. "It shouldn't. That's not how the Gates work. It should give us access to all the worlds. I think."

"But we don't know for sure," Brock added. "We really don't know shit."

"I'm not going back to Erde," Hayden said firmly. "It's too Dark there."

"Enyxa can still get us here," I said. "We have to try to get to Earth. As long as she can get to us, we'll go Dark anyway, on Erde or anywhere."

Instinct told me the bitch couldn't simply show up on Earth as she had on Erde and here. Our societies and ways of living may have been spiraling our world toward Darkness, or maybe Darkness was leading us down that spiral, but she didn't rule us. Earth wasn't Dark yet. And we needed to get out of the Dark. I didn't know how much longer we'd last.

"I agree," Bex said. "We have to try."

Hayden groaned. "I don't like it, but I go where you go."

Brock said nothing. His face held his perpetual scowl, which wasn't like the Brock I'd known on Earth. He was changing, and not for the better. All the more reason we needed to get out of here.

I didn't know what else to do but swim for the Gate and hope it would open for us like the one on Erde did, so I did exactly that. The others followed me into the water. I prayed hard as we approached where I felt the Gate to be. As soon as I dove under the water, the lights sprang toward the surface. I popped back up.

"Bex and Hayden, go first. Try to Forge."

Before they could plunge under, however, the walls of light reached upward, and the water sucked downward, taking all of us with it. By the time our feet hit the bottom of the lake where we'd landed, the cylindrical walls were solid and the water gone. We'd barely caught our breath when a hole began opening in the Gate. It wouldn't Forge them here, apparently, so my initial instinct had been right. They couldn't Forge on a Dark world.

Rather than jumping through the newly formed hole this time, I peeked in. Mountains and a lake spread out before us.

"Looks like it could be Earth," I said hesitantly. So far, everything had looked like it could be Earth at first glance, even Erde.

"The fuck it does," Brock said just as a beast that looked somewhat like a horse but was covered in feathers galloped by. Wings lifted from its back as it turned toward us and snapped with teeth like an alligator's rather than an equine's. I jerked back, into the group behind me who'd been leaning forward to see, too.

When we all pulled back, the hole closed up.

"Here's one," Hayden said from my right.

We all turned toward a new hole gaping open. A green field stretched out with a stream running through it. Creatures grazed in the distance, and they looked like normal cows.

"Is this it?" Bex squealed with excitement.

A huge ball, the size of a blimp, with wings and scales flew at us. We flinched away, and the hole closed up just in time. Several more began opening, giving us glimpses of worlds that looked like Earth but weren't.

"There are so many worlds that are similar to Earth." Enyxa's voice filled the space around us. "In this universe and beyond. Worlds in other dimensions, planes, and realms that *are* Earth. Just not yours. If you think I'll let you find your way back to your own world, you're more delusional than I thought. Which is good. Will only make the Darkness come faster."

All of the gaping holes with all their familiar-but-not-quite-right scenes began to make me dizzy. Enyxa's words brought renewed despair that we'd never find our way home. She would never let us. My body felt heavy. My soul small. When a new black hole began yawning open, I couldn't fight the force of it. I let it suck me through. The others followed.

We landed on a floor of ice, surrounded by more ice. The only light came from a blue glow within the frozen water, illuminating enough to show that everything around us was coated in ice. We were in a cavern, facing nothing but darkness outside. Instinct told me the entire world was frozen over.

"Nice choice for a layover." Enyxa's voice again. She appeared in front of us, her black-and-white hair covered in frost. "This is one of my favorite worlds. The cold and endless Darkness make me happy. You lot won't last long here, which makes it even better. I don't think this will be a layover after all. No, I think this will be your final destination, for this life cycle, at least."

Hayden growled as he pulled Bex's shivering body into his arms. "You underestimate us."

Enyxa turned a dark eye on them. "You two might last longer. But these others—Broderick and Jacquelena—they haven't much chance. I can feel their Darkness growing, and it's quite lovely. Let's see, shall we? Broderick, why don't you tell these friends of yours what happened next with you and Asia?"

"Fuck you," Brock snapped.

Enyxa laughed, a tinkling sound full of delight. "I'd love to, darling, but you're just not my type. Yet." She sauntered around him, trailing a pointed black fingernail over his cheek. "Soon, though. A few more trips down memory lane, and you'll be there. I can't wait to show you everything. But first, tell us, Brock. Tell us what you did to the person you call the love of your lives. Tell us what happened to your family."

A snarl lifted Brock's lip, but he refused to talk.

"Ah. Be that way then," Enyxa said, her bottom lip jutting out in a pout. "I'll share the story for you. I'm sure Asia will enjoy reliving it all, too."

The cords in Brock's neck strained, and he squeezed his eyes shut, but none of us could block out the visions Enyxa forced on us. We fell to the freezing floor, our bodies trembling as we tried to huddle together for the heat. I was actually grateful when our icy world disappeared, and we dove into the memories that belonged to Brock and Asia, seen through Asia's eyes since Enyxa couldn't get Brock to cooperate.

CHAPTER 16

Asia

MY CHEST CONSTRICTED, making it difficult to breathe as I stared at Brock's baby mama standing in front of his house in a pink sleeveless shirt and white shorts with her long brown hair hanging loosely past her shoulders. Kami. The same person to whom I'd been talking on Facebook and encouraging to take charge of her life. She had taken my advice to make the right decisions for herself and to stop letting others make them for her. And that apparently entailed returning for her baby ... who happened to be my boyfriend's son. How could this be happening? What were the odds? Was she coming back for Brock, too? I blinked against the sting in my eyes.

As I remained frozen in place, Kami held her arms out and stepped forward to take Connor from me. I instinctively turned away from her, toward Brock, and handed him the baby.

"I want to hold my son," Kami said, her voice distant in my ears as Brock and I stared at each other.

"Why were you at a Single and Pregnant support group?" he asked me, ignoring Kami's demand. "You don't have a baby ..."

His voice trailed off as he obviously realized that having a baby was only one possibility for someone who'd go to that kind of support group. All kinds of questions crossed his mind, I could tell ... I could *feel* somehow.

"What happened?" he demanded, jumping to the worst conclusions. His eyes darkened with accusation. My throat tightened, and I could only shake my head, unable to form the words of explanation. I hadn't planned on telling him until absolutely necessary. I certainly hadn't figured out how, and here I was, on the spot.

"Can we talk about this later?" Kami snipped. "I'd like to hold my baby. I came a long way to see him."

When Brock saw that I wouldn't talk about this now, he blew out a harsh breath through enflamed nostrils and turned his head toward Kami.

"What the hell do you want?"

Her brows lifted, crinkling her forehead. She spoke slowly and deliberately. "I. Want. To. Hold. My. Baby. How many times do I have to say it?"

Brock pressed Connor protectively against his shoulder. "You gave him up. You can't just drop him at my doorstep, and then suddenly appear months later wanting to hold him. What do you really want, Kami?"

She stared at him for a long moment, and then held her hands up, palms toward the sky. Her tone changed, pleading now rather than demanding. "I screwed up, okay? I admit it. And I'm sorry, so very sorry. I let others tell me what to do, and it was wrong. I *know* that, and I've regretted it ever since. I want to do what's right for all of us, so I'm here now, Brock. I'm here for Connor ... and for you."

His dark eyes narrowed at her. "It doesn't work that way. You *dumped* him on my doorstep. Didn't even wait to make sure he'd be okay."

Kami's eyes watered. Her voice came out in a whisper. "I knew he'd be okay with you. I hated doing it, though, you have to believe me. That's why I'm here. I want to make it all right."

"I don't even ..." Brock shook his head as his voice trailed off, and his chocolate gaze swung to me, his eyes darker than normal. I could feel his hurt and confusion and wished I could talk to him, but I couldn't. Not here. Not now.

Kami must have noticed something pass between us, too, and she apparently didn't like that her plans wouldn't go as smoothly as she'd hoped.

"What does she have anything to do with us?" she snapped.

"Kami," Brock said between clenched teeth without removing his gaze from me. "Did you really think I'd wait around for you?"

"I didn't think you'd be fucking the first thing to walk in when you had a baby to take care of!"

Now Brock's eyes broke away from me to glare at her. "Asia and I—"

"Asia and you have nothing! That's pretty damn obvious since you don't even know about her past." She turned her sharp blue eyes on me. "Does anyone know the real you, Asia? I certainly don't. Didn't expect to find you here with my man and my son after everything we'd talked about."

Brock's eyes came back to me again with a new emotion filling them: distrust. I shook my head.

"No," I finally croaked. "I had no idea. We didn't talk about *that* much."

"Except you knew I'd had a baby, and then you took off and ended up right here with my son in your arms." Kami gasped. "Oh, my god! Were you even pregnant in the first place, or was that all a big scam for attention?"

"I ... I ..." I stammered under her accusation.

The tone of her voice turned from shock to cold. "You're one of those sick fucks who pretend to be pregnant and then steal some poor mother's baby, aren't you? That's why you're here, isn't it?"

"No!" A switch flipped, and I returned to myself. I took a step toward Kami, putting us toe-to-toe, and bowed out my chest. "Poor mother? *You?* My ass. Who do you think you are?

You abandoned your own son. You had a great guy and a sweet baby, and you *left* them! How can you make such accusations? If I'd had what you did—"

I choked on the angry sob building in my throat and forced myself to draw in a deep, calming breath before I completely lost my shit.

"But you didn't have it," Kami sneered, taking advantage of my pause. "So here you are, trying to take *my* life."

"The life you didn't want?" I couldn't help but say it.

"See! You are, aren't you? You're a fucking imposter. You're nothing but a lying, scheming little bitch."

My breath caught audibly, and Brock stepped between us. Good thing. Otherwise, I might have punched her.

"You know nothing about me," I seethed, glaring at her around his arm.

"And that's the problem, isn't it?" Brock said, and my head snapped up to look at him. His tone and words were unexpected. "Kami's right. I don't know much about you at all."

"Brock—" I started, feeling like I'd been slapped. He didn't believe her, did he? "Nothing she's saying is true."

"So you didn't meet at the support group?"

"Yes, but—"

"But nothing," he said. "I feel like I don't know who you are, Asia. After everything I've told you, everything we've been through, I don't really know anything about you, do I? But I do know this. You don't belong in my life."

My mouth fell open. I thought my heart would fly out of it. Instead, it became lodged in my throat, choking me. I stared blankly at him, waiting for him to qualify that statement with something like, "until you tell me what happened" or "until I know all about you." But he only glared at me, his eyes full of as much accusation as Kami held.

"Brock," I whispered, my hand pressed against my throat.

In answer, he turned his back toward me and handed Connor over to Kami. She smiled up at Brock and then at Connor, her expression triumphant. My stomach heaved as if I'd been punched. My insides battled against each other, part of me wanting to stay and explain, and another part wanting to run away. I simply turned on my heel and strode toward the garage and my apartment. If either of them noticed, they didn't try to stop me.

Once inside, I thought the sobs would come, but they didn't. I dropped to the couch, and stared at the wall as my mind tried to process what just happened. Did Brock really believe Kami's accusations of me? How could he? He knew me better than that! So I hadn't told him everything. That much was true. But how could he believe I was that type of person? That I could be so heartless and manipulative? She'd shut him out, treated him like dirt, and he believed her over me? Wouldn't even let me explain?

I fell over onto my side and curled into myself, my body sinking further into the couch cushions as a new realization washed over me. It didn't matter if I had explained. My past had nothing to do with our present, which was why I hadn't told him in the first place. And the present situation was that Connor's mother wanted back into their lives. Who was I to stop that?

I swallowed this truth pill, but it was long and hard to do so. Darkness started settling in on me, not only outside as the afternoon became evening, but also onto my heart and soul. Once again, I was completely alone. And so fucking hollow.

Hope showed up at my door the next morning with two Starbucks cups in her hands.

"I had to get away from the arguing for a while," she said, holding a cup out to me. "They've been at it all night."

I took the cup and stepped aside, silently inviting her in. We both sat on the couch, side by side. Hope put her cup on the table and enveloped me in a hug.

"I'm so sorry," she whispered. "This shouldn't be happening to you. To any of you."

"Did you hear what she said about me?"

"The lies?"

I pulled back to look into her eyes. She gave me a soft smile.

"Yes, I know the truth, Asia. You didn't really think I'd let you into my house, into my personal life and the lives of my son and grandbaby, without knowing everything about you, did you? I saw the hospital records." She chuckled at what must have been a shocked look in my eyes. Of course, I understood why she'd do a background check, but she shouldn't have found what she obviously had. Not just because they were private medical records, but because they were supposed to have been destroyed. "I have my ways of finding out what I need to know. And I know you are a good person. A kind, generous, intelligent young woman who'd never do what that little hussy accused you of."

"Hussy?" I choked out.

"She abandoned the two people I love most in the world. Left my grandbaby—her own son—on a doorstep! No, I don't like her. And I certainly don't like what she's saying to Brock about you."

"He said I don't belong in his life," I muttered.

She pulled me back against her and tightened her arms around me. "He's wrong. And I'll make sure he knows it."

Her kindness broke me, and I finally cried as she held me.

"Please don't tell him the truth," I said once I pulled away and scrubbed at my wet cheeks. A dark spot stained the shoulder of her shirt. "Because it doesn't really matter."

"It *does* matter. But don't worry. I'll make sure he gets it from you."

I blew out a sigh as she left. Hope was right in one way. It mattered to me that Brock knew the truth. But only because I didn't want him thinking that I was a manipulative liar who'd scammed her way into his and his son's lives. I wanted him to know because I cared about what he thought of me. I cared about him period.

Which made the heartache so much worse.

I'd been wondering if he cared about me at all, at least enough to find out the truth, for a day and a half before he finally came over. We stood at my open door staring at each other over the threshold for a long moment. Then he glanced over his shoulder before pulling me into his arms.

"I've missed you so much," he murmured into my hair as he squeezed me tightly. I took a moment to inhale his familiar scent and linger in the embrace of his strong arms before he let me go, and then I stepped backwards so he could come inside.

"I don't understand," I said as soon as I closed the door.

He turned to face me and pushed a hand through his dark hair. "I'm sorry I said what I did. It was mean and wrong. I *know* you aren't the type of person to do what Kami was saying. I was just ... overwhelmed. In shock. I mean, you confirmed part of her story, so I didn't know what to believe. And Kami ... besides what she did to Connor and me, I wouldn't have thought her capable of making up such lies. I'm sorry, Asia. I'm so sorry."

"So you don't think I used her to get to you and Connor and manipulate my way into your lives? That I tried to steal your baby?"

He chuckled, though it held no sound of humor. "Of course not. I know there are some fucked-up people who do that, but you're not one of them." He pressed his hand against the left side of his chest. "I know it here in my heart, and in my soul."

A thousand-pound weight lifted from my chest, and I felt like I could breathe for the first time in over a day. I did just that—breathed deeply—as Brock rested his hands on his hips and watched me.

"Thank you," I finally said.

"There's nothing to thank me for." He glanced at the couch. "But we do need to talk."

I nodded. He walked around the coffee table and took a seat on the edge of the sofa. He rested his elbows on his knees, wrapped a palm around a fist, and looked up at me. I remained standing on the other side of the coffee table, too wired with anxiety to sit down.

"You were pregnant?" he asked. "That part's true?"

I nodded again as I inhaled another breath.

"I had a miscarriage last summer," I said quietly.

My hands moved automatically to my stomach, as they used to when I'd had a life growing in there and after I'd lost it. The habit had died many months ago, but I suddenly felt just as empty as I had the moment I woke up in the hospital. I closed my eyes, squeezing them shut against the memories of how it had all happened. When I opened them, Brock was staring at me. The anxious energy of only a moment ago had completely drained away with the words I'd never said before. I moved over to the couch and sat next to him, but I couldn't look him in the eyes so I stared at my hands as they tried to wring the life out of each other.

"I was a little over four months along. Everything, all of it, was horrible and messy, and not something I want to remember. My life had been turned upside down twice, leaving me an emotional mess, and I'd finally gotten over it—at least, as much as someone can. It's in the past and has nothing to do with us, so I didn't tell you. I didn't want you getting all weird with me, especially when it came to Connor." I sniffed and swiped at my cheeks to find them wet. I hadn't realized I'd been crying.

"The father?"

My jaw clenched, and my spine stiffened. I looked up at Brock, right into the eye. "Doesn't deserve to live."

His brows raised slightly, and I could tell he had many questions about what that meant, but the fucker didn't deserve two breaths for me to explain. I'd vowed to never speak of him again. Thankfully, Brock nodded, getting the message loud and clear. "So you went to the support group?"

"Yeah, the end of last spring semester, shortly after I found out I was pregnant. I'd seen Kami there the one and only time I went. I didn't talk to her at all, and then I went home for the summer the moment exams were over. I had to get out of that place. Home ended up being no better, and my summer turned out to be the worst one ever. I tried to go back to school in the fall, but I was different. I couldn't handle it. I was on my way out of town, headed down here, when I stopped at a coffee shop and ran into her. We only talked for a few minutes. She never told me what happened with her and her baby, I swear, but I could tell she regretted it. I thought maybe she'd aborted it or given it up for adoption. I really had no idea about you, Brock. I mean, even after I met you and knew about Connor, it never crossed my mind. You weren't even in Boston. And maybe bringing it up to you would have helped both of us, but I just didn't see how. I didn't want to relive any of it. And that's all I've been doing since yesterday."

"Damn, babe. I'm so sorry you had to go through it." He wrapped his arms around my shoulders and pulled me against him again. More tears leaked from my eyes.

"God, I haven't cried this much since it happened," I said when I finally pulled away.

We sat sideways on the couch, facing each other. His eyes averted from mine, and the corners of his mouth turned down. I dropped my head, knowing I was about to cry some more.

"I'm sorry for all of this," he said, his voice a hoarse whisper. "I know you're telling me the truth. I can feel it." He picked up my hands and lifted them to his mouth to kiss my knuckles. "I wasn't lying when I said I love you, Asia. I still do."

I slowly lifted my head to look up at him. "I hear a *but* in there."

He closed his eyes, grimaced as though he didn't like what he saw on the backs of his lids, and nodded before opening them. "We've been talking through things day and night, and Kami wants to try to make it work. Between us. Her and me, I mean." His voice shook on that last bit, and he blew out a breath. "I have to try, Asia. I owe it to Connor. He deserves to have his father *and* mother."

I pulled my hands from his grip and bit on my trembling lip, refusing to let any more tears fall in his presence. I nodded and said, "I understand. It's the right thing to do, and I'd expect no less from you."

With another exhale, he swiped a hand over his face, and then stood and walked over to the door, where he paused. He didn't turn back to me, but spoke to the wall.

"I wish you'd been the one to come to New York for that party instead of her." He dropped his head, pressing his forehead to the door. "This really sucks, and it's going to be fucking hard, but we can't see each other. At all. It's not fair to any of us. You can't be a part of my life, Asia."

I understood what he meant, but that didn't lessen the pain that stabbed through my heart as he walked out my door without another word. Even with all the crying I'd already done, the emotions of the last two days overwhelmed me. The agony in my heart and soul were too much to bear. I ran for my bed, pushed my way under the covers, and bawled until my pillow was soaked.

The irony of the entire situation was not lost on me. I'd come here to escape the nightmare my life had turned into the night I conceived, and I'd actually found happiness when I thought I never would. But here I was, sucked back into the horror story, reliving everything, facing the demons I thought I'd slain, and all *because* of the one person who'd completed me, who'd brought that happiness into my life. And I'd been the one to bring it all down. My sage wisdom that was supposed to help a young woman empower herself was the very thing that destroyed me. How appropriate.

As much as I wished Brock would come running back to me with a changed mind, I knew he never would. And I really didn't want him to. This whole situation was not about me. There were many lives and well-beings at stake, including baby Connor's. If Brock and Kami could grow to truly love each other and the three of them could be a happy family, my broken heart would be worth it.

I just didn't know what to do about my broken *soul*. Would I ever feel that wholeness again like I did with Brock? Somehow I doubted it. I thought that was a once-in-a-lifetime experience. That kind of connection couldn't exist with more than one other soul in this world. Ours just wasn't meant to last. We weren't Twin Flames, like Jacey and Micah in that book that now sat on the shelf in my closet. We'd be able to live without each other, and these last few months would eventually morph into nothing more than a fond memory. Brock would become some guy I used to know.

As much as I knew this all needed to happen so I could move on, my whole body ached with the thought of it. An actual physical pain throughout my joints and bones.

Time. Time will heal the wounds, and I'll be fine.

It took exactly one day and night for me to realize I needed more than time—I also needed space. I couldn't stay at Hope's estate. Although Brock and I had been through this before, it felt different this time with another woman in the house. I told Hope while working that I didn't want any details, but she insisted I knew that Kami was staying in one of the guest rooms. Of course, my imagination took that to mean that her stuff was staying in the guest room, but that didn't mean her body was. The thought made me sick to my stomach. As I walked through the house toward the back door after work, I could hear the three of them as a family in the kitchen, and my soul throbbed. That night, long after Connor's bedtime, giggling and laughter from the hot tub outside traveled across the yard and to my apartment, even though my door and windows were shut tight. My stomach heaved, and I had to run for the bathroom.

No matter how hard I tried, I couldn't get away from them, and although I wanted to, it wasn't exactly fair to ask them to avoid living their lives because of me. I was the outsider. The one who didn't belong. The intruder. I was the one who had to go.

"I wish you'd change your mind," Hope said the next evening as she stood in my bedroom, watching me pack. She plopped onto my bed and scowled. "I'd happily kick her out."

I smiled. "You have to give her a chance. Whether you like it or not, she's the mother of your grandchild."

"I don't like it. I like *you*. You're the one who should be staying, not her. What am I going to do without you?" She threw her arms in the air with exaggerated despair.

"I'm not leaving you, Hope. I'm still going to work for you, remember?" I'd gone to her earlier with the news that I was moving out. We'd discussed my work and how I could do most of it virtually so I could avoid being at the house as much as possible.

"Where are you going to go?"

"I'm sure I can find a place. I already have an appointment set up for tomorrow to look at an apartment over on Palm Boulevard."

She frowned. "That's too far away."

"It's only eight miles."

"Exactly. Too far away. I'm worried about you."

"I'll be fine." I sighed. "Physically, anyway."

"You belong here, though. And you belong with Brock. I haven't changed my mind on that, young lady."

"Well, he has."

She waved her hand in the air. "He's being a dumb male. I know what he's trying to do, and it *would* be best for Connor if it actually worked, but it won't. Connor doesn't deserve to grow up in the disaster that's waiting to happen."

I glanced at her and was surprised to see her eyes glistening. She truly believed what she was saying.

"At least he'll always have you," I offered.

She nodded. "Yes, but he deserves more. Both of those boys do. You deserve happiness, too. I wish you'd stick around."

"We've been through this. I can't be around them."

Her finger jabbed into the air. "Mark my words. Kami's little honeymoon won't last long. Brock will be miserable—he already is—and Kami will end up leaving them anyway, abandoning Connor once again."

"But I can't be the reason it doesn't work for them."

Hope grabbed my hands and held them between hers as she looked up at me. "Oh, Asia, honey, you always were the reason."

CHAPTER 17

6 MONTHS AGO

Asia I ROLLED OVER on what I assumed to be my bed, the movement taking every bit of effort I had. My body felt heavier than an elephant's, as though it were made of metal and a giant magnet was implanted in the mattress, holding me down. My head felt even more massive, and I could swear oatmeal replaced my brain in my skull. I didn't even remember falling asleep, but I'd apparently been dead to the world. What time was it anyway? I heaved my arm over and reached for my phone on the nightstand. I studied the numbers, my mind unable to make sense of them: 10:49.

It was still night? I tried pushing away the cobwebs filling my head to reorient myself. I'd been packing, I remembered. Hope had been here. I couldn't remember anything else. Had I passed out on her? I didn't remember her leaving. She must have thought me to be a basket case. No wonder she worried.

Before I could remember any more of my miserable life, I put my phone back and rolled over again, hoping to fall right back to sleep and stay that way until morning when I'd wake up clear headed. Right now, I just wanted to shut my brain off … and my heart. As my eyes began to close, I noticed the light slipping in between the curtains. I squinted harder.

That was daylight seeping in.

Oh, my god! I bolted upright, suddenly and immediately awake with a pounding heart. It was 10:50 in the *morning*? How long had I slept? More than the standard eight hours, but I still felt so tired. I glanced at the clock on my phone one more time, and then fell back against my pillows. It was almost 11 a.m. The appointment for the apartment had been at ten.

I shuffled out to the kitchen and made my coffee, then called the rental manager to reschedule. I told him work had tied me up; he told me the apartment had been rented to the people who showed up when I didn't. Great. That meant at least one more day here. A glance out my window showed both Brock's and Kami's cars gone. At least that was a bonus for the day.

Hope had already given me the day off so I could apartment hunt, as much as she protested the idea. But I couldn't summon the energy to even shower and dress, so I camped out on my couch almost all day, dozing off and on. I couldn't help but wonder if I was getting sick again. The last thing I needed was to become as ill as I'd been in Chicago. A little after three in the afternoon, I forced myself outside for some fresh air. As I was about to walk out, the leather-bound book on my coffee table caught my eye. How did that get there? Had I pulled it out last night and couldn't remember that either? I supposed that was possible. For some inexplicable reason, I grabbed it on my way out the door. I didn't have a destination in my mind, but my feet carried me to the beach, where I fell to my butt, needing a rest. What was wrong with me? I'd been working out with Brock and had become pretty fit. How could I be so exhausted from a two-block walk?

After only a few minutes of staring at the waves, listening to them crash on the sand, and inhaling the salty, humid air, my body grew restless. Dead-ass tired, but jumpy at the same time. I felt all wrong, like I was in the wrong place, doing the wrong thing, feeling the wrong feels. *The book.* Based on nothing more than intuition, I felt like the book had all the answers. I pushed it in front of my folded legs on the sand and threw it open. My fingers flipped through the pages until I found what I was instinctively looking for: Jacey's drawing of a mansion.

That's where I need to be.

I didn't understand the sudden desire—no, *need*—to go to this mansion in a book that Brock and I had deemed fiction, but it came strong and urgent. And oh, so very real. My fingers skimmed over the sketch, and I felt as though a hook had lodged into my gut and something reeled me in toward the picture. I didn't know how long I sat there staring at the drawing and wondering how to get to it, but long enough for the sun to begin burning my skin. I rubbed my hand over my arm and clamped it around my wrist. And then I realized the burn came from the inside out.

I looked down as I slowly peeled my fingers away from my forearm, and gasped.

"No fucking way," I muttered under my breath. Goose bumps swept over my skin.

I had a mark on my arm just like Jacey and Micah's in the book.

Although I had to squint, I could see the formation of a flame showing through on my skin. I pushed the pages of the book back to the beginning and began skimming the story, refreshing my memory. Still, the mark on my arm made no sense. Neither did the pull to the mansion. How could I possibly be like them? They couldn't even be real!

I shut the book, my heart pounding. Wet sand dusted the front of it. I hadn't realized I'd been so close to the water—that enough time had passed for the tide to come closer. I tried to brush the sand off, but most of it just moved around. As my fingers swept harder, little symbols around the image embossed on the front cover began to glow a silvery-blue. Only for a moment and then they disappeared, barely noticeable etches in the leather. But the glowing marks remained like a vision, and although blurry, I somehow knew what they meant.

The Tree of Hope

The Phoenix Guardians

Seven ... something.

That symbol faded in my mind too quickly to decipher, but I'd become focused on one particular mark anyway:

An'bris

I knew that name. I knew it *was* a name. But how? Following my instincts again, I turned to the inside of the back cover. There, faint, barely visible in the glow of the late afternoon sun, was a list of names. Ja'mai, followed by Jacquelena and Jeremicah, and under each of those more names, ending with Jacey and Leni on one side and Micah and Jeric on the other. After Ja'mai was An'bris again. My eyes stopped there, where it listed Broderick and Anastasia. That had to have been us. Right?

"Oh, my god!" I shrieked out loud. "We're somehow like them."

I didn't know what it all meant. How we were like them. What we were supposed to do about it. Even as I stared at the page with the names—including mine and Brock's!—the ink faded again, all of them disappearing.

The sky overhead suddenly fell dark as though a storm cloud had passed over the sun. I looked up, and sure enough, a dark gray cloud churned. A figure down the beach about twenty yards caught my eye. He wore a dark hoodie and dark jeans and had spiky blond hair. All I could think about was Jacey's Billy Idol wannabe in the book. More figures in dark clothing dotted the beach. Were they closing in on me, or was that my imagination? Could they actually be the Shadowmen from the book?

I wasn't about to find out. In a nanosecond, I was on my feet and sprinting for home. I ran the whole way, sure they were after me, and with each step, the truth settled further. We were meant to receive this book and read it. We were somehow tied to it. Brock and I were in some way like Jacey and Micah. I had no doubt.

As I flew for the driveway, something small and white streaked toward me. A squeal jumped out of my mouth when it flew past, and I glanced over my shoulder. A cat. It was just a cat. But a man in dark clothing still ran after me, and the feline ran at him. He suddenly stopped down the street, on the far side of Hope's property. The cat stopped too and paced back and forth. I paused at the gate that crossed the driveway. The man's head turned toward the house, down at the cat, then back to me. And then he spun and ran off. I didn't take it for granted. I punched in the numbers for the people gate, ran in, hit the button to close it, and ran for my apartment.

Not until I was inside did I look back through the window to check the driveway. None of the dark figures remained, but I knew they'd been chasing me. *Were* they Shadowmen? A chill ran down my spine. Nobody's cars were in the driveway except mine. Hope parked in the garage, but Brock, Kami, and I all parked outside. They were gone.

I tossed the book on the coffee table, grabbed my phone, and dialed Brock's number. It went straight to voicemail. Was it turned off, or was he avoiding me? I called Hope next.

"Do you know where Brock is?" I demanded as soon as she picked up. "I seriously need to talk to him."

"It's about time," she said. "Unfortunately, he's tied up at school. There's some issue with his classes, I guess."

"Crap." I glanced at the clock on the stove. It was nearly six o'clock. He couldn't be there much longer, and the rational thing to do would have been to wait for him. But rationality had disappeared as soon as the mark on my arm had appeared. Another look at it, clearly defined and growing brighter, only made me freak out more. "I have to find him, Hope. I can't wait any longer. Something's going on, and I *have* to see him. Do you know where I should go?"

"I'll take you."

"What?" She'd hung up, though, and a minute later, a horn was honking from the driveway. I peeked out to see her car parked next to my Camaro.

"Come on," she yelled out the window.

I grabbed my purse and ran out the door.

"I could have driven myself," I said as I slid into her passenger seat and reached for my seat belt.

"He has Connor with him, and the two of you need to talk. I'll take the baby so you can have some alone time." She glanced down at my arm. "Nice tat."

I rubbed my hand over the mark on my skin. I didn't have the time or inclination to explain that it wasn't a tattoo. I was simply grateful that she was driving, because I realized now I probably couldn't have. I was seriously freaking the fuck out.

We pulled into the Lot F on Brock's college campus at the same time he was crossing toward his car with Connor in one arm. He glanced over and cocked his head at the sight of his mom's car as she drove in the direction he walked. We found his Audi and parked behind him two seconds before he reached it. Hope threw the transmission into park, jumped out of the car, and jogged up to Brock while I could only sit there and stare. I reached over and turned the car off, and then climbed out, but stayed on my side, watching him, my whole body shaking. What if he wouldn't talk to me?

"Give me Connor and your keys," Hope ordered. Brock looked at her like she'd lost her mind.

"What's going on?" he asked.

"Time's run out. You and Asia need to move it."

What? I'd only told her we needed to talk. Where did she want us to go?

"What are you talking about, mother?" Brock demanded. "It's been a long day. The school's lost all of my records. They don't even show that I'm a student here!"

My breath caught.

"All the more reason," Hope said, reaching for Connor, and I about choked on the air stuck in my lungs. I clamped my hand over my mouth as I stood there stupidly, staring at them. Hope snuggled the baby close against her chest and held out a hand. "Your keys. Now."

"Mom—"

"Don't argue with me, Brock! You're running out of time!"

He dug his hand into his jeans pocket, but didn't pull his keys out. He glanced over at me and quickly away. "I can't. I made a promise to Kami that I wouldn't see *her* any more."

My heart rolled and sank, and my stomach dropped to my knees. He referred to me as though I were the devil. The weight of his words crushed me, and I wanted to drop to the ground, curl into a ball, and never get up again.

"Brock Richard Verdor," Hope said with that tone mothers get when they've lost patience with their children. She moved until she was toe-to-toe with him and glared up into his face. "Listen to me. Do you remember what I told you as a child? That there would be times when you must listen to me and obey, no matter what?"

Their gazes locked at this cryptic question, and then Brock cocked his head and nodded. "I remember."

Hope glanced over her shoulder at me, up at the darkening sky with more clouds churning overhead, and then at him. "This is one of those times. Go with Asia. Don't look back, no matter what."

"What about Connor?"

"I'll take him home in your car. The car seat's already in it. Don't worry. I'll take care of him." Her hand remained open, and Brock finally dropped the keys into it. "Now go! Don't waste time, or it'll be too late for both of you!"

Brock dropped a kiss on Connor's forehead and another on his mom's who quickly embraced him with one arm before pushing him away. He sauntered slowly toward me, his expression a mask of uncertainty. When Hope turned for Brock's car, I saw her face for the first time. Tears streamed down her cheeks.

What the hell was going on? What had she been trying to tell him? She seemed to know something about our situation.

As she opened the rear door of Brock's car, she looked over at me and gave me a small, sad smile. Then she ducked down to strap Connor into his car seat.

"What's going on?" Brock asked as he stood on the opposite side of Hope's car.

My gaze swung to his face. Mixed emotions crossed over his features. I thought I saw a momentary hint of love in his eyes, but mostly confusion and impatience. He didn't want to be here. He didn't want to be with me.

"I'm ... I'm so sorry," I whispered as I held my arm over the roof of Hope's car. "I didn't do anything, I swear. It just happened."

Brock's eyes slid down to inspect my arm, and then about bugged out of his head. He lifted his own arm up and pushed back the long sleeve covering it before laying it over the roof. A flame showed on his skin, too.

"It showed up today while I was in the Registrar's office, arguing with them about my status."

Our eyes locked for a long moment.

"What the hell, Brock? Did you forget about me? I had to walk all the way here from the mechanic's!"

Our lock broke at the sound of Kami's voice.

"Shit," Brock muttered under his breath before turning toward her.

Stopping in front of his car, she glared at me and then at him. She tilted her head, jutted a leg out, and placed her hands on her hips.

"You *promised*," she snapped with narrowed eyes.

"I ... I—" Brock stammered.

Hope stepped in. "Kami, come with me. They have some things to discuss."

Kami's gaze swung to the older woman. "The hell they do!"

"Don't make a scene, honey," Hope warned. "Everything will make sense soon. I promise. Just get in the car. We'll meet them at home."

She'd walked over to Kami by then and wrapped her hand around the girl's elbow. She guided her toward the passenger side of Brock's car. If Kami could shoot flames out of her eyes, I'd be burning to a crisp. Thankfully, Connor began fussing, and Kami turned her attention inside the car, and climbed into the front seat.

My knees buckled with relief that we weren't going to have a scene here. I dropped into the passenger seat of Hope's car. Brock already sat next to me where his mother had been sitting only moments ago. He'd chosen me over Kami.

"What's it mean?" he demanded. "The marks?"

Well, he chose curiosity and weird shit over Kami.

"It has to do with this book," I said, grabbing the journal from the floor in front of me and placing it onto my lap. "Our names showed up in it and then disappeared."

"What the fu—?"

A horn blared outside. Hope looked over the seats at us with reverse lights glowing white. Brock turned the engine over and backed up so she could move out of the parking spot. While we followed her toward the exit of the lot, I explained everything I knew to Brock. I turned the pages of the book to the drawing of the mansion while we waited behind a short line of cars at the stop sign.

"I've been dreaming of this place," Brock murmured as he studied it. "I felt like I'd seen it before, but had forgotten it had been in this book."

"What happens in your dreams?"

"We're trying to get there. You and me."

His hand slid from the gearshift to rest on top of mine. Hope was next in line to exit, and he pulled up behind her.

Once the car came to a complete stop, Brock looked over at me. He gave my hand a squeeze, then removed it and turned to watch the traffic.

"Why's that car going so damn fast?"

As I swung my gaze around to see what he saw, I watched Hope pull the Audi out of the parking lot. My arc continued to the left, where a light-colored truck was barreling down the street at breakneck speed. My heart stopped in my chest.

"NOOOOOO!" I shrieked.

"STOOOOPPPP!" Brock yelled.

Our shouts were drowned out by the sound of tires screeching on asphalt, metal crunching into metal, and glass shattering as the truck plowed into the side of Brock's car. The driver's side. Where both Hope and Connor had been sitting. Flames erupted immediately, engulfing both vehicles.

Brock's screams filled my head, melding into a heart-wrenching harmony with my own.

CHAPTER 18

Leni

"No, GOD, NO! *Connor*," Brock wailed, his cries bouncing off the frozen walls as we all returned to the present.

My eyes and face hurt, and I pressed my hands against my cheeks. A sheet of ice layered my skin, my tears frozen solid. Sobs wracked through me, shaking me harder than the cold did. Poor Brock. Poor Asia. Poor Hope and Connor. Poor Kami, too, who may have been a bitch, but hadn't deserved to die like that. I wrapped my arms around Brock as best as I could. His body had curled into the fetal position as he continued to cry out his baby boy's name.

"I'm so sorry, Brock." I cried with him. Bex draped herself over us, and her body shook as she sobbed, too.

"He's gone," he wept. "My son is *gone*. He was just a little baby."

"It's a terrible thing, losing a child, isn't it?" Enyxa asked.

I hadn't realized she remained in the cavern with us.

Brock's body fell still underneath us. His sobs ceased. He pushed us off of him and rose to his feet. As Bex and I sat on our butts with Hayden, Brock strode over to stand right in front of Enyxa, where she sat on a boulder, one leg crossed over the other. He jabbed a finger in her face.

"Don't act like you know *anything*."

She let out a sound that was something between a laugh and a sigh. She shook her head. "Oh, Broderick, I know exactly how you feel. Time to share some of my story. How *I* went Dark."

She rose to her feet and sauntered around the cavern slowly as she began, her stiletto-heeled boots clicking on the ice.

"Believe it or not, eons ago I was like you lot. Satan had Separated me from my Twin Flame."

"Satan?" Bex gasped. "He's still real?"

Enyxa threw her head back and laughed. "Oh, yes, darling, *very* real. Not every world calls him Satan, but that's what you know him as. If you could remember everything, you'd remember that you've all met him, too."

Bex shivered next to me, and I didn't think this time was due to the cold.

"He ripped our soul in two and sent me back to Earth on my own, just as I did to all of you and the rest of the Original Seven many times since then." She looked over at us as she continued her trek around the cavern, dragging her fingernail along the icy wall. "Oh, yes, more than once, to all of you. But I get ahead of myself. We're talking about *me* right now. Satan took my other half, and sent me to Earth alone. I was still of the Light at first. Once our souls had gone through the many life cycles and experienced everything we needed to, we'd become a Union, just like you lot had been. We'd been solidly in the Light for millennia. The Light remained strong in my soul. For a while …"

Her voice trailed off momentarily. Brock stood where he'd been, his arms crossed over his broad chest, watching her with the same mesmerized attention as the rest of us.

"My lives were hell, though. Not literal Hell. That came later. But they were horrible. Lifetime after lifetime of an empty feeling inside—the loss of my other half. I kept making the same stupid mistakes over and over of believing that I'd found him, but instead finding myself in a relationship with a man who didn't love me. Some even hated me, or worse, didn't care about me at all. Some beat me black and blue, leaving me in puddles of blood. Raped me, sometimes every night. *Murdered* me."

Enyxa's voice came cold as she stood right behind us, her Darkness waving over us, *into* us. Next to me, Bex scooted closer to Hayden, who wrapped his arms around her. I reached out and took her hand in mine, giving it a squeeze.

"Life after life of men who treated me like the scum on the soles of their feet. Life after life of watching my parents die, living as an orphan, or worse, with people who said they'd take care of me but only abused me and treated me like a slave."

A tingle ran down my spine, and I stiffened. Maybe I was only imagining it, but I swore Enyxa herself ran that fingernail of hers down my back. I was too scared to look over my shoulder to find out.

She moved on, rounding her way back to Brock until she stood in front of him. "Life after life of watching my own children die in my arms. Sometimes from disease, others from accidents. Many times by burning to death." She leaned closer to him, her eyes sparking as she recalled the memories. "Over and over again, I smelled their flesh frying. Heard their screams for me. Tried in vain to save them. Over and over again, I watched the life leave their innocent eyes, their tiny bodies fall limp or burn into ash. *Hundreds* of them." She pushed a finger into Brock's chest. "Yes, Broderick, I have real knowledge what it feels like to lose a child."

He staggered backwards, closer to us. Enyxa turned to face us all.

"It was enough to make anyone go Dark, even someone as Light as I'd once been. But not enough to satisfy Satan. When I finally succumbed, he had to make it worse. Make me relive every horrible moment from the time he Separated us and throughout every miserable lifetime. As Light as I'd been, it had taken hundreds of lifetimes to get there, and he forced me to go through them all on repeat. Until I finally gave in to him. Until I accepted his offer to serve with him, as his equal, and accepted a piece of him into my soul. He rewarded me with some of his Darker worlds. I've taken others. Just as I'll be taking Earth once you lot go Dark."

"You've done this to us!" Brock accused. "You caused these tragedies in all of our lives, haven't you?"

Enyxa laughed. "Yes, I have, but not completely on my own. You'll learn that later. And before you ask, yes, I'll be making you relive Every. Single. One. Of those tragedies. Every last agonizing moment. You think this life has been bad? Wait until you recall all of your past lives. You think losing your child this time is unspeakable? Wait until you remember *all* of the children you've lost in your many lives, Broderick. Wait until you, Nathayden, relive all the pain you've caused in others' lives, including Rebethannah's. Wait until you, Rebethannah, recall all the times you've been beaten, abused, and raped because you'd denied Nathayden's love for the attention of other men." Enyxa turned the full force of her gaze on me, and her mouth stretched into a wide grin. "And you, Jacquelena. Oh, the memories you'll recall ... but the best one of all will *destroy* you. All of you. You will be mine, soon. I'll wait as long as it takes, because this will be so much fun."

Enyxa sauntered over to the mouth of the cave as the sounds of the accident bounced around the cavern and Brock's memory returned to all of us. An image of the accident and the cars exploding into flames showed in front of us. Brock fell to his knees, weeping again.

"By the way, Broderick," Enyxa said as she stood just outside the cave. I couldn't imagine how he could hear her over the feral sounds he made. "You should have never trusted Hope and her surreptitious ways, especially that night. One of your many mistakes. But it worked out perfectly for me ... just as I'd *hoped*."

She let out a wicked laugh, as though she'd told a hilarious joke. No, not a joke. A pun.

I narrowed my eyes. "Hope's someone, isn't she? Someone to the Guardians? Or to you?"

Enyxa's dark eyes twinkled. "Oh, she's someone all right. Well, she *was*. Sadly—or not—now there is no Hope."

She stepped backwards, her foot finding no ice to land on, and she disappeared into the darkness, her laughter carrying on the air. I scrambled and slid on my hands and knees, barely able to stop the skid over the ice in time before I fell off the ledge myself. For as far as I could see, darkness stretched and the ice glowed blue far down below us. We were at least a hundred feet up, on the side of a cliff. Unfortunately, Enyxa's body didn't lay splayed out on the ground. Her existence wouldn't end so easily.

I crawled and skidded back over to Brock and tried to hug him. He shrugged me off.

"Just leave me alone," he muttered, his voice hoarse. He sat on his butt, his knees pulled to his chest, and his arms wrapped around his shins.

"You can't let her win," I said. "I can't give you Asia's love, but I can give you friendship. You need it, Brock."

"It's too late for me. My son, his mother, my mother ... they all died, Leni!" He shook his head as fresh tears rolled over the rims of his eyes. "Mom ... God, I don't even know what to think of her now. If she's even my mom after what Enyxa just said."

"Don't listen to Enyxa. I'm beginning to think she's full of lies."

He shook his head. "I don't think she's lied to us at all, and what she said makes sense. Hope was burning to death, but hell-bent on telling us what to do. Why were there flames in the first place? Those cars should have never burst into fire! But somehow they did, and she was in the middle of the flames, screaming at us, yelling at us to go west, to the manor. She wanted me to leave her and my crying son! Why? Why was that so important at that time? Maybe we could have done something for them, but she was more concerned about us getting away. I fought it at first, but Asia was convinced—or maybe fooled is the better word—and eventually dragged me away."

"You needed to Forge," I reminded him.

He looked up at me with narrowed dark eyes sparking with anger. "*Did* we? Did we really, Asia and me?" He shook his head. "I don't know what to fucking believe any more. *Who* to believe." He pressed the heel of his palm against his forehead, his fingers pushing his dark hair straight up. "I don't deserve someone as great as Asia. I deserved Kami. If you want to say the universe was bringing two souls together, it was Kami and me. The universe worked *against* Asia and me. You know our story now. How can you say it's anything like yours and Jeric's?"

I opened my mouth, but I didn't have an answer for him.

"You can't," he snarled. His voice came out quieter, the anger deflating. "We've always known we were different. Maybe now I know why."

"What do you mean?"

"Someone was forcing it. Maybe it was us, wanting to be together even though we shouldn't have been. Maybe, though, it was Hope or Enyxa ... or both, working together so we'd end up like this." He blew out a heavy sigh. "It doesn't matter, though. I've lost them all anyway, and I can't fight it any more. I can't take Enyxa putting me through that one more time. The first time was enough. I'm done, Leni. Done with all of it."

He bent his head into his knees and rocked himself, shutting me out.

Enyxa wasn't done with us, though. More memories assaulted me, starting with Jeric's accident that smashed his family between two vehicles and threw him into the ditch, leaving him deaf and an orphan. Then she took me back into Micah's life, and I watched as his Marine brothers were shot down. She took me through the varied forms of Jacquelena, starting with Jacey and how she'd died by Micah's side. The murder of that version of Bex, Pops' death and the funeral, back through all the issues Jacey had and the pain she survived, including the fire that killed her parents. Then we went to the previous lifetime, when Jeric and I were Ja'mai, a Union soul, and the agonizing moment when Enyxa Separated us. Then before, reliving all of the tragedies and horrors of our times.

Rebethannah and Nathayden, and Broderick and Anastasia were always present in the memories. Other couples, too, whom I couldn't identify now, but I wondered if they'd been part of the Sacred Seven—the *Original* Seven, as Enyxa had said. Amongst us all, we experienced the loss of parents, siblings at young ages, our own children, and each other. At least one of us was abused, raped, or murdered, or all three in each life cycle. We lost dear friends. We hurt other people. Other people harmed us. We even went back to another life, another world, another time when we'd been Ja'mai. Another agonizing Separation by Enyxa.

As she promised, we relived all of the bad times, experienced the pain—ours and others'—all over again. When I came out of it, my soul was so Dark and empty, the cold of this world became unnoticeable. I saw past Bex and Hayden, whose bodies were intertwined. I imagined their souls were, too, Bonding to help each other survive the horrors. Brock and I didn't have that luxury.

"No more. No more, no more, no more." Brock pled desperately under his breath, his hands clamped over his head as he rocked back and forth, oblivious to the rest of us.

His despair washed over me. My own rose to mix with it. He was right. We couldn't keep reliving the accident that killed his baby boy, let alone all of these other tragedies. I had a feeling we'd only seen a glimpse of what Enyxa had in store for us, and my heart and soul couldn't take any more. Staying strong was too hard. Too painful. Jeric's absence made me weak, and Enyxa would keep us apart for as long as it took. Would make us relive all the atrocities forever if we let her. Why go through all of that agony? Why try to survive when I knew in my soul that it was all in vain? We were lost forever now. No reason to fight that fact. Not when the Darkness was easy. Welcoming. Calling for me. I curled into a ball, closed my eyes, and gave in. Let it have me.

I drifted off into an unexpected peace.

"Oh, *hell* no!" Bex's voice pierced through the curtain of Darkness. It was distant at first, but she'd apparently returned to her body because it came clearer and firmer with each word she spoke. "You two get the fuck up. If you don't care about yourselves, at least think about Hayden and me stuck on this world by ourselves. And think about Asia and Jeric. They'll go Dark with you, right? Is that what you want, Leni?"

I groaned, wanting to protest, but she knew exactly what to say.

"No. Not my Jeric," I murmured, and I rolled over onto my side, too tired to stay upright.

Something cold clamped around my arm and shook me.

"Then get your sweet little ass up, and let's get the hell out of this place," Bex ordered. She tugged at me, forcing me back upright. "How do we do this? We haven't left the place where the Gate is, so how do we get it back?"

Thank God I didn't have to answer her, because I really didn't know and possessed no energy to think about it. Fortunately, the Gate lit up all around us as if responding to her need. I squeezed my eyes shut against the bright light as I listened to Bex and Hayden grow excited about an opening, and then deflated when Bex realized it wasn't Earth. They did this several times while Brock and I still sat on the ice, curled into ourselves.

"What happens if we stay in here until the appropriate hole opens up?" Hayden asked.

My head lolled side to side on my neck. "I dunno."

"Can we do that?" Bex asked. "Would it let us just stay in here?"

"Could just bring us back to the last world," I muttered. "Or take us to the Space Between."

"What's that? What happens there?"

"We die," Brock said flatly.

I didn't know if that was entirely true, but didn't have the energy to argue. I wondered instead if there was some way for us to get to the Space Between, and then if Brock and I could summon our other halves there. Of course, Brock was probably right and that would mean our physical bodies would have to die, but it could possibly mean our souls would be reunited. Our bodies were only temporary anyway.

The Space Between could be our last hope.

"Ohmagosh! That looks like the real Earth!" Bex squealed. "I've seen that place before, when I dated a guy in Tampa. I've been on that bridge!"

I peeled an eye open and peeked through. A familiar site of Tampa Bay and the surrounding city showed through the expanding hole. Both of my eyes popped fully open, and I crawled closer to get a better look. The Sunshine Skyway Bridge stretched across the bay to our left. The city sprawled out in front of us, beyond the water. We seemed to be right in the middle of the bay itself ... as though on an island.

"It can't be," I breathed. I reached behind for Brock. "Brock, look! Is it real? Is it *our* Earth?"

He didn't answer me. The hole opened wider, the world beyond became clearer, and I gasped at the sight straight ahead.

A rundown hotel. A big mansion sitting in the center of it. How could that possibly exist on any other world?

"Oh, my god! That's the Phoenix Manor! Come on!"

I reached behind me again, grabbed Brock's wrist, and sprang toward the hole.

CHAPTER 19

Jeric   THE FEELINGS WERE suffocating. The Darkness smothering. Vague and distant memories that I couldn't bring into focus and knew I didn't want to. The emotions that came along with them were more than enough, and they weren't mine. Not all of them anyway.

Asia must have been writing in the Book of Phoenix, because I woke up feeling her story again. Relived along with her the horror of the accident that killed Brock's son and mother. That shit brought on my own memories of the wreck that took my hearing and the lives of my sister and parents, but I somehow summoned the power to walk down the hall to check on Asia. The Book lay on the floor in the middle of the hallway outside her room, and she refused to open the door.

I'd picked up the Book and barely made it back to my own room before succumbing to the sadness and the Darkness. That's when the onslaught began. Like a fucking whip of emotions, one snap against the flesh of my soul after another. Pain, loss, sadness, depression, fear, horror ... crack, crack, CRACK.

And then the peace of Darkness. The beautiful serenity. So easy to sink into ...

No! I wouldn't give in. I wouldn't let the Darkness win. I'd hang on, if not for myself, then for Leni.

I forced myself off the floor where I'd been sitting against the wall with my knees to my chest and walked over to the dresser where the iPod was. Music had always been my refuge when I was younger. Where I went when I needed to escape the real world. How I dealt with being a teen trying to figure out life. I'd fallen out of the habit as soon as I lost my hearing, but had picked it up again in the last few days.

With the earphones stuck in my ears, I tapped the shuffle button and sat on the bed. I leaned against the headboard and closed my eyes, shutting out the rest of the world. I tried to clear my head and lose myself in the lyrics, the harmony, the riffs of the guitar, and rhythm of the drums ... the individual notes the singer held. Several songs played before the weight on my chest lifted.

And then Closer by Nine Inch Nails came on.

The image of Leni dancing immediately popped into my head and played behind my eyelids. She looked at me with those sea-green eyes, holding her gaze on my face as her arms lifted and swung to the beat, her shoulders moved to and fro, her tits strained against her top, and her hips swayed side to side. Her strong legs moved her body, and she did that move strippers do—squatting down and coming up slowly, her pelvis making slow circles, her perfect ass sliding back and forth, in and out of reach.

She danced her way closer to me, circled her arms around my neck and rocked side to side, just close enough for her tits to brush against my chest. Then she turned and backed into me, moving that round globe of her ass against my dick. I imagined placing my hands on her hips, stroking my fingers over her thighs ... because that's all I could do. Imagine.

She felt so close, yet was worlds away.

I grabbed my tablet and banged out a few lines of a song I'd started for her, but the need to touch her, to feel her body against mine again became overwhelming. If I couldn't be with her, I could at least be surrounded by her things. Two minutes later, I was banging on Asia's door.

"What?" she snapped as she threw open the door. "Can't you take a hint? Besides the fact that it's seven o'clock in the fucking morning?"

Was it? I hadn't even noticed the time.

"Can I borrow your car?" I asked. A couple of Guardians had retrieved the Camaro from where we'd abandoned it on the side of I-4 in our rush to bring Bex to the Gate. Asia's brows scrunched, and her lips parted, but I butted in. "I'm going to Lake Haven. Need to pick up a few things from the camper."

She blinked. Again. Rubbed the sleep out of her eyes. Another moment passed as she processed what I meant, not buying my excuse. "Jeric, the Lakari—"

"Fuck 'em. Let them come for me. I'm ninety percent there anyway. And when they do, I'd rather be in Leni's camper than this prison."

"What if they come back? Brock and Leni?"

I leveled my gaze on her. "Do you really think that's going to happen?"

My hope had all but deteriorated, and I sure as hell was sick of sitting around this place doing nothing but waiting and growing more miserable by the second.

Asia had no answer for me, except to say, "I'm driving."

She needed a few minutes to put on some real clothes and pull herself a little more together than how she'd answered the door—looking like a hermit. As I waited, the anticipation built, and by the time she was ready, the urge to get out of here had grown so strong, I nearly opened the window and made the eight-story leap to the ground. But since Leni and I weren't together, I couldn't rely on my Phoenix abilities and strengths to survive the jump. So I tore down the stairs, out the door, and to Asia's Camaro with her right on my heels.

She slid her big sunglasses on her face to cover her red, swollen eyes, and then peeled out of the parking lot. She pushed the Camaro to its potential as we headed north toward the Florida-Georgia state line, finally away from the Phoenix manor and the watchful eyes of the other Guardians. They'd shit a brick if they knew we'd left on our own, but then again, maybe they didn't care. Maybe they'd come to the conclusion Asia and I had that the odds of us surviving were approaching zero. And once we were gone, they could return to business as usual and not have to worry about choosing us over the rest of Earth.

When Asia turned into the RV park and I saw the camper, I had a moment of thinking I couldn't deal with going near it. But by the time she parked in front of it, the moment had passed. I needed to be inside it as badly as I needed to be inside Leni herself. I jumped out of the car, and Asia took off for the apartment down the road that she and Brock shared.

I didn't have the key, so I had to jimmy the lock with a credit card. Once inside, I flew to the bedroom, belly-flopped onto the bed, and gathered the blanket and pillows to my face. I rolled around in them, wishing they were her. One hand fisted around something softer than the sheets—the peach-colored camisole she'd slept in that had been stuffed under her pillow. I pressed it against my nose and inhaled my girl's scent deeply, trying to soak it all the way in so it could fill my blood and saturate my bones. I closed my eyes. My arms flopped outward. I imagined the Darkness taking me away like this, enveloping me in its promise of silence and peace.

But reality didn't cooperate.

Only minutes into my solitude, sharp pain wracked through my gut. My thighs clenched up to my chest, and my shoulders pulled down. When I thought the spasm had passed, I barely moved when another shot through me. Like a giant hook speared into my stomach and yanked on by some unseen force. Yanking me back toward the manor.

Fuck.

I didn't want to go back. I wanted to fight it. But the pain only worsened the longer I lay there, curled on my side, moaning. I managed to roll to my knees and push myself up, untangling myself from the sheets. A car horn blew outside, not right outside but not as far as the highway either. I glanced out the window. The yellow Camaro was fishtailing toward the camper. Asia must have felt the painful draw to the manor, too.

I grabbed Leni's backpack sitting in the corner of the room and stuffed it with as much as I could manage to gather. Some clothes for me. A few of her things, including the camisole. The car honked again.

"Jeric," Asia hollered. My gaze flew around the room, and then I backed toward the kitchen and the door. Nothing caught my eye that could be helpful. Another spasm tore through my gut, and I ran out to the car. "Can't ... stay ... have to ... go ... back."

She could barely talk, panting her way through the words as her face screwed up in pain.

"Are you sure you can drive?" I asked, and in answer, her body curled into itself and her head pressed on the steering wheel's horn. I pulled her back, then hopped out of the car and ran around to the driver's side. She'd already moved over to the passenger seat. I was barely in and backing out when a dark form dropped in front of the car. Other Lakari dropped around us, taking their human figures. "Hang on."

I yanked the steering wheel to spin the car and at the same time threw the transmission into gear. We hit a couple of the Lakari, who shattered and disintegrated. The others returned to their Dark soul forms and followed us, knowing how vulnerable we were. On total gut instinct, I turned right out of the RV park instead of heading for the highway.

"Where ... are ... you going?" Asia asked. One of her arms held tightly against her stomach, and her free hand gripped the edge of the seat, her knuckles bone-white.

I didn't answer her. As soon as the Lakari thought they had us, the manor had lost its pull on me. Instead, I felt the need to go in this direction. We passed through town, and then I turned right, then left. I made the turns on total gut feeling.

"What the hell, Jeric?" Asia demanded as I stood on the brake at a sudden dead end, nothing but trees and water ahead of us. "It's swamp land. And now we're trapped!"

A six-foot tall, chain-link fence topped with barbed wire edged the trees in front of us with a red and white sign hanging on it: "No Trespassing by Order of the Lake Haven City Council. These springs are closed to the public." I had no idea why I needed to come here, but my stomach didn't hurt as bad and Asia could breathe better, so there must have been a reason. She was twisted in her seat, looking through the back window with wide eyes, so I glanced into the rearview mirror. Several Shadowmen stood at the other end of the road, the only way out of here.

We were in no shape to fight.

"Why are they just standing there?" Asia whispered.

"No fucking clue ..." I'd barely finished the word when a new hook stabbed into my gut. Asia whimpered.

"The ... manor," she choked out.

The need to be here disappeared as quickly as it had come, and I had no idea what we were doing here. No idea why the hell the Shadowmen were at the end of the road. No idea how we were going to drive back to the manor through this pain.

I gripped the gearshift and pulled it into reverse, then stomped on the gas. The car charged down the road, and I spun it again. A large, dark shape barreled down the other road, about to cross in front of us. I slammed on the brake, and so did the driver coming toward us. The Shadowmen didn't fly back into their spirit forms, though. Instead, more dropped down to the road, circling the Camaro. I kept my foot on the brake, but gunned the engine. Sand spewed from the back tires. If I could get through the Shadowmen, there was just enough room to pass the truck that had almost hit us. Surely they'd leave the human in there alone.

Pain charged through me again, though. Blinding this time. I couldn't say if it had been Asia or me who'd had the presence of mind to put the car into park. We were both screaming. The Darkness pressed in on us from all sides of the car, the dark of night as the Shadowmen swarmed in on us. My eyes barely caught a white streak through the Darkness before they squeezed shut from the agony. The sounds of nails scraping on glass were followed by siren shrieks. I clamped my hands over my ears. The car door opened. The Lakari were coming for us, excited for their long-awaited success. I leaned toward the console and blindly kicked out at whatever tried to make its way in, my last ditch effort before succumbing to the inevitable. I was surprised when my foot connected with something solid.

"Can't believe I'm saving your stupid asses." A male voice but heavily laced with a feminine edge. Mat. My eyes sprang open. The Darkness was gone. "Yeah, we followed you. Scared the fuckers off with a little help from that cat. Now move over."

Asia and I exchanged a glance. She cringed with another bout of pain, then moved between the seats into the back.

"You're too damn big to crawl over," Mat said with an exaggerated sigh, and he pulled me out of the driver's side and walked me around the car before shoving me into the passenger's seat. He waved at the driver of the truck that had almost hit us—Kel—before sliding into the driver's seat. "Told him I get to drive this bitch if we were doing this. You know, all you had to do was tell us you wanted to come up here. We would have guarded you."

"We didn't *want* chaperones," I growled as I stared out the window, my arms crossed over my stomach. We were already headed back to the highway. The Darkness of the Lakari stayed with us overhead, but with Kel and Mat nearby, we weren't as vulnerable as we had been.

"You apparently *needed* them, though."

"Depends on how you look at it," Asia said quietly from the backseat.

Mat glanced at her in the rearview mirror. "Honey, don't you two go gettin' suicidal on us. We're doing everything we can to help you out. If we're doin' it for nothin', that will seriously throw my panties in a bunch."

We drove back to Tampa in silence. Asia and I were silent, anyway. Mat turned on the radio and belted out song after song. I wished I were deaf again. I pressed my forehead against the window and scowled the whole way back. Each mile we came closer to the manor brought more relief from the pain, until it returned to the same agony I'd been living with since Leni disappeared. I'd become used to it, I supposed, because I didn't think anything could be worse until we'd been so far away. Or maybe the Darkness had set in and numbed it some. Either way, this was at least tolerable.

We were back at the manor by late afternoon. I trudged my way upstairs to my room, threw Leni's backpack on the bed, and pulled out the camisole. Without turning the lights on, I lay on the bed fully clothed, facing the ceiling, and held the little peach top to my nose. I breathed her in as I drifted off.

"*Jeric.*"

What the hell? I bolted upright. Morning sun streamed through the crack in the curtains, and Leni's voice came loud and clear in my head. I knew the sense of smell was powerful, but this was more than a memory. I could feel it in my soul. I could feel *her* in my soul.

"*Jeric, baby, I'm here. We made it!*"

Yesterday's flight down the stairs was slower than a turtle compared to how I bolted down the stairs now and out to the bay. Super-fucking-man wouldn't have anything on me. I felt

Leni out there, close but not close enough. Even from here, I could see the light of the Gate shining through the water. I ran into the bay, and when it became too deep to run, I prepared to swim.

"Leni!" I yelled before I sucked in a breath to take the dive down.

But a huge black shape soared through the water toward me. Not until it broke the surface did I learn that it wasn't a single shape, but several. Dozens of Lakari flew upwards, searching for their comrades in the sky. They didn't have to go far—the Lakari were always overhead. Their appearance was like a signal, and all of them swarmed down.

I ran back for the shore where I'd be able to fight better on solid ground. The earth quaked underneath my feet. Guardians poured out of the manor, but Asia already stood on the edge of the bay. As I ran out of the water and across the beach to the grassy lawn of the manor, the Lakari screeched overhead, the sound like fingernails on a chalkboard. I turned around and looked up to see them all meld into a large, black cloud that soared away.

"Do you feel them?" Asia asked, running up to me. She wore a man's shirt, Brock's I assumed, that reached her knees and tight legging things underneath. Her voice was filled with more hope and excitement than I'd ever heard. A complete turnaround from how she'd been when we'd arrived back yesterday.

"Yeah. I heard her, too, you know—" I twirled a finger around my head and peach fabric flapped between my fingers, spraying drops of water. "In my head ..."

My voice trailed off as I opened my fist with Leni's camisole still in it. Asia looked down at the soaking wet material, and the look on her face meant she knew exactly what it was.

She tugged at the hem of her shirt. "Looks like you had the same idea I did. I've been wearing Brock's shirt since we got back."

My jaw clenched.

"Yeah, well, I'm not *wearing* it, Asia," I muttered as I stuffed the top into my back pocket.

We waited on the edge of the water along with the other Phoenix for news from the Guardians who had been on duty. The longer we waited, the more the truth settled in. I *had* felt Leni's presence in this world again.

But I didn't any more.

"Just the Lakari came through," Kel announced a few minutes later. His eyes found Asia and me, and he shook his head.

"Bullshit," I said.

"We felt them here," Asia added. "What happened to them?"

"There were only the Lakari," Kel said. "They had to work to get the Gate closed because more were trying to push through. More of those monsters, too."

"No!" I growled, and I pushed my way through the crowd of Guardians that had gathered to stand in front of Kel. "They were here, damn it!"

"Dude, I'm sorry. They weren't. Only a horde of Darkness trying to push its way through."

I grabbed the front of his shirt and lifted him nearly off his feet, although he was about as big as me. "She was fucking here, Kel. You're in charge of those idiots down there. What the fuck happened, goddammit?"

His hands shoved against my chest, and since his Twin Flame was in this world with him, he was much stronger than I was. I stumbled backward several feet, forced to let go of him. "Back the hell off, man. I don't know what you two think happened, but nobody but Lakari came through that Gate. Didn't you see them?"

I wanted to swing at him, but a small hand wrapped over my wrist, stopping me.

"You're not helping," Asia snapped at me. "They're gone. They probably weren't even here in the first place. The stupid Book or Enyxa was just fucking with us."

A growl rumbled low in my throat as I glared at Kel, then his mate Mat, and then the other Guardians who were gathered around. Asia was right, though—if Leni had been here on this world if even for a second, she was gone now. The agony in my soul because of her absence confirmed that fact. I pushed my way past Kel and stomped for the manor, my soaked shoes squawking the whole way.

"Jeric?" Melinda called to me. My eyes skittered over to where she stood by the doors to the mansion. "If Lakari keep getting through even with the Gate sealed, the decision will have to be made. If you want to put it to a vote again ..."

I let her trail off, ignoring her and refusing to acknowledge her message. This was a bad time to be reminding me that we'd have to collapse the Gates if we couldn't keep the Lakari out of our world. I strode right past her and down the hall for the stairwell. Asia caught up with me and climbed the eight stories by my side, although we didn't speak for several flights.

"We have to figure that damn Book out," I said as we passed the fifth floor. "You read some of the symbols on it before, right?"

"They don't tell me anything but our past names. I can't even read them all."

"Well, try harder, damn it."

"Fuck you, Jeric. You try! I've had the Book the last few nights, and it only brought me misery. It's your turn." She stormed up another flight. "It was *your* other half who planted the clues, remember?"

"We don't know that for sure. And *you've* read them better than anyone except her." I was doing everything I could to suppress the anger that remained from the news Kel had delivered, but I wasn't doing a good job at it. Asia didn't deserve to be at the receiving end, but she was holding her own on dishing it back out. I needed to calm down before I punched the wall—or drove her into punching me. We climbed the last flight as I swallowed down the anger that persisted in bubbling up. "You realize what's happening, right? We need to know if that Book can bring them back because the way things are going, I'll have to order to collapse the Gates. Sooner rather than later."

"Then you figure it out, Jeric. I'm done with it all, especially with that stupid-ass Book." Asia slammed the door to the eighth floor open and stalked down the hall to her room.

I turned in the opposite direction toward my room. As soon as I was inside, I peeled my wet t-shirt off and pulled the camisole out of my back pocket. They hit the fiberglass with a splat when I tossed them into the tub before pushing my way out of my soggy jeans and boxer briefs. A long, hard run would have helped my mood, but I couldn't leave the manor, and going down to the treadmills in the gym meant dealing with people, which would only fuel the anger.

Asia could have been right about the Book or Enyxa messing with our heads and making us think we felt our Twin Flames when we didn't, but I couldn't help but think the Guardians who'd been on duty had fucked up and locked them out. If the Gates were sealed, how could the Lakari get through on their own? Guardians would have had to create the opening, and if we hadn't done it on our side, then someone must have on the other.

Unless the Dark side really was becoming powerful enough to break our seal.

I turned on the shower as hot as it would go and stepped in. The physical sting of the hot spray gave me something to focus on besides the anger. Once it washed away, the full force of what it all meant slammed down on me. I dropped to my knees in the tub and picked up the peach-colored top. It no longer held Leni's scent, washed out and lost down the drain. Just as I was losing her, slipping away like the water through my fingers.

I crossed my arms over my stomach, leaned over my knees, and did what I hadn't done since I'd awoken from the coma and learned my whole family had died: I sobbed my ass off as the water poured down on me until it turned ice cold. Cold as my soul was quickly becoming.

CHAPTER 20

Leni BLACKNESS FILLED THE hole in the Gate. Darkness flew past us. Just as I'd crossed through the hole into our own world with Brock, Bex, and Hayden right behind me, I slammed into something solid. Like a rubber ball bouncing off a hard wall, we ricocheted backward through the sea of Dark souls that had suddenly swarmed in, and against the far wall of the Gate, which pushed us off into another direction. My body cartwheeled and somersaulted around the cylinder. I lost myself in the Darkness that had filled it, unable to gain any kind of orientation. I screamed and reached out, thankful to latch onto both Brock and Bex. We careened around again, spun, and soared out into a gray light.

We landed with a splash into freezing cold water. I kicked my way to the surface, and the others popped up around me. At least we'd all made it, wherever we were. The sky was an overcast gray, and the water was a darker slate color. The rough waves told me it was a sea—not a pond or lake, and definitely not Tampa Bay. City buildings stood in the distance on our right, a grouping of tall wind turbines rose out of the water ahead of us, and what appeared to be a castle or fort of some kind stood on the shore to our left, the closer one that we swam for.

"I am so sick of this!" I screamed as we waded out of the water. "We were there! I *felt* him! What the hell happened?"

Anger consumed me, and I held onto it, because otherwise it would be a deep depression that would suck me down its black hole. And I didn't know how many more times I could climb out of that. How many more times I could fight off the Darkness.

"They closed the Gate on us," Brock guessed, his voice a growl. "Idiots thought we were Lakari."

"Oy! Where did you lot come from?" A dark-haired man dressed in black pants and a thick, gray coat stood on the beach in front of us. I thought his thick accent could be British … like I thought Hayden's could be Australian. Possibly, but not likely.

"Where are we?" Hayden asked.

The man cocked his head as we all shivered before him, and then he ran off, over a rock piling.

"What an asshole," Brock muttered. I glared at him. I couldn't disagree, but his attitude was grating on me. Probably because it fed my own shitty mood, which only made me angrier with him.

"Come 'ed," the man yelled. "Come with me!"

We hesitated at first, but this very human-like being seemed to be our only hope of learning where we were. So we climbed up and over the pilings to find a parking lot with a red van sitting in it and the man standing at the open rear doors, pulling something from the back cargo area. He looked human and spoke English, although heavily accented, but the van didn't look exactly right to me. It was taller and narrower than the vans we had at home, and the steering wheel was on the wrong side of the cab. My heart leapt, though, at the white lettering on the passenger door: Hughes Fishery of Liverpool.

"Liverpool?" I asked. "That's where we are?"

"Did you get turned 'round on your swim? This is Fort Perch Rock in New Brighton," the man said. Did he really think we'd been out for a swim in these kinds of clothes and this kind of weather? He nodded to the distant shore with the city buildings as he handed me a gray wool blanket. "Liverpool's on the other side of the Mersey."

I looked up at the old stone fortress in front of us as I wrapped the blanket around my shoulders, although I could barely feel the cold from the adrenaline suddenly shooting through my system. I contained my excitement, though, not wanting to get my hopes built up that we'd actually made it to Earth after all.

"England?" I hedged.

"Of course. What other Liverpool is there?" He handed blankets to the others.

"As in home of the Beatles?" Brock asked. Even his tone, which had been so dark and heavy lately, had lightened.

"The one and only. What's da matta with you lot? Where'd you think ye'ra?"

"Who's the queen?" Bex asked.

He looked at her as though she asked what color the sky was. "Queen Elizabeth. Who else?"

Could we really be on Earth? *Our* world? Could we be so lucky that when they blocked us at the Tampa Gate, they knocked us only slightly off course?

Several figures appeared out of nowhere and surrounded us, all dressed in black that provided a steep contrast to their snow-white skin. Three of the dozen or so were women.

"She's probably not queen any more," one of the newcomers said, his voice deep and gravelly. "Me thinks me mates ate her last night."

He tossed his blond head back and laughed, exposing long fangs that jutted where his eyeteeth should have been. Then, moving faster than a blur, he held our rescuer pinned in his arms, and his head dove for his captive's throat, shredding it like a dog attacking a small animal and lapping up the blood.

Bex and I both screamed until Hayden clamped his hands over our mouths. We fell silent immediately, and he let go.

"OHMAGAWD!" Bex shrieked as soon as he did. "Are ya'll *vampires?*"

If I hadn't been watching the gore with my own eyes, I might have laughed. These people weren't the Lakari, but I could feel the intense Darkness of their souls, their auras almost solid black. Brock must have, too, because he dropped his blanket as quickly as I did mine. We both charged at our deranged attackers. We moved fast, but they moved even faster. I was able to slam my fist into a woman's throat, but instead of her form shattering like glass or disintegrating into smoke, it felt more like a rock-solid wall. My hand crumpled under the force. She grabbed for me, but I threw her off and spun out of her reach. Only to find myself in someone else's arms. In less than two heartbeats, we were all pinned by one of these monsters, their long fangs poised at our throats, where they all froze. I tried to fight, but I couldn't. I couldn't kick, scratch, or squirm my way out. I couldn't move at all.

My whole body had become completely paralyzed.

A green light shot across the parking lot and hit the woman holding Bex. She dropped to the ground like a dead weight, and then disappeared into thin air with a faint popping sound. Bex didn't move a hair, though, also paralyzed. We all remained frozen in place as more people, dressed in black leather outfits like some kind of superheroes—or maybe villains—spread out before us. With only six of them, they were outnumbered at least two-to-one, but they somehow had complete control over the situation.

A guy not much older than us seemed to be their leader, and if he were chosen by appearances, I could see why. He had an inhuman beauty to him, even if his sandy brown hair was a little longer than I preferred. It somehow made him all the more otherworldly. Of course, we obviously were on another world than Earth, but looking at the others we'd met so far, he was a prime specimen for this place. His leather pants and black shirt hugged him tightly to show every muscle, and if I thought Jeric and Brock were built nicely, they had nothing on this guy. He had the form of a god, and with the fierce look in his eyes, he could have easily been a warrior angel or a beautiful demon.

He stood a few yards in front of the others, his arm held straight out in front of him, his palm facing us. From what I thought were green eyes, his sparking gaze swept over the group, back and forth and side to side, as his body remained tense and alert. On either side of him stood two more men—a tall blond and a shorter but powerfully built bald man. A green light, like the one that had soared across the lot a moment ago, danced over the blond man's fingers. Next to him stood a tall, perfectly built woman with long, snowy hair but a young and gorgeous face and skin as white as those who'd originally attacked us. On the other side of the leader and the bald guy was a small, blond woman and a tall, thin, dark-haired woman whose eyes I swore glowed yellow like a cat's.

"*You know what can happen if you try to fight us.*" The female voice with an American-like accent sounded in my mind, and nobody's lips had moved. What kind of world was this? They obviously had special powers. Were they like the Phoenix Guardians, but of their Gates? We'd only been able to mind-talk in certain situations, when our souls were projected and when Jeric had been deaf. "*Give them a chance, my love.*"

The beautiful man's hand dropped. My body felt released.

"Stupid fools. Their blood smells too sweet to resist." One of the original attackers—the woman I'd thrown off—jumped for me again.

The others lunged for us, too, like a den of lions on a small group of antelope. Brock and I called on our Phoenix abilities to fight them off, but Hayden and Bex didn't have our strength and speed. In fact, we were barely able to defend ourselves, our powers too weak since we were Separated from our other halves. We punched and kicked with our limbs blurring, but our opponents were stronger, harder, and faster, and no matter where our blows landed, they hurt us worse than them. Someone's fangs scraped across my wrist, and I immediately went limp. Bex screamed next to me.

Then one by one, the attackers began disappearing with barely audible popping noises.

When they were all gone, the other group remained, the man's palm pointed directly at me. Bex, Hayden, and Brock stood close to me, all of us with our hands up in surrender.

"*Wait! Not them!*" The young-sounding female voice again.

The guy cocked his head. Another *pop* sounded, and a young woman, auburn-haired and dressed like the others in black leathers and combat boots, suddenly appeared next to him. She placed her hand lightly on the guy's arm, and he dropped it and stood up straight, and then she turned her gaze on us. Sheesh. Talk about inhumanly beautiful. She looked like an angel with the prettiest, biggest, almond-shaped brown eyes I'd ever seen. I practically wanted to take a knee in front of her.

"You're different," she said, and she had the same voice as the one that had been speaking in my head, but less tinny sounding.

She walked up to me. My friends gathered closer, tightening our group. She stood a little shorter than me, and her body was only slightly smaller than mine, but power emanated from her soul, waves of it crashing over us. And something else—a goodness like none other. If Enyxa was the epitome of Darkness, this young woman was the Light.

"Ya'll aren't gonna kill us like you did them, are you?" Bex asked, her voice pleading. "We *are* different. I swear to God and baby Jesus we're nothing like them."

"Don't worry. We didn't kill them," said the small blond woman who stood by the bald man.

"Then what happened to them?" Hayden demanded.

"They did what they always do when we arrive," said the tall blond guy, the corner of his mouth lifting. "Ran away scared."

Bex let out a small sound. I couldn't blame her. If those rock-solid people—one of whom had ripped another man's throat out—were scared, who were *these* people?

"But are you going to kill *us*?" I asked, trying to sound braver than my insides felt. My stomach ached as though it'd tied itself into a big, tight knot.

The girl in front of us tilted her head and gave us a small smile. "We don't kill unless necessary. Only if there's no hope at all. And I sense hope in all of you. Not a lot, but it's there."

"Who are you?" I demanded.

"I'm wondering the same about you," she said. "You're obviously American. And I sense ... something ... not entirely evil, but ... it *is* tainting you, isn't it?"

A chill ran down my spine. How did she know that? And if we weren't on Earth, how did she know we were American? Were their countries here that similar to ours?

"Alexis," the beautiful man growled, and even when it held a warning, he had a bone-melting voice. Almost as nice as Jeric's singing voice, but not quite.

"It's okay, Tristan," she said, turning her head to glance over her shoulder at him. "They're not Daemoni. You know that."

"I don't know *what* they are," he said as he crossed the few paces to stand next to her. He towered over her—over all of us, even Brock and Hayden.

Alexis turned back to us, eyeing us carefully. "Yeah, you're not Amadis, either, and not exactly Norman."

"What the hell are Daemoni, Amadis, and Norman?" Brock rumbled. I wanted to stomp on his foot. We seriously did not want to pick a fight with these people. They had unusual powers we didn't stand a chance against, especially when two of us were only halves of our wholes.

"Daemoni are Satan's minions. The vampires you just met are some of them," Alexis said, and she smiled as my eyes about popped out of my head.

"Ohmagosh," Bex whispered. "I was right? Vampires? You have real, live vampires on this world?"

"They're not exactly 'live'," the blond guy responded with a smirk. "But yeah, you just met some. And since the secret's out, we may as well tell you. You happen to be looking at a were-tiger, a witch, a were-crocodile, a warlock, and another vampire."

He pointed to each of them as he said it, starting at our left with the tall, thin woman, pointing to himself when he said warlock, and finishing with the beautiful blonde next to him. I noticed he didn't define Alexis and Tristan.

"So what are you two?"

"We lead the Amadis army. The Daemoni are trying to take over the world for Satan, and we're trying to stop them and protect the Normans—the normal humans. And with the way you two moved—" Her dark eyes bounced from me to Brock and back again. "—you obviously aren't Norman. So *what* are you?"

I bit my lip, then simply blurted it out because I didn't know what else to say. "We're the Phoenix, Guardians of Earth's Gates."

Her brows pushed together. "What Gates?"

"The Gates between worlds."

She looked over at Tristan. The way they moved with each other and looked into the other's eyes, they obviously had a deep connection. Soul mates? Twin Flames?

"I don't know," Tristan said. "As far as I know, there are no Gates to the Otherworld."

"Owen?" Alexis asked.

The blond guy behind them shook his head. "Dude, I'm clueless."

"There must be Gates here," I said. "That's how we got here in the first place."

"Right," Bex said. "We just need to find that one again, go through it to get back to Earth, and we'll be out of all ya'll's hair. No harm, no foul."

"Um ... you *are* on Earth," Alexis said, placing her hands on her hips.

Two more small bodies popped into sight from nowhere, both of them female with big blue eyes and white hair, one with traces of purple and the other with shades of pink. How could we be on Earth when there were all these creatures and people who appear out of thin air and disappear as easily? Either she was lying, or we'd lost our sanity to the Darkness.

"We've got this," said the one with the pink hair to Alexis.

The other one waved her hand toward all of them. "Go on. You lot need to save the world, remember?"

More English accents. I was completely confused.

"Great," Owen muttered. "Just what we need—faeries."

My gaze flew to him. He gave me a nod, his sapphire blue eyes smiling, as though saying, *Yeah, we have those, too.*

"Stacey and Debbie, right?" Alexis asked the ... *faeries.* Now I knew we were definitely not on Earth. I didn't care what this Alexis chick said. Maybe they called this world Earth, but it wasn't *the* Earth. Not *my* home, thank God. The Lakari and everyday humans were enough to deal with.

"Yes, I'm Debbie," said the one with the purplish hair.

"Stacey." The other one dipped into a curtsy.

"Wotch her. She can be naughty," Debbie said, although the way she eyed Hayden, I thought she might be pretty naughty herself. Bex tensed next to me, and I grabbed her arm as a warning.

"Not naughty. Just fun." The twinkle in Stacey's eye confirmed this, especially as her gaze lingered over Brock.

"There's nothing fun about this," Alexis replied, and the faeries scowled as their attention was pulled from the men. "We felt a ripple in the veil and came to check it out. Do you know what happened?"

"It's nothing you need to worry about," Debbie said, edging her way closer to us. "We'll take care of them."

"How are they faerie business?" Tristan asked, his voice harsh and demanding. I was definitely sure I wouldn't want to be on his bad side. "And why should we trust you with them?"

He sounded upset with the faeries, who looked at each other pointedly.

"It's not exactly faerie business," Stacey said. "It's Otherworld business. They caused the ripple in the veil when they passed through. We need to take them back through it." Her blue-eyed gaze turned on us. "What you call the Gates."

"The hell you are," Tristan said. "They're under our protection now." His eyes fell on me—they were hazel, not entirely green like I'd thought before. Gold flecks dotted the green around the pupil, making them unusually stunning. "Where do you want to go? We'll take you."

I swallowed. "To Earth."

He opened his mouth, but Debbie jumped in. "To *their* Earth."

The force of everyone's gaze landed on her with these three words. She pursed her lips together and wrung her small hands.

"She means to their dimension," Stacey said.

"What the hell does that mean?" demanded the snowy-haired woman who'd been standing back with Owen.

"Hush," Owen muttered to the woman he'd called a vampire. Wow. He had balls.

"It's a good question," Alexis said.

Debbie winked at her. "And *you* know the answer."

Alexis cocked her head, her reddish-brown ponytail falling over her shoulder. She squinted as she seemed to be thinking hard about something. The way Tristan studied her and narrowed his own eyes, I wondered if they were mind-talking.

"*Really?*" she said eventually. "There are multiple Earths in different dimensions?"

"Alternate universes," Tristan said with understanding in his voice. "That's a new one, even for me. I had no idea the theory was true."

The thin, dark-haired woman with yellow cat eyes spoke up. "With God, anything is possible, isn't it?"

"Of course you'd say that, Sheree," the white-blond vampire muttered with an eye roll. "Always gotta bring God into it—"

"Enough," Alexis snapped, cutting off the vampire. She turned her attention back to the faeries. "So that's what's going on here? There are really alternate universes and worlds? That's possible?"

"The possibilities beyond this world and this life you know are endless, young one," Debbie confirmed.

"It's cool, though, chick," Stacey said. "You're the same kinda. You defend your people and worlds. Your enemies appear to you differently, but they're all on the same side—the evil side."

"It's curious that you ever met," Debbie said. "You're really not supposed to. Crossing dimensions is nearly impossible and leads to this confusion. It's a bit awkward, isn't it?"

"Awkward? These people are bat-shit *crazy*," Bex whispered for only us to hear.

Several people's mouths twitched, fighting smiles as if they'd actually heard her, though. Maybe they had. They had different powers than the Phoenix, but heightened senses would be logical for us to share. Bex must have realized this because she stiffened next to me.

"Can we please just go home?" she pled, her voice overly loud and extra sweet now. "We don't want to overstay our welcome."

"Did you make this happen?" Tristan accused of the faeries, ignoring Bex's plea.

Debbie's hand went to her chest, and her blue eyes widened innocently. "Wot? Us? No!"

"No, not us," Stacey said, "but if we don't get them back to their dimension, they and their world will go tits up in a hurry."

"You can take them back to their dimension and their Earth through the Otherworld?" Alexis clarified.

"We can get them to their dimension. From there, they'll have to find their own way to their Earth," Debbie answered.

Bex and Brock both groaned. I suppressed my own complaint. Stacey had practically called us peers, but I felt intimidated by Alexis and Tristan. I didn't want to look any weaker than we already did, although internally I was throwing a temper tantrum about having to deal with the Gate again. Like Bex, I just wanted to go home.

"Come now," Debbie said, curling her arm around Hayden's and stroking his muscles. "Oh, aren't you strong? And so handsome. Maybe I won't let you go but will take you home instead."

Bex let out a low snarl.

"*Faeries*," Tristan warned, his voice low and threatening.

Debbie sighed, and then used her free hand to grab Bex. "You, too, dear. Come with us, and we'll take you back to where you came from."

She started off toward the freezing water, tugging Hayden and Bex along with her. My insides waged an internal battle, refusing to enter any more water or to freeze my ass off again, but I fought it and started off, too.

"Hold on," I said, turning back to Alexis. "What did you mean that you don't kill? You don't destroy the Dark souls?"

"Only if there's no hope. But there's almost always hope, if you look for it. Unless they've completely given into the evil, you might have to search hard, but it's there. And we *have* to show mercy to those souls, no matter what they've done, or we're no better than them. We lead them back to the good side. That's our job. Is that yours?"

"Sort of. We lead them back to love and Light."

She gave me a smile. "Same thing, right?"

"Yeah." I nodded and returned her grin. "I guess it is. It was, uh, good to meet you."

"Definitely."

"Very ... interesting," Tristan agreed.

I gave them a little wave, and then turned to catch up with Debbie, Hayden, and Bex. Brock followed me, Stacey's arm draped around his waist and her free hand petting his muscular arm as they walked. Brock neither encouraged nor dismissed her. He was in his own Dark world again. Thank God and sweet baby Jesus, as Bex would say, that the faeries didn't force us to return to the icy water. Once we reached the edge of the shore where we'd first arrived, they circled their arms around us, clasped hands, and lifted their arms upward.

The world—this Earth of a different dimension—disappeared and a blinding light surrounded us.

"Cheers," one of the faeries said, and that was the last we saw or heard of them.

I felt like a penny sucked up in a vacuum, being pulled forcefully through a tube with no control of where I went. My body bounced up against some kind of wall and ricocheted off like before. I hoped that meant we were back in the Gate. If only I could see. If only I could find the opening to Earth—*our* Earth. The one where my Twin Flame waited. The only place I would ever feel complete.

Darkness surrounded us instead of the blinding light of the Gate as we continued traveling through the vacuum. Then a light began to shine from far away, growing closer by the second. A prism of colors came into view—what looked like Jacey's version of the Space Between. My heart raced at the thought of going there, but we blasted on past it, unable to stop even if we wanted to, and nothing but blackness engulfed us again.

Until we finally landed on a cold, hard surface. Ice. My vision came slow to me, and when it did, I could no longer suppress the temper tantrum.

"NOOOO!" I screamed at the top of my lungs, stomping my foot on the frozen floor that glowed blue from within. "Why *here*? Why the fuck this god-awful place again?"

Anywhere else. How many other millions of worlds could we have gone to instead of here? I would have even taken Erde over this world. At least there was light, as miserable and gray as the place was. The screaming monsters were terrifying, but at least there was food. There were trees and the ability to build a fire for warmth. The people there were completely Dark or close to it, but there *were* people. And not all had succumbed. The world hadn't totally given into the Darkness. Not like here, where there was no hope left.

"You're here because this is where I want you."

I spun to find Enyxa standing in the depths of the ice-coated cavern, still wearing the black suit that looked painted on and her spiky-heeled, thigh-high boots. I jumped and soared across the small room at her. Brock somehow beat me to her and tackled her to the floor. I landed on my feet and slid several inches, and I had to leap over them before they steamrolled me down.

Brock yelled nonsensical, angry sounds as he swung his fist at her. She caught his arm in her hand, and he immediately fell still. His face twisted with torture, and his body collapsed to the ground as he screamed with a terror I never wanted to experience. But I didn't have a choice.

Enyxa brought us down with the memory of how she'd Separated us, making the pain as she ripped our souls into two clearer than ever.

"The Darkness is thorough here, isn't it?" she asked as we all lay writhing on the cold floor. "As I said, one of my favorite places. It'll help you along. So will this—a memory I've been waiting a very, *very* long time to share with you. Remember how I said I was once like you? I meant it in every possible way. Let's go back to the beginning, to when we were Union souls for the first time and sent to Earth to guard the Gates. To the beginning of the Phoenix Guardians, a few millennia ago. To when we were the Original Seven."

My breath caught.

"Yes, Jacquelena, as a Union soul, I was part of that Seven. We were known as Ny'xan then. When you and Jeremicah are One, you are known as Ja'mai. Broderick, you and your other half are An'bris, and Nathayden and Rebethannah are Ra'den. There were three other Union souls, but we'll get to them soon enough. We Seven Unions were responsible for guarding Earth's Gates and keeping Satan and his followers out. But we failed. More specifically, *Ja'mai* failed, since you were, after all, our leader.

"Satan forced his way through a Gate and attacked us, knowing he couldn't take control of the world as long as we survived. He ripped our souls in halves, starting with Ja'mai. He was too arrogant and proud, however, and underestimated us. Instead of taking care of each of us and ensuring we were completely destroyed, he tossed the Separated souls aside to move on to the next Union to split. We—Ny'xan—helped Ja'mai's torn souls through the Gate, giving our leader safe passage to the Space Between. We helped each of the others, too, while Ra'den and An'bris continued to fight the demons infiltrating our world. At last, only An'bris and Ny'xan remained."

Her gaze swept over to Bex and Hayden, and then to Brock, letting this sink in, before returning to me.

"Satan grabbed both of us and reached into our bodies at the same time to retrieve our souls. We fought like the warriors we were, but he was too Dark and powerful. He yanked our souls out. He ripped An'bris' in half first and tossed the pieces to the ground, then went after our soul. Both halves of An'bris made it through the Gate and to the Space Between. Satan threw my piece into the Gate, setting it on a path to always return to Earth, and he took my Twin Flame's half with him to the Dark worlds, although we didn't know it then."

She made us relive the agony as she spoke, but I had a feeling she was holding much of it back, ensuring we could hear her story.

"We all returned to Earth as Separated souls for the next cycle," she continued. "All of us except my other half. While we were in the Space Between, you promised me, Jacquelena, that you would find me. You swore to me that you would find my soul and you would help me stay in the Light until we were able to find my Twin Flame and make us whole again."

Enyxa paused, stood and walked over to me, towering over my form on the ground. She squatted in front of me and stared me down with her black-as-night eyes.

"You *promised*," she hissed, her voice colder than the ice I lay on, sending a new shiver down my back. "You promised, and you lied. You never found me. You never helped us. You abandoned us!"

"We … we didn't … we had no idea," I stammered.

"You were our leader! You were supposed to be there for us. Instead you let us go Dark. It's *your* fault we lost each other!"

I rolled onto my knees, lifted myself to her eye level. "We. Didn't. Remember. You *know* we never remember. We've been through how many lifetimes since then?"

"Don't give me excuses!" Her voice rose into a shrill shriek. "It's all YOUR FAULT, JACQUELENA!"

She brought us body and soul into the memory of the original Separation. At that time, we'd been a Union for so long, had existed as Ja'mai for so many life cycles, we no longer remembered anything different. And then Satan himself broke through the Gates and through our defenses. He entered our world, destroyed our peace, severed us from each other and everything we knew. It had been the most painful Separation, when Satan had been the one to rip us apart. I knew this now as I relived the full extent of it, screaming through the renewed agony.

Then Enyxa took us through her memories again, through her hundreds of horrific lives as her soul grew Dark while our souls had been finding each other, re-Bonding, and eventually becoming Unions again. And then to the first time she Separated us. She destroyed another of the Original Seven, permanently Separating them and forcing them to go Dark. She did it again and again, each time waiting for us to grow into Unions, ripping us in halves, and taking one more of us. Until the last time, and only the three of us remained. She'd tried to destroy Rebethannah and Nathayden then when she took his half to the Dark worlds with her. We'd fed ourselves right into her hands by bringing Bex to Hayden—by bringing all of us to the Darkness.

We'd effectively demolished the Original Seven.

"You've had this vendetta against us all," Brock snarled, bringing my focus back to the present. He was on his feet, his chest puffed and his arms flexed. "*You've* caused all the tragedies in all of our lives!"

Enyxa beamed widely. "Yes, Broderick, but you already knew that. Everything that's happened since I went Dark— every single heartache including your son's death, even bringing you and Anastasia to be Forged together over and over again, and allowing you to bring Rebethannah to Nathayden— *all* of it was to lead to this very moment. But now you know who is truly to blame. If Ja'mai had been a real leader, we'd all be Union souls, living in the Light on Earth. If Jacquelena had kept her promise to me, *none* of us would be here right now. You would have never gone through the horror of losing your child and your mother. You would be with your other half—who you're *supposed* to be with."

"What does that mean?" Brock barked. "Who am I supposed to be with?"

Enyxa rolled her eyes. "You have to look within to know that. The real problem is why you are here and not with your other half in the first place."

Brock turned toward me, his chocolate-brown eyes nearly as black as Enyxa's. His lip lifted in a snarl as he glared at me, his biceps flexed, and his chest lifted as he inhaled through enflamed nostrils. He looked every bit as powerful as that Tristan had, and the blame that filled his eyes paralyzed me just as effectively.

My heart broke for him and everything he'd been through. It cracked into shards for Bex and Hayden and all of their pain, and more for the rest of the Seven that no longer existed. It shattered completely for all of the souls that had gone Dark because of me. I took the full weight of all the blame. Everything Enyxa said was true, I knew now. I remembered it clearly.

It had all been my fault, and none of us would be here if it weren't for my failures.

CHAPTER 21

Aria   I TRIED TO awake from the nightmare, but I wasn't sleeping and this Darkness wasn't something I could so easily escape. I'd gone through a bout of severe depression after the miscarriage, but that was nothing compared to the despair I felt now. A Darkness so thick and heavy filled every pore of my skin, every cell of my body, every molecule of air in my lungs, suffocating me under its weight. The black pit I'd been in before was nothing more than a ditch compared to the sinkhole I sat at the bottom of now, the light of the world so far away, I was no longer a part of it. I was alone, completely and utterly alone here, with only hopeless, negative thoughts surrounding me, pulling me further down into the Darkness.

I couldn't feel Brock's presence because of the Separation of worlds, but I somehow knew that he, too, was growing Darker. Although writing in the Book had made me feel closer to him, I hadn't been able to write about the accident. Still, the memories had come on their own, just as heartbreaking and devastating as the actual event. I'd felt him pull away then. I knew why.

He blamed me. Rightly so.

Which was why I deserved everything happening to me now. I deserved the heartache, the agony, the Dark sickness that was taking over my soul.

Something pounded on my door. I slid deeper under the covers, hiding, wishing the Darkness would consume me completely.

"Asia!" Jeric pounded again, making the door shake. "Asia, we can't do this by ourselves. Let me in!"

I huddled down further and pulled a pillow over my head, muffling his pleas so I could resist them and he'd eventually go away. My own despair was enough. Jeric was wrong. We had to do this by ourselves, because taking on any more than I already had would kill me. Then again ... wasn't that what I wanted? I'd just been wishing for the Darkness to take me away once and for all.

"Asia!" The door slammed open and banged into the wall.

I sat up, holding the pillow to my chest and squinting at Jeric's form in the brightness of the hallway behind him. He flipped a light on. I threw myself back down and covered my head with the pillow again.

"You're scaring the shit out of me," he said as the door clicked shut. I didn't peek, but I could tell he'd moved to the end of the bed. "Nobody's seen you in nearly two days. Which means you're not eating or anything. Are you *trying* to kill yourself?"

"Would it matter?" I muttered. I doubted he heard me through the pillow.

"Fuck yeah, it would matter. What would Brock do if he came back to that?"

"Brock's not coming back. Neither is Leni. Get over it and give in."

The end of the bed sank. I groaned, threw the pillow off, and scooched up to lean against the headboard. I narrowed my eyes and glared hard at him.

"What are you doing?" I demanded.

"Not letting you give in. Weren't you the one telling me the other day to stop feeling sorry for myself? Well, back at ya, sister."

"Screw you, Jeric."

"Fuck yourself, Asia."

I scowled. He returned it.

"What are you doing, Jeric?" I asked again.

He studied me for a long moment, blew out a hard breath, dropped his head into his hands, and leaned his elbows on his knees.

"I don't know," he admitted, and I sighed at the sound of his forlorn voice. "I thought I'd try to pull you out of it and bring myself along, but I just can't do it. Brock would kill me if he came back to you gone, but I can't bring myself to care any more. Because they're *not* coming back, are they?"

"Even if they were, Brock wouldn't care," I muttered. "He hates me. I can feel it."

"Bullshit. You're Twin Flames."

"Are we?" I snapped.

Jeric twisted his head and peered at me between his forearm and bicep. "What the hell does that mean?"

I frowned and picked at a thread on the blanket. "I've never really felt it. Neither has he. We've never had what you and Leni do, or Kel and Mat, Melinda and Uri …. Brock and I have always been different. And I know why now. We *aren't* Twin Flames. We *aren't* each other's other halves. We were somehow made to believe we are, but we don't really belong together."

Jeric lifted his head up and cocked it to the side. "That's impossible."

"How do we know? We know nothing, do we? You got the memory of the accident?"

He cringed and nodded.

"That should have never happened! If Hope and I hadn't shown up all persistent and demanding, Brock and Connor would have been gone and far away from that parking lot long before that truck came barreling down the street. But no, I had to fuck things up. I had convinced myself that it was supposed to be him and me together, and I forced him into believing that, too. Dragged him all the way over here, and now our halves have been Forged together when they don't belong. If I'd left it alone, if I'd let him be with Kami instead of jumping to conclusions and tracking him down at school, she and Connor wouldn't be dead now. Maybe *they're* the Twin Flames."

"How can you say that? Can souls even be Forged if they're not Twin Flames?"

"Apparently, yeah."

"And what about the matching marks you both had?"

"How do we know one didn't show up on Kami's arm, too? How do we know Enyxa didn't somehow make that happen, just like she's done everything else?"

Jeric didn't answer. He'd apparently felt that today, too— that Enyxa had been setting us up all along.

"Don't you remember your past lives together?" he asked.

"Barely. But here's another thing: we don't remember our last life at all. Not. At. All."

"Not even after you Bonded?"

"No! Because we didn't Bond then. We *never* found each other last time. Why would that be unless we weren't supposed to be together in the first place?"

He rubbed his hand over his face, then shook his head. "You're grasping at straws, Asia. You don't believe it. That's the Darkness making up lies."

"It's not!" I dropped my face into my hands and groaned. "Or in a way it is, because it's all Enyxa's doing. She's brought us to this point. *She* brought Brock and I together, not our souls or the universe working in weird ways, and definitely not any Guides. Enyxa made it happen. I feel that truth so strongly, it's like she actually admitted to it."

"How the hell can she do that? Force you together?"

I threw my hands in the air. "Obviously with some kind of help."

"I don't buy it. How the hell can you be so sure?"

I looked up at him, inhaling a deep breath as I reconsidered what I was about to say. I had to do it. He needed to understand the truth. It was the only way he'd leave me the hell alone.

"I died last summer." The words came out flatly, and I watched as he processed this. His brows scrunched together, and he nodded for me to continue. Again, I asked myself if I really wanted to tell this story. I'd never wanted to relive this again, but he left me no choice. "Not this past summer that just ended, but last year. When I had my miscarriage ... the baby wasn't the only one who died that day. My miscarriage wasn't something sad and unexplainable that randomly happens to many pregnancies. It was deliberate. I wasn't supposed to wake up."

Jeric stared at me for a long moment with those piercing blue eyes of his. "I'm already lost. Start at the beginning."

I sighed and pushed my hair back from my face, catching a glimpse of the newly colored strands—they were a deep, dark blue now instead of pitch black. I'd been going for a lighter blue, an attempt to lighten my mood, too, but apparently my soul was already too Dark to lighten my hair any more than this.

"Fine," I said. "Rewind several months back, when I'd met this guy at college named Drew. He was a frat boy, ran in the same circles as me. The obnoxiously rich circles, that is." I snorted when Jeric's forehead scrunched. "Yeah, I was a rich bitch back then, thanks to my asshole step-father, and I was always after the most eligible bachelors, even if they were dickwads like him. Drew was king of them all. Son of a Senator, but you'd think *he* was the politician with the power. Smooth as butter and hot as shit. We weren't serious or anything. Fuck buddies. Booty calls. Whatever you want to call it. But my pills got messed up, or maybe I was just the unlucky one-hundredth of a percent when they failed. Anyway, I got pregnant."

My throat began to thicken, and I had to take a moment to clear it.

"Drew, the great guy that he was, wanted me to get an abortion. He assumed I'd take care of it, and ... I ... I was going to." I could barely speak any more. Tears leaked out of the corners of my eyes. I averted my head and let them fall. "I set up the appointment, went to the clinic and everything. But when they called my name, I froze. I couldn't go into that room." I pressed my hands to my stomach. My words came out all teary and barely understandable. "I ... I couldn't kill my baby, Jeric."

His weight lifted from the end of the bed, and he came around to Brock's side and sat down. He put an arm around my shoulder, and I leaned into him and sucked in a jagged breath so I could go on.

"I ran out of the clinic and all the way home bawling. Later, when I came to accept my decision, I went to the support group. Kami was there, a few months further along than me. She had a tiny little baby bump already. That's the only reason I remembered her being there—she was the only one who did." I rubbed my eyes. "Anyway, I couldn't have an abortion, I knew that for sure, and I went home for the summer thinking I'd figure out exactly what I was going to do. I was sick the first month and a half of summer break, until I reached the second trimester. By then, *I* had a bump, and it'd become *my* baby. I decided I was going to have him or her and be the best mother I could be. My stepfather was livid. I was an embarrassment to him and his elite country club reputation. *My* pregnancy somehow made *him* look bad to his top executive clients. He said I'd be keeping the pregnancy a secret and giving the baby up for adoption, or he'd disown me. I didn't really care if he did."

"What about your mother?"

I rolled my eyes. "She's just a damn doormat. She let him walk all over her from the moment she met him, and he rescued us from a life of poverty. That's what she called it when her own parents disowned her because I was born out of wedlock, but she really had no idea what poor is. So yeah, Mark thought he'd threaten to do the same to me, thinking I wouldn't want to be like my mom. And I *didn't* want to be like her, but not in the way he thought. He didn't know me at all. The only thing my mom did was not let him kick me out until after the baby was born. But then, right after the Fourth of July, Drew showed up at my parents' house. He didn't live around there, but his dad had a place close by for when he was in Washington. Drew wanted another booty call, I guess, but wasn't expecting to see me pregnant."

My throat started closing again as the memories returned.

"What happened?" Jeric asked quietly when I didn't continue.

I chuckled, the sound flat with no humor. "Saying he was pissed off doesn't even begin to describe it. He looked like a cartoon character, the way his face turned beet red and his eyes bulged the moment he saw my bump. We were already inside, in the kitchen, and I saw he was about to lose his shit, so I rushed him outside to the deck. I didn't need Mark to hear the argument. I tried to explain to Drew that I was doing this all on my own ..."

"You lied to me!" he'd yelled. "You said you took care of it!"

"You never bothered to find out," I'd said. "You didn't give two shits about us. So go on back to your life and don't worry about it."

"Don't *worry* about it? Until you come after me in two years for child support? Yeah, right, you conniving little bitch. What do you think my dad's going to say about this? You'll ruin my whole family!"

Mark had been outside and heard the argument after all. He came running up the deck stairs. "What's going on? Who are you?"

"Drew Cavendish, sir." The polite politician coming out.

"Cavendish? As in Andrew Cavendish?"

"That's my dad."

"God damn it, Asia," Mark snapped at me, his hands on his hips. "A Senator's son? You had to screw up with a *Senator's* son? What the hell were you thinking? What the fuck is wrong with you?"

He glared at me as though I'd been the only one there the night I got pregnant, as if I'd gone and done it on purpose.

"She was supposed to get a fucking abortion," Drew snarled as he took a step closer to me. Mark did the same. I backed up against the railing that circled the deck.

"You lied to us, Asia?" Mark demanded. I shook my head. I felt so tiny and out of control as they both towered over me. "You said the father didn't care if you had the baby."

"I said the father didn't care period," I said, trying to be bitchy, but sounding weak.

"Why didn't you just get the abortion, Asia?" Drew asked. "Why do you have to fuck things up so badly?"

"That's all she knows how to do," Mark muttered. "If you don't want the baby, Drew, and we don't want it, we can still take care of this. There are certain clinics that will do it this far along."

"*I* want it!" I said, finally finding my voice. "*You're* not taking care of anything!"

"Shut up, Asia," both men barked at the same time.

My breath caught at the looks in their eyes. Their gears were obviously turning. They were seriously trying to figure out how to get me to a clinic to "take care of my problem." My baby wasn't a fucking problem!

"Go to hell. Both of you!" I ducked away from where they'd tried to corner me against the deck railing. "I don't need either of you and none of you have the right to tell me what to do with me and my baby."

"You're not doing this!" Drew yelled as he ran for me with his arms extended and his hands clawed like he wanted to choke me. But instead of wrapping his palms around my neck, he pressed them to my shoulders and shoved.

"I don't know everything that happened next," I told Jeric. "I remember lying on the concrete patio below the deck, staring up at the summer evening sky as something warm and wet pooled around me. I remember darkness closing in on my vision, blotting out the blue sky and stars, and I let myself be swallowed up by it." I sniffed at the memory and exhaled slowly. "And then I woke up in a hospital room, no longer pregnant and with a severe concussion. All I know is that I'd moved to the top of the deck's stairs right before Drew came after me. He and Mark both said I stepped backwards and rolled down the steps. I *know* he shoved me. When I freaked out about the baby, the doctors and nurses said I'd never been pregnant. The whole thing had been wiped from my medical records. They said I'd hit hard enough that I'd actually died for a few moments when the paramedics first arrived, and they blamed the head injury for thinking I'd ever been pregnant."

"They paid off the doctors and everyone else to clean up the whole situation," Jeric said.

"You know how much that had to have cost them? They should have been facing attempted murder charges, even second-degree charges for the baby. But their mother-fucking money kept them out of jail and saved Drew from embarrassing his family. Assholes."

"That's why you went after Mason like you did."

I winced. Although Mason had deserved the broken glass stabbed into his nuts, I couldn't believe I'd actually done that. I didn't think I'd had it in me. But I'd grown so damn tired of rich, arrogant fuckers thinking they were invincible and getting away with everything, including murder. Mason might not ever serve time, but he certainly hadn't gotten away with what he did scot-free.

"Yeah," I finally admitted. "He was just like them."

I swiped at my cheeks again, and Jeric pulled his arm away. The feeling of being so close to him had become awkward, so I scooted back over to my side of the bed.

"What's this have to do with you and Brock not being Twin Flames?"

I sighed, leaned over, and buried my face in my hands again as more tears came. After a moment, I sat back up. "I remember dying. I remember the Darkness—not just in my vision, but in my soul—taking over. I know now that's what it was. I remember someone saying to me, 'Not yet. Not until I'm done with you.' A female voice. That one phrase had brought me back. It had been the lifeline I held onto whenever my thoughts turned to suicide because I couldn't stand living that life any longer. But knowing what I do now, I can only believe that had been Enyxa. She'd wanted to make sure I lived so I could break up Brock and Kami. She wanted to hurt him and used me to do it."

"How can you say that?"

"Because the Darkness had already started to take me then. I didn't know that's what it was when I'd gone into a deep depression, but her Darkness stayed with me and began to grow already, Jeric. By the time I went back to college, I'd become a completely different person. I wanted nothing to do with my friends, even the ones I'd known since elementary school. Nobody meant anything to me. And I couldn't be there any more. I needed to go south. For some reason, I *knew* south was where I needed to go, and I thought it had been to escape that ridiculous life I'd grown to hate so much. But now I know differently. It'd been Enyxa all along, driving me and setting us up. Nothing between Brock and me has ever been real."

At least, not on his end, but I didn't say that to Jeric. Then he'd think I was making shit up, trying to make it all look worse than it was because I was letting the Darkness get to me. That's how it works—Darkness and depression make you see all the negatives and it convinces you that's all there is until you completely believe it. Until you see the actual and horrible truth with perfect clarity. So in a way, the Darkness *was* getting to me. It was helping me to see clearly that my love for Brock had always been unrequited. That I'd been delusional in thinking that he and I were made for each other—even more, that we'd actually shared a soul. He and Kami belonged together. He'd basically told me that, and God and the angels or the universe or whatever had kept trying to bring them together while tearing him and me apart. And now she was dead and so was their son, all because of me and my selfish demands.

Brock was going Dark now, and that was my fault, too. He had every right to hate me. I hated myself just as much.

The air in my room became thick and heavy, pressing down on me, on my chest. I couldn't breathe.

"I need air," I croaked, jumping off the bed.

I already wore another of Brock's long t-shirts with black leggings under it, so I only had to stuff my feet into my Doc Martens before I could rush out of the room. Jeric followed on my heels. I didn't know why. Probably because he didn't trust me to be alone.

I didn't trust myself.

The Lakari had been constantly swarming over the manor and the bay like a cloud of oversized bees, so it was no surprise they were out there when I ran out of the mansion, onto the lawn, and back to the place where Jeric and I had stayed on guard when Leni, Brock, and Bex had first disappeared. Every once in a while, one or two of the Dark souls would dip down as if threatening us. More like taunting. We probably shouldn't have been outside, making ourselves vulnerable to their Darkness—even more so than we already were. They surely sensed us on the brink of becoming one of them.

We took our sentry posts again at the edge of the manor's lawn where the bay began. I looked out over the water toward the Gate, but the hope I'd felt only a few days ago that our Twin Flames would return had all but slipped away with the tide.

"I got an email from Yoshi today," Jeric said, breaking the long silence. "Tokyo's been having a lot of problems."

I didn't reply. He didn't expect me to. This was probably what he'd come to my room to tell me earlier. We watched the waves lap at the sand for a while.

"The news media's been all over the increase in murders, crimes, drug use, and suicides lately," he finally added. "Uri couldn't help but point out to me this morning that the biggest spikes are in cities near the Gates."

I had no idea why he felt the urge to share all of that with me. In case we'd forgotten just how dire our situation had become? Because we needed our last bit of hope to disappear completely? Or maybe it was because deep down, he, like me, couldn't wait for everything to reach its worst because that meant the Darkness would come. He'd told me about the peace of the Darkness taking him away right before he and Leni had been Forged. I'd begun to feel it myself more than once already. He'd said the nothingness had been comforting. The opposite of the pain we suffered right now. So maybe he was ready to hurry it all along.

Maybe he was waiting on me to give him permission to end it all.

"If you're telling me that you need to collapse the Gates, Jeric," I said, turning to look him in the eye, "just fucking do it already." I turned my back to the water ... to the Gate. "There's no more hope for us."

He scowled as he shoved his hands into his jeans pockets and stared across the water. I left him there and strode toward the large wooden doors of the manor. He caught up with me a second or two later and walked silently next to me. We were still forty yards from the doors to the mansion when they opened, and Uri and Melinda came out, escorting another woman.

I stopped dead in my tracks at the sight of the familiar face.

"What the hell?" My hand flew to cover my gaping mouth. "*Impossible.*"

She was supposed to be dead.

CHAPTER 22

Jeric "I HAD A feeling we'd find you here," Melinda said as she and Uri walked toward us with a woman I didn't recognize but who felt familiar anyway. She held a white cat in her arms that reminded me of Ghost, but with no markings, there was no way to know if they were one and the same. "We've been looking for the two of you."

"What are you?" Asia asked, sounding breathless at my side.

I glanced sideways at her, thinking she said that wrong and meant *who,* not what. The sight of her stopped me from correcting her, though. All blood had drained from her face, leaving her skin white as snow. Her eyes, almost black in contrast, looked like they might bug out of her face if they opened any wider. Her hand hid her mouth, and she appeared to be hyperventilating.

What the hell was wrong with her?

"Asia?" I hedged.

"What are you?" she repeated, louder this time. Uri, Melinda, and the strange-but-familiar woman had come out of the mansion and stopped about halfway to us. Asia's voice scaled several octaves as she continued. "How are you here? You're supposed to be dead. I saw you burn!"

"There's a lot to explain," the woman began.

"Damn right there is! Is Connor alive, too?"

The woman pressed her lips together. "Asia—"

"*Is* he?" Asia demanded.

"I'll tell you everything. I promise. It's a long story, much of it hard to believe, but I *will* tell you. First, we have to get Brock and the others back before it's too late."

"You know how?" I asked, skepticism mixing with hope.

"I do."

"Why should we trust you?" Asia asked. "How can we believe anything you say when you made us think you were dead? We *mourned* you!"

"Asia," Melinda said. "This is our hope."

"I know who she is," Asia snapped, and I finally did, too. Brock's mother, Hope, which I should have known as I noticed the resemblance now. She had Brock's dark hair, except hers had some gray in it, and the same brown eyes. And now I understood Asia's reaction to seeing her.

"I mean, she's *our* hope," Melinda said. "She can help us with the Gates and Enyxa and getting everyone back. But we're running out of time."

Asia crossed her arms over her chest and jutted her hip out. "I've heard that before. From you yourself, Hope. While you were supposedly burning to death! You rushed us out of there. Told us to hurry. Why? So you could make your mystical escape and leave us thinking you were dead? To fake Connor's death so you could run off with him? To force Brock and me to Forge when we shouldn't have?"

"Asia!" Hope pulled back, holding the cat tighter against her. "You don't think—"

"I don't know what to think any more!" She threw her arms in the air and stomped several paces away.

"How can you help us?" I asked Hope while Asia walked off some of her anger and shock.

"Do you have the Book of Phoenix?" Hope asked. "The answers are there."

One side of my mouth curled tightly. "We've found nothing in it that can help."

"You're not looking in the right way. I can show you."

Asia flew back over to us. "How the hell do you know anything about the Book? How. Are. You. *Here?*"

Hope sighed. "I told you I'd explain everything later."

"You're not touching the Book until you at least tell me that," Asia declared. "Because you know what? I think you're working with Enyxa. And until you can prove you're not, you aren't getting anywhere close to that Book."

A few Guardians had gathered around, concerned at the sound of Enyxa's name, but also curious. I wasn't about to get them involved until we knew more. I tried to wave them off.

"Let's go inside, and Hope can tell you what she's already told us," Uri suggested. He opened the wooden door and held it for the rest of us.

We followed Melinda and Hope inside with Uri taking up the rear, through the mansion part of the manor and into what had once been part of the hotel. Melinda and Uri led us to the same meeting room where they'd told us about the Sacred Seven. So I shouldn't have been surprised to see Mira and Theo, my and Leni's Guides, in there, waiting for us. We hadn't seen them since they'd left to guide more Phoenix souls at the same time we'd left the manor for our first mission—the one that had brought us to our current situation. That had only been a few months ago, but Theo looked like he'd aged another ten years, and the old man didn't really have much room to grow any older. Mira rushed to me, flitting her hands over me in a grandmotherly way. She hadn't acted like a real grandmother to me since before my accident, but here she was, all concerned.

"I'm fine," I muttered.

"You can't be."

"Okay, I'm not. Nothing you can do about it, though."

"We brought her here as soon as we found her," Mira said.

"*You* brought her here?" I lifted a brow.

Mira nodded and explained in a near whisper. "We were supposed to be helping some young souls, but I felt her presence nearby. I called Theo, and we went investigating. I guess because we're Guides, we had an unusual pull to her. Theo called it instinct. You'll never believe where we found her."

"Explain," Asia ordered, speaking over everyone else and cutting Mira off. She didn't sit at the conference table. Nobody did. She leaned her butt against the edge of the table and crossed her arms over her chest, glaring at Hope. "From the beginning."

The woman stood at the front of the room, stroking the white fur of her cat, and we all faced her, expectantly. Her dark gaze slid over each of us.

"Starting from the beginning would require days or weeks, and we don't have that kind of time. I'll tell you what you need to know for now, and as I said, I promise to tell the rest later. After everyone's safe." She drew in a breath, buying a few more moments, then blurted it out. "I'm Ete'hope. A Union soul. A *very* high level Union soul ... or what people here on Earth might think of as a low level angel."

Several gasps came from the healers and the Guides, and then they each took a seat. Asia and I only stood there, dumbfounded. At least, I was. I thought Asia was still nothing but cynical.

"That's how I was able to survive the fire," Hope went on. "It would take a lot more than that to kill me."

"Connor?" Asia demanded. "Kami?"

Hope frowned. "Kami was a soul headed for Darkness. Unfortunately, she didn't make it."

"Connor?" Asia asked again, her patience wearing thin. I could hear it in her voice.

"His soul is safe," was the only answer Hope gave. "I've been watching over this world for a couple of millennia, since Ny'xan's soul was split in half. In fact, I was in charge of choosing the Original Seven to take over guardianship of Earth's Gates, and I chose you from a pool of long-time Union souls. When Satan managed to get past your defenses and enter this world, he split Ny'xan, taking the masculine half with him to the Dark worlds and leaving the feminine half—Enyxa—to return to Earth. The Original Seven were no longer Seven, and that was a problem. I tried to help Ny'xan and her Twin Flame, and after a lot of searching and risking my own soul, I was actually able to find and rescue his half. But she'd become too Dark by then and single-mindedly focused on revenge."

Hope paused, biting her lip. Asia and I both took this as an opportunity to sit down. Standing while listening to this was no longer an option. This was the kind of shit that knocked you off your feet.

"Enyxa made herself Earth's enemy," Hope went on. "Everything she's done with every other world has been part of her plan to destroy Earth. I needed the rest of the Original Seven to return to Earth as Union souls so you could defeat her. But every time you came close to reaching that level, she would find her way to you and split your souls. And each time, we lost one of the Seven."

"And you didn't do anything, almighty angel?" Asia snarked.

"I've done what I can for their souls, but I can't interfere in the affairs of Earth, including the Phoenix and even the Original Seven, unless all of Earth's souls were at risk."

"Which they are now," I said.

"Yes. Now I can help you."

"How?" Melinda asked.

"Yeah, how?" Asia demanded. "You said using the Book of Phoenix, but we've tried everything possible."

"Not everything," Hope said.

"What do you know about it?" I asked.

Hope gave a small smile. "Actually, I haven't been able to interfere in anything of consequence, but I have helped you a little in the past in different ways. Like this guy." She held up the cat, which jumped out of her hands, strode over to me and wound himself between my legs. "I call him Buddy, but I think you know him as Ghost, Jeric? He's been my eyes and ears, especially while I was healing from the burns. Before him was Sammy. I have a few animal souls roaming this world, helping the Guardians when they can and keeping me abreast of news."

"That explains a lot," I muttered as I reached down and stroked Ghost's coat.

"Like what?" Asia demanded.

"Like how he helped Leni and me fight the Shadowmen the very first time. Like how Sammy rescued Jacey from the fire."

Asia clicked her tongue. "What's that have to do with the Book?"

"It's another way I've been able to help," Hope said. "In an attempt to get you Guardians back on track. Part of the Separation includes a loss of memory, and you know what kind of problems that's caused. So you don't recall this, but I encouraged Jacquelena and the rest of you to create artifacts to help you remember from lifetime to lifetime. But after a while, they always became lost or destroyed. So I actually helped with the creation of the Book of Phoenix, making it different. I had you three dyads—what was left of the Original Seven—imprint your souls into the pages so you would know the Book and it would know you. I also channeled some of my powers into it. Including the ability to summon each other from other worlds."

I jumped to my feet. "Are you fucking serious?"

Hope's brows lifted. "Completely serious."

"Yeah, right," Asia muttered. She stood, too, and placed her hands on her narrow hips. "If that were the case, why are they gone? Why didn't Leni just summon Nathayden here for Bex?"

"The Book can send you to other worlds, too. It works both ways," Hope said. "Leni obviously didn't remember this, or trust me, she would have brought Nathayden here instead."

I paced a few times and wiped my hand over my face before stopping in front of Hope. "You can bring Leni and Brock back? You know this for sure?"

"Yes," she said simply. "And Rebethannah and Nathayden, wherever they are."

"How?"

"With the Book. And the Gates. We'll need to open the Gates again."

"And there it is," Asia said, throwing her hands in the air in an I-told-you-so way. "How do we know you aren't using this to open the Gates for Enyxa and her Lakari?"

"I am."

Gasps filled the room again, followed by complete silence. If a pin dropped on the carpet, we all would have heard it.

"It's the only way to defeat her," Hope explained. "We need the remainder of the Original Seven on this Earth, and we need her here, too. She can only be defeated in the world she truly belongs to, and that's here."

Asia snorted. "Sounds like a plan to destroy us all and the rest of Earth's souls."

"Asia, why don't you trust me?"

Asia leaned toward her. "Because you already set me up. Brock and me."

"I *helped* you. I protected you from the time Brock was conceived, becoming his parent myself so I could be close. I pulled you south, I made sure you came to us and made you—and only you—see that help wanted ad."

"You didn't even give me the job at first!"

"Because I knew you weren't ready for it. I saw your reaction to baby Connor, and I knew you needed more time. I sent Buddy to watch over you in the meantime. Who do you think told Brock about the Camaro for sale?" Hope waited for an answer, but Asia only stared, eyes narrowed, nostrils flared. Hope sighed. "I ensured you two met this time. I knew it would be harder than normal for you since you didn't find each other in your last cycle, so I've done everything I can to make sure you made it together. I protected you from the Lakari and even from the soul sickness. I gave you the best running start I could, holding off the consequences as long as possible. Until Kami came along and became a threat to your relationship."

"It wasn't *me* he was supposed to meet, though. It was her!"

Hope cocked her head to the side. "Do you really believe that?"

"It's obvious, isn't it? We don't belong together. We never did."

Hope crossed the five yards to Asia and put her hands on the girl's shoulders. "Asia, love, you need to get out of your head and search your *heart* and ask yourself if that's true." She tapped Asia's chest with a finger. "You know the truth right here, in this space within you that you call your soul. And search the *Light* part of it, not the Dark. The Dark will always say what it needs to feed itself."

Asia stared at the older woman/angel/Union soul/Enyxa's minion/whatever she was, but I saw no sign of her changing her mind. I cleared my throat, needing to move on.

"You're serious about opening the Gates?" I asked. "*All* of them? And letting Enyxa in?"

Hope turned from Asia and gave me a sharp nod. "We have to use the Book to summon the others at the same time. As long as there are souls from the Original Seven on this world and together, Enyxa can't take control. And as long as you and Jacquelena don't become Dark, the rest of the Original Seven will survive."

"I don't trust her," Asia muttered, as if that was news.

"And not all of the Gates," Hope added, ignoring Asia's declaration. "Just one. Gather as many warriors as you can because there *will* be a battle."

"This is exactly what we did the other day," I said.

"But now you know more," Hope replied. "Now you have me on your side."

"And if we go down?" Asia challenged. "The remainder of the Seven? If they don't come back and Jeric and Leni go Dark?"

"You have to trust me and the Book," Hope said, and she suddenly held the Book of Phoenix in her hands. The Book that had been in my room.

"How did you get that?" I demanded.

"It knows me," Hope answered. "Because it belongs to me as much as it does to you. How do you think you and Brock first found it, Asia? When you both tried to get rid of it, why do you think it kept reappearing?"

Asia didn't answer. Even if she was coming around to accepting Hope's plan, she wouldn't admit it now, so I looked around at the others in the room who had managed to stay out of the conversation.

"I think we should try it," Uri said. "But in the end, it's your call, Jeric."

"The Phoenix will stand behind you no matter what," Melinda added.

"We found her for a reason," Mira said. "She's a being of the Light."

Theo took the longest to say anything, his old eyes narrowed in thought. "I'll tell you what I tell Leni all the time. Follow your instinct. Listen to your soul. It knows best." He looked over at Asia. "You, too, little lady. Hope is right. You'll find what you need to know, what matters most, in that space within you and only you."

I clasped my hand on the back of my neck and paced a couple more times. I glanced over at Asia. She looked away from me. Hope spoke up before Asia could say anything.

"I hope I'll earn your trust again one of these days, Asia," the older woman said. "And here's what I pray is a step in the right direction." She held the Book up in the air. "If I was really working on Enyxa's side, if I was really just wanting to get her here, I could use this Book and open the Gates myself. All of them. I could let thousands of her Dark souls in all over the world, letting them destroy the Phoenix Guardians, and you with them. But I haven't done that. I'm giving you a choice. And I'm trying to help you, giving you a chance to bring in an army and do this in the most strategic way possible with the least amount of risk." Hope turned her gaze on me. "Jermicah, you must be able to see that. You must trust me, or the whole world is doomed."

Asia gnawed on her lip behind Hope, twisted a finger in her blue hair, and then gave me the slightest nod. I couldn't tell in her dark eyes if she'd actually changed her mind, or if she saw what we'd both wanted earlier today before Hope had arrived: the fastest route to Darkness to end our pain once and for all.

It was a shit-ass choice, though. Even if I did want the Darkness to take me when there was no hope of seeing Leni again, I didn't want it consuming all of Earth's souls. And we'd be taking that risk. On the other hand, this could be my chance to save my girl. To save her soul. Maybe even save the world.

I needed her here with me to light my way and show me the right decision. But, of course, that was the whole fucking problem. And I missed her more than ever.

CHAPTER 23

Leni BROCK GLARED AT me with murder in his eyes. With hatred so pure and unadulterated, it could only come from Darkness. And I couldn't blame him. If I'd been in his shoes, staring down the one person who'd been ultimately responsible for every tragedy I'd experienced in this life and past ones … the reason we were all here, losing our souls … I'd want to kill me, too. As expected, he flew at me.

Hayden jumped in front of him, pushing him backwards across the ice. "You don't want to do this, mate."

"The hell I don't!"

"Just let him," I said in misery from my seat on the floor. "I deserve it. I'm done anyway. I'm tired of fighting it all."

"Don't you give up," Bex snapped as she dropped to my side.

"Leave me alone, Bex." I lay down on my side with my knees pulled to my chest.

"No. You wouldn't let me die. I'm not letting you."

"Let me go," Brock snarled.

"I'm not letting you do something you'll regret," Hayden said. He pinned Brock to the cavern wall.

I closed my eyes, unable to look at him any more. Any of them. How could Bex be trying to save me after all the heartache I caused in her lives? How could any of them stand to look at me?

A giggle sounded from somewhere in the distance, although it wasn't really. Enyxa hadn't left our cavern. She knew we were close to crossing to her side. But she'd sounded so far away because I'd been the one leaving. My soul had been anyway.

"Isn't this working out perfectly?" she cooed. "Did you know the Phoenix could have saved you with the Book? But they won't. They're too afraid of me and my army. And now you're so close to going Dark!" She'd nearly squealed it, if evil could squeal. "You will become my children, and what's ironic but you know is true, Jacquelena, is that I'll be a better mother than you've had in lifetimes. I take care of my children. And once you become one of mine, so will your other halves on Earth. Rebethannah and Nathayden, un-Forged and weak, will follow right behind. And then the Original Seven—what the Guardians had been stupid enough to call *sacred*—will be completely destroyed. And you know what that means, Jacquelena?"

I moaned in answer, not giving two fucks what it meant any more. There was nothing I could do about it anyway.

"It means the Gates will open to *me*, the last of the Original Seven. I'll finally be able to take over Earth, and I'll be a better leader than Ja'mai could ever be. As long as any of you are there, I can't have it, but you'll be gone! Earth will be mine. Not even Satan's, but mine. All *mine!*"

It took me a long moment to process what she was saying because I'd already let myself go. I'd already been working on releasing my soul from this body so it could follow the Darkness to the peace of finality. But Enyxa had gone on and on, droning in the background of my mind, not letting me go completely.

And her meaning began to take form. We'd been shut out of our own world because they'd been so afraid of the Lakari and Enyxa. The Phoenix Guardians had been forced to choose between our souls and all of Earth's. They'd obviously chosen the rest of humanity. I couldn't blame them. We'd been the ones to mess up in the first place, way back in the beginning, causing this catastrophe. We deserved to go Dark. The rest of Earth did not.

But there was something else Enyxa had just said: As long as we, the Original Seven, were on Earth, she couldn't enter. She couldn't take it. But as soon as we'd all gone Dark, Earth was hers anyway.

There really was no choice.

I managed to summon every bit of feeling I still had, every drop of love left in my body, every thin thread of connection we might still have. I focused on the Book of Phoenix, praying like I'd never prayed before that it would receive my last ditch effort of communication, and I silently screamed:

JEEEEERRRRRIIIIICCCCC!

CHAPTER 24

Jeric THE HEALERS, THE Guides, Hope, and Asia stared at me expectantly, waiting for my decision. I rubbed my brow ring as I looked at each of their faces and saw for the first time how much trust they put into me. How much faith they had that I would make the right decision not only for all of us but for all of humanity. They looked to me as the leader of the Phoenix Guardians. Even Hope, who could have moved forward on her own, but left the ultimate decision to me. I'd never felt so much fucking pressure in my life. But I knew what I needed to do.

It was time to become that leader once and for all.

"The last time someone told me what was best for everyone, I couldn't bring myself to trust them," I started. "I'm—"

"Hope! The Book," Melinda interrupted with a panic.

Asia sucked in her breath. "I've seen it do that before."

Hope tossed the Book onto the conference table as black smoke poured out of it. She opened the cover with a swipe of her finger over the lock—a show of evidence she'd been telling the truth. She turned through the pages, and the smoke began to clear. She found the one where the words had been burned into, clearly in Leni's handwriting:

"Jeric! Open the Gate and bring us home. It's the only way to save Earth!"

My fingers skimmed over the words, and I could *feel* Leni reaching out to me. I could feel her soul looking for mine. A small smile twitched at the corners of my mouth. If I hadn't been sure before that I was doing the right thing—as risky as it was—I knew now. I put my hands on the table to brace myself and looked up at the others again.

"As I was saying, I'm not making the same mistake again. Let's do this."

After a few minutes of planning, Melinda, Uri, Mira, and Theo left the room to begin spreading the word to the Guardians, not just at our Gate, but all over the world. We needed to bring as many here as possible without leaving the other Gates completely unmanned, just in case something went wrong. So there was much to be coordinated.

"You two come with me, and I'll show you how to use the Book," Hope said to Asia and me.

She picked the Book up and walked out of the meeting room. I began to follow, but Asia didn't. I stopped in the doorway and turned, silently questioning her. Her gaze avoided my face.

"Asia," Hope said from behind me, "if you want your proof that I'm here to help, you're about to get it."

Asia bit her bottom lip, then blew out a breath and finally strode toward the doorway. We followed Hope down the hall, into the mansion part of the manor, and out the wooden double doors that led to the lawn and the bay.

"Like the Gates, many of the Book's powers are activated by water," Hope explained as she walked to the water's edge.

"Well, it came out of the bay the other day after soaking in it for two days," Asia said, "and the water didn't do anything except wash away what had been written inside."

"Not permanently washed away," Hope corrected. "And no, it wouldn't react if it was water-logged. That would make it too easy for the wrong person to find it and accidentally activate its powers. The water has to be applied lightly and with purpose. Like this."

She bent down and swished her fingers in the water, then held her hand above the Book and let it drip onto the corner of the cover. The symbols that had been etched into the leather at that spot glowed a silvery blue. Somehow, as I stared at them, I knew exactly what they meant: Jacquelena.

"These symbols are your souls' imprints," Hope explained as she lit up more symbols: Broderick. "Highlighting them like this creates a stronger connection. Wetting different parts of the cover provides different results, such as opening a portal to another place on Earth or even creating a Gate wherever you are to take you to different worlds."

She pointed to the areas of the image embossed on the cover that contained the various powers, but she didn't actually activate them.

"So that's what Leni did when they disappeared?" Asia asked, her voice showing real interest.

Hope nodded. "And that's what we'll do to get them back. The intent and desire of the user determines the direction of travel. She must have been focusing on taking Rebethannah to Nathayden, rather than bringing Nathayden to Earth. The Gate will illuminate around the Book and take anyone within its walls. The problem with that, though, is that the Book is Earthbound. When you use a Gate created by the Book, you have to want to leave for good ... or be sure there's someone here who can bring you back. Like what we're going to do."

She opened the Book and flipped to the page that had been burned. "You can write in it as a one-way record-keeper, as Jacey did, but you can also intend for your writing to be felt by one of your own. And messages can come from other worlds, so when you're in the situation you are now, you can't exactly talk back and forth, but you can communicate."

As if the Book heard her—maybe it did, or Leni did, or whatever—new words appeared on the page. More from Leni:

"Enyxa's here. We'll try to fight her, but I don't think we're strong enough. We're too Dark. She'll try to come through the Gate as soon as you open it, so be ready, Jeric. Please, God, say this message is getting through."

"Perfect," Hope said. "Enyxa's exactly where we want her."

"With our Twin Flames?" I asked in disbelief. "Not exactly!"

"Yes, exactly. It is up to you and your Twin Flames to defeat Enyxa. This is part of who you are. But first, we need to get the rest of the Guardians here as quickly as possible. I'll show you how to create those portals for them."

Before she began, we confirmed with Uri and Melinda that the leaders at each of the other six Gates had been notified and Guardians were on standby. Then Hope plunged her hand in the water again and started tracing certain parts of the image with her fingertip, leaving a trail of water.

Within a few minutes, Guardians from around the world began dropping into the water and onto the lawn around us as though falling from the sky. Yoshi and Tasha came, along with several Tokyo Guardians. They all took one look at Hope and bowed deeply. What did they know that we didn't? Asia and I exchanged a look.

"The Darkness within you blinds you from the truth," Hope said, as though reading our minds.

It took an absurd amount of time for all of the Guardians to arrive. Or maybe it wasn't that long, but my patience was quickly dissolving. If all went well, I'd be holding my girl by the end of the night. If it didn't go well, we'd all be dead and Earth would belong to Enyxa. Both possibilities sent shot after shot of adrenaline rushing through my veins. I couldn't stand still and went from leader to leader to check on the status of their

Guardians, discuss our plans, and alter them when someone provided a new idea. Eventually, they all told me to chill the hell out, and I was diminished to pacing.

Asia, on the other hand, became more and more withdrawn.

She sat on the beach near the water's edge with her knees pulled up to her chin. She absent-mindedly traced designs in the sand next to her as she stared out over the water and the sun hanging low in the afternoon sky.

I strode over to her. "Are you up for this?"

She didn't look up at me. "Of course."

"For real? Because I can't have you doing something stupid. I need you to overcome the Darkness."

"I can do it, Jeric. I will be the warrior you need me to be."

If only she'd sounded more convincing. I began to wonder if she should be inside, protecting the bodies of those Guardians who projected. She didn't seem to have the proper awareness to be out here in the middle of the action.

"Stop worrying about me," Asia said. "You've been there for me this week. I'll be there for you. I'll fight for you until my last breath."

I cocked my head at this last statement. Maybe lack of alertness wasn't the problem. Maybe suicidal tendencies were. I was about to ask when Mat and Kel came jogging up to us.

"Everyone who's coming is here," Kel said.

"We're ready then," Hope said, suddenly appearing by my side.

All of the Guardians—hundreds of dyad pairs—had gathered on the lawn, once again looking to me to lead them. I blew out a heavy breath before addressing them.

"My comrades, my friends, my fellow warriors," I began and immediately felt like a dumbass for how stupid that sounded. Like I was some military leader in a scripted movie about to give a powerful speech to motivate the troops. Then again, I supposed that was precisely what I was about to do. "We have no choice but to do exactly the opposite of what the Phoenix

Guardians of the Gates are supposed to do—we're going to invite evil into our world rather than keep it out."

A quiet murmur floated through the crowd.

"I know it sounds messed up," I continued over the din. "But it's the only way to defeat Enyxa and rid Earth of her Dark souls. Imagine what that would mean."

The crowd became louder, now with excitement.

"It would mean Earth's souls have a better chance of staying Light. It would mean our jobs as Phoenix Guardians would become less risky. It could even mean we'd have a chance to live a full life and grow old with our Twin Flames."

Some whoops and hollers sounded from the audience now. We may have not been able to remember much else, but we could all recall how short our life cycles on Earth had always been, all because of the Lakari. Just because we were warriors shouldn't have had to mean we could never have a future—a real future—with our other halves, but that was how it had always been for us. My biggest fear since rejoining the Phoenix had been the fact that I could lose Leni at any time. That possibility existed anyway, I knew, but as long as Enyxa and the Lakari were around, it wasn't a possibility. It was a sure thing. We could change that with this battle.

I looked out across the crowd. "So I'm asking you to join me in the battle that's about to start. It's the biggest battle in our history, and I know it's a big risk. I'm sure we'll lose some of our friends. We may even lose the battle completely, which would mean losing the war and Earth itself. But if we don't fight, if we don't do this, we lose anyway."

"Let's do this!" someone yelled from the crowd. Several people cheered and wolf-whistled in support.

"We *can* do it because we have Hope on our side!" Yoshi said with a fist pump into the air. The crowd cheered loudly as Hope took my hand and gave it a squeeze. She really was our last hope.

"It's time to rise up, Phoenix Guardians," she said, raising her voice to be heard. "It's time to do what you're supposed to do: protect Earth's souls."

I was pumped up more than ever and shot my fist into the air. "Let's show Enyxa that her Darkness doesn't belong here! Evil does *not* win on Earth!"

The Guardians erupted into battle cries and war chants. The whole thing *was* on the cheesy side, straight from Hollywood, but it worked. A good pep talk had always invigorated me before a fight, and this one had done the same.

The Phoenix began dividing up into who would fight physically, who would project their souls for the battle, and who would be inside with the healers to protect the bodies of those who projected. I had no choice but to be out here on the lawn, fighting physically.

"Asia, go inside and help the healers," I said to her, noticing how uninvolved she'd been in everything.

"No. I told you I'd fight."

"You're not in the right frame of mind. The last thing I need is for Brock to come back and find you dead."

"I'll fight my hardest, I promise you that. You don't need to worry about me."

I studied her face, the despair that filled her eyes. She moved closer to me and wrapped a hand around my arm.

"Please, Jeric," she begged. "Don't send me inside. I need to be out here. I need to fight. And ... I need to be here—right here—when he comes back. It's the only way I'll know."

I didn't know what she meant by that. Surely she'd feel the presence of Brock's soul the moment he returned to our world even if she was inside the manor. But the pleading look in her sorrow-filled eyes made me give in.

"Don't make me regret it," I growled.

"Don't worry about me so much. I promised you I'd fight, and I will. I'll do whatever it takes, remember?"

I stared at her for another moment, and then nodded. "Whatever it takes."

"Everyone's in place," Hope said from the edge of the water. "Time to open the Gate."

I called out the order, and all of us in physical forms on the lawn tensed up and braced for the battle that was about to begin. The Dark souls above us immediately grew excited, swirling into a cloud that expanded by the second as more flew from all corners of the world to join them. A rumbling sound came from the bay. The water rippled toward us, and then grew into larger waves. A steady stream of Darkness rose from the water where the Gate was and merged into the black cloud overhead.

Then physical figures burst out of the water and more fell from the air above. Some four-legged and monstrous, and others two-legged but just as beastly. All of them angry and hell-bent on attacking us, running and stomping through the water toward land. All of them sending out wave after wave of Darkness. The Lakari from above began dropping onto the lawn in human form, ready to fight.

The Darkness that blasted me disintegrated the hope I'd had only moments ago. Asia and I may have been too Dark already to put up much of a fight. And if it was too late for us, it was too late for everyone else.

So I couldn't think that way. Asia and I had promised each other to do whatever it took, and I wouldn't break that promise. Not to her, not to my Leni.

I fought the beasts and Shadowmen as hard as I could, punching and kicking and using my sword. But for every one I slayed, three more came. Enyxa's Dark souls must have been pouring out of all of her worlds and invading ours. She'd been planning for this for millennia. She'd had them all at the ready. Hundreds of thousands of souls she'd made go Dark, maybe millions. We had barely a thousand Guardians.

We may have had Hope, who fought as hard as the rest of us, trying to protect our world, but the only way to win was for Leni, Brock, Bex, and Nathayden to join us.

But even as Dark souls continued pouring out of the Gate, they never came.

"We have to use the Book to summon them," Hope called out to me. "Asia! Jeric! Hurry!"

I sliced off the head of an alien beast I'd been fighting and ran toward the water's edge. Asia met us there. Following Hope's lead, we each scooped water into our hands and poured it over the area of the cover image that depicted the Gate under the island with the tree. The water in the image glowed.

"Now press your fingers to it," Hope said, "and call them back by their souls' names."

Hope and I both pressed two fingers to the silvery-blue part of the image. Asia's small hand, however, paused in midair above ours.

"Hope," she said, her voice quiet and desperate, "are they going to remember us when they come back? Or will their memories be stripped away again?"

My eyes flew up to her face. I'd forgotten about the theories we'd exchanged that explained why we all lost our memories after a Separation. Yoshi and Tasha had speculated that the Space Between or the Gate did it, or it simply had something to do with returning to Earth. I'd suggested it had been Enyxa. However it happened, that would really fucking suck. I couldn't imagine Leni not remembering me or everything we'd been through together. We'd be okay, but it would suck. But for the others ... Brock and Bex ... would losing their memories be a good thing? Would Brock be better off if he had no memory of having and losing his son? Would Bex, too, if she didn't remember being beaten to near death by someone who claimed to love her? Was that what Asia wanted? Did she want Brock to remember her and their life together, or did she hope he'd forget the horrible memories? This must have been what had her so quiet the last few hours. Hope looked at me with the same questions in her eyes, before softening her gaze as she turned to Asia.

"I can't make any guarantees," she replied, "but it had been Satan who had originally stolen your memories the first time, in a simple act of evil. It worked effectively, though, so Enyxa mimicked the curse every time she Separated you, so you wouldn't remember the rest of the Seven and how to save them."

"So it's not the Gate or the Space Between that's been stripping our memories?" I clarified.

Hope made a face. "All souls lose memories of past lives when you're born anywhere, every time, but for Guardians, that loss should be only temporary, until you Bond and Forge. It's been Enyxa who's prevented that recall all along."

"And she could still do it, since she's with them, right?" Asia asked.

Hope sighed. "It's a possibility, yes. But Anastasia, no matter what happens or what's already happened between the two of you, you and Broderick will know each other and you will love each other. That's something I can guarantee because you *are* one and the same soul."

Asia blinked several times and sucked her lips in as she sniffed. Then she nodded and dropped her fingers to the Book's cover. "I guess there's only one way to find out."

Hope smiled.

"Then let's call them home." She closed her eyes. "Bring Jacquelena, Broderick, Rebethannah, and Nathayden back to this world, this place where they belong," she ordered the Book, and Asia and I echoed her. "Besides water, the most important ingredient is belief. You must truly and completely *believe* from the space within."

I put my whole damn soul into believing my girl would return to me, as well as the others, and I murmured the chant under my breath. The light of a Gate sprang out of the water directly in front of us. I watched and waited with bated breath. A form darkened the light, followed by several more.

None were the souls we'd summoned.

CHAPTER 25

Leni   THE SLIGHTEST BIT of warmth filled my soul for a short moment. A feeling of Jeric's soul briefly brushing against mine. Impossible, I knew, but maybe it was a sign that he'd heard my messages. Maybe he was trying to respond to me. I really had no idea if this was true or not, but I had to fight through the Darkness weighing heavily on me and pray that he heard me ... that he would open the Gate for us. I also had to hope that we had enough Light left in us to enter the Gate into Earth.

And to keep Enyxa from following us.

She paced around the cavern, waiting for us to succumb to her Darkness. Our physical bodies, already weak, would likely die before we turned completely, and we'd have to go through as many life cycles as it took on Dark worlds like this one and Erde, churning through the pain she threw at us over and over until the process was complete. She must have thought we were close to giving in this time around since she remained by our sides. Or maybe she simply stayed for the entertainment of watching us spiral into the Darkness.

When she was on the far side of the icy cave, far enough away that she couldn't push me back down, I gathered every last bit of energy I had remaining to shove the Darkness aside and pull myself to my hands and knees. Every cell of my body felt like it was made of lead, and I strained just to remain upright. Although the world we were on remained colder than cold, sweat beaded on my forehead as I reached for the knife I'd stuffed in my boot.

"We ... have ... to ... fight her," I said to the others as I struggled to breathe.

Brock didn't move, but Hayden and Bex did. They rose to their feet and pulled out their own weapons. Enyxa only laughed.

"You dare to fight me?" she asked, her tone teasing like an adult would use with a child in a tickle fight.

For a moment, I fell for it, thinking how ridiculous of me to even consider challenging her. She was strong and powerful, a queen of the Darkness. And why should I fight her when giving in to her was so much easier? When giving in meant I'd become one of hers and she'd take care of me?

But only for a moment.

"Damn right," I said as I shoved myself to my feet and lunged at her, knife poised to plunge into her neck.

Blackness filled my vision. I flew through the air. My back cracked against something hard—a wall of solid ice—and I fell to the floor. My memory of the fire that killed Jacey's parents flashed through my mind. As soon as I realized what she was doing, I pushed the memory away and focused on Jeric and my love for him.

Enyxa snarled. As though silently planned, Hayden and Bex attacked her. With a swipe of Enyxa's arm, they flew across the room as I'd just done, screaming against the memories Enyxa forced onto them.

"Brock," I whispered through clenched teeth as I nudged him with my boot, barely able to reach his leg with the tip of it. "Snap out of it, Brock, and help us."

He didn't budge. I blew out a breath and tried again with Enyxa. I managed to slice my blade over her shoulder before she sent me across the room, but by the time I returned to the present after another horrible memory, her wound had closed. I'd landed between Hayden and Bex who were crouched next to me. Enyxa stared at us from the center of the room, her black eyes sparkling with laughter and her mouth stretched into a toothy grin. She was enjoying this.

"You can't beat me," she said, and she let out a wicked laugh that lifted the hairs on my arms.

Hayden tapped three fingers on the floor in front of him. He tapped it again, this time with the tips of two fingers.

"You'll *never* win," I said, and Hayden's single finger hit the floor.

The three of us sprang upwards and outwards. We tackled Enyxa, but only managed to land a few blows before she threw us off of her again. I slammed into the wall once more with several loud cracks. I didn't know if that was the ice on the wall or my bones breaking, but pain wracked through me. I slid to the floor next to Brock, who remained in the fetal position, ignoring everything going on around him. Darkness enveloped me. More memories slammed down, and these were too awful to bear. With one last-ditch effort, I silently screamed for Jeric until my soul could barely hold on and tears spilled over and froze to my cheeks.

Lights sprang out of the ice. A circle of them reaching for the cave's roof.

Enyxa let out a shout of glee. "Oh, Jacquelena, I think I *will* win. Thank you for your help."

With a siren's shriek, she stepped into the lights. Snarls and growls filled the cave as her hellhounds entered and followed her. They all disappeared into the Gate.

We need to go, too. I thought the words, but couldn't act on them. My body hurt too much and felt too weak to move. My soul felt heavier and Darker with each beat of my heart.

"Come on," Bex said, shaking my foot. She crawled over to me. "We have to go in the Gate."

"I can't do it again," I said. "What if we don't go home?"

"Who cares?" Hayden said. "As long as we get the hell off this place."

Small arms slid under my pits and pulled me up to sitting. Bex braced me from behind. She'd somehow become the strong one trying to save my life. But it was becoming too late for me.

"We're going through the Gate, and ya'll are comin' with us," she said as she scooted for the lights. "And you're going to believe real fucking hard that we're goin' home. You can do this, Leni. You *need* to do it. For Jeric, if no other reason."

I was too helpless to fight her and too weak to help her. She tugged me toward the Gate.

"Brock," I said. "We can't leave him."

"We're not leaving anyone," Hayden said as he squatted at Brock's feet. He grabbed the other man's ankles and pulled.

"Brock, come on," I tried to yell at him. If I could muster this much energy, so could he. "Let's find Asia, Brock."

"Why?" he moaned. "So I can break her heart again?"

"Stop it," I snarled. Or I tried to. It came out more like a soft hiss, too weak to be a real command. "Just come with us through the Gate."

"So we can end up on another fucked up world gone Dark? Guess that's where we belong anyway."

Ignoring him, Bex and Hayden yanked at both of us and managed to pull us through the Gate's walls. With the last shred of hope I possessed, knowing how much Earth's souls needed us, I concentrated every fiber of my being and my soul on returning home and to Jeric.

Darkness consumed us. And Brock was right: that's where we belonged.

CHAPTER 26

Jeric A WOMAN STEPPED through the walls of the Gate, with curves that made Leni look like a boy, all of them emphasized by her tight, black bodysuit and boots that reached over her knees. Her long, black and white hair blew wildly, and her black eyes were even crazier. They matched the maniacal grin that spread on her face as she looked around. All of the fighting ceased as everyone froze, staring at her. I'd never met her before in person—that I could remember anyway—but I knew for certain this was Enyxa.

Following her came three dogs the size of cargo vans, each with three heads nearly as big as their bodies. Their black fur was matted and mangy, and their black eyes showed white as they lolled around their sockets. With the putrid stink of rotten eggs, saliva dripped from their foot-long fangs, and I had to cover my nose and mouth with the inside of my elbow to keep the sulfuric smell from gagging me.

"Yes, I'm here," she said. "The party can begin."

The Lakari jumped back into action, and our Guardians fought back. Enyxa spoke in a strange, guttural language, and many of the other monsters returned to their attacks. Another phrase in another language and the rest sprang into the fight.

The Darkness had become so deep in our immediate area, blacker than the darkest hour of night, and I could barely see around the manor's lawn, but I could definitely hear the battle resuming. The sounds of gnashing teeth and metal against metal filled the air. Grunts and groans and battle cries, too. A wail of pain every now and then. Both Guardians and monsters going down. Lakari disintegrated and flew to the sky to regroup. Enyxa cackled like a stereotypical cartoon witch.

Asia and I only stood there, though, with Hope by our side. Staring at the lights of the new Gate and waiting with our breaths held. Hope and I tried to summon them again. Asia remained a statue, her lips sealed. No more bodies or souls came through the Gate opened by the Book of Phoenix, but more Dark beings continued flowing from the main Gate out in the bay.

My stomach knotted, and I wanted to throw up.

"They're not coming," I finally said, my words garbled because of the lump in my throat. I tore my eyes from the lights and looked around, taking in the scene of violence and death, of shadows fighting and others lying dead on the ground. We were severely outnumbered. Not that it would matter in the end, but the less Darkness in this world when we went down, the longer the human souls could hold out. "We need to close the—"

A green-skinned, troll-like beast, size XXXXXL, bowled into the three of us, slamming into my left side. I went down, falling on top of Asia and Hope. Ignoring the crunching sound I'd heard when it hit me and the pain shooting through my left arm, I jumped up and swung my right foot toward the beast's chest, the highest point I could reach. Asia and Hope sprang up, too, with blades extended. They carved gashes into the troll's torso, but it only smirked lopsidedly, exposing its crooked, pocked teeth.

"It takes more than that to kill a Weiran," someone said from behind us—Enyxa's voice. "One of the most invincible Dark races in this universe. A nearly perfect soldier."

"But not completely invincible," Hope said over her shoulder, and she slapped her hand over one of the cuts in the Weiran's skin. A bright light flowed into the alien's body, coming out at its various openings, including the gashes we'd sliced into it. Its scream was like a sonic boom. The earth shook when it fell.

Enyxa snarled, and I took advantage of the moment. With my blade held high, I charged at her. Her arm swept out, and without her even touching me, a force flew into me, slamming into my chest and sending me sailing. I landed several yards away on my back, my breath flying out of me and pinpricks of light shooting across my vision.

"You want to play that way, young angel?" Enyxa said, and she let out a wicked laugh. "You're on!"

A wave of Darkness blasted at me. It blanketed me, soaked into me, consumed me. A vision of Leni's body sprawled out on a sheet of blue ice filled my mind. Her opened eyes stared upwards, not sea-green and beautiful, but cloudy gray and empty of life. Enyxa's own memory of what she'd left behind to come here. The pain I'd been living with for the past several days didn't compare to the agony that ripped through my heart and soul now. I tried to cover my head with my hands, as if that would help, but physical pain in my arm knocked me back to reality. Asia's screams sounded from somewhere nearby.

I forced my eyes open, in time to see Hope blast her light at Enyxa. The bitch sprang upwards and flipped in the air. The light blasted into an alien, and it exploded. Enyxa landed and ran off, out of my line of vision. I rolled over and tried to push myself to my knees with one arm. The ground quaked underneath me, and I looked up and around. One of those fire-breathing elephant-like things that had been coming through the Gate was barreling through the water, headed right for me. A shot of adrenaline forced me to my feet.

"Close the fucking Gate!" I yelled right before the beast rammed at me.

I lifted my knife up and slashed at its neck. Black blood spurted, spraying me, and it blew out a burst of fire. Someone in the direction of the flames screamed. Asia flew over the top of it and pierced her blade between its shoulders before sliding down its side. She landed next to me, panting, as the monster reared up, blowing more fire with its anger. Its tree-trunk-like front legs waved in the air before they crashed back to the ground, leaving divots in the earth and forcing us to stumble backwards.

"We're only making it mad," I said, and even I could hear the defeat in my voice. The image of Leni's dead body hadn't left my vision. The Darkness weighed me down more than ever.

"I ... I can't fight like I used to," Asia said, still working to draw in breaths. "I couldn't even jump all the way over it, let alone actually hurt it."

"We can't fight like the rest of them," I agreed, jutting my chin toward the other Guardians. They weren't entirely successful, but at least most of them were holding their own for as long as possible. Without our other halves here, Asia and I were comparatively weak and worthless.

The beast swung its head toward us. A Guardian came running in our direction, wielding a long sword. She jumped upwards and arced the blade downward, severing the trunk just as it hit us and knocked us down. Upon impact, the appendage shattered into hundreds of wriggling pieces, but the monster itself was only angered more. The skin at the amputation site split apart and several thin, white tentacles curled out of it, toothy, snapping mouths at their ends.

"That's disgusting," Asia muttered. The other Guardian screamed, swinging her sword wildly as the tentacles swayed toward her. She managed to land a few swipes, cutting the monster, but it wouldn't go down.

"Its eye," I said, staggering to my feet once again. It was a guess pulled out of my ass. No more than a gut feeling. But stabbing the beast in the eye was the best thing I could come up with to defeat it. "Get it ... in the ... eye."

It took every ounce of effort I had to raise my knife in the air again. No way would I be able to jump to reach its eye when I felt like the entire planet was strapped to my waist, pulling me down. So I arced my hand behind me and swung the blade up, letting go at the top of my swing. The knife spun end over end. I stumbled backward and fell onto my ass from the effort. As I hit the ground, the blade's point plunged right into the beast's orb.

A fountain of black blood spurted everywhere. The creature wailed, blowing fire in the air. People screamed. The monster wobbled on its legs, and then it started leaning over, toward Asia and me. We tried to scramble backwards, but it fell onto us, crushing our legs and pinning us under its weight. My head cracked against the ground again. The little black pieces that remained of its trunk wriggled and jumped their way onto Asia's body and mine. Dozens of the fuckers latched onto us, little spindly teeth or barbs piercing into our skin. I tried to brush them off, but they were hooked on like leeches.

Instead of sucking my blood, however, the opposite seemed to be true. The things were spurting thin streams of venom into my flesh—an ice-cold venom of Darkness that leaked into my blood and carried throughout my system. As if my heart and soul could take any more of the Dark.

I couldn't move my body. My legs, shattered and pinned by the alien monster, and my broken arm screamed in pain when I tried. My good hand scrambled to fling off the leeches, but there were too many of them, each streaming Darkness into my blood, my heart, my soul. It overcame my last bit of energy. My arm fell to the ground. Splotches of black burst like fireworks in my vision.

I rolled my head to the side to see Asia lying on the ground next to me in the same predicament—half of her body wedged under the creature and her skin dotted with alien bits shooting Darkness into her veins. Her head lolled toward me. I was sure the defeated expression on her face and the despair in her eyes mirrored my own.

"Maybe we'll meet them in the Space Between," I whispered hoarsely.

Her glassy eyes watered, and she gave me the slightest smile. "I never thought of you as the optimist."

"If there's any chance of finding my Leni, I'll hang onto whatever hope I can get."

Her focus moved from my eyes to something behind me. "Good news is it looks like they closed the Gate."

I forced my head to roll to the other side. The lights in the distance, out by the island, had gone dark. The main Gate was closed. The lights nearer to us, barely off shore, began to dim. The Gate the Book had opened was closing, too. My own soul Darkened even more along with its lights.

I'd failed my girl. I'd failed the Phoenix Guardians. I'd failed the world. The only thing left to do was to submit to the Darkness.

CHAPTER 27

Asia AS THE GATE we'd opened with the Book of Phoenix dimmed, a tear leaked out of the corner of my eye and slid across the bridge of my nose before falling to the ground under my cheek. I thought, at first, the sense of loss inexplicable since I had given up hope for Brock and me long ago, but it hit me hard nonetheless. Then I realized it was the thought of *everyone* losing Brock that broke me. That shattered my heart into a million pieces. A world without him—a universe without his soul—was unimaginable. Devastating. The loss of his soul completely wasn't fair to all of those who loved him, especially his other half. That other half wasn't me, I knew in my head, but I felt the pain as if it were my own.

The ice-cold Darkness from the little slug-like things all over my skin seeped into my blood, and I waited for its numbness to take over. To push the pain away completely. To Darken the last bit of Light that remained in my soul and to fill that space within me that had become so empty. I'd been longing for the promised peace of the Darkness for what felt like half a lifetime. But if I hadn't been ready for it before, I was now, especially as I watched the Gate before me fall completely dark. I closed my eyes.

A blast of Darkness hit me again, as if to say, "Come with me." Along with it, Enyxa flooded me with the worst memories of this lifetime. Walking into the abortion clinic and running out of it, losing my baby anyway, fighting the deepest pits of depression in my room, leaving my life and everything I knew behind, living out of my car, seeing Kami return for her family, hearing Brock say those words: "You don't belong in my life." The memories crushed me. Ground the pieces of my heart into powder. Opened my soul so the Darkness could wash in.

But it wasn't Darkness that filled me.

Warmth. Light. Hope. Love.

"*NO!*" I silently screamed, wishing I could explain to whoever was trying to help me—probably Hope—that it was too late. That the Darkness was what I wanted.

Thankfully, the feelings subsided. They were too weak to overcome what already possessed me.

"I'm sorry," someone whispered above me. "So sorry."

A heavy weight fell on top of my chest. The Darkness within it was nearly as thorough as my own. The being's essence lifted, and I only knew this because it pulled at my own, wanting to take me with it. My soul rose, too, unable to fight it. Not *wanting* to fight it. Because this was the one I belonged with. This soul, as Dark as it was, was my true other half. My Twin Flame. Wherever it had come from, whatever Dark world it had been on, it had finally found me. I felt it in the space within me—in every fiber of my soul.

"*Welcome back,*" my soul whispered to the other one, and they both crashed into each other.

If I hadn't known for sure before, I definitely knew now. We filled each other with utter completeness. Our Darkness swirled together, as did the little bit of Light until the black became a dark charcoal gray. The more our essences mingled and combined, the stronger mine became. A new hope blossomed, bringing with it love. We gave it back and forth, sharing it with each other until it became one love, both of ours, nobody else's. Love like no other, so complete and solid like I'd never felt before. A bond so tight, it could only belong to Twin Flames. *This* was my true love. My Twin Flame. My other half of our dyad pair.

"*You are mine*," his soul sang into mine.

"*Forever and always*," I confirmed into his.

"*I don't deserve it.*"

"*Don't ever doubt it.*"

"*Never again. Your love is my life force.*"

We looked down at our bodies. If I'd been in my physical form, I would have wept. If my soul wasn't a part of his this very moment, I would have never believed it. I'd already written us off, believing we'd been Forged together even though we didn't belong together. But all of that doubt disappeared the moment I felt his soul with mine again. The Darkness had tried to deceive me, but the Light won. Brock's body was draped over my torso, his thickly muscled arms wrapped around me. Hope knelt by the two of us, her head bent, probably crying.

"*She's alive!*" His emotions ran through me.

"*She's been our Hope all along. Let's give her a little now.*"

She looked up at us, at our souls, as if she could see us. Maybe she could. But we slid into our bodies anyway. Brock lifted his weight off of me, and I opened my eyes to find his dark ones hovering right over me. He lowered his head and pressed his lips gently against mine. Hope let out a cry. The joy in it was nothing compared to what filled me.

"You're back," I whispered.

"Only because of you. I've been to Hell and back, literally I think. And I almost gave in. I almost bought the lie Enyxa tried to feed me. But when we finally landed back here, I knew this was where I belonged. With you."

"You remember me? Everything?"

He cocked his head. "How could I ever forget you? You are my one and only love, Asia."

"After everything I've done ..." Even knowing now, feeling it in my soul that his and mine belonged together, I still didn't know if this current person—Brock Verdor—could truly love me, who I was right now, in *this* life.

"You've done nothing but love me, Asia. Don't blame yourself for what Enyxa did to us. Just focus on us, babe. Focus on what matters most."

I blinked away the tears of gratitude and gave a tiny nod, the most movement I could muster against the pain of my crushed legs. "Us. Our love. That's what matters most. I feel it in every space within my soul."

His lips turned up into a smile. I wanted to feel them on me again. I wanted to kiss him until I could feel nothing else but his lips moving against mine. I wanted his mouth to drive away the pain and bring the bliss it always delivered. But what I wanted would have to wait. The sounds of war still surrounded us, and our fellow Guardians needed our help.

"Let's shove this bitch back to the Dark where she belongs," Brock said as he rolled completely off of me and lay next to me. His fingers intertwined with mine.

"I'll guard your bodies," Hope said.

Brock and I projected our souls from our bodies again. We swirled together for a moment for another boost of strength.

And then we went to battle. Together. As one, as we were always meant to be.

CHAPTER 28

SOMETHING CHANGED. I didn't know how long I'd been in the Dark, how long I'd been *Leni* wherever I was now, but I felt the change in my chest ... in my heart. A bit of Lightness that made it pound out one more beat, as shriveled as it was. And then another. My heart rate picked up pace, although blood already rushed in my head, drowning out everything else. It began to quiet, though, allowing other sounds in as my vision cleared as well. I blinked against the blackness surrounding me, trying to make sense of what I heard—roars and growls, cries of pain, metal clashing against metal. It sounded like a battle.

My surroundings became clearer as I grew fully alert. I stood in water, facing the shore. It was night and hard to see, but I thought a large shape loomed just ahead. I squinted. A big building? Between it and me were dark shadows moving against the darker night. Fighting. Why? Where was I? What was going on? I shook my head, trying to clear it, but nothing made sense. I couldn't remember how I'd arrived here. Why I would be standing in a body of water. I didn't even know if I was in a lake or a sea, although the waves pushing at me told me it was at least bigger than a pond.

What had I been doing before? Was I brought here? Who would throw me into the middle of a battle like this? Or had I come here on my own? Was I supposed to be a part of it? Nothing but a deep black filled my mind. No memories of a past. Nothing at all.

Panic began to rise. My heart rate spiked even faster. I tried to draw in air, but couldn't. What was I going to do? I needed to get out of here.

And then ...

I felt it. In that space within me that had been so empty. My soul. My *soul* felt another. It recognized the other and immediately responded. Growing inside me, the little bit of Light remaining in it brightening. Jeremicah. The other half to me ... Jacquelena. That's right. And my Jeremicah was here.

Here ...? *Here!* Earth! I'd made it back to my Earth! To my home! To my Jeric!

Everything flooded back to me. The worlds, the Gates, struggling to return to this place, to this man, my love and my other half.

His soul was very Dark, like my own had become, but I felt it nonetheless. And just feeling his so close Lightened mine considerably. A heavy weight lifted from my shoulders. Strength returned to me. And even with the battle waging fiercely in front of my eyes, hope exploded.

We had a chance.

But there was so much to do. A war to win.

Now that my awareness returned, I realized Bex and Hayden stood in the water with me, although Brock was gone. I wished there was time to send Bex and Hayden's souls to the Gate to be Forged, now that we were in a world where Darkness didn't rule, but there wasn't. I ran through the water with them right behind me. My knife was in my hand, and I targeted the physical beasts first—gozzards and Weirans and those centipede things that made me shudder, as well as others I hadn't had the pleasure to meet and kill on the Dark worlds. My speed hadn't fully returned, but I still moved quickly, latching onto shoulders and backs, and stabbing eyes and throats before jumping to the next beast. The Phoenix Guardians were hugely outnumbered, but Hayden and I made a pretty big dent in the number of alien monsters, with some help from Bex.

The first break we had, I ran over to Jeric's body laying half under a dead gozzard.

"Oh, no!" I pressed my hand against his cheek and stroked his lips with my thumb. "Don't give up, babe. I'm here."

He was so still, but I could feel his soul. He wasn't gone yet.

Asia lay next to him with Brock already sprawled over her and a woman kneeling next to them, her face buried in her hands. At least Brock had found Asia. We'd been able to bring him back, but his soul had become so black with all of the times Enyxa had put his horrible memories of losing his son on repeat. He'd pretty much given up before we brought him home, and I could only hope Asia's love was enough to return the Light to his soul. I could only hope he was wrong about them being forced together. The way he'd come straight to her when we arrived and held her now, I had to believe they were meant for each other. They just had to believe it themselves.

A hand clamped over mine that was pressed to Jeric's face. I looked back at him. His blue eyes were open and although full of pain, also somehow smiling.

"Jeric!" I threw myself on top of him, and he groaned underneath me. He was hurt. I sat back up. "I'm sorry. So sorry."

"Don't be." He squeezed my hand. "You're here. Everything else will be okay."

I nodded and looked around. "Yes, but there's still a fight to be won."

"Go. I'll be waiting right here."

I studied the gigantic gozzard squishing him and Asia. Although some of my strength had returned, I knew there was no way I could move it myself. A Weiran cut off all thoughts of that anyway as he threw a fist at me.

I ducked and rolled away from the others, hoping to keep the troll's attention on me. He turned toward me with a snarl, both of his fists coming together with my body right in the middle. I rolled again, then sprang to my feet, launched myself into the air, and landed on the back of his fat neck. I aimed for the eye with my knife, but he twisted and batted at me, and the point stabbed into his ear. He didn't like that, either, and wailed, but it didn't take him down. He tried to shake me off, then hit at me again, landing a blow into the side of my head. Stars shot across my vision, but I didn't let go. I hung onto the knife's hilt and tightened my legs around his neck. He stopped trying to throw me off for a moment, and I seized the opportunity. After wiggling the blade free from his thick hide, I tried again. This time it landed in his eye. He fell to his knees with his arms reaching out. They plowed into the gozzard, moving the other beast off of Jeric and Asia as he fell face forward. I leapt from its neck before its shoulders hit the ground.

As I swung around to look for another attacker, my gaze landed on Enyxa and her hellhounds halfway across the lawn. Her black eyes locked with mine. She gave me what I thought was a taunting wave. There was nothing taunting about it. A force of Darkness slammed into me, knocking me down.

I fell hard on my knees and then on my side as she blasted me again and again, reminding me once more of all of the atrocities I'd done to others, including her, and the agony I'd suffered. I clamped my hands over my ears and squeezed my eyes shut, trying to block her out. But there was only one way to overcome her. One way to defeat her. One way to win.

The Light.

And the Light came from love. I reached my arm out toward Jeric, but he was several feet too far away. He looked at me and reached his own tattooed arm for me. I tried to scooch closer to him. It took all of my determination and will to budge a few inches. His mouth moved, but I couldn't hear him over the din of the fighting around us. I wiggled a little closer, but Darkness began to crowd into my vision.

"*No!*" I silently shouted against it. "*You will not take me!*"

There was a tugging at my soul. I felt Jeric's right over me. *Project!* That's what he'd been trying to tell me. It had been so long since I'd been able to, I'd forgotten that I could now. But it would be stupid to do so. Enyxa was probably waiting for us to do exactly that so she could send one of her Dark souls to destroy our bodies.

"Go ahead," said the woman who'd been kneeling next to Brock and Asia. She stood now, looking as though she was guarding them. "I'll watch your bodies. Don't worry."

I didn't know who she was, but I had no choice but to trust her.

"I'm Hope," she said, and now I knew why she looked familiar—like Brock. I didn't know how it was possible that she was alive, though. I'd seen the memories of the accident replay more times than my heart could take. But at this moment, I could only believe she was that: our Hope.

I threw myself out of my body and straight into Jeric's soul. Our forces combined, swirled together, filled each other's empty spaces.

"*Damn it, Leni, I've missed you so much,*" Jeric's soul said into mine. "*I've missed* this *so much.*"

"*I almost can't believe we're doing this. I didn't think we'd ever be able to again.*" Love and disbelief nearly overwhelmed me. I wanted to stay in that moment, to stretch it out into eternity.

If Enyxa didn't blast more Darkness our way, I might have done just that.

"Can we kill this fucking bitch already?" Brock asked from beside us. He and Asia had pulled apart, their projected forms floating next to us, both of them a light gray now, nearly the color their souls should be.

Jeric and I pulled our souls away from each other.

"Hell yeah!" Jeric said.

"You'll have to take her soul," Hope said as if she were part of the conversation.

Could she see us? She seemed to be looking directly at us, but how could she? How did she even know who we were and anything about us? Jeric's soul shared with mine in less than a second who and what Hope was. I had no words, but was glad to have her on our side.

"Get her soul," she instructed. "You'll know what to do with it, Jacquelena."

The four of us floated down to ground level, side by side, Asia and I in the middle and the guys on our flanks. Enyxa stared at us from across the lawn, seeing us in soul form. She gave us a mocking grin. Bex and Hayden stepped up, pushing Asia and me apart.

"We sense you," Bex whispered in answer to the question I didn't ask but had been thinking.

Enyxa laughed.

"We're here, too," said Kel, and he and Mat stood on Brock's far side.

"Us, too," said an Asian man. Jeric told me his name was Yoshi and the woman with him was Tasha. They stood on the other side of Jeric.

"If you're in your physical bodies, take the hellhounds," Jeric instructed. "If you can get through them, go for Enyxa herself."

That was my man. Giving orders like a commander. Like a leader ... the leader he was supposed to be. I beamed, my soul shining brightly.

"On my three," Jeric said, and he quietly counted down.

We all soared for Enyxa and her hellhounds. She laughed at first. The dogs snarled and growled, and then went on the attack. While her hounds went after the other Guardians, Enyxa targeted our souls, trying to blast us with more Darkness, but we split and swooped, and it missed us. She threw another hit toward Asia and Brock. I felt them take the blow, their souls rolling through the air, but Jeric and I took advantage of Enyxa's distraction. We flew directly at her, brightening ourselves as much as possible, and planned to hit her hard with our Light, hopefully hard enough to knock her soul out. But we flew right *through* her.

"What the hell?" Jeric asked.

We swooped back around, taking in the scene below us. Bodies, belonging to both Guardians and creatures from other worlds, lay strewn around the manor's lawn. Many still fought, mostly against Lakari. As far as we could tell, all of the aliens had been killed. But the Lakari outnumbered us twenty-to-one, easily.

"If we can defeat her, the Lakari will follow her to the Dark worlds," I said.

"Let's—ah, shit."

We watched below as one of the hellhounds snapped Mat off the ground with its mouth and shook him like a rag doll. Kel already lay lifelessly on the ground in front of its paws.

Hayden and Bex, however, who hadn't even been Forged and strengthened yet, managed to kill their hellhound. They went after Enyxa next. Bex held her knife in the air as she ran to the face of evil. Hayden ran with a dagger in each hand. Brock, Asia, Jeric, and I charged at Enyxa simultaneously, giving Bex and Hayden a fair chance. We slammed into her at the same time. Her body shattered into pieces. They all flew up above us to reform.

"Ohmagosh, I've seen that before!" Bex exclaimed, remembering the Shadowmen's attack at the K-bomb party. I didn't know she'd even seen that much.

"She can't hold her form," Jeric said.

"Get her soul!" Hope yelled at us.

"Project," I told Bex and Hayden before Jeric and I flew up toward Enyxa.

She dropped out of our reach, though, to the ground, and returned to her physical form. We soared at her again. This time as we passed through her, I took hold of whatever my fingers could grasp. Being in soul form myself, I could only grab onto her soul. I yanked at it. Jeric came back and latched onto me. Together we pulled, stretching Enyxa's soul as she let out a blood-curdling scream. Finally, her soul detached. Her physical "form" fell to the ground and disintegrated. A black, smoke-like substance, but more tangible and with thin strands of white running through it, shaped itself into Enyxa's form. She twisted and turned in my grip, trying to pull free.

"Doesn't feel very nice to be torn out of your body, does it?" Jeric asked.

She snarled and fought against me. I held on as tight as I could.

"Bring her here," Hope called. She'd stepped away from our bodies a few feet and into the water, where she knelt down, wetting the cover of the Book of Phoenix. The light of a new Gate began shining under the water. When it hit the surface, though, a fire burned in a circle on top of the water.

"NOOOOO!" Enyxa shrieked. With a hard jerk, she flew out of my grip.

"Get her!" I yelled.

She swooped out of the Guardians' reach and upward toward a cloud of Dark souls. We couldn't let her reach it.

"Hurry!" Jeric yelled as he soared faster and higher than any of us.

His fist swung out, and he punched her in her soul's throat. The force sent her off course, directly into Brock and Asia. They all tumbled in the air. Bex and Hayden's soul forms were closer, and they went after them. By the time they all stopped, Brock and Hayden both held a squirming Enyxa.

We all dropped down in front of Hope and the ring of fire, the guys holding Enyxa tightly. I almost felt sorry for her with her black-as-night soul. Well, except for the few streaks of white.

"Look what I have, Enyxa," Hope said calmly. She held a ball of dark gray, almost black, light in her hand, like a sphere of shadow. It began to unfurl, wisps curling upwards and out.

Enyxa fell completely still. The white strands of her soul brightened.

"Gabrixander?" she gasped. We all knew immediately who that was: Enyxa's other half. At one time, they'd been a part of our Phoenix family.

"Yes," Hope confirmed. "I've been holding him for you for nearly two millennia. Unfortunately, you were too focused on your vendetta to realize the true reason you've been wanting to return to this Earth all of this time. Because he'd been here."

"My love," Enyxa cried, and the sound of her wails pierced my heart.

Who knew she still had any love? The white of her soul grew even more. And I realized I should have known. Wasn't that what she'd been telling us? Wasn't love the reason she'd been so focused on her revenge? All of this, over the millennia, everything she'd ever done to us and the rest of the Guardians, had always been for her love, for her other half, and for the need to avenge her loss of him. To alleviate the pain of her broken heart and soul.

"You two can join each other now," Hope said. "You can be together, at least, in the Dark worlds."

Brock and Hayden moved her closer to the ring of fire. Hope held her hand out with the gray of Gabrixander's soul—a slightly lighter gray now—dripping over the sides of her cupped palm. After having no physical form for so long, he was unable to take any shape. Enyxa reached out for him. He glowed brighter. Brock and Hayden held her over the flames. They were about to drop her in, and Hope would let her other half follow so they could rejoin, even if it was in the pits of Hell. Even if they did finally find each other again and could reunite with the hope of love forever.

Hope ...

"*We don't kill unless there's no hope.*" That chick Alexis's words echoed in my mind. "*If there's even the slightest bit, we save them.*"

I hadn't understood her meaning then. The only Dark souls we'd had experience with at the time—the Lakari and the aliens of the Dark worlds—were Dark through and through. They'd succumbed, given themselves completely over to evil. There was no hope for them. I'd thought maybe Alexis had meant their equivalent to our Broken and Lost, who only needed help to the Space Between so they could find the Light and their loves. But, I knew now, she'd meant more than that. She'd also meant that the souls who appeared to be all Dark, who had been gone to the other side for even thousands of years, could still hold a trace of love. Of hope. Strands of Light left in the Darkness.

"*Wait!*" I screamed before the guys let her go. Following my intuition, what I felt to be true deep in my heart and soul, I soared in front of them, hovering over the ring of fire myself. "She has hope. So does he. There's *hope* for them! We can't kill them! We can't let them go like this!"

I flew at Enyxa's soul, slid my fingers between the Dark and Light parts, and pulled as hard as I could at a white fiber. The guys held Enyxa tightly, their fingers digging into her black shoulders, and pulled her backward. Bex came over and helped me. Those who had been on that other Earth with me understood what I meant. They knew what I was trying to do. Asia and Jeric only stared at us for a moment, but with a word of encouragement from Hope, they joined in the tug of war with Enyxa's soul. Asia, Jeric, and Bex pulled me back as I held onto the Light piece, stretching it until a little bit unraveled, then stretching it more.

Touching it like this, I realized the Dark parts were part of Satan. I could feel him and how he'd attached himself to her. And I could feel through his deep, deep Blackness that he'd only been using Enyxa all of this time to get his hands on Earth. As soon as she would have claimed this world, he would have taken it from her. She had been barely more than his puppet all of this time. She must have finally felt this truth, too, because her Light part in my hand began undulating and wriggling, trying to pull itself free from the black.

And then a horrible sound of fabric ripping apart, except it wasn't fabric.

We all knew the sound well. We also knew the pain. We'd all experienced it before. My soul hurt for Enyxa as she shrieked in agony while we tore hers into two, Separating the Dark from the Light. We flew backwards when they finally detached from each other. Asia, Bex, Jeric, and I, with the Light part of Enyxa's soul crying in my hands, stopped on the far side of the ring of fire. Brock and Hayden hovered opposite of us holding the black remnant as it hollered in a weak threat. As though tossing a piece of garbage into the bin, they released the shreds of soul into the fiery Gate, sending it back to Hell, back to Satan, where it belonged.

Lakari swooped down, a gush of Dark souls pouring into the Gate after their master. A river of them screamed by us and downward. Away. Out of our world. Once and for all. As if the Gate to Hell knew they'd all been sucked out of our Earth, it closed up with a swoosh, and the flames disappeared.

Enyxa jerked out of my grip and flew to her other half. They tried to join with each other, swirling together, but they were too weak on their own. Hope gathered them together and cupped them in her hands.

"Very good, Jacquelena, you followed your instinct and saw their love," she said as her body lit up and glowed a bright white. "Let's get them to the Space Between."

Jeric's soul clashed into mine, his pride for me washing through me. I returned the feeling, so proud of him for being the leader he was meant to be, before we shared a moment of peace. Then we pulled apart and, along with the others, followed Hope out to the permanent Gate in the middle of the bay.

"While we're here, you and Hayden can finally Forge," I said to Bex.

"Thank God and baby Jesus. I have no idea how we even survived that. That shit was crazy!"

I laughed, and so did the others.

When we reached the island with the weeping willow tree, Hope paused.

"That's my tree," she said.

Asia gasped. "I knew that! The Tree of Hope!"

"I planted it in the very beginning. I put a tree by each one of Earth's Gates," she said. "Maybe some day I'll tell you why."

She plunged downward then, the two souls still in her hands. We followed her down. The lights of the Gate sprang up. More Guardians joined us. Hundreds of souls. Hope held the two up.

"I hold here the two halves of Ny'xan, one of the Original Seven," she said. "May they find each other and their peace once again. May they grow together and return to us the strong souls of the Light they are meant to be. Until we meet again."

"Until we meet again," every Guardian said in unison.

Hope let them go, and they soared into the Gate. Everyone cheered and hollered when they disappeared inside. The sounds must have been strange to anyone else, and a pod of dolphins swam toward us to check it out. After a brief celebration in our soul forms, Jeric promised everyone a real party later. All of the Guardians except the remainder of the Original Seven left. Brock, Asia, Jeric, and I stood by as Bex and

Hayden entered the Gate. We didn't need to hear their vows. It was too late anyway, and they'd already proven themselves worthy.

When the Gate disappeared several moments later, a ball of blinding white light remained—their souls conjoined. In other words, making love in the way only souls can do.

"Well, then," Brock said, chuckling as he turned away. "We're out of here. You two enjoy that Bonding."

He took Asia's hand, and they flew upward together.

Jeric wrapped his soul around mine. "I think *we* have lots of Bonding to do, too."

The feeling sent tingles through me. We bounded upwards together and flew over the city lights as One, enjoying our reunion for all it was worth.

CHAPTER 29

I WEEK LATER

WARMTH ON MY face awoke me. I squinted my eyes open against a bright light with a large form silhouetted in it. I didn't have to wait for my eyes and brain to focus to know that was Brock standing in the sunlight streaming through the window. My soul felt him before I'd fully gained consciousness.

"Hey, beautiful," he greeted as he squeezed my hand and lifted my knuckles to his lips.

He shifted out of the light, allowing me to see his ruggedly handsome face better. His dark hair was as disheveled as always, as though he'd been pulling at it, which he probably had been. His chocolate eyes smiled warmly at me. Without moving my gaze from the face I missed so much, I could see from peripheral vision that I wasn't in the same room I'd spent the last week in, healing. No, this one was more familiar, although it felt different now. Bright. Not like the dark one it had been while Brock was gone.

"The healers let me bring you to our room," he said. "I didn't even wait for help. I carried you up here myself."

I smiled. "It's not like you left my side anyway."

He'd even slept in the chair next to me the first few nights, then in the bed with me when the healers allowed. We'd spent most of that time outside of our bodies, Bonding.

"No. But I couldn't wait to get you alone. I've been going crazy waiting for you to wake up. I've already wasted too much of my life without you."

My heart swelled, and my soul sang. I squeezed his hand and brought it to my lips to return the gesture of kissing his knuckles.

"I love you, Brock," I said around the lump in my throat.

He fell from the chair to his knees and rested his chin on the side of the bed.

"You give me life, Asia," he replied. "I will never doubt us again. I will never push you away. In fact, I will never let you go again."

I sucked in my bottom lip and gnawed at it as I looked into his deep brown eyes. "Before you say that, I have to tell you something."

"Nothing will change my mind, babe. Nothing can be worse than what we've been through already."

I nodded, although I wasn't quite sure I agreed. "Just let me get this out there. Jeric was right. You deserve to know everything about me. And then you can decide for certain."

I tried to sit up, but my legs couldn't quite cooperate.

"You're not fully healed yet," he said. "You're doing better than Jeric—he apparently took the brunt of the gozzard's weight and has that broken arm, too—but you're not quite up to snuff. Let me."

He came around to his side of the bed and crawled in next to me. Then he lifted my torso up and situated himself around me, then pulled me back against him. His muscular arms encircled my shoulders and his hands found mine in my lap, over the covers. Under the blanket, I wore only his extra-large shirt and panties. He picked my hands up and intertwined our fingers as I leaned back against his chest. His head leaned in, and he kissed my temple.

"What's on your mind?" he asked.

I drew in a deep breath and almost chickened out. "You've already been through a lot. Maybe now's not a good time."

His breath fluttered through my hair, and he lifted our hands to push some stray strands away from my face. I'd changed the color to a silvery lilac after he'd told me the other day that it had been his favorite color on me. I'd made it long, too, because I knew he liked to pull on it.

"I'm here with you. Life is good. Our souls are Light again. So unless you're about to tell me that you don't want me here ..."

I squeezed his fingers. "Never. But hear me out. I've done something really horrible—"

"Asia. Stop. I know you were taking the blame for what happened to Connor, but that was never your fault, babe. I *never* blamed you one second for that. Mom has some explaining to do, whenever she gets back from whatever she's doing, but not you. You took some of that pain for me, Asia. I would have never made it through that time if not for you. I would have gone Dark immediately."

I nodded against his chest. "I know that now. I'd always felt terrible about that, and it had caused a lot of strain between us before ... before you ... went to Hell and came back. But I understand now. I mean, it's good to hear that from you. You have no idea how good." I paused and sighed. "But this thing I have to tell you is definitely all me. Jeric can verify it."

Brock tensed up behind me, and his fingers tightened around mine. When he spoke, I could tell it was through a clenched jaw. "While I was gone ...?"

"What? No! Nothing like that!" I extracted a hand from his grip and lifted it to his cheek, soothing his jaw. Then I blew out a breath and spilled. "It was the night you disappeared, but first, I have to go back, to when I had my miscarriage."

And I finally told him everything. Everything about douchebag Drew and dickhead Mark, about my pregnancy and miscarriage. About being shoved down the stairs and my medical records being wiped out. About how they'd bought their way out of trouble and how badly it had pissed me off when Mason had done the same thing and then nearly killed Bex. And then, with a heavy dose of guilt mixed with fear of how he'd react to my atrocity, I told him what I did to Mason. He cringed.

Then he sat in stunned silence for a long moment.

And then he laughed.

He laughed so hard that he had us both bent over, his chest shaking me. His arms tightened around me as he settled down and sat back against the headboard again, pulling me with him.

"You really stabbed a broken bottle neck into his dick?" he asked, his voice mixed with disbelief and humor.

"Yeah, I pretty much did. It's bad, I know, and I still can't believe I did it. But the fucker deserved it."

"He most certainly did."

He laughed again and then crossed our arms over my chest, hugging me tighter.

"You're my hero," he whispered against my ear. He chuckled again. "I don't remember teaching you that move, though."

"The situation called for improvisation. Jeric had already beaten him to a pulp."

"He saw you do it, huh?"

"Yeah. I think it gave him a whole new perspective of me."

He laughed. "I don't doubt it. Nobody messes with my girl."

"Or the ones she loves."

His lips pressed against my cheekbone. "That includes me?"

I tilted my head and turned my neck, our mouths less than an inch from each other. "More than anyone."

He caught my lips within his full ones and kissed my worries away. When my neck couldn't hold that position any more, he kissed over my cheek and jaw and down the side of my throat, until his mouth landed on my favorite place. His lips parted, and his tongue swept out, swirling against my skin. I shuddered in his arms, then pulled his hands up to my chest and cupped them over my breasts. My nipples strained against the material of my shirt—I wore no bra—aching for his touch.

"Can we ...?" I asked breathlessly.

He moaned against my neck. "We're not supposed to. You can't be moved like that yet."

"But there are other ways to pleasure each other."

His mouth moved up to my ear, and he nibbled on my lobe. "I like your way of thinking. But I'm not going to do anything that might hurt you."

Despite his words, his erection pressed against my lower back.

"I'm pretty sure it would feel good, not hurt."

He pulled my lobe between his lips and circled it with the tip of his tongue before releasing it. "When I make love to you, Asia, I'm going to make *real* love *with* you."

"Oh, you most definitely will." I pulled his arms from around me and motioned for him to lie next to me. "Wait. Take your shirt off. I miss seeing you like that."

He pulled his shirt over his head, and I smiled at his beauty, although it only made me ache more for him. Once he lay down next to me, we turned to face each other. I trailed my fingertips over his glorious pecs and abs, then back and forth above the waistband of his jeans, making his muscles jump under my touch. Then I slid my hand over the large bulge in his jeans.

"Asia," he moaned, his eyes hooding over, the darkness of them smoldering.

"Touch me," I whispered. "I need your hands on me. I need to feel your body *and* your soul."

His hand slid under my shirt and up my side, over my ribs. He cupped my breast and rubbed his thumb over my tight nipple, then rolled and pinched it between his fingers.

"More," I whimpered as I undid his jeans and slid my hand inside, freeing him from the confines. His hand moved downward, under the covers, between my legs. He leaned in, and his mouth found mine at the same time his finger stroked against me. I became liquid at his touch.

"I don't want to hurt you."

"Then keep doing what you're doing," I moaned.

His whole hand became involved in pleasuring me as mine pleasured him, and we stroked each other more frantically and urgently until we both felt the release we needed—the release of our souls from our bodies at the height of our physical climax.

"This is what I really needed," my soul said to his. "Feeling you in all the spaces within me."

"Right where I belong," he agreed. "Where my soul belongs. As a part of yours since the beginning of time."

"And into eternity."

Our souls swirled more tightly together, forming an almost solid bond like when we had first been Forged. No longer would either of us doubt these words. Never again would we let anyone try to convince us differently, including our own selves.

We belonged together. Our souls two halves of the same One.

CHAPTER 30

4 WEEKS LATER

Jeric LENI JUMPED OUT of the Camaro after me, and I'd barely had a chance to shut the door before Brock peeled away. After several weeks of being stuck at the manor, we were all ready for freedom and privacy. While some of us had to physically heal, others cleaned up the manor after the big battle. We burned the Dark creatures' bodies. We buried our own after sending their souls to the Space Between. Yoshi and Tasha almost hadn't survived. Mat and Kel hadn't. Neither had Uri and Melinda. We said "Until we meet again" more times than I wanted to remember, but I would remember anyway. Every single one of them.

After we mourned them and Sissy, we celebrated. We celebrated our victory and our comrades' lives. We celebrated the fact that we may not be able to lead normal lives, exactly, but with Enyxa and the Lakari no longer a threat to this world, we might actually be able to live to old age with our Twin Flames. Something we'd never been able to do in the past. We all planned to take full advantage of this.

We all were ready to celebrate this fact alone with our other halves.

"I can't believe I'm home!" Leni squealed as she threw open the door of her Airstream camper after jimmying the lock with the edge of an envelope that had been stuck to the door. She stepped in and spun in a circle with her arms held out. "So many times I thought I'd never see this place again. Hell, I thought I'd never see *Earth* again." She turned toward me and beamed, her sea-green eyes brighter than I'd ever seen them. "Or your gorgeous face."

I shut the door behind me with a big, dorky grin. Seeing my girl and her love for me would never get old. I'd cherish both for as long as I existed in this body and beyond. I opened my arms for her, and she danced her way over to me. My dick was already beginning to swell.

"What's in the envelope?" I asked, looking for a distraction so I could contain my excitement.

Although our souls had Bonded often, we hadn't been able to be together physically until now. The healers hadn't allowed it until two days ago, but then Leni made us wait until we could be truly alone. The past two days had been nearly as torturous as when she'd been gone. So now that I could finally make love to her in all possible ways, I didn't want it to end before it even began. I wanted it to last as long as I could possibly draw it out.

Her caramel curls fell over her face as she looked down at the paper still in her hand. She slid a finger under the flap to open it and pulled out a card. We read it together.

"Hope's invited us to a party. A field party." Her voice sounded as perplexed as I felt. "Isn't that Ty's property? Did you ever find anything ...?"

I rubbed my brow ring. "Yeah. And no. Maybe Hope has something up her sleeve."

"She has lots of those, doesn't she?"

She swung her arms around my neck and looked up at me. Her boobs pressed against my chest as she leaned into my body. My arms fell around her, resting on the small of her back, my hands on her round ass. She wasn't looking for an answer. The question had been rhetorical. She was looking for a kiss. At least, I hoped that's what she wanted because I leaned down and crushed my mouth to hers. The invitation fell to the floor, quickly forgotten.

Her full lips were soft and delicious as always, but I needed more. I licked at them, pressing into the seam between them, until her mouth parted. I sucked her bottom lip into my mouth, and she let out a little whimper before nipping at my own. Her tongue found mine. Her fingers tangled in my hair and pulled. Her body pressed into me, her tits rubbing against my chest. I moved one hand up her back and into her curls while grabbing her ass with the other and holding her pelvis against me as I jerked against her belly, my dick straining against my jeans.

"Damn it, Leni," I groaned against her lips. "I want to fuck every inch of your body with my mouth before I make love to you. I want to make you forget every moment you were in Hell and show you heaven again. But it's been so fucking long, and I'm about to come right now."

She giggled as her hand slid down my neck, my chest, my abs, and to my cock. She cupped the bulge and stroked it. I groaned again.

"We have as long as we want to do it as many times as we want," she said as her fingers moved to the button of my jeans and deftly popped it from the hole. Her hand slid under the waistband, pushing the zipper down, her fingers teasing me, and I about came undone.

"Uh-huh," I said, wrapping my hands over her wrists and pulling her hands far, far away.

She smiled mischievously, her green eyes twinkling.

"Okay." She sank downward, her nose skimming over my shirt as she went down to her knees. "I'll do it this way."

My dick wanted to jump into her mouth, only inches away, but it was still trapped by cotton and denim.

"You're gonna kill me," I said.

I reached down, grabbed her by the waist and lifted her up, all the way off the ground. I threw her over my shoulder and held her with one arm across her thighs. My hand smacked her ass, and she squealed and kicked and laughed as I carried her back to the bedroom. I spanked her again before tossing her onto the bed. She landed on her back and smiled up at me.

"Are you going to behave?" I asked.

Her grin widened. "Hell no!"

She sprang up at me, somehow tearing her top off as she did. Then she reached for the hem of my shirt and pulled it over my head while I undid her bra, freeing those perfect tits that I loved so much. I wanted to spend time with each globe and its pinkish-brown nipple, already hard and pulled tight, showing them just how much I missed and loved them. But she was already finishing the job of undoing my jeans and pulling them down, taking my boxer briefs with them. The freedom was unbelievable, but the ache for release only intensified by a million, especially when she grabbed my balls with one hand and wrapped her hand around my shaft with the other and squeezed. She began to sink to her knees again, her lips already parting and her tongue slipping out. I'd be a goner if she so much as touched me with that pink tongue.

So I pushed her back onto the bed, curled my fingers over the waistband of her yoga pants and panties, and yanked them both off. She squirmed, her boobs bouncing side to side, as she pulled her legs free. Then she bent them at the knees and let each fall to the side, opening herself for me.

"Fuck me now, and then we can make love," she said, her hand reaching up to stroke my chest.

"How do I argue with that?"

She pinched my nipple, then pulled on the ring. "You don't."

Unable to fight it, I crawled onto the bed over her, pausing at her chest. I just couldn't let them go another second. My elbows bent, and I dropped down to flick her pebbled nipple with my tongue. Shit. That was too much of a tease. I swirled my tongue around it, but it tasted too damn good to let it go at that. My lips clamped around the whole thing, and I sucked it into my mouth, cupping the softness of her boob with my hand as my tongue rolled her nipple and my teeth scraped over it. She moaned and whimpered, and her pelvis lifted toward me, trapping my dick between us. She stroked herself, slick and hot, against it as my mouth devoured her tit.

"It's been too long for me, too," she cried. "I *need* you, Jeric. I need you inside me. Now! *Please.*"

One of her hands grabbed my hair, pulling my head up to hers, while the other reached between us and caressed me while guiding my tip to her opening. Her whole body trembled underneath me. She gazed at me with hooded eyes, and then lifted her shoulders off the bed and melded her mouth over mine. Her tongue plunged into my mouth as my cock plunged into her. She was tight and slick and fucking perfect. I filled her all the way, feeling her squeeze and convulse around me. We both moaned, and with only a few more strokes, we were shouting each other's names.

"Harder, Jeric, *faster*," she cried, and I pumped into her as hard and as fast as I could, feeling the build for both of us.

A few thrusts after that, and the earth quaked. I exploded inside her, and our souls shot out of our bodies.

"Now we make love," she whispered once we came down from the high and lay side by side, panting.

Her fingers trailed over one of the tattoos on my arm—the puzzle piece showing a heart with a lock on it.

"And tomorrow, I'm getting a real tattoo," she said as her green-eyed gaze lifted to mine. "Do I still get the key?"

I rolled onto my side and cupped my hand to her face. "You already have the key. You have my whole damn heart, Leni. And my soul. My everything."

"You *are* my everything, Jeric."

I rubbed my thumb over her bottom lip. "Damn straight. I am yours forever. And you are mine."

"Yours. Always. Now make love to me." She sucked my thumb into her mouth, and I did just that. Made love to her all night long with the intention of doing so every night for as long as we both lived ... hopefully until we were old and gray.

EPILOGUE

Bex

HAYDEN SAT ON my old, grungy, plaid couch, his brows pulled down over his eyes as he stared at the screen of a tablet the Guardians had given us. I'd tried explaining computers and the Internet and everything to him, but it was a lot to take for someone coming from his world. It was kind of fun to watch him look at everything here with a childlike wonder. My old friends would probably say if brains were leather, he wouldn't be able to saddle a june bug, but I thought it was sweet. We both had a healthy appreciation for the simple things in life, like being able to live in this trailer. I'd been embarrassed to bring him here at first, but Hayden had never had a home to live in before. It may as well have been a palace to him.

Of course, we were only able to live here because of help from the Guardians. We didn't have a pot to piss in or a window to throw it out of, literally. Uncle Troy had disowned me, acted like he never knew me. Hope and Leni had explained that it was part of what we go through as Phoenix Guardians—everyone forgets we ever existed. Since he was my last living relative that I knew of, it kind of hurt when Uncle Troy failed to recognize me, but I never liked him much anyway. It was annoying, though, that we had to pay rent to live in the trailer that had been my own mama's.

Walking around my own hometown of Lake Haven as a complete stranger was the weirdest thing of all. Everyone kept wondering how I knew their names, and I just couldn't believe they didn't remember me in the slightest. But after everything I'd been through—I'd been to Hell and back and had brought the other half of my soul with me!—I supposed it wasn't really that big of a deal. Still, this life would take some adjusting to.

At least I had Hayden. I felt like I could survive anything with him by my side. We had a lot of getting to know each other to do, so we were taking things slow, at least on a physical level. But Bonding our souls together was more intimate than anything I'd ever experienced, and more pleasurable, too. So we were doing just fine with that, while learning all about each other. The best thing was knowing he was mine. All mine. And I was his. Our love and our connection went deeper than anything anyone could understand, and nobody could take that away from us.

"Are you ready to go?" I asked him as I strode across the kitchen and into the living room.

"You're excited for this, aren't you ...?" His voice trailed off when he looked up at me, and his brows rose high up on his forehead.

I thrilled at the look in his gray eyes as he took me in, wearing a halter-top, low-slung, cut-off shorts, and cowboy boots. The weather wouldn't allow me to wear my favorite outfit much longer, and I already had a sweater packed in my bag for tonight, when the air would cool off after sunset. But right now, late October in Florida was still pretty hot.

But not as hot as Hayden's gaze made me feel. Ironically, I wanted to shiver under the heat of his eyes as they moved down and back up. He cocked his head to the side.

"This is normal attire for these parties?" he asked.

I shrugged. "Pretty much. Of course, I don't know what this one is gonna be like. Hope didn't exactly call it a K-bomb, and since nobody in town knows us, I don't know who's even gonna be there. It's all kinda weird, but knowing Hope, I'm sure she's got something planned. I'm super curious, though, because it's on Ty's property. I wonder if ..."

I shook my head, cutting myself off. I'd been trying not to let my hopes soar too high that Ty was okay. Not after Leni and Brock had told me his truck had been found by the springs. That's where dead bodies had been found in the past, too, although his hadn't. Jeric and Asia had driven out there while we were gone, and never saw Ty's truck, so I could only hope he had moved on. Where, I didn't know, especially since he'd just bought that property, but nobody in town had seen him. At least, that's what they told Jeric, who they knew had been training Ty for his fights. They wouldn't talk to me at all, thinking I was some stranger trying to stick my nose where it didn't belong.

A horn blared outside, and Hayden stood up. I couldn't help my smile. Or the way my thighs clenched. One of these days, I would have that man inside me. We were quickly failing at taking it slow. It had become harder and harder to do so. He may have been from a different world, but he was all man—one fine specimen, too. Several inches over six feet tall, short, light-brown hair, and chiseled features like a god. His light gray eyes were especially striking against his deeply tanned skin, and I always felt like he was piercing my soul with his gaze. Well, I guess he kind of was. And he was so protective of me. I always felt safe, like I was wrapped in a cocoon when he was nearby.

I took his hand and led him outside to Brock and Asia's Camaro. The Orlando authorities had confiscated my car from asshole's condo parking lot, believing that it had belonged to my poor Sissy, and since I had no ID they'd accept, I'd never be able to get it out of the tow yard. So for now, we relied on others for transportation.

Asia slid out of the passenger seat, her hair a beautiful lilac-silver and a pair of big shades covering her eyes, and climbed into the backseat. She wasn't wearing her normal all black, but a white tank that slid off her shoulders with a denim skirt that barely covered her girl parts. She did have on her combat boots, though. I followed in after her, and Hayden's big body sat in the front. Even if he wasn't too big to sit back here, we would have let him have shotgun. So far, nothing had excited him as much as riding in the Camaro.

Like I said, we were taking things slow. Before long, I'd be the big excitement of his day. He reached around the seat and placed his hand around my calf and squeezed. An electric spark jolted through me, and I could feel what he was telling me: *You already are.* God, I loved this man.

"Good thing I brought sunscreen," I said to Asia, pulling a bottle out of my bag as Brock drove us through town. "Your skin's whiter than mine."

"Trust me, I've already drenched myself in it. I don't know what I was thinking, wearing this."

"You look hot," I said, nudging her shoulder with my own. "Are you feeling better?"

"Perfect." She grinned. She had such a pretty smile that I'd never seen much of in the past. She really was doing better in all kinds of ways. "You?"

I returned her smile. "Perfect. I am kind of nervous about this party, though. Hope really hasn't told ya'll what's going on?"

Asia shook her head. "Nope. But I sure hope we're about to find out."

Brock drove us out to the dirt road that ended in the middle of nowhere. Leni's old red pickup already sat in the grass, but no other vehicles. Brock and Asia had brought some lawn chairs and a cooler that the guys unloaded from the trunk, and we made our way through the field to the lake.

Jeric and Leni had apparently just arrived, too, because Jeric was setting their cooler down next to a picnic table, and Leni was dropping their chairs to the ground. But then I noticed the rest of the spread—a hog roasting in the pit and a table covered in food that could feed a whole town.

"Did ya'll do this?" I asked with surprise.

Leni shook her head, her light brown curls bobbing over her shoulders. "Not us. Must have been Hope."

I looked around. "Did you see her?"

"Not yet," Jeric said.

"Asia, babe," Brock said, "maybe you should have reminded her about her own party."

She laughed. "I haven't worked for her in ages."

"But you know how she is. She's my mom, and I love her, but she can be pretty flaky."

"I think that was a show."

Brock shrugged, but let it go. I was glad to see he was coming back around to Hope. He'd been pretty mad at her at first, confused and angry, especially about Connor, and none of us could blame him. As far as I knew, she hadn't really explained much yet. We were all hoping she'd be doing that today. But Hope was his mama, and family was precious. Although my lesson had been most recent, we'd all learned this the hard way. Now, we were each other's family.

We set up our chairs in front of the lake, and each sat down with a beer in hand, and then the silence settled on us. It was eerily quiet with no music playing like there usually was. Even the birds seemed to have fallen silent. Everyone but Hayden and me stiffened, moving to the edges of their chairs. They all turned their heads up toward the sky, as though expecting something to drop from it—something not good.

But the unexpected movement came from the lake in front of us. A geyser sprayed up several feet into the air, making us all gasp.

"Never seen that before," I said, my hand gripping Hayden's. He'd already jumped to his feet, ready to protect me.

When the water fell, though, Hope stood out there in the middle of the lake. And she wasn't alone.

"*Ty?*" I shrieked. "Ty Daniels?"

I ran for the water, but he beat me to the shore. Ty's arms wrapped around me, and he swooped me off my feet and spun me around.

"You're okay?" I asked breathlessly once he set me back on the ground. My gaze traveled from his head to his feet and back up, making sure. He wore his usual t-shirt, jeans, and cowboy boots, and somehow, they weren't wet. And he looked perfectly fine.

"Life's been ... interesting lately," he said. "But, yeah, I'm good, Bex."

"And you remember me!" I squealed, clapping my hands together.

"How could I ever forget you?" The sweet look he gave me was different than those he'd always given me in the past. He knew things had changed between us, but I still backed up to Hayden and took his hand before introducing them. The others then welcomed both Ty and Hope, and Ty grabbed a beer before we all sat down again, except for Ty and Hope, who stood in front of us.

"How did this—" Jeric motioned his hands toward Ty and Hope "—happen?"

Ty looked at Hope, and she gave him a slight nod.

"I'm like ya'll," he said with a proud smile.

We all stared at him stupidly with our mouths hanging open so wide, we could have caught flies.

Hope snickered at our reaction. "I'd like you all to meet Tobialaric, who you've known as Ty. He and his other half were one of the Original Seven."

"*What?*" I jumped up and ran over to give Ty another hug.

"That's why I was always pulled to you," he said after letting me go again. "I guess my soul recognized yours, just not in the way I thought."

"So where is she?"

Ty frowned. "I don't know yet."

"She's here, though," Hope assured. "On this world. The timing is right. I made sure of it. He just has to find her."

"How ...?" Jeric asked again.

Hayden pulled me over to sit on his lap so Ty could have my chair as Hope began.

"I explained to you before and you all saw that I was able to find the other half of Ny'xan and bring him back to this world. Well, I've been able to do that with the rest of the Original Seven. It's been my goal to reunite you, but it's been difficult. The timing with everyone's souls returning to Earth at about the same time has been nearly impossible. I've had to keep the souls contained until I could capture their mate's soul, too. During your last cycle, I was able to get Tobialaric's and his other half's pieces and send them to the Space Between together. I've just recently sent the other two pairs into the Space Between—two of them you haven't seen in many, many life cycles, but you do know the others. One as Connor and the other as Sissy."

My breath caught in my throat, and my hand flew to my mouth. Tears filled my eyes as I looked over at Brock and Asia. They beamed at each other, their eyes lit up with hope.

"Since you can all live long lives now," Hope continued, "which means the possibility of raising your own families, you may be lucky enough that their souls find you again, maybe upon conception."

The smiles on Brock and Asia's faces couldn't have grown any bigger without breaking their faces. Jeric and Leni exchanged a look, too. Hayden tightened his arms around me, and I leaned against his hard chest.

"Maybe someday," he whispered against my ear, and a new excitement for the future ran through me. I may not have my Sissy any more, but hopefully I'd meet her soul again soon.

"These halves, like Ty, have been Separated for many life cycles," Hope continued. "You saw how Enyxa and Gabrixander were. She hadn't even sensed him on me until I actually showed him to her. It's going to be hard for these others to find each other and believe in their Bond. That's why when I found Ty coming around the springs, I took the risk to reach out and help him. It took me weeks to convince him."

"What were you doin' at the springs, anyway, Ty?" I asked. "You know how dangerous they are."

He shrugged. "I couldn't help myself. I guess my soul knew Hope was there ... and the others."

Our heads all snapped back to Hope.

"Others?" Leni asked.

"The ones I just sent back," Hope said, and her lips twitched at the corners. "The springs aren't really dangerous. The bodies that had been found hadn't even been real—if you struck one in the right place, it would blow up in smoke. They belonged to Lakari who had come too close, and I used them to keep curious town folk away. You see, the springs are my safe place. My refuge. A haven for Guardians' souls, as well, where I keep them safe when nowhere else, not even the Space Between, can help them. This is where I came to recover from the accident—an accident caused by Lakari, of course. I brought Connor's soul here, too, and kept it with the others until the timing was right. I went out for Sissy's, and that's when Mirangela and Theodethan found me, returning here. Just in time, too."

"She said that's why we all end up here in Lake Haven," Ty said. "Our souls naturally gravitate to this place."

"Because the rest of the Seven were here?" Asia asked.

Hope nodded. "That and because the artifacts are here, too, when they're not safely with their owners. The Book, the Orb, the Stone, the Cup ... there are several. But those are for another time. Right now, it's time to celebrate."

She lifted her chin, and her gaze focused behind us. We turned to look over our shoulders. Several vehicles were pulling up to the dead end, and people were spilling out, grabbing their coolers and chairs. Some guys were already unloading a cargo van and a big truck with band equipment. I jumped off Hayden's lap with surprise, and everyone else stood, too.

"I invited the town," Hope said. "Thought you all should get to know them. I think you'll be staying here a while since the Gate is taken care of."

"Will we really get to live long together?" Jeric asked, taking Leni's hand.

"I can't guarantee anything, of course," Hope said, "but the odds are definitely in your favor now."

"And we can have families?" Asia asked, hope high in her voice.

"You better," Hope said. "I miss my grandson. I think he's ready to return." She gave Asia and Brock a wink. "One more thing I'm sure you're all interested in. Mason Hayes stabbed another prisoner and killed him. The State's seeking the death penalty, but no matter what, he'll be behind bars for the rest of his life. He won't be buying his way out of this, I guarantee it."

I hadn't realized just how heavily this had weighed on me until she shared that bit of news. I suddenly felt five hundred pounds lighter. I felt like I could truly heal and move on and not forever be looking over my shoulder, wondering if he was close. With a laugh that bubbled out of my soul and over my heart, I threw my arms around Hayden's neck, and he pulled me off the ground in a hug. My life could go on now, and I couldn't wait to start it with him.

The crowd began pouring into the party area, but before we joined them, I grabbed Ty's wrist.

"We'll help you find your girl," I promised him.

He gave me a nod and a smile. "I know. I was pretty damn disappointed when I found out you weren't her, but then so much made sense. She's out there, Bex. I feel it."

We shared another hug before I took Hayden's hand, and we joined the others in greeting the newcomers. Pretty much everyone I'd grown up with, known since preschool, was there, but they had no idea who I was. Even Kaylee and her husband and the rest of our high school class, and Aunt Faye and Elizabeth, who had apparently moved back when the Darkness had receded from Lake Haven.

But that was how things were for us, the Phoenix Guardians. And they were my new family. My sisters and brothers who I'd known for millennia, and with whom I'd been to Hell and back. And Sissy would be joining us soon, I hoped, maybe as my own child, or maybe as Leni's or Asia's. I prayed her soul would find us so we could protect her as she grew up. That was for another day, though. A future that looked brighter than ever.

Tonight, we were celebrating.

Leni handed me a red plastic cup, and I groaned at the smell of hunch punch, but laughed when I saw the rest of our group had one as we gathered into a circle.

"To life," she said, lifting her cup in the air. "To family. To the souls who have found their other halves and the ones who will soon. To this beautiful world called Earth that I never want to leave again." She turned toward Jeric. "And to love for eternity."

"Here, here," Brock said, and we all bumped our cups together before chugging the hunch punch, then letting out a whoop.

"Shall we get this party started?" asked a sexy male voice that came through the speakers.

The band was set up on a portable stage, and several people cheered in the crowd, which had grown immensely. Hope really had invited the whole town.

"Jeric, my man," said the guy speaking through the microphone, his guitar hanging at his hip. "You have something to share?"

Jeric grinned and planted a kiss on Leni's forehead before jogging over to the stage and jumping up on it. The other guy handed him the microphone, then stepped back and took his guitar in hand.

"A little something I wrote for my girl Leni, but I think many of you can relate."

The song opened with a tune I liked so far, and my body started swaying against Hayden, but when Jeric began singing, we all froze. The lyrics about love and longing and hope were beautiful and his voice completely mesmerizing. And when he was done, all the girls had wet eyes and wet panties, too. Leni threw her arms around him when he returned to her, and they locked into a sweet embrace.

"Before we really start up," said the guitarist on stage, "let's everyone raise our cans and cups to our hostess, Hope Verdor."

Our group cheered the loudest, and both Brock and Jeric whistled loudly. I looked around, but she seemed to have disappeared. But I knew she wasn't really gone. She was watching over us from somewhere, the Light eliminating the Darkness.

The guitarist held his beer can up.

"Here's to knowing that when life is at its worst and the world feels darkest, we just have to look within and remember that we *always* have Hope."

THE END
TO A BEAUTIFUL BEGINNING

ABOUT THE AUTHOR

KRISTIE COOK IS a lifelong, award-winning writer in various genres, from marketing communications to fantasy fiction. She continues to write the Soul Savers Series, a New Adult paranormal romance / contemporary fantasy, with *Promise, Purpose, Devotion, Power,* and the latest release, *Wrath,* book five, available now. She's also written a companion novella, *Genesis: A Soul Savers Novella,* which details the compelling history of her Soul Savers mythology. Over 300,000 Soul Savers books have been sold, with *Promise* peaking at #54 on the Amazon Top 100 Paid list and at #1 in the Amazon Fantasy category.

Kristie's second series, The Book of Phoenix, is a New Adult paranormal trilogy. *The Space Between* and *The Space Beyond* are currently available, and *The Space Within* will be available Summer 2014.

Besides writing, Kristie enjoys reading, cooking, traveling and riding on the back of a motorcycle. She has lived in ten states, but currently calls Southwest Florida home with her husband, three sons, a beagle, and a puggle.

CONNECT WITH ME ONLINE

I love to hear from and connect with readers.
Please don't be shy.

Email: kristie@kristiecook.com
Author's Website & Blog: http://www.KristieCook.com
UK Fan Site: http://www.kristiecookfansite.co.uk
Soul Saver Series Website: http://www.SoulSaversSeries.com
Facebook: http://www.facebook.com/AuthorKristieCook
Twitter: http://twitter.com/kristiecookauth

If you'd like to get an automatic email when my next book is
released, sign up here:
https://www.facebook.com/AuthorKristieCook/app_16630360
3381066. Your email address will not be shared and you can
unsubscribe at any time!

Word of mouth is very important for any author. If you
enjoyed the book, please consider leaving a review, even if it's
only a sentence or two.

PROMISE

The sensation of being watched clung to me like a spider web, invisible threads bristling the back of my neck and down my spine. I brushed my fingers across my shoulders, as if I could drag the feeling off and flick it away.

It was ridiculous, of course. Not just ridiculous to think I could pull it off so easily, as if it really was strands of a web, but it was even more absurd to feel it in the first place. Nobody ever held that much interest in me. Occasionally, people stared with curiosity when they picked me up on their "weird radars," but usually they just ignored me. No one ever watched so intensely.

Yet the hairs on the back of my neck stood on end at the feeling as I visited my favorite Washington, D.C., monument for likely the last time. I sat on the stone steps with the stately Thomas Jefferson behind me and gazed over the Potomac River tidal basin, enjoying the peace just before sunset. Well, trying to enjoy it anyway.

I blamed the ominous feeling on my unruly imagination, with it being twilight and the sky looking so foreboding. It was the perfect backdrop for one of my stories. The sun hung low—an eerie, orange ball glowing behind a shroud of haze, a column of steel-blue cloud rising around it, threatening to snuff it out. I envisioned something not-quite-human watching it from the shadows, waiting to begin its hunt under the cover of darkness.

That's all it is, just my fascination with mythical creatures, I told myself. *Uh-huh. Right.*

Surrendering hope for a peaceful moment, I hurried to the closest Metro station. The feeling of being followed stuck with me on the train ride home, but at my stop in Arlington, I forgot the sinister sensation. Some kids from school stood near the top of the escalator as I stepped off. I'd witnessed before their favorite summer activity: dressing in all black and hassling people exiting the Metro station. So mature, but what can you expect? They were younger—they hadn't graduated with me over a month ago—and apparently, still stuck in the rebellious phase that I'd never been through myself.

I usually took the elevator to circumvent them, but had been too distracted tonight.

"Hey, there's the weird girl who heals," one of them said loudly to the others. "It's s'posed to be really freaky to watch."

"Hey, freak, got any tricks to show us?" another called.

I pretended not to hear and crossed the street to avoid them. My eyes stung, but no tears came. I wouldn't allow them. It was my own fault—I'd been a klutz with the Bunsen burner in Chemistry and my lab partner saw my skin heal the burn almost instantly. People harassed me about it every day the last two months of school. If I didn't let them get to me, they were usually just annoying. Usually.

Night had crept its way in during my ride home. I walked quickly through the bright commercial district and turned down the darker residential street for home, still four blocks away. Footsteps behind me echoed my own. I quickened my pace. *Two more days. That's all. Just two more days and we're out of here.*

"C'mon, dude, we just wanna know if it's true," a boy's voice said.

"Yeah, just show us. It doesn't hurt, right?"

I glanced over my shoulder. Three teens followed me and I caught the glint of a blade in one of their hands. I realized their plan to satisfy their curiosity—slice me open and watch the wound heal. *What is* wrong *with people? Of course, it hurts!* Bungalow-style homes lined the street, each with an empty front porch. Not a single person sat outside on this summer's evening. No one to witness their fun and my agony. My heartbeat notched up with anxiety.

Pop! Crack! The streetlights along the entire block blacked out at the sounds. I inhaled sharply and halted mid-stride. The footsteps behind me ceased, too.

"What the *hell?*" Surprise and fear filled the boy's question.

A couple appeared from nowhere, three houses down, standing in the middle of the street. It was too dark to see their features and I could only tell their genders by their shapes. The woman's high-heeled shoes clicked on the pavement as they walked toward me. The man, big and burly, pulled his shirt over his head and handed it to the woman. Without breaking stride, he took off one shoe and then the other, leaving him with only pants. *What the . . . ?*

I considered my options. The woman and her half-naked companion blocked my way home, but I wouldn't just raise my chin and walk brusquely by them, pretending they meant no harm. Because I just knew they did. I stood trapped between the boys with the knife and the bizarre couple. Somehow, I knew the knife was less threatening.

"Boo!" The woman cackled as the boys took off running. As she and the man closed in on me, the alarms screamed in my head.

Evil! Bad! Run! Go!

My sixth sense had never been so frightened. I couldn't move, though. Fear paralyzed my body. My heart hammered painfully against my ribs.

The couple stopped several yards away. The woman studied me as if assessing a rare animal, while the man lifted his face to the sky, his whole body trembling. I followed his gaze to see the thin, gauzy clouds sliding across a full moon. The woman cackled again. Panic sucked the air from my lungs.

"Alexis, at last," the woman said, her voice raspy, like a long-time smoker's. "We'll get such a nice reward for you."

My eyes widened and my voice trembled. "D-do I know you?"

She grinned, a wicked glint in her eyes. "Not yet."

Or ever, if I can help it.

I turned and ran. My pulse throbbed in my head. Breaths tore through my chest. My mind couldn't focus, couldn't make sense of this absurd couple and what they wanted with me, but my body kept moving. The bright lights of the commercial area I'd just left beaconed me to their safety.

The woman abruptly appeared in front of me before I was half-way down the street. The shock sent me hurling to the ground and my head smacked hard against the pavement. Stars shot across my eyes. My hands burned from asphalt scrapes. Fighting the blackness trying to swallow my vision, I rolled onto my side, gasping for breath. A sticky wetness pooled under my temple.

My eyes rolled up to the woman, who now pointed what looked like a stick at me. Her lips moved silently as she waved a pattern in the air. I felt pinned to the ground, though nothing physically restrained me. Panic flailed uselessly below the surface of my paralyzed body, making my breaths quick and shallow. I was done for. They could do anything they wanted with me. There was no escape now.

My vision faltered. Now two women stood over me, two sticks pointed at me. Two moons wavered behind them. I didn't know if it was fear or the head injury that caused everything to slide apart and together again. I squeezed my eyes shut.

But I couldn't close my ears, couldn't block out the gnarl. My eyes popped open with terror, expecting to see a wild beast, but the feral sound came from the man. His eyes rolled back, showing only whites. His hands clenched into fists. His muscles strained, the veins protruding like ropes along the bulges. His body shook violently until the edges of his shape became a blur.

"I can't hold it," he growled.

"Then don't," the woman said. "Don't fight it. It's time!"

A ripping sound tore through the night as the man lurched forward, his skin shredding. A gelatinous liquid spurt out of him like an exploding jar of jelly. His pants tore into ribbons as his body lengthened and grew. The shape of his limbs transformed. His face elongated, his nose and mouth becoming a . . . *Holy crap! A snout?!* I gasped, a scream stuck in my throat. By the time his front

. . . *legs* . . . hit the ground, fur covered his body. He was no longer man. He was— *A freakin' wolf?!*

The beast moved closer, a low growl in its throat. Its stench of decaying corpses and rotting leaves overwhelmed my sensitive nose, the disgustingly sweet odor gagging me and forcing me to breathe through my mouth.

Pop! Another woman appeared, again out of nowhere. Her pale skin glowed and her white hair shimmered in the moonlight.

"I smell blood," she said, her voice a flutter of wind chimes. "Mmm . . . delicious blood."

The scrapes on my hands had already healed, but not the cut on my head. It must have been deep enough for a normal person to need stitches. For me, it could take ten minutes to heal. So my blood was still fresh.

I could only smell the wolf's rancid odor as it hovered over me.

"Back off, *mutt,*" the white-blonde snarled as she stepped closer. "This is too important for the likes of you."

"How dare you!" Stick-woman gasped. "We had her first!"

"Alexis is mine. Always *mine!*"

What the hell is happening?! What do they want with me? Whoever they were, they wanted to do more than just terrorize me. I could hear it in the way the blonde said I was *hers.* She wanted me to hurt . . . or worse. Cold fear slid down my spine and hot tears burned my eyes.

Pop! My heart jumped into my throat as another man materialized in the darkness and strode toward me. *Not more!* The wolf growled. Both women hissed. Goose bumps crawled along my skin.

The man stepped in front of me, placing himself between me and the others.

Good! Very good! Safe! My sense slightly calmed me.

"You're alone?" the blonde asked. "Ha! You haven't a chance."

The wolf lunged at my protector. He raised his hands and thrust them out toward the beast and it flew back as if blasted by something unseen. I heard a thud and a whimper as it hit the pavement. I blinked several times, disbelieving what I just saw.

The women hissed again. The first one raised her stick, pointing it at my protector. The blonde took a step toward me.

Pop! Another person appeared, between the two women and my human shield. The women responded immediately—their teeth gleamed in the moonlight as their lips spread into grins.

No way could my protector stand up against this second man. The new one was taller, wider in the shoulders, thicker in the torso and arms than my protector, who was now out-numbered and out-muscled. The second man took a single step toward us. I didn't dare look up at him, afraid of what I might see. But I felt his eyes rake over me. My trembling turned to quakes.

My sixth sense continued shouting conflicting alarms, everyone's intentions so strong. *Good* and *Evil* both screamed in my head and I couldn't tell which this new person was.

But then he turned to face the women and their expressions darkened. And I knew. He was on our side. I swatted down a leap of hope, though. The attackers still out-numbered my protectors.

The wolf, now back on all fours, stalked toward us. The fur on the back of its neck rose. Hunger shone in its eyes as its lips curled back in a snarl. Its pace quickened, my heart galloping with it. It lunged once more. I tried to scream. My constricted throat only allowed a whimper.

Then the wolf flew backwards again and fell to the ground a second time. The bigger man's hand hung in the air, palm straight out facing the wolf, as if he'd hit it, but I never saw the contact.

Both women eyed me with obvious greed. Then their eyes shifted back to my brawny protector and confusion and even fear flickered across their faces. He turned his hand toward them. Their eyes widened, looking as terrified as I felt.

They disappeared with two *pops*.

"I've got Alexis! Take care of that one!" The lankier man easily lifted me into his arms and sprinted toward my house. The beast's stench continued to fill my head, a persistent odor that wouldn't leave even as distance separated us.

A wolfish howl behind us diminished into a human cry of pain. I shuddered in the arms of the stranger.